Ravished Wings

by

Maria Osborne Perry

As Cu'lugh walked through the door he heard Odette's surprised whimper. She was just rising to her hands and knees and her face was bright and nervous at once. He contemplated her with deliberate sternness and she bowed her head at once. Oh, how he loved her golden hair as it draped her milken shoulders and spilled over the bronze floor plate of the cage. He drew a little closer and caught the reflection of her face in it. Wonderfully chagrined was that lovely face, the brow knit anxiously and the lips pressed together as she struggled against the urge to beg.

This book is a work of fiction. Names, characters, places, and incidents either are products of the author's imagination or are used fictitiously. Any resemblance to actual events or locales or persons, living or dead, is entirely coincidental.

RAVISHED WINGS
Copyright © 2002 Maria Osborne Perry
ISBN: 1-894869-63-X
Cover art by Martine Jardin

Published by Zumaya Publications, 2002
Look for us online at: www.zumayapublications.com

It is an open question whether any behavior based on fear of eternal punishment can be regarded as ethical or should be regarded as merely cowardly.

Margaret Mead in Redbook

"For my true love and knight-in-shining armor, Robert Perry."

Chapter One

rompted by a nightmare, Odette ran to the bedchamber where her mother and father slept. Try as she might, they did not stir; and when at last she held her own breath and saw that their chests neither rose nor fell she knew they would never awaken again.

Her mother's handmaidens tried to soothe her, and the menservants respectfully carried the bodies to a funeral pallet in the Great Hall as the first rays of dawn yawned over the eastern mountains. It illuminated the forest paths before the invading Franks. No warning had come from the boundary sentries and the sleeping village was taken by utter surprise. Flaming arrows hailed into rooftops and through windows and bars, igniting the homes and the keeps and the stalls of the livestock. The waking Saxon men, with little time to draw their weapons let alone properly gear for battle, tried to disperse their women and children into the sanctuary of the groves as the hooves of the Frankish horses thundered onto the streets.

Warriors and innocents alike were cut down; and those who reached the woodland found the brambles torched by an envoy of the crusaders at the priest Boniface's bidding. Fifteen guardsmen stayed to defend the chieftain's household while twenty others charged out into the fray.

Only then did Odette's older sister Vanda emerge from her rooms, her dour spinster women following at her heels. The confessor their father had allowed her wandered out of his dirty chamber and, told of the siege outside and the bodies on the pallet, lifted his arms heavenward and shouted an exultation to his god for answering his prayers.

Odette stood beside the pallet, curling a lock of her mother's black hair about her fingers. She looked up dully and saw one of her father's men butt the priest's temple with the handle of his war ax. The man crumpled to his knees, laughing despite the blood that flowed down his face and throat. The guard who had struck him turned to the women and ordered them to go with the children to the shelter of the cellar beneath the pantry. His words seemed a world away to Odette, and it took the concerted effort of two women to pry her hands from Silfr's hair.

One of them picked Odette up and ran with her out of the Hall and through the longhouse to the pantry. The darkness of the cellar was total, so she could not see who it was had taken her; but she could feel the heat of the massed humanity all about them and hear the choking cries of the other children. The arms of the woman holding her were like two steel bands, pressing Odette protectively against a pair of naked breasts.

Odette, subdued by the heat and the stifling fear, closed her eyes and imagined it was Silfr who held her and they were simply waiting for her father to return from one of his hunting parties. Soon enough , however, the sound of battle carried into the longhouse; and the Franks stormed in, challenging the Saxon defenders with bestial, blood-lusty growls and whoops. An eternity seemed to pass as iron and brass clashed throughout the rooms above and the smoke of fires drifted through the lattice of the cellar's only window. As Rulf's men fell they cursed the invaders and the exhaled curses of the dying seemed to seep through the floorboards and suffuse the humid air.

At length the fury outside subsided so that all Odette could hear were the shouts of the victorious and the desolate screams of women. At last heavy footfalls tramped into the pantry, and the woman holding Odette shuddered when someone kicked back the bearskin placed over the cellar door, clutching the child so tightly she could hardly breathe. The door was drawn open and the light of day washed down the stairs to reveal the cringing hidden.

Odette felt the woman make an uncertain sound. Turning her face she looked up and saw not the face of a cruel warrior peering down on them all, but that of her own sister.

A hand pulled Vanda back and a crowing voice, thick with the invader's accent, ordered them upstairs. The other Saxon women were draped in heavy furs and led away to Boniface's encampment, but only the fatal thrust of a Frankish blade through the ribs extracted Odette from the diligent arms that had held her so long. The woman swayed and brushed Odette's brow with a kiss, and as she fell to the floor her killer ripped the child from her faltering grasp.

Odette only then saw her face—Inga, one of Silfr's handmaidens, a blithe, guileless young woman who had faithfully pleasured the chieftain's unmarried warriors. Inga had taught Odette how to braid her hair and to weave flowers into intricate garlands and to make flutes out of the reeds that grew by the wilderness streams.

Odette's terror and shock vanished, replaced by wrath. She turned on the towering killer, screaming, kicking and striking at him with her small fists. Her vision shrouded by her tears she did not see the reaction on his face, though she heard his derisive laugh. Her mind was blank but for the anger and grief that compelled her, and the unspeakably horrible thought that some murderous coward might hurt Vanda and the other women as this one had Inga.

Suddenly, she turned and fled from the pantry and ran through the kitchen. Down the softly shadowed hallway she continued, hurdling the two hacked bodies lying beside their fallen war axes. Into the Great Hall she dashed, breathless and her heart twinging with dread.

A cluster of women turned toward her. She looked them over expectantly, but they were strangers, these black-gowned women who served Vanda. They had remained so well cloistered in her sister's rooms that Odette knew them only by their gowns and pale complexions. One of them spoke her name in a soft, surprised way that only exacerbated Odette's sense of urgency.

Frankish warriors busied themselves pilfering the weapons of the dead, oblivious to the seven-year-old walking around the somber serving women to approach the pallet. It remained on the rowanwood table, but the bodies of her mother and father were gone. The white roses were scattered to the floor, their petals squashed into the pooling gore.

Odette felt the blood drain from her head and she caught the pallet as she fell. A gasp rose from the serving women, and one of them walked to her and helped her sit down. The woman made a soothing sound and spoke words Odette could not understand as gently she pulled free the errant golden strands of hair matted to Odette's tearstained cheeks and pressed the cross of iron to her lips.

* * *

The following day Charles Martel took residence in the longhouse in the fecund valley beside the Teutoburger Wald, where the renegade chieftain Rulf had led his tribe after leaving their conquered homeland beside the Mosel. With the aid of her women, Vanda prepared a feast in his honor, and in that of the priest Boniface, who had worked throughout the night without sleep or rest to oversee the thorough burning of the sacred groves and the search for Silfr's swanmaiden's mantle. Somehow they had known that Rulf had buried the mantle somewhere in the groves, an act of homage to the Goddess Freyja in gratitude for his beloved bride.

But the labors of the missionaries had failed to unearth the mantle, though Boniface declared they had *succeeded* in their quest by the act of denying the thing's existence save in the heretical fantasies of the pagans.

Odette sat beside her older sister during the meal, staring at the silver plates and golden drinking vessels spread out on the banquet table. All the finery her father had had smithed in gift to her mother upon the celebration of their marriage. It mattered not to her what this priest harped on or what the cold-eyed Frankish leader insinuated. Theirs had been a marriage true and sacred before the eyes of the gods.

But as they explained to Vanda the rights their Church assumed over the land, Odette was comforted at least by the understanding they had no intention of harming her sister. By the end of the meal Charles had proposed even that Vanda wed his own brother. Odette felt her stiffen and, glancing down, saw her sister's fingernails gouge the wood of the bench. But Vanda smiled and nodded compliantly, asking only if this brother were a Christian.

Martel blinked dully, and the smile that crimped the corners of his mouth seemed a little too animated.

"But, of course, dear kinswoman," he replied with a sheepish glance at Boniface. "To raise a pagan to the position of vassal lord would little behoove our recent enterprise. And Thierry is young and gentle to the fairer sex, and I have no doubt you possess the talents to subdue any hint of youthful intractability in him that may have eluded my discernment. Why, he was the same young man you met this morning in my camp—perhaps you noticed his smitten face?"

The priest made an ugly sound, but Martel dispelled his disapproval with good humor. "'Tis good in the eyes of God, my friend, Thierry is enamored. Marriage may be repellent to those avowed to chastity, but the politics of the Church can only benefit by mutual interest of the parties whose unions cement the loyalty of the respective tribes."

The priest grunted and sipped the water in his goblet. His eyes swept across the table, over the vapid, staring faces of Vanda's women and Martel's men stuffing their stomachs. But at length his glare settled, heavy and contemptuous, on Odette.

"What say you of that one, vassal of Christ? The whore's spawn?"

Martel regarded Odette only briefly, his smile benign and faraway. "The child is nothing. I think you put too much care in what the pagans contemplate. They have just been conquered and their numbers will be dispersed as you have requested. No one shall look to a girl child for any claim."

A second time Odette heard Vanda's nails scrape on the bench.

The woman looked at her suddenly and the smile that met Odette's eyes was warm, mesmerizing. Vanda touched Odette's chin and smoothed her hair. Odette flinched and almost drew back, for never in the seven years of her life had Vanda graced her with more than a passing glance in the halls or the reproof to go away those times Odette found the courage to knock on her door.

"I shall see to it, good father," Vanda said, her voice husky and assured, "that my sister is raised to know God and His commandments. Never again shall paganism or harlotry taint these halls."

The promise must have satisfied Boniface, for he raised his hand in blessing. After he had departed Martel asked Vanda for her permission to send for his brother the next day.

"You are lord of this house, good sir," she responded.

Then, with his permission, Vanda rose to go say her evening prayers, taking Odette by the hand and leading her down the hallways to her private rooms.

At the door they stopped, and Vanda inhaled slowly and patted the little white cap she'd had Odette wear since the morning. Odette gazed at her, feeling the grief rise up within her again, and took cheer in the sisterly embrace she was pulled into.

Vanda exhaled slowly and the iron in her arms tightened like bodice cords about Odette's ribs. "Keep your heart open to all you shall be soon instructed, sweeting sister, and embrace, willingly, desperately, all the Godly virtues of which you have thus far been ignorant. I see the avarice in your eyes; it blazes as undeniably as your sordid pedigree! But God *does* accommodate those whose hearts are steadfast in His demands, and my piety shall be rewarded, just as my father's apostasy was in its own…*fashion.*"

As Vanda's arms slowly released, tiny black dots swam before Odette's eyes. And as her vision cleared and she sought for a reply to this hard thing Vanda had declared she heard something—or, rather, *felt* it—approach in the hallway. A chill without force of breeze or substance sighed over them both. Odette's flesh tingled, and her nostrils were seized by the smell of decay and tempered madness. Vanda stood and turned and a look of indescribable relief faded the crimson from her angry face.

"Hrowthe," she whispered and then Odette noticed the shadows prancing on the walls. Before her eyes they resolved and formed a man. He wore robes the color of soot much like Boniface, yet the fabric was as clean as his porcelain skin. His face appeared ancient, and yet something glinted under his hollowed features, something discernible and vital though dimmer than any ordinary aura that bordered the human body. A countenance of vitality and youth Odette witnessed there beneath the furrows and hardened skin, a youth—and more so a humanity—refuted by the semblance he had decidedly assumed.

Instinct promised in its disturbing manner that no adult mortal was in danger of seeing this figure as anything but human. But the trust and affection in Vanda's face as he drew near told they were no recent acquaintances.

His encrusted eyes studied Odette's face; and if he suspected her knowledge he did not say. Instead, he gave Vanda a gentle reproof.

"Is it piety you truly want from this child of Silfr? You cannot have it both ways, my dear one."

Vanda's cheeks flared again and her cobalt eyes glowered, but her mouth twitched as the flood of hostility cooled. "Very true, Hrowthe. I am weary of this ordeal, that is all."

She looked down at Odette and, bending down, pressed her cheek against Odette's head. But Odette could not forget those threatening words spoken moments before, nor that this was her sister, sired from the same loins from whence she had been created. She felt violated in a way that paled even the murderous actions of the Franks. Death, however violent, possessed only measurable suffering, a thing that could not torment after the deliverance.

And to feel the sweetened breath upon her temple and heated lips press upon her brow while her sister's every limb quaked with hatred…this was torment.

Odette's heart quickened and she bolted free of the small, fiery palms. Down the hallway she fled and through a door that led outside. There, in the moonlight, she looked for the comforting sight of her mother's walled garden, but the air was thick still with smoke and the wails of children bereft of family as well as home.

Chapter Two

highs, long and voluptuous and silken, wrapped about Cu'lugh's hips; and the lips he knew so well pressed against his mouth, breathing moist and warm into his mouth. Only a vision, but it stirred the blood within him, delaying freezing death. He tried to focus on her face, her green eyes that were always just beyond meeting his own; but the drowsiness eclipsed them.

Still he knew she was there, in some form or another, as she'd been since he was but a small boy. A vision—a demon, his mother would have said; his father, too, though Pepin of Herstal had kept at least a dozen concubines. Unlike some created sensual vision, though, the dimensions of the golden-haired girl were defined, solid; and her fragrance, her touch lingered. Even when he had other concerns her pliant, breathless moans remained with Cu'lugh as tangibly as the voices of his companions and friends.

Besides his younger brother Thierry and Thierry's mother Angla, the girl was the only other creature who had never failed or used him; if that were demonic, so be it. A thousand times had he stroked her quivering flesh and suckled her pert breasts, and just the memory of these mental rendezvous had quieted the pain of his legitimate brother's mockery. The fragrance of her he had carried with him to the distant lands he'd traveled in search of adventure, other lands where he'd offered his military talents to leaders more appreciative than his father. He had taken delight in many women yet known only quick boredom or disappointment, and he knew these disappointed affairs had been affected, too, by a hauntingly sweet moan that would not release its possession of his soul.

The purpose of this latest adventure was to confirm Thierry's death for the younger man's mother, but it had been the haunting emptiness never filled that had spurred him into the wilds of Germany, to the land of the twice-quelled Saxon tribe. She was there, somewhere, in this lonesome world; perhaps not in the semblance he'd dreamed all his life, but she was there…waiting, summoning with her mischievous smile and eager kisses.

Now he was going to die; and he knew he'd been a fool, that there was nothing else to blame for his predicament than his spurious pursuit to make real a vision.

The cold crept deeper into his body, congealing his blood and lulling his brain into a sleep from which he would never awaken. He grieved for Angla, waiting so anxiously to know the fate of her only son and that of Thierry's young wife Vanda, who was alone despite Charles's vow of protection from any and all who might question her claims to the fief.

It was nearly Beltane, springtime, and in Frankland the trees were budding and the green returning to the grass of the fields. But not here, not in this wilderness so far from home; and for all Cu'lugh's experience as a mercenary soldier his best preparations were futile against the insidious snowstorm. He had known he was near the fief when it struck, and he took shelter in the forest, though all instinct told him to skirt this strangely denuded forest, so silent as he entered not even the sound of a single bird stirred within the boughs. His horse fell not long after he'd goaded it in, and he tried to warm it with his bedding and his own cape.

But a venomous blast swept through the terrain, sucking the horse's breath away and permeating the frigid air with a thick, foul perfume, compelling him to draw the cape about himself again just as a howling wind swept through the barren palisades like a pack of spectral mist wolves, blinding him, unbalancing his sense of direction. He wandered, stumbling, until he felt a small opening in the wall of a deep stone ravine; and therein he hid as the screaming wind shook the ground outside. In the mercilessly bitter air, his limbs had begun to grow numb and his thoughts to ramble when first he felt the presence staring at him from the entrance.

His goose-fleshed skin felt as if flayed by ice shards beneath the unseen scrutiny; and even as the drowsiness drained his life away he was aware there was more than one. They bickered in whispers, agitated and suspicious. He knew their craving to pounce and tear his limbs from his body and feast on his organs and blood—for the satisfaction of it as well as to end the jeopardy of allowing him to live. Yet, they hesitated in this virulent desire and waited, shuffling in the snow on feet that perceived not the cold or the roughness of the forest floor or cared that from their malignant bodies the smell of decay arose. Their heavy, ravenous eyes never left him and he could feel their bloodless tongues lolling thirstily over their parched lips.

And though death was all that waited to answer the loyalty and selflessness that had brought him to this wretched land, more than ever before the golden-haired vision gave him solace.

*　*　*

The Blodsauker priests heard the wind die down and the rustle of wings coming toward them through the drifted canopy. They turned their heads as one and watched the raven light down on the snowy ground and bristle her wings. Although to them she was a living woman like any other, she was under Hrowthe's protection and, indeed, had given them this forest to inhabit as well as the building supplies and hands necessary to build their temple in the city. They met her yellow eyes with solemn nods and one of them pointed to the mouth of the grotto. She squawked and lifted her wings again and turned her hard glare into the recesses. For several moments she contemplated the freezing warrior.

At length she fluttered her wings again and screamed; and they watched, not certain what to do, if anything, as her avian body spasmed and thrashed on the ground. Moments later the raven semblance began to break, recede; and her form grew and elongated, a grotesque mass of twisting sinew and flesh and blood. The feathers disappeared and the skin grew light, the wings transformed to elegant arms and the taloned legs turned softly curved. She screamed; and the Blodsaukers flinched, fearful of her, for in their subconscious they remembered the Berserker priests, their avowed enemies, who had searched down so many of their kind and destroyed them.

But Vanda was patron, not enemy, and had been chosen by God Himself to build a temple for the brotherhood and provide the sacrifice for the Great Rite of Fealty. So had Hrowthe, their wisest and most erudite, proclaimed; and so they had come, at his request, to this kingdom in the wilds of Germany to wipe away the vestiges of Freyja's sacrilege. By abstaining from sating the appetite of their sacred position the priests had empowered their goal, and the steadfastness of their conviction was revealed by the ruin of the forest, once sacred to pagan gods. Now they guarded it against trespassers, for Hrowthe's gift of farseeing had told of possible interference from tribes jealous of Vanda's wealth. Not even was Charles Martel to be trusted, he who had given her title to rule the land upon the death of her husband.

For who was to know when the problems with the Moorish heretics would end and the Church fathers turn their attention again to the German lands? It was not in the interest of the ignorant Catholics to allow a woman, no matter how pious, to rule. They did not understand it was the utter rejection of the sins inherent to the female sex that Vanda had embraced; and that rejection was what made her worthy to serve God personally.

She stood before them, naked but unarousing, her body a temple consecrated by the power of abstinence and the controlling force of her objectives. One of the priests removed his shabby tunic and offered it to her. Wrapping it about her shoulders, she went to the mouth of the grotto and knelt. An uncertain smile graced her lips, and with her fingertips she brushed the warrior's frosted face. She whispered to the priests to fetch two of her guards, who waited at the edge of the forest for her command.

The power of her maternal heritage glowed in her rosy countenance—the strength and unforgiving temper of the ancient Burgundian queens, the resilience and zeal of her more recent Christian ancestresses. Like Gundrun, the Volsung princess, she realized she was different from other mortal women; and that the difference necessitated she maintain a strong hand in governing her inferiors and her aides. She kept only enough Saxons to maintain the fief's crops and livestock. The others had long ago been bartered into servitude of Boniface's brothers, who had been assigned by the Pope to build cities in the domains wrested from pagan tribes.

She had recruited Lombards and other foreigners to manufacture those goods required, to run the smithies and other trades of her land; and she possessed the deft talent of dangling marriage before noblemen so lusty for her land and the chance to call themselves lord of it they thought nothing of sending her cart upon cart of gold and silver and exotic spices and fabrics.

Nor did Lady Vanda squander her wealth. But for the maintenance of her private apartments, her city was managed on a frugal budget. With her stern ordinances in place, few of her mercenaries or traders would risk life or wealth to be caught committing the sins of the flesh with the handful of women that dwelt in the female section of the serfs' quarters. Hrowthe had told the brethren Vanda was the epitome of the female perfected, and it was true. They doubted not she would receive the treasure of the Nibelung for her part in the Rite—and that she would use the treasure just as she claimed, to bolster her army and keep her kingdom a safe haven for those seeking shelter from the corruption of the old pagan misconceptions.

So had the respectful Blodsaukers vowed that when the Rite was completed they would take turns guarding her kingdom until her death—or that blessed day for which they had each gorged their veins upon human blood and knowledge for the sake of humanity's deliverance from the falsehoods of mortal existence. If that day came while she still lived, surely at God's side would Lady Vanda hold a special place.

Now, as the warrior gasped for breath, they bowed their heads, though not one could imagine why she would allow this brother of Lord Thierry to live.

* * *

While still in the semblance of the raven Vanda had pored over the warrior's thoughts, investigating for sign of treachery and for confirmation that he was, indeed, her dead husband's brother. She'd pulled away with a hoard of information and was satisfied, though his pagan sentiments and love for her husband were unsettling. It was the warrior's own greed for power and relentless need to prove his worth to a long-dead father and pious mother, however, that made him a ripe instrument to remedy the very problem that Thierry had wrought.

Vanda could not believe her good fortune. Her own mercenaries were either too frightened of the unknown or unchaste by pagan standards to even hope to find the boundaries of the unearthly realm of Athla. That Thierry had entered was proof enough he was unworthy to rule, even in but name, a Christian land; that he'd taken Odette there was unforgivable. But now had fate brought one whose very sins would allow him into Athla.

Vanda laid her mouth on Cu'lugh's and blew her warm breath into his throat. He stirred again, his eyelids working until he broke the ice that matted his lashes together. He stared at her as if confused, but as a human she could not read his thoughts. She smiled and saw a tiny reaction, as if he struggled against the freezing death. She flattened herself over his shivering form.

She remembered the images she'd gleaned while yet in her raven's guise—of Thierry, and of Thierry's mother, whom this knight loved more than his own. There was a flitting image so bright it had nearly blinded, but that she'd put away without concern for its nature and returned to her true form.

She would have to give this man the comfort he'd sought by coming here, to show him Thierry's grave. That single thought caused her some pain, for never

9

would she forget that once Thierry had adored her and taken pains to please her for the chance of being permitted a second entry into her bed. Then his tender conscience began to question her over the running of the fief he'd entrusted her with and the fate of the girl, whom he had himself taken into Burgundy. Such a shame that her husband had not understood that for his sake alone had she graciously put the bastard out to fosterage instead of killing her as Charles had proposed.

For all Cu'lugh's misconceptions, his faults too many to count, his greed made him malleable as much as Thierry's conscience had made him, in the end, unbearable.

Vanda felt Cu'lugh's body shudder and he said something in her ear. When she gazed down at him she could see that consciousness had returned.

"Welcome, brother Cu'lugh," she said. "We feared you lost to death's embrace, but I see my arms proved more determined."

Chapter Three

In Odette's dream her mother was as vital and close as if she'd never died. Silfr was all white, flawless skin and black hair, her dark eyes patient; but her voice was urgent as she told Odette to fetch a certain egg from a certain nest by a certain brook. Odette watched herself flit through a grove outside the city, the lush grass cool under her bare feet, until she came to a clearing and a gurgling brook. At the edge stood an apple tree laden with fruit and at its roots was a nest. Three large eggs lay cradled within: two of dull amber, the third green and speckled with pink. This was the one she sought and gingerly she picked it up and folded it carefully in her apron.

But when she turned a man stood before her, dressed in hunter-green breeches and a tunic of beaten leather. Dark of eyes and hair and mustached, he was unlike any Saxon man, but she knew him somehow and relaxed when he smiled.

"Your egg is broken." It was all he said, but it was enough to make her blush and grow hot with embarrassment; and when she unrolled the fabric of her apron she saw that, indeed, the egg had broken and a small serpent with scales of gossamer rainbow hues lifted its tiny head to her. It hissed at her in such a way she wanted to stroke it, but as she lifted her fingers to touch the glossy head the clearing suddenly darkened and a wind swept down, so fierce it roiled the surface of the water.

Odette sheltered the serpent between the apron and her belly and looked up. The man was gone, and where he had been there stood an ancient crone. The wind whipped her grey-streaked black hair about her face and her raspy cackle broke through the tumult; and as she raised her twisted and swollen hands Odette saw long, long, sharp nails.

"You chose poorly, Odette."

The next moment she descended and her claws wrapped about Odette's throat. Odette could not breathe or move, and despite the sense of impending doom she knew that, but for the darkness, the crone held no power.

Sunlight suddenly struck Odette's face. The crone's fingers slipped away and her cackle dwindled and Odette awoke, safe in the bright-walled room she had grown to love. Beside her bed was a tray laden with fresh fruit and soft bread drizzled with honey. The handmaiden who had drawn back the curtains apologized but said it was as well, for Queen Honi was coming shortly with important tidings.

The kings of Athla were bound by sacred law to consult the judgment of the leading vitkis, the priestesses of Freyja, before making any decision that affected women and children. In Athla, the role of men was two-fold—masters and protectors—and any abusive perversion of this privilege was subject to the gravest of penalties. Evolved from the ancient principles of seith, the practices set forth by the goddess Freyja and Her lordly consort Od, the culture of Athla was based on the fundamental belief in the balance of the opposing yet complimentary elements of femininity and masculinity.

Odette had known since the first day Thierry had brought her to the household of King Larsarian and Queen Honi that the time would arrive when she would have to say good-bye to the carefree childhood that Athlans promoted for their children. She would leave the court and her friends and be schooled under the experienced hand of a vitki specialized in training the young women to please men. She could not know the date when this was to befall, for it was deemed by custom such precise knowledge would ruin the happiness of childhood. But she'd been warned of what would come, and she had accepted it; though she feared this education, shrouded in mystery, almost as much as returning to Burgundy. Again and again she told herself Thierry would return for her before the time arrived for her education, that Thierry would succeed in convincing Vanda it was best for all involved for Odette to return to her homeland, even if she were declared a bastard and could expect no more privilege than a position as one of Vanda's handmaidens.

Although much time had passed and King Larsarian had assured Odette she was just as much a citizen as any born in Athla, she still feared losing the unconditional love she'd come to know in this strange and wonderful land only to be entered by the chosen and worthy few.

When she was ten years of age Thierry had taken her to a small estate in Burgundy to be raised by acquaintances of her sister. Odette had wanted to love her guardians, Bierns and Irene, and tried to please them. But the couple were suspicious of her every thought and critical of her every move. Irene said she would end up facing God's eternal punishment for favoring gowns and other standard feminine apparel to the masculine breeches and rough shirts she herself wore. Irene's eccentric demands did not end at the wardrobe; she expected Odette to labor in the fields, not planting or harvesting but laboring at those tasks customarily undertaken by men—plowing and cutting timber, even helping the men to cut the horns on the oxen and geld the steers. Odette did not possess the strength or experience to keep up with the men and when Irene discovered her male servants often sent Odette away while they toiled she accused her fosterling of trying to enchant the servants into taking over her work.

Irene also accused Odette of trying to enchant her husband, even though Odette was too young to comprehend her meaning. Bierns, a hermit within his house, had been all too eager to pacify his domineering wife's cynical views regarding Odette. He grew increasingly violent, quick to strike Odette across the face at the first drop of a tear she might shed under Irene's accusations and reproaches, as if such exhibitions would disquiet his wife's suspicions.

The couple's odd behavior had at first pained Odette greatly, but their relentless denunciation at last made her indifferent, at least to their words. She dreamt of a day when Vanda would call her home again; but when Thierry arrived with news he was taking her not home but to other guardians her dreams sifted away like grave ash to the four winds, so sure she was that it was to a household even less loving than that of Bierns and Irene. She remembered little of the journey through the Wastelands except that abiding despondency.

But King Larsarian and Queen Honi were as different from Bierns and Irene as clear water to muck. Upon her arrival they had revealed to her that her mother had been a kinswoman of Queen Honi's.

Odette loved Queen Honi deeply; and Honi let her play with the children of her serving women just as Silfr had so many years before. Unlike the women of Athla, children were free to roam the city and the countryside as they wished. King Larsarian indulged Odette as fully as any father, and with her companions she spent most of her days playing in the streets or exploring the hills and dales of the city's pastureland. At night she would return to the castle and there keep the hours until bedtime with the queen, who enjoyed telling wondrous stories as she brushed and braided Odette's long golden hair; and they often played games until the king ordered his wife to bed.

Odette grew accustomed to seeing the serving women working in their pretty livery, which would have made the priests of the Christian realms gasp and fume. As well as wearing scanty garments, Odette knew, these women were subject to embarrassing punishments dealt out by the castle stewards, and part of their duties involved pleasing those who held power over them, whether it were the stewards or the king's noblemen.

Queen Honi herself had to dress to please the king and she was not exempt from chastisement any more than her servants. This did not shock Odette entirely, even after years in the dispassionate household of Bierns and Irene. Silfr, her mother, had been as subject to the will of Odette's father and for that reason had been held as his most treasured ornament. The king and queen loved with the same devotion and passion as her parents, and so Odette had quickly come to feel at home in Athla and in the royal household.

Last night, however, the queen had said Odette was to stay indoors today, that she would not be able to join her companions for some time. Odette's heart quickened now with a wild and unsettling desire to flee her rooms and hide in the streets. She thought of her friends and the grottoes of the forests where they had played the day before, and of the stream in the northern glen where sometimes she went to fish. They would wonder what had happened to her...and soon enough guess the answer and know she was not returning to them.

After a time two of the queen's servants came and dressed her in a simple dress of white cotton with a skirt crisscrossed with ribbons of pink satin. They also brought her favorite shoes, the simple leather ones she wore almost daily, and new stockings of a sheer white fabric. They took from her wardrobe a cape of grey flannel and spread this across the foot of her bed. For the first time Odette truly noticed how vulnerable these girls were in the thigh-length chemises they wore, denied undergarments to conceal the secret portals between their legs. For once she minded their company, resenting the smell of their perfume and the subservient way they addressed the steward who looked in from time to time. And, very unexpectedly, Odette felt even a twinge of resentment for Queen Honi and, irrationally, toward the image of her mother that seemed close to her thoughts.

When the serving girls left Odette sat on the side of the bed, rolling a ball of colored yarn scraps across the blankets. Her heart beat rapidly and every few moments she looked up expectantly at the white-stained door. At last it opened and she leaped off the mattress, ready to fling her arms about the queen. But she held back, for Honi was not alone.

Odette recognized the woman with the cool grey eyes as one of the queen's friends. She did not visit as frequently as some of Honi's friends and Odette couldn't recall her name. Tall and very fair of skin, the woman had deep auburn hair bound in a braid rolled tight at the back of her head. She wore leather breeches and riding boots like a man, and her face, oval and hard despite its prettiness, reminded Odette of a young boy's. Tucked in the belt at her lean hip was a narrow-lashed flail. The lady's long fingers toyed idly with the smooth rounded handle that was sheathed with iron-studded leather.

Odette looked at the queen, admiring her soft gossamer pantaloons that billowed out from a golden girdle at her waist. Her breasts were unveiled this morning, the nipples capped with gold thimbles, and her throat was adorned with a hammered golden collar. Honi's hair was woven into a single braid that fell from the crown of her head all the way to the back of her knees. Despite her bright garments, however, the queen's blotched cheeks and red eyes betrayed her unhappiness.

Odette reproached herself for a moment's resentment toward Honi. "Please do not weep, dearest Honi," she said. "I know what you have come to say."

Queen Honi embraced her savagely. "Sweet Odette," she murmured. "Yes, the time of innocence is past." She wiped the tears from her face with the back of her hand and smiled a little. "I weep not for you, dearest, but myself. You have been as a daughter to me. But now I understand my own mother's tears the day I was led away to be taught those things which all my life I'd heard were the most beautiful and sacred of the womanly arts. You see, dearest, that which may seem almost impossible to bear now shall pass away, even though I fear I shall grieve long for those times we might yet have spent together."

Odette felt tears in her own eyes now. "You have been very good to me, Honi, always." It was truth—she had known nothing but contentment in Athla.

"You have known such loss, and now, by law and custom, I must send you away. How I would have preferred to keep you here, pampering you forever. At least my good king and husband has allowed me to chose your teacher instead of summoning them here to bid for the right of your tutelage and education as is usual."

Odette glanced at the other woman—the teacher, surely, and Odette could not stifle the sharp dislike brewing in her heart.

"I do wish we could have had more than this single mortal year together," the queen lamented.

One year? No, it must have been longer than that, Odette thought.

"Have I grown so quickly?"

The queen shook her head. "No, my love, do you not remember? Well, it is better that way, I suppose. You are eighteen years of age, by reckoning in your world, and before coming here you dwelt in the household of Duke Bierns of Burgundy and his wife, Irene, for ten. I remember that first night Thierry brought you here—a frightened, despairing child. It is well the last year has seemed longer."

"You have treated me so well, Queen Honi," Odette said, "I shall always treasure my time here."

Honi smiled brilliantly through fresh tears. She sighed and looked hesitantly at the woman. "This is Helrose, Odette, my good friend. We were trained together in the sacred arts. As I chose to wed and give myself completely as a love thrall to the king, Helrose chose to become a teacher. She is a Mistress of seith and as such bows to no other woman."

Odette looked at Helrose, and the lady's stony, unreadable eyes made her tremble.

"I am honored, Helrose."

The woman's mouth spread into a one-sided smile, making her pretty features look like carved alabaster. "You shall address me only as 'my Mistress,' Odette. You shall never speak to me without permission, save it be an emergency, and you shall obey my every word—or face whatever punishment I deem fitting. Can you remember this?"

Odette flushed at the sharp words and she edged instinctively toward Queen Honi.

"It is all right, child," Honi said softly. "This is the way. The schooling is rigorous and the teachers strict, as it must be, but no harm shall come to you, I promise."

Odette shook her head. "No, no," she whispered. "I-I think she wishes for me to be…like you! And I mean no disrespect, but I am not ready for that!"

The Mistress took a step toward Odette so that she seemed a tower of unmovable pale stone. Her voice softened a bit; the inflexibility relaxed a moment. "Do you know how Honi and I were taken away for schooling, Odette?"

Odette shook her head.

"You have seen the serving girls punished by the king's stewards—chastened publicly, harshly. It seems cruel to you, yes? Imagine being taken from your home by such a man, carried through the streets and taken to the Guild of the Instructors, and there stripped of your garments before an assembly of strangers, taken away again by the one bidding the highest for the honor of training you in the sacred arts. That is how it fared for us—with no choice, no hope of redemption, even when our mothers and fathers passed each day before the houses of our teachers, saw us from the streets. You were raised in the Outer Realm, Odette, and these things seem strange to you…and so you should be grateful to our king who spoils his wife and allows her to choose for you a teacher enlightened to the ignorance instilled there."

Odette saw a trace of a smile pass between the two women. She had no doubt this Mistress spoke true, and yet her dread was inconsolable.

"Please, Honi, may I not have but a little longer?"

The queen clasped Odette's face tenderly between her hands and kissed her brow. "No, you must go now, Odette. If you resist the king will chose your teacher for you, one not as understanding as Helrose."

"I am a patient woman," said Helrose, "and I know it will be most difficult for you, raised in the Outer Realm as you were. But I shall be strict, have no doubt; and the best comfort you can find is to remember why our young women undergo this training. Have you any idea, child?"

Odette blinked. "No…I mean, perhaps—to learn the sacred arts of seith, the balance between men and women."

Mistress Helrose nodded slowly. "Yes, that is part of it. The balance of male and female, the essence of both principles we all carry within ourselves. You must understand, as all young people, the intrinsic attributes of the respective sexes. The male, physically the dominant of the two, must learn to control and ennoble his dominant position. The female must learn submission with dignity and without yielding her individual personality. These generalities I speak of are natural, but not inflexible; and it may well be that one day you will be inclined toward the mirrored balance, and become a dominant mistress as permitted by the holy statutes.

"But first you must learn the sacred arts that were practiced by Freyja Herself as an act of homage to Her beloved and as a means of fulfilling Her own divinity. Obedience and submission are the key lessons. As I said, this does not mean you yield your own personality or opinions and thoughts, for hollow is the vessel from which the wine is taken. You shall learn not only how to give men pleasure but how to be appealing to them, to temper your emotions, your anger and moods and become deserving of their respect, protection and desire. It is a hallowed way, Odette, to follow the example of the Goddess, Who, while She is the great lifegiver and bearer of pleasure, must submit to the pleasure and will of the God—the bringer of trials and death."

Odette's thoughts were frantic, and she blurted out, "But I can love the goddess without all of this!"

Helrose sighed. "No, Odette. It has been tried before, in your realm. What do you believe keeps our realm safe from the suffering, disease and war that infects Midgard? Allows us to live so long that your people believe we are elementals or demons or legends? What has allowed us to feel and govern with our own force of will the natural processes of our bodies with such precision that overpopulation is never a concern?

"It is not that we are better than your father's race, Odette, but that we long ago chose to embrace the marriage of body and soul so that we can enjoy and learn and love. We know the soul need not return time and again to learn what it needs, but can, when cleansed of futile delusions, create and enjoy all the rewards of a heaven within one lifetime.

"And when the time comes we do die—whether by accident or rare treachery—we return to this realm as soon as a womb becomes available or by simple manifestation. Our souls are not bound to misconceptions that we cannot learn but for suffering endlessly in fire and brimstone or by reincarnating time and again in bodies ignorant of the truth."

Odette's skin crawled. "I-I do not believe this, you are mistaken!"

A small smile eased Helrose's hard features. "You cannot believe now, but you shall. The only difference between Athlans and folk of Midgard is our faith that we are all active extensions of the Eternal Ones instead of segregated, lost elements."

"Are you saying I shall never die?"

"I do not know. The misconceptions run deep in the psyche of the Midgardians, so deeply that they spread to and taint even the perceptions of those growing in the womb. But if you cannot expel the misconceptions entirely, at least you can enjoy our life while you are here. That, too, will be part of your education."

Odette wanted to say that she'd enjoyed life already while in Athla. Why did she need to give up her friends, the carefree days of playing in the fields and running heedlessly in the streets? But she knew there was nothing more she could say to justify this argument; the choice had been made for her.

And anger for that began to swell within her. How dare this woman speak of freedom in the same breath as she expounded the need for slavery? Certainly, she did not feel as fortunate as this Mistress had implied she should.

Then again, the queen had specially chosen Helrose, and perhaps that was because this woman, despite her cool demeanor, was more like the queen than her position allowed her to admit. It was a desperate thought to cling to, but it helped still Odette's outrage.

Even so, she trembled as the queen wrapped the flannel cape about her shoulders, tying the red ribbon neatly at her throat. She was still trembling as they embraced in farewell, but summoned her composure as best she could to follow Mistress Helrose out of the bright room.

Chapter Four

As they walked through the castle Odette could not help but stare now, for the first time since coming to Athla, at the serving girls who went about their tasks in their collars and tiny chemises. The voices of the house guards and knights gathered in the meeting hall disturbed her somehow, the masculine inflections sounded so much deeper than before. The very stones of the walls seemed suddenly restrictive, and for the first time she paid heed to the sighs and suppressed whimpers, a slap of leather against flesh resounding from a chamber down the hallway. How she could have disregarded all these things she could not imagine; and she bit her lip once or twice, hoping the pain would make her ignore it all again.

She breathed a little easier once they were outside the castle, but then Mistress Helrose turned to her and warned her again not to speak unbidden except for dire need.

"Now, address me as you should," she commanded, and Odette noticed in the morning sun a dusting of freckles over the lady's nose and cheekbones.

She felt a sharp angry pang in her gut to say it: "My Mistress."

The Mistress nodded and strode across the thick lawn of the grounds and into the sparkling-clean cobblestone street. Odette noticed the way the guards bowed to Helrose, and their bold glances that swept over her revealed that they knew precisely why she was in the company of the Mistress. She blanched and lowered her eyes.

Mistress Helrose proceeded down toward the western section of town. Past the houses of the guild masters they passed, and the raised open temples of marble and bluestone with their columns of granite and marble roofed with burnished gold. As they neared the square Odette glanced back to look once again at Larsarian's castle, and she wondered if she would ever set foot again within the familiar walls. It saddened her to realize she'd not asked if the queen would ask after her, and already she missed Honi painfully.

Her eyes began to tear and she deliberately scanned the sharp snow-capped mountains surrounding Athla, taking some solace in the lazy mist tumbling down Heimdallr's Gorge to the north. Towering beyond to the west was Bragi's Song, the wide waterfall that fed the river that cut through the valley. As she gazed upon the distant foaming water she thought about the fields she and her playmates had played in, so thick and lush—the flowers of a thousand varieties that grew there, the trees under which they'd danced, some so large they dwarfed the castle.

Athla—no, it was not Midgard, where life was so fragile and transient. But now she longed so to be there, safe from the reach of Mistress Helrose and the law that now governed her life.

Odette's heart rebelled at being forced to give up the only security she'd known since her parents died. She thought of turning and fleeing suddenly down one of the narrow alleyways, of finding a route out of Athla, one that might lead her home...

"Do not dawdle, Odette!"

Odette inhaled briskly, holding her tongue that wanted to lash out against the order. How she hated the haughty woman! But she knew any attempt to flee would only bring the reckoning of the street sentries, and so she caught up with the Mistress and followed her into the western square.

This was one of the liveliest sections of the city during the daytime hours, where merchants without permanent shops brought their canopied carts to sell their wares, everything from household goods to food and jewelry. Well-dressed men with heavy money pouches on their belts gossiped with shopkeepers under the heavy awnings, while children ran in and out the doors of the respective establishments. Pedestrians and vendors alike congested the area, and the Mistress was forced to slow her quick pace so Odette could keep up.

Odette remembered not so long ago being stopped by one of the proprietors of the shops. He had thought her by her maturity to be a runaway from one of the houses of training and dared to call a street sentry. How she and her friends had laughed when a passing nobleman identified Odette as the queen's young ward and kinswoman.

"A child yet," the nobleman had said.

She and her companions had laughed at the apologetic proprietor even more as he shook his finger in her face and promised that one day she would regret her mockery.

Now Odette panicked at the thought of running into him again and she searched for him skittishly. She did not see him amongst the throng. But everywhere she saw women as she'd never truly seen them before. Barely clad— and not clad at all—wearing collars to designate they were owned by someone. Silken cords, bands of leather, chokers of precious metals—whatever their master or mistress wanted. Not one of these women was spared the tell-tale sign, not even those with babes in arms and certainly not those wearing the gold bands of matrimony on their left wrist. Yet, they went about their affairs with no embarrassment. Several even greeted the Mistress in passing, as if they not only accepted their slavery but that a few women actually escaped or eluded the condition. Odette wondered how they could be so friendly to Helrose.

I shall never allow myself to be so completely conditioned—and this arrogant Mistress shall never know my congeniality!

Mistress Helrose turned to give her another impatient look to hurry up. Odette resented that look, and she resented the men who paraded by leading their women on chains or gaily dyed leashes.

One woman advancing toward them was as well-clad as Mistress Helrose. A wide-shouldered blonde in suede riding clothes, she led by a leather leash a young man who was naked but for the silver collar about his neck. Odette was so startled she stopped in her tracks and stared at the two—and at the young man's endowments that swayed with his every plodding step. His skin was covered with a film of dirt and his brown hair was disheveled. There was a savage glower in the bright eyes that stared out from the unshaven face, and Odette saw that he deliberately avoided meeting the eyes of those they passed. The woman leading him walked as if in a great hurry, and as they passed by Odette saw half a dozen pink welts on the young man's thighs and buttocks. Without meaning to she gasped, and the woman glanced back, smiling coolly.

A firm hand grasped Odette's arm, making her jump.

The Mistress's eyes were narrowed and angry. "Young lady, you are to follow, not gape like some mannerless bumpkin."

Odette started to protest but something held her back. From behind the Mistress, she saw several men watching from where they sat at the mead house across the square. They laughed—good-naturedly, but Odette was unforgiving. She felt the anger swell in her chest and her hands clench into fists at her hips.

One of them called out "Mistress Helrose, what is this flower's name?"

The Mistress offered him a wan smile.

"It has been long since you patronized my establishment, Uung. If you wish to find out her name you must come by again." Mistress Helrose drew her fingers quite deliberately through the length of Odette's hair, letting it fall slowly over her shoulder so it looked like strands of gold cascading in the sunlight. Indignant, Odette drew back.

"Leave me be," she muttered crossly.

At once the woman reached out and pinched the lobe of Odette's left ear between a thumb and forefinger. Odette gasped again, astonished, and slapped the intrusive hand away, only to feel the next moment her head wrenched back when the Mistress grabbed a handful of her hair. The men at the table laughed louder now; and Odette did not know what was worse, the embarrassment or the icy stare of the Mistress.

"I will certainly come to try one of your elixirs again," the man said. "I look forward to being served by this little wildflower!"

Odette forgot her discomfort in the terror the man's words produced. She heard Helrose's voice, low and penetrating. "Shall I allow you to serve this man right now, Odette—in all ways he may enjoy? Is that what you wish?"

Odette's voice was shockingly compliant to her own ears. "No, my Mistress."

Mistress Helrose said some word of parting and apology to the men; but as soon as she released Odette's hair she grasped her wrist firmly and pulled her rudely along through the crowded way. Odette had never known such stunning humiliation; and she tried to avoid the eyes of the passersby, praying none would recognize her as the carefree girl who just the day before had run wild with her friends through the city.

At length the Mistress slowed, and Odette saw the gates to a private courtyard of a large residence. She was familiar with it, for her friends had told her it was the residence of one of Athla's most renowned healers. It was the last building on the western quadrant of the city, towered over by the great willows that were nurtured by the stream the property abutted. It was this water, she'd heard, clean and laden with minerals, that provided the essential ingredients for the elixirs that Athlans were so fond of drinking.

Odette had never set foot on the property or even ventured the back way through the city to the stream, but she knew from her friends that an iron fence enclosed the entire property. Adults patronized the place day and night to sip the elixirs and wines and herbal waters that were the healer's specialty.

The manor house was grand, built of warm brown stone and with large stained-glass windows. The roof was of gently lolling cream tiles. As the Mistress entered the gates Odette saw the tiles of the courtyard had been glazed and laid in such a fashion as to create a great image of paired white swans gliding across water.

The tables for the patrons were empty and Odette supposed the proprietor had not yet opened for business. Serving girls scurried about, all in slight chemises and brass collars, cleaning the tables and benches, untangling the breeze-twisted ribbons that hung from rose-covered trellises, watering the flowering herbs that grew in bronze pots set all about. From the corner of her eye, Odette saw the breeze lift the hem of one girl's pretty ivory chemise, displaying her private parts. The girl did not waste time pulling it down, and Odette could not help but wonder if such a gesture was forbidden.

The serving girls inclined their heads as Mistress Helrose hurried past. Odette tried to ignore their skirting, curious glances. As they advanced closer to the manor Odette saw several tall posts edging the courtyard from which hung on crosspieces large beehive-shaped cages of smooth wrought iron bars, floored, as well, with iron bars. She was about to ask permission to inquire what they were for when she saw something near one of the willow trunks that made her gasp. She heard a round of stifled giggles from the serving girls.

"It is nothing, Odette," the Mistress said, and to Odette's regret the lady stopped her course. She looked at the thing that had made Odette gasp: a low-built pillory about two and a half feet high in which was confined a girl with tousled brown hair. The girl's waist was thrust through a large eyelet opening between the upper and lower plank, and her wrists shackled to the front of the lower. Two locks beside the eyelet sealed the planks together. A small platform positioned the girl's lower abdomen and hips so that her naked buttocks were raised slightly above her head. Her legs dangled so that her toes barely touched the tiles. From a rope on the side of the pillory hung a long, thick wooden paddle. Odette did not have to wonder what it was used for.

Unlike the other girls, this one was utterly naked but for her collar. She wriggled uncomfortably in her bonds, and by her reddened eyes and damp face Odette knew she'd just recently been weeping.

"That flower sought to be clever when first set out for punishment, keeping her eyes shut as if to close out the consequences of her misbehavior. Thus, you see, Odette, she has lost the privilege of her maiden's chemise."

Odette felt guilty for staring at the girl, yet she could hardly draw her eyes away.

"You shall be given a chemise as well, dear," Mistress Helrose continued, "but take heed—wearing it is a privilege that, once forfeited, is difficult to regain."

The Mistress inclined her head to one of the other girls, who rushed ahead to open the manor's lily-carved oak door. Mistress Helrose pushed Odette into a Great Hall that, with its walls of smooth, grey stones and high wooden beams, reminded Odette somewhat of her father's feasting hall. A long banquet table stood in the middle of the room, surrounded by heavy oaken high-back chairs; and banners, trophies and other ornaments hung on the walls, though in the shadowy light Odette could not make out the details of them all.

But whereas the hearth in her father's hall had been a round stone structure that dominated the whole of the room, the hearth here was set into the farthest wall. Tall and wide enough for five men to stand within, its grate was cold now; and another serving girl swept the ashes away.

The girl looked up, bowing her head so quickly when she saw it was the Mistress who entered that her braid of brown hair swept softly across one cheek. The Mistress called her and she trotted forward and knelt at the lady's feet.

"Yolande, where is—-?" the Mistress began, and then turned toward a tall, lean figure entering through a door in the distant corner of the room. "Ah, there you are, brother."

Odette shivered as the man approached, though why she wasn't sure. He shared his sister's fair complexion, and his long breeches and overcoat were of dark, sober cloth. The heels of his boots clicked sharply as he approached. Odette could not help but stare at his face, so handsome he was with finely chiseled features and deep-set eyes of the most vivid blue she'd ever seen. His hair was soft and dark and fell softly about his shoulders.

He caught her stare and smiled, a gesture much like his sister's but more profound in its hardness. Odette shivered and turned her eyes away.

"So, this is Odette." There was something pointed about the way he said it, something that verged on reproach. She raised her eyes carefully and saw that he carried, as did his sister, a flail. Odette felt angry again, in part because she'd not expected to find a man in a position of authority at her teacher's house and in part for the near-malice of that smile he wore.

"The queen's brat."

Odette bristled and noticed how Helrose's brow rose and her tone flattened. "Eryan is my brother, Odette, and as do all my flowers, you shall address him as *my Lord*, as with our other stewards. We have a washerwoman and a seamstress who are to be called *my Lady*. The same rule applies in speaking to your superiors as with myself. Lest I bid otherwise, you shall obey their every instruction as if it were my own."

Odette could hardly believe fate had played her so wrongly. The gods expected such a price for her deliverance from Burgundy? Not only service to Mistress

Helrose, but men as well?

This is wrong, wrong, she thought; and suddenly she hated Athla with all the passion with which she'd appreciated it. At least in the world beyond its borders her body would have been safe from the eyes of men, either by concealment in masculine garments as the insecure Irene had preferred or in those drab, voluminous and shapeless gowns endorsed by the women-fearing Church fathers.

"I see she is yet ignorant of proper manners, sister," Lord Eryan remarked.

Helrose smiled blandly. "I shall leave much of her enlightening to you, brother. But we need to speak. Yolande, take Odette to the wardrobe room and find suitable garments for her."

Chapter Five

dette quailed as the Mistress gestured her to follow the girl. Through a door to the south wing of the manor Yolande led her. It opened into a long hallway with a staircase at the very end, and a soft, hazy light filtered down the stairs from a window on the second floor. Yolanda entered one of the many doors along the hall into a windowless room. Several chests stood against the walls, as well as two tall wardrobes. A great silver mirror stretched across nearly the length of the back wall. Standing before this, Yolande whispered that Odette should undress.

"You spoke," Odette said.

"Yes. It is permitted when neither the Mistress nor any of the stewards are about, as long as we speak quietly."

Odette regarded the girl with an uncertain emotion, for though she felt a certain amount of pity for Yolande, she sensed resentment and impatience from her. The girl muttered as she hunted through one of the wardrobes, and when she returned held out the familiar chemise and a handful of silken cords, the kind used for braiding hair.

"I will help you change now."

Odette walked over to the door, which stood ajar, and eyed it nervously. "Only in private."

Yolande wedged herself between Odette and the door. "You must learn to disrobe without shame—it is part of our training."

Odette closed her eyes, not entirely believing she was truly enduring this, especially from one who should have understood her feelings. "It is but a small thing to ask for, is it not—my first day here?"

"A small thing?" Yolande's mouth hardened. "Lord Eryan is right about you—now stop being so haughty and disrobe."

Odette tried to dismiss the remark, thinking the girl must have experienced an exhausting morning. She eyed the things in Yolande's hands and smiled bitterly.

"No collar?"

"Lord Eryan will see to that."

Odette could not believe the unfeeling words or the contempt so plain in Yolande's eyes. She struggled for air and the walls seemed to be slowly closing about them both. "No, Yolande, I shall never wear those horrid things!"

A savage desperation came over Odette. She thrust Yolande's hands away, knocking the chemise and cords to the floor. The girl's face reddened and she hissed angrily.

The moment Yolande stooped to retrieve the scattered items Odette slammed the door and threw her weight against it. Yolande glowered at her.

"Please," Odette whispered desperately, "this life is not for me! Help me, Yolande, please! There must be a way out of this place, out of Athla altogether!"

Yolande did not answer, only threw her load down again and, reaching up, grasped Odette's hand tightly, trying to wrench her down. Odette growled and kicked Yolande in the shoulder lightly, breaking the girl's hold. Yolande turned and lunged forward on her knees, catching the hem of Odette's cape.

"Stop trying to draw their attention," she spat.

Odette's fear and its accompanying anger broke open like a hot spring too long dammed. She screamed with such intensity that Yolande jumped and her eyes bulged.

"Stop this before its too late, Odette!"

But it was already too late—footsteps, brisk and heavy, sounded in the hallway and the next moment the doorknob twisted.

"Open this door immediately!" It was Lord Eryan, and his tone of icy anger made Odette's legs feel weak and unsteady.

"How could you do this to me," she demanded of Yolande, who had moved back now. Odette saw the fear in the other girl's eyes, just beneath the blazing scorn.

Lord Eryan put his weight to the door, over and over, until Odette's feet slid back and allowed him entrance. She shrank in the corner behind it, terrified beyond thought. He strode in and stood over Yolande, and Odette saw he gripped the handle of the flail tightly in one hand. Yolande shook her head wordlessly and pointed to the corner where Odette stood.

His husky voice made her very soul tremble. 'Odette."

With his free hand he grasped her wrist. She screamed as he pulled her, stomping both her feet wildly.

"I shall not wear this unseemly garment!" she wailed and twisted her arm violently in the effort to escape. She broke free and started to run to the other side of the room when his arm caught her at the waist and she heard footsteps.

"She *refuses* our generous wardrobe," he said in his mockingly calm tone.

He grabbed her hair and yanked her head to one side so that she was forced to meet Mistress Helrose's disapproving face. The cool demeanor of that disapproval only fanned Odette's rage; she screamed and kicked one heel backward, striking Eryan's shin. Ignoring the pain in his cry she wriggled with all her might against the arm that enclosed her waist. Then she felt a terrible sharp pain in her left nipple— the Mistress had pinched it between her thumb and forefinger and now began to turn it and wrench it as one prying a weed from a garden. The pain was unbearable. She stilled, panting, and growled at both of them.

The next moment she heard Lord Eryan throw the flail to the floor. He lifted her arms by the wrists above her head and held her so that only the tips of her toes touched the floor. Odette kicked in frustration as the Mistress went to comfort Yolande, who was crying and sputtering as she relayed all Odette had done.

The Mistress returned, reached up and untied Odette's cape, handing it to

Yolande. Then from a pocket on the hip of her breeches she pulled out a pair of tiny shears, the kind often carried on cloth brooches by matrons in Midgard. Helrose cut into the shoulder seams of the beautiful ribboned gown.

"No, please," Odette pleaded.

It did no good, of course. Soon enough Mistress Helrose had rent the seams of the beautiful garment and it fell to the floor. Odette's breasts were bare and she blushed, closing her eyes as she felt the Mistress tug on the side of her silken underpants. Odette gasped to hear shears split through the seams, and as the cloth slipped over her hips and down her legs she began to cry. The Mistress unbuckled her leather shoes and removed these, too, and lastly, the dainty white stockings were pulled down her calves and over her feet. Odette was naked now in Lord Eryan's grasp, and she twisted this way and that in the urgency to free herself and run away and hide.

The Mistress slapped her face and Odette's struggle stopped. She expected reprimand, of a length to surpass Irene's angriest tirade; but instead of reproach, the Mistress fished from her pocket a key and held it up before Odette's eyes. Odette stared at it, not daring to think what it locked or opened. Helrose then gave Lord Eryan a knowing nod. He let go of Odette's wrists and with a snap of his hands caught her about the waist, spun her about and threw her up over one shoulder. Odette was so startled she could not make a sound, and with her golden hair sweeping against the back his knees he carried her from the room and down the hallway.

Odette's shock had subsided enough for her to know a new fear. Lord Eryan opened the door in the hall and she felt the merciless light of the sun caress her naked flesh. She heard murmurs from the girls who worked in the courtyard, and knew that everyone there was now a spectator to her humiliation. She squirmed on Lord Eryan's shoulder and thrashed the air with her feet and beat her fists on his back and screamed angrily, thinking there was surely some merciful soul who would hear her from the public square and come to her defense.

Suddenly, Lord Eryan stopped, but not to release her. Mistress Helrose stepped past them, reaching for something. Odette heard a faint but distinct scrape of metal.

She was heaved into one of the cages, not too roughly, but with enough force she was thrust against the far bars. Before she could fling herself at the door Lord Eryan shut it firmly and Mistress Helrose turned the key. The lock dropped with a leaden sound. Odette glared at them, and with her temples drumming with anger and fear, pounded her fists against the bars.

"Let me out!"

Lord Eryan's brow was dark and creased with agitation, but Mistress Helrose remained imperturbable.

"Continue this tantrum and you'll find yourself tethered and gagged, young lady."

Odette panted to control her scream, for she knew the woman would not hesitate to do just as she vowed. Past the Mistress the naked girl was still bound in the pillory, and the others watched as smiling and curious customers strolled up from the square.

Why did I not obey?

Odette felt the tears, hot and heavy, roll down her cheeks; and she lowered her head and sobbed, angry but regretful.

This response must have contented the Mistress, for she and her brother walked back into the manor. The serving girls gathered about Odette's cage, whispering amongst themselves. Odette huddled against the back, wishing she could just break the bars and run from them. But at length they returned to their work.

The bars of the cage were so much more confining than she could have ever imagined. Her least movement made it sway, lending her the added concern that it might fall. After a time, though, she realized the crosspiece held it quite securely, and she began to relax a little. She folded her legs together, inclining her face over her arms and concealing herself as much as possible with her hair.

Her legs eventually began to ache so she had no choice but to move a little. Raising her head slightly she saw the serving girls had the courtyard spotless and the tables ready. One table was set with stone jugs and an array of clean silver cups. Customers were quickly filling up the seats and benches. Odette turned her back to them and folded her legs tightly to one side, bowing her head so her hair shielded her face entirely.

For a long time she sat this way, trying to ignore the sounds of their conversations and laughter. But just as she began to feel numb from her position she felt a hand on her hip. She jumped, horrified and tried to scoot away from the intrusive touch while keeping her legs folded. Through the spaces of the bars she looked at the grinning man who had touched her. Odette shrieked. He moved about the cage slowly, caressing her with his appraising eyes, and to Odette's alarm a second man came up beside him and regarded her with the same bold smile. She fell back on her buttocks and with her heels pushed away from them. The one who had touched her wore a white shirt and pants of beige velvet; the other was dressed in the powder-blue uniform of the queen's personal guards. Neither spoke to her. Finally they moved away slowly, the one in beige blowing her a kiss as they went to find a table.

She watched as they detoured over to the pillory. The one in beige slapped the buttocks of the captive girl. It was only one slap; but the girl guessed what next they planned and she squirmed fretfully, whimpering. The men walked to the front of the pillory where the girl could see them and the young guard bent down, tilted her head sideways and kissed her mouth for a long, greedy moment. They went on, then, taking a seat at one of the tables. Odette saw the girl's mouth pucker as if she was in great discomfort, though it didn't seem exactly to Odette as if she were in pain. A little time later another group of men approached and toyed with the girl's breasts and filled her vagina gently with their fingers. She groaned deeply, and the frustration on her face made Odette blush.

Odette wanted to hate the girl for allowing herself to react passionately, or at least Mistress Helrose for promoting the girl's passion. But when the girl groaned again Odette's thighs flared with a sudden and intense heat, and the humiliation of it made her start to cry again silently.

Another man appeared from the manor. He was tall and muscular beneath his cotton tunic and leather breeches. His blonde hair was swept back in a single tail. He had an easy smile, so different from the demeanor of Lord Eryan. His presence brought a certain uneasy alertness to the ranks of the serving girls, and when he addressed them their heads bowed. But their faint blushes were not lost on Odette. He was almost tender in his speech, even complimenting their work before he sent them all into the manor. His primary tasks seemed to be overseeing the needs of the patrons and the obedience of the fresh bevy of girls who came trotting out from the manor.

These were dressed in skimpy ruffled aprons and nothing else besides the brass collars on their necks. They served the customers with only a minimum of words, smiling readily, diligently, no matter how many ogling eyes skimmed over them or how many hands tweaked their thighs or nipples.

Odette sighed and shook her head, refusing to believe this was acceptable behavior. The customers began to come up to her cage and pinch her buttocks or thighs or stroke her hair casually, as if she were but some pet to them; and she tried to believe she would awaken from this distressing dream at the call of her friends outside her bedroom window at the castle where all was familiar and secure.

Yet, there was not one note of malice in the patron's caresses and touches, as if it were but natural she be subject to such attentions. She was surprised to overhear comments on her beauty, for besides her biased kinswoman Honi she couldn't remember anyone ever saying she was pretty.

Her sister had been pretty with her dark hair and startling blue eyes, her slender limbs and tiny waist. The beauty of Odette's small-boned mother, Silfr, had inspired ballads in her homeland just as much as had her devotion to the chieftain. Odette's eyes were not blue like Vanda's nor exotic black like Silfr's, but green. Her hair was neither gleaming black nor rich brunette—certainly not blonde as Honi's—but that rich gold of filtered honey. Her features she'd inherited directly from her father, even down to the high forehead of which she'd always been self-conscious; and though Rulf had been an attractive man, Odette had always regretted that the petite features with which both her mother and half-sister had been graced had eluded her.

At length, Odette was torn between hating the presumptuous patrons and taking consolation, perhaps even a little pride, in their compliments.

The pair of young men who had teased her earlier finished their drinks and called for the steward. The one in the beige breeches asked, "Is the little green-eyed flower in the cage available for pleasure?"

Odette was so alarmed by this question she gasped sharply. They laughed to hear it, and the steward, too, but to Odette's relief he stifled their inquiry.

"She is a virgin," he said. "You will have to wait until after her Unveiling."

"And when is that scheduled?"

The steward was quiet a moment. "No more than a month, surely. But any of our bloomed flowers are available for your pleasure. They are all fully trained."

Odette shuddered. *It is true what the Mistress said!*

She was miserable, wondering what this *Unveiling* meant, and if she, as the other girls, would be made *available* to customers when it was done.

She shut out the banter of the three men and hugged her legs to her breasts tightly, glad that her hair fell over her like a canopy. It alone offered a touch of privacy. The sun was moving toward the center of the heavens and the reflection of it made the cage bars very warm against her skin. She began to grow sleepy and her arms and legs ached to move. But she refused to give in to the pain. It was what they expected—that she give in to the restricting bars and move about seeking a comfortable position, uncaring of the eyes upon her. Yes, it was punishment, effective punishment, all the more humiliating for the inner admission that her behavior had merited it.

Suddenly, she heard a loud *crack* and a pained cry that trailed off into a fretful whimper. She turned slightly in the cage and lifted her eyes under the veil of her hair to see the steward standing behind the girl in the pillory. The paddle was raised in his right hand.

He must have been content with the single crack across her buttocks because he dropped the paddle and unbolted the upper board. He raised it, gently lifted the girl off the platform and, picking her up into his arms, delivered her to the table where now sat the two young men who had asked for Odette's pleasure. He placed her into the lap of the one in the beige breeches. The young man tilted the girl's face up and, turning her chin carefully, kissed her exposed throat. She moaned, shuddering, and as his mouth grazed over her throat he cupped her breasts in his hands, massaging the nipples, making them grow hard and pink. The girl's head fell limp against his shoulder and her hips bobbed on his lap.

Odette hid her frantic tears against her knees.

Not all the punishments or training in the world will make me surrender like that!

But the throb between her thighs seemed to mock her thoughts, and so she enveloped herself with indignation, hoping it would ease the discomforting ache.

Chapter Six

fter a time Odette felt someone else draw near. She was terrified whoever this was would see or guess the moment of passion she'd felt at watching the girl with the young men and began to tremble and squeeze her legs even more tightly.

"You should not do that, little flower. Here, open your eyes."

She did so with a whimper and found not a patron but the blonde steward, and his beauty was so fierce and startling that she inched back as far as the bars would allow.

"Your tears should be long over, little flower." His voice was much kinder than Lord Eryan's. He reached through the bars, offering Odette a linen napkin. "Wipe them away now."

She dried her cheeks and nose with the napkin and found it difficult not to stare at his handsome features. Her thighs tingled fiercely and she blushed, though she found the strength not to cry again.

She spoke to him before thinking of the consequences, "Why do you call me *flower?*"

He laughed gently. "All Mistress Helrose's students are called flowers." He folded his long arms across his chest. "You are not to speak without permission, you know that?"

She nodded timidly, but knew by his patient tone she had nothing to fear at the moment.

"Odette, Odette..." His voice was beautiful and she found herself wanting him to say her name again. "You look enough like the queen that I can understand Lord Eryan's frustration," he went on, "but worry naught, flower. Just be pliant and sweet-natured and he shall soon be mollified. Our Lord Eryan is prone to moodiness and melancholy, but he is a proficient overseer."

His subtle hint of some frustration in Lord Eryan piqued Odette, and seeing her questioning look the steward said, "I am Alban—Lord Alban to you—and have served here longer than any other. Yours is a pretty face, little flower, you must not discolor it with tears any longer. Mistress Helrose is a strict teacher, but your wellbeing is important to her. Punishment should not be looked upon as cruel, Odette, but as a method of correcting undesirable behavior and instilling humility. A young lady learns either pride or self-loathing if her punishments do not come quickly and without consideration to modesty. I hope this you will remember."

Odette nodded, although the Christian moralities in which she'd been indoctrinated argued, vehemently, against what he said.

"Remember, and you shall learn the full value of all your lessons." He reached into the cage again and ran his fingers through her hair, his fingertips just barely touching her shoulders; but the sensation made her skin feel as if it had been scorched.

"The Mistress wishes for you to be taken back to the house shortly," he continued. "See, this is not so bad. Lydene, whom you have watched with such horror, spent the entire night locked in the pillory, allowed out only to relieve herself and forced to endure the attentions and chastisements of the night guards. Now cheer up, Odette. I shall release you soon enough—although, in truth, seeing you confined this way is a treat for the eyes."

Odette blushed so hard her face hurt and Lord Alban smiled and patted her head before turning away. For all his kindness his presence was more distressing to her than that of either Mistress Helrose or her brother. However, she felt strangely more relaxed and was able to rest against the bars, pulling her legs to one side with as much modesty as possible. She still bolted at the customers' touches, but her resentment was not so fierce as it had been before.

The two young men went off, leading Lydene between them; and Odette, knowing instinctively their intentions, was torn between horror and envy for Lydene's freedom. When one gentleman offered her a stick of honey candy she almost smiled, and would have accepted had not Lord Alban came running up and told the gentleman it was forbidden to feed the punished girls.

A trio of men came to the courtyard sometime later. They were loud and their clothes dusty. Odette had a keen sense they were Outer Realmers, though she did not know what exactly inspired the suspicion. The trio was impatient for service, and so crudely did they speak to their serving girl that Lord Alban intervened and told them to leave.

The men only laughed. "You are a gallant man, to defend the ears of whores," said one of them, and Odette's heart jumped as the man reached for the dagger strapped to his leg.

Alban's reaction was quick; he drew his own dagger before the man had hardly moved. Immediately, the other patrons sprang to his aid, brandishing their own blades, swords as well as daggers. The faces of the three men paled as they surveyed the circle of blades.

"Rynmer, go fetch the street sentries," Alban ordered, and the man he'd spoken to darted at once across the courtyard into the square.

The stranger shoved his dagger back into its sheath and raised his hands amicably. "I apologize, sir, I did not know—"

"No," Alban said flatly, "that is quite clear. To correct your misunderstanding, sir, it is not enough to be allowed entrance into Athla. You must respect our laws to retain your welcome...and our laws do not allow for the abuse of women, either physically or verbally."

Odette saw one of the trio raise a greasy eyebrow toward her cage. "And what say you to *that*, proprietor?"

Alban sighed. "I have no doubt that you, as an intelligent man, understand the difference between abuse and punishment."

Soon Rynmer returned, accompanied by two stout street sentries.

"These are the crude fellows, Alban?"

Lord Alban nodded, and the sentries ordered the trio to rise and accompany them. Odette watched as the trio conceded, grumbling under their breaths with every step. When they were gone the patrons settled back to their respective tables, and Lord Alban spoke words of reassurance to the uneasy serving girls. The milieu was again one of good nature and quiet merriment.

Lord Alban approached Odette's cage and took from his belt a key. As he unlocked the door Odette's heart pounded with a mixture of relief and new anxiety. When he reached in and grasped her hips a bolt of electricity tore through her thighs and breasts. He pulled her out quickly and set her feet on the tiles; and again Odette felt terribly aware of her nakedness and drew one arm over her breasts while with the other attempted to hide her sex. The cage door shut behind her with an ominous heavy sound that made her jump and she bowed her head.

He pulled her arms away, setting them firmly at her sides. "That is not well done, little flower," he reproached. "It is a very disrespectful manner of presenting yourself."

Odette did not want to *present herself,* and had to fight the urge to shield her body again. To her horror Lord Alban grasped the length of her hair in his hand and bade her walk before him to the door. Her agitation rose again at having to submit to this indignity, but at least, she told herself, she was leaving the cage behind.

Inside, he led her to the wall beside the door to the hallway and turned her so she faced the stones.

"Wait here, do not turn your head," he said.

As his footfalls faded Odette's irritation grew into anger. She pouted, abashed to have to stand this way, like some errant child.

Was the cage not enough?

The Great Hall was silent. After several minutes she took a chance on turning her head, and could not help but admire the genteel beauty of the room. The healer, whoever he was, must indeed have satisfied the king greatly to own such a fine house and rich furnishings. An image, wicked but comforting, formed in her mind of the gentleman healer ordering Mistress Helrose into one of the cages out in the courtyard. She smiled to picture Helrose, chagrined and blushing, exposed to the same frank eyes that had ogled her.

She heard footfalls coming from another part of the room and quickly turned back to the stones. She felt someone come out of the shadows and felt breath on her shoulders. A warm hand pressed against her buttocks, making her quiver, followed by suppressed giggles.

Someone said, *"Shh!"* and then another hand slid to her breast and tweaked her nipple cruelly. Odette gasped and spun about to find Yolande and another girl. Their smiles were cruel.

"I would suggest you press that nose firmly against those stones," Yolande said.

Odette shook with rage, but she knew Lord Alban would be back shortly, so she complied, though she growled under her breath "Keep your hands away."

Yolande only snickered and again touched her buttocks, this time massaging them roughly, then prying them apart a little. Odette shivered, alarmed to find her nipples had grown hard and her thighs were throbbing.

"This is the way it is, Odette," Yolande crooned. "You are one of Mistress Helrose's 'flowers'—a precious herb to be plucked and bruised with loving hands, your essence distilled for the pleasure of others."

As the girl continued to massage her backside Odette felt a shameful urge to move her hips; and though she hissed at Yolande to stop and the other pleaded it was time they left, she would not relent. Yolande probed a finger between Odette's buttocks and massaged the opening of her anus. Odette moaned, hot, aching and sure her knees would buckle.

"Leave me be!"

Yolande did release her, not out of mercy but because of the sound of heavy footfalls approaching. As deep, masculine voices wafted into the hall Yolande and her friend scurried away, leaving Odette red with shame as she faced the unfeeling wall.

The footfalls came up behind her and she was turned from the wall by her hair to face both Lord Alban and Lord Eryan. How differing their looks: the towering blonde Alban with his easy smile, lean Lord Eryan with his dark hair and sober features and pale handsomeness.

"Are you ready to obey without making a spectacle of yourself, young lady?" Lord Eryan demanded.

She nodded.

He grunted uncertainly and, pushing her hair from her shoulders, turned her about this way and that. She could feel his eyes poring over her flesh coldly.

"Your mistress is in an indulgent mood," he said at last, "and will allow you another chance to don the chemise. But this shall be your final chance. Your collar shall go on, with or without your compliance if it takes the steward and I both to put it on you."

Odette was aware of the mockery that laced his tone, though, in fairness, it seemed part of his nature. When a moment later he took her by the wrist she looked pleadingly to Lord Alban. But he said nothing; and when suddenly Lord Eryan spun her about and delivered several sharp spanks to her buttocks, bringing a startled cry to her lips, she heard a lazy, amused purr from deep in the steward's chest.

Eryan ordered her to walk down the hallway to the very room she'd entered before with Yolande. She thought she would weep again when he thrust a lavender chemise into her hands.

She slipped it on, discovering the bodice was slightly boned between the double layer of fabric so that it cupped her breasts snugly. Lord Eryan tied the cords himself, very tightly, so her breasts were thrust so high the aureolas of her nipples peeped over the front.

"This is how you are to fit the chemise after bathing and whenever the bodice rides up." Odette glanced into the silver mirror and blushed, for the flimsy, pretty thing drew the attention of the eyes to the naked flesh beneath the fabric.

He next put a collar about her throat, wide and brass like those of the serving girls. The metal was heavy and cold against her skin. She feared he might fasten it too tightly, but his deft fingers adjusted it only snug enough to prevent it from slipping down to her collarbone. With a small key he locked it in place; and as she heard the tinny clink of the pins fall into place Odette's skin broke out in goose flesh.

"It will come off for routine polishing only," he said, and gestured for her to sit down on the small bench. When she was seated he separated and draped her hair evenly before her shoulders and with a tortoiseshell comb began to brush out the tangles. When both sections were smooth he wove them into braids at either side of her head, tying them with ribbons the same shade of lavender as her chemise.

"There," he said at last, "you look the proper slave." The word *slave* echoed in Odette's temples, winding deep into her soul and touching the marrow of her identity. At least the frightful word seemed to more aptly describe the lot of the novices of Freyja than *flower* or even *student*, and for his candor Odette had to respect Lord Eryan.

He bade her stand and turn slowly. As he contemplated his work Odette thought she noticed a softening in his temperament.

"Now, Odette, it is proper for you to kneel when the Mistress enters your presence. And as perhaps Yolande explained before your wanton display, it is permissible for our girls to speak amongst themselves, quietly, when they are alone. The chemise you retain for however long you merit the privilege."

Odette's mind was reeling with curiosity now. "May I speak, my lord?"

He smiled a bit. "Yes, Odette."

"What am I to do when my menses commence? Am I not to be allowed undergarments?"

"You have experienced menses?"

She nodded shyly.

"Even during your stay in the king's household?"

She thought it a witless question, but upon reflecting she realized, no, she had not had her monthly bleeding once since Thierry brought her to Athla. "No, not for some time."

"It is not a problem you shall be vexed with until after you are fully trained. Then, if you wish to bear children, you will resume your menses so as to prepare your body for fruition. Things are different here in Athla, Odette, than in Midgard. The bodies of our women are not regulated by false notions of mortality that have robbed men and women of the ability to control the mechanics of procreation. Had you been a much older woman when you arrived here, no doubt your body would have met difficulty in throwing off those regulations. As it is, your body has accepted the ebb and flow of our realm. You shan't be troubled by menses until you are prepared—mind and soul—to conceive, and then not again unless you desire to conceive again."

Odette was astonished. "That is wondrous."

He lifted a reproachful finger. "You asked permission to speak once, not twice," he said, and then sighed. "But I will allow you for a time to speak, as it seems you have some reasonable questions."

His demeanor honestly soothed Odette now, and she spoke to him of the man she had seen in the street earlier, the one collared and leashed at a woman's hand.

"If he were well groomed, he is one who has chosen the contrasting initiation, which is endorsed by the code of diversity for a young man who wishes to volunteer himself into the service of a Mistress or Master, in order to refine his own nature. Was he well groomed?"

Odette shook her head.

"Then he was a criminal, likely an offender of the Great Statute," Eryan said, and seeing the question in Odette's eyes, explained. "The Great Statue is our principle that while a man may hold a woman as property and chattel he is prohibited from abusing her—abuse defined as anything outside approved and appropriately administered punishments. The man you saw probably came from the Outer Realm, for it is rare to find a man of Athla who would dare even think of abusing his woman. This man you saw was quite fortunate; he obviously found the king's leniency for his crime. Banishment is the usual penalty for those who break the law the first time. Had he killed or permanently maimed the woman he would have received death. I pray this criminal learns his lesson."

"What does the Great Statute define as outside the approved and appropriately administered punishments, my Lord?"

"Anything that brings a broken bone or open wound...burning and disfigurement, of course. And taking the life of a woman, unless it is to prevent the woman from committing immediate murder, warrants the death sentence."

Odette nodded, beginning to see a certain wisdom in the harsh laws, at least as it pertained to the Athlan beliefs.

"And what of women," she asked. "I mean, surely there are those who commit wrongs far worse than disobeying their men."

"There are the rare incidents, my dear. Those deemed suitable for retraining may be returned to society. There is banishment for those whose histories prove they are too dangerous. During my lifetime, I have known only two instances when the situation could not be corrected privately, in the home, as is preferred. The first involved a woman who killed her husband. She was from the Outer Realm, and so smitten was her husband that he gave in to her pleas to be spared physical corrections. She was also, unfortunately, very greedy. She tired of him soon and, while he slept, stabbed him and took his horse, having loaded the beast's back with all of his wealth she could carry. But he was not dead—not dead enough, at least—and his neighbors stopped her before she reached the boundaries of Athla. As if she were good enough to have ever found her way back to the Outer Realm even if she wanted! The husband died and she went before the king's judgment. I do not know what befell her except that she indeed was taken outside the boundaries, left alone in the Wastelands. If she ever found her way back to Midgard I should be very surprised.

"The second incident involved a woman who had renounced our ways. Her civic antagonism was so strong that she poisoned the king's wife, whom she saw as a symbol of all she hated. This was a long time ago, and I am not certain, but if memory serves adequately the woman was forced to drink her own concoction in Freyja's Temple."

Odette thought about these women. Despite her shock at her own sudden subjugation, she could not understand such overheated animosity, let alone animosity leading to such vile and drastic actions.

Eryan fluffed the ends of Odette's braids. "Now, is there anything else you would like to know?"

Odette watched silently as he retied the cords of the chemise to make the little knot prettier. The masculine scent of him seemed to pull the walls closer. She feared if she moved her breasts would spill out from the bodice and so grasped for something, anything, to say that would keep her in the room a little while longer.

A question rose suddenly, one that had piqued her briefly when Lord Alban first spoke to her.

"Do you not care for the queen, Lord Eryan?"

The muscles of Eryan's face tensed. "My feelings for our queen are neither here nor there—but I see you share her penchant for curiosity into matters not your concern." He looked at her evenly and Odette thought she heard a trace of the mocking coldness once again. "You would be wise to keep that curiosity in check, my dear."

Chapter Seven

He commanded her to follow him, and she moved awkwardly, uncomfortably aware of how her breasts seemed to heave over the bodice and how devoid of concealment were her buttocks. Back to the Great Hall he led her. The place was empty now and the silence almost deafening. He continued on to the door past the hearth and entered a long room with a floor of spotless red stones. It was the kitchen, and Odette saw with a moment's pricking gall that Yolande and one of her friends were kneading bread at the wooden table that stood in the middle of the room. Another girl tended a cauldron of boiling water hanging over a brazier set into one wall. Lord Eryan motioned Odette toward a man standing at a butcher's block. He was dressed in a cook's uniform and carving a large hunk of meat. He was taller than Lord Alban—surely one of the tallest men Odette had ever laid eyes on—all brawny muscles with a bull's neck, though the fingers of his massive hands were surprisingly long and dexterous. He lifted a heavy blonde eyebrow at Lord Eryan's approach, and there seemed to Odette to be a glint of impatience in his grey eyes.

"Bjorn, this is Odette. I am sure you can find something for her to do."

The cook smiled at her pleasantly enough. "Wash your hands, girl, and help me with these scraps." She nodded and stepped over to a counter where stood a clay dish filled with clean water. As she cleaned her hands she heard some words, low but unquestionably heated, exchanged between the two men. When Lord Eryan departed Bjorn gave a deep sigh.

"Take this outside and bury it in the refuse hole by the gate." He handed her an iron pot brimming with bones and stripped fat and motioned with his head toward the door that led outside. "There's a pile of straw nearby to cover it with."

She did as he instructed, finding herself in a yard picketed by tall willows. Directly facing the door stood two posts with a line hung between them for drying clothes and beyond that, through the willows, she could see the glassy surface of water. To the far right of her was the midden hole, heaped over with hay from the bin beside it. As she discarded and covered the scraps she glanced about, admiring the dark green of the grass and savoring the lulling lap of the water as it moved.

As she opened the door to the kitchen she was stopped by a voice thundering from within. Slowly, she pulled the door ajar and peeked in hesitantly. The girl at the brazier cast her a warning look and Odette crept in as quietly as she could, noticing almost immediately that a measure of flour had fell on the floor from the wooden table. Yolande trembled where she stood, her eyes shiny with brimming, angry tears. Bjorn took a large wooden spoon from a peg on the wall, and in two long strides stood over Yolande.

"Why, girl? Why can you never take care with a task? Am I not more indulgent with you than the others you squawk about to your friends? Yes, I've caught your little conversations; I know how you resent it here. Is it not enough I have always been patient with you?"

Yolande did not answer. Truly, it appeared to Odette that she bit her tongue to keep from speaking. Bjorn shook his head irritably and motioned for Yolande's companion to go stand beside Odette, then he commanded Yolande to bend over the table and lift the hem of her chemise.

By Yolande's blanched gape and the shock on the faces of the other girls Odette guessed punishment was not something familiar to the girl. Her hands moved fretfully at the hem of her chemise but she seemed unable to lift it. Finally, Bjorn grasped her by the shoulders, turned her around and inclined her forward over the table. He ordered her to hold firmly to the edge. She complied slowly, gasping when he yanked the chemise up with his own hands. Bjorn patted her buttocks lightly with his left hand a moment, and Odette saw Yolande grimace. Then with his right the cook raised the wooden spoon and brought it down. The cook spanked her long and thoroughly, so that her backside soon was an even shade of crimson; and Odette could not help but smile to watch Yolande grit her teeth as her hips danced so desperately that her braid jiggled over her shoulders.

When at last the spanking was over Bjorn ordered Yolande to sweep up the flour and afterward go to a far corner of the room to stand with her nose pressed to the joining of the walls.

"Odette, help Mya with the bread," Bjorn said as he returned to cutting the beef. Soon he had the meat prepared and placed in the oven. He wiped his hands on his apron and, stepping over beside Yolande, whispered something in her ear. Odette glanced up and saw him lift her chemise again. With his hand he spanked several more times, renewing the red that had started to fade from her buttocks. This time Odette heard Yolande make a distinct crying sound, as if this more intimate punishment vexed her even more than the spanking over the table.

As Bjorn turned back to his cooking he whistled a bawdy tune, drowning out the sound of Yolande's indignant sniffing.

* * *

Customers were turned away at eventide and the members of Mistress Helrose's household gathered in the Great Hall for the evening meal. Odette had grown very hungry by the time she helped set the Mistress's table with brass plates and crystal goblets and cutlery of finest silver. After she and the other girls from the kitchen brought the food and refreshments they sat with the rest of Mistress Helrose's students on the bare floor near the hearth. The girls ate off wooden plates and shared a jug of mineral water. Lydene had been returned promptly as the sun set by the two gentlemen who had enjoyed her pleasures. They were invited by the Mistress to share her meal and sat down alongside Lord Eryan and a few other guests. Two girls wearing little white aprons embroidered with cornflowers over the fronts of their chemises served the wine and ale and other beverages from sparkling glass pitchers.

The Mistress had changed from her riding clothes into a simple, high-necked gown the shade of Burgundian wine. Her hair was unbound now and fell in shining auburn ripples about her shoulders. Yolande seemed to have recovered her composure, and as she had retained the right to wear her chemise Odette suspected Bjorn was more lenient than Lord Eryan would have cared to know; and she felt a little resentful as she watched Yolande eat. *And she said I was spoiled!*

Lydene, oblivious to her mussed hair and the rosy stain remaining on her breasts and in her cheeks, ate ravenously. She was not the only one of Helrose's flowers who had been stripped of her chemise—five others shared this fate. Odette was intrigued by two of these, who besides their brass collars wore slender brass belts about their waists locked in place at the back. From the locks hung leather appendages that appeared to insert into the girls' anuses. From the front of the belts sheathed golden shields fell over their pubic mounds and delved through the triangles of soft hair between their thighs. The shields expanded at the end to separate their nether lips and mold gently over the front of the mounds of flesh within. Their nether mouths could be seen whenever they knelt or moved, as if left purposely exposed. From the sides of the belts straps hung down the outer sides of their thighs to garters of leather. An iron chain bound each set of garters, tethering the girls' legs so as to limit the length of their strides.

Odette heard one of the men who had taken Lydene say "You set a generous table, Mistress Helrose. And this wine is impressive—as mellow as your elixirs!"

Odette lifted her eyes. So Helrose was the healer! *I might have guessed,* she thought, disappointed.

"Thank you," Helrose said. "Tell me, how generous was our little Lydene today? Did she endeavor to please?"

The two men exchanged glances, and then the one in the beige replied evenly, "She did not argue today."

The Mistress's eyes turned toward Lydene, whose face had turned scarlet. For a moment Odette thought Helrose would comment but she turned the conversation abruptly.

"And what think you of my new flower?"

Odette's eyes immediately lowered and she heard the same young man say "I would have taken her today had your steward allowed."

A woman guest asked, "Shall she be ready soon, Helrose?"

"In a few days," the Mistress replied and Odette felt the air knocked from her breast.

"I hear she was none too willing this first day," laughed another man.

Odette felt a heaviness on her brow and, looking up warily, saw Yolande was staring at her. The girl's lips were tight-set and pale, her hazel eyes baleful. Odette deliberately grinned at her and turned her attention to her food. It was easier to ignore the conversation from the Mistress's table when she knew she was not the only flower whose pride had been dashed that day.

Later, when she and the other girls had finished their meal and sat or lay silently on the floor, Odette heard her name spoken and looked up. The Mistress gestured for her to come to the table, and Odette complied without delay, remembering to kneel when she reached Helrose's chair. She ignored the scrutiny of the other guests, especially Lord Eryan, sitting so starchily beside his sister.

As she waited for the Mistress to speak she saw the two serving girls kneeling on the floor at the far end of the table, their foreheads pressed to the floor and their arms stretched before them with their palms turned up. One of the guests, a merchant in a soiled tunic, sat idly stroking the hair of one of the girls. Odette closed her eyes a moment and looked up at the Mistress.

"It is considered forward to meet my eyes unbidden." Mistress Helrose's voice sounded more cautionary than displeased, but Odette dropped her eyes at once.

The Mistress touched the back of her collar, sending a ripple of goose bumps down Odette's spine. Suddenly, she felt small and helpless again, and she blamed the collar, and imagined wrenching it from her throat and dashing it against a wall.

"You have decided to accept your chemise. Answer me, Odette, do you feel the color favors you?"

Odette opened her mouth but the answer trembled in her throat. The Mistress yanked one of her braids. "Do you think the color favors you, Odette?"

"Yes, my Mistress."

"I must agree." The Mistress did not speak again for several moments and Odette could feel Lord Eryan's cool, stern eyes surveying her.

"You know, I was very dissatisfied with your earlier behavior, young lady." She pulled up on the braid sharply, forcing Odette to her feet. "You shall cross my lap."

Odette felt unsteady on her feet, for she could not believe what she'd just heard.

"This moment!"

This time Odette obeyed. The Mistress's legs were like warm, smooth stone beneath her gown. She pulled Odette forward a little so that Odette's arms fell over one side of her lap and her legs draped the other side, only the tips of her toes touching the floor.

"Place your hands behind your back," the Mistress said. Odette complied, feeling her heart race wildly. Mistress Helrose raised her chemise, exposing her buttocks, and Odette heard an approving murmur rise from the guests. It was all Odette could do not to struggle as the Mistress cinched her wrists together with one firm hand.

"You shall obey the rules, Odette. In that, you have no choice."

Odette nodded earnestly, afraid the next moment it was the wrong thing to do; but the Mistress did not remark on it. Instead, she touched Odette's left thigh, drawing her fingertip slowly, lightly, over the flesh just below the buttock, across the curve and onto the other thigh. Odette tensed at the almost ticklish touch, and the Mistress, noting this, gave a disproving sound. She removed her hand and Odette lay over her lap, enduring the lengthy moments.

Suddenly, the palm of the Mistress came down smartly across her buttocks. Odette tensed again, expecting more spanks, but Helrose's attention returned to Odette's thighs. She stroked the same tender areas with her fingers, stroking, then pinching it. The next moment the Mistress spanked her here, too, more smartly than she had Odette's buttocks. Odette held her breath, expectant, miserable; she felt her wrists released.

"Keep your hands together," the Mistress ordered.

Odette obeyed, and felt fingers again stroke her thighs, while Helrose moved her other hand to Odette's bodice and pulled the fabric away from her nipples. Odette gasped loudly at the sudden exposure and the Mistress spanked her several times.

Helrose kneaded Odette's right nipple beneath her fingertips. Odette suppressed her shocked moan and tried to lie acquiescently as Mistress Helrose spread her thighs apart. A ripple of heat shot up Odette's spine, making her squirm, and the Mistress laughed softly, pressing her fingers deep between Odette's thighs until they touched the nether lips. She patted the lips firmly and roamed Odette's sex with her fingers, stopping and touching gently the flesh just within, the same part where on the two gartered girls hung the little shield plates. Some small organ awakened under Helrose's touch, and as she began to massage it between her finger and thumb Odette felt it swell and throb, filling her with a maddening need that made her hips undulate.

The ministration made her virginal nethermouth moisten and swell; and as the Mistress began to stretch and ply her right nipple harshly, her other breast seemed to ache for the same shameful attention. The forced passion stunned her and she closed her eyes and clenched her legs together tightly as she dared against Helrose's intrusive wrist. Relentlessly the Mistress worked the organ, occasionally flicking a fingertip roughly over the exposed tip and sending an electric jolt throughout Odette's body. Odette moaned, bringing a ripple of laughter from the onlookers.

Abruptly, the Mistress stopped whetting the budding organ and withdrew her hand from Odette's thighs. It came down across Odette's buttocks, much harder than before.

"Open your eyes! You shall never keep them closed when you are punished or handled."

Odette's eyes flew open, but the punishing hand did not cease. Odette's buttocks soon felt as if they were being scalded and her hips moved frantically in the attempt to dodge each new blow. She knew how crimson her flesh must be, how utterly exposed she was before these guests and Helrose's stewards. Desperate with humiliation she tried to wrench out of the Mistress's hold, to slide back on her feet and propel herself up.

But Helrose's experience and strength quickly subdued her. Letting go Odette's nipple, she caught Odette's wrists together and yanked Odette back atop her lap and held her securely in place.

"*Naughty girl!*" In her anger the Mistress's palm bore down now at a furious pace. Odette thrashed under the spanking and kicked the air with her heels, all too aware of the tears streaming from her eyes. Adding to her misery was the humiliating awareness of how damp her thighs were and that the little organ aroused to life by the Mistress now fluttered and beat for attention.

And as her buttocks throbbed under Mistress Helrose's punishment and her tears fell to the floor, an unexpected surrender came over Odette. It quelled the indignation the startling day had prompted and banished altogether the fear she'd known since leaving Burgundy. Even as she cried out with each spank, she felt a new and abiding solace that not all Honi's love and indulgence had ever provided.

When at last the spanking ceased Odette realized how loudly she cried, though she could not seem to stop. Her buttocks felt swollen, truly scalded; but the Mistress was not quite finished, and holding Odette's wrists together she wrenched her thighs roughly open. She plucked Odette's nether lips apart once more, and Odette shuddered when she touched the fluttering, heated organ.

"A trembling pearl," the Mistress cooed softly. "Do you see, dear Holbarki?"

Someone rose from the table and a shadow fell over Odette. She felt another finger touch the tiny organ, sending a slight bolt through her womb, her breasts, her thighs.

"Yes," came the masculine assent, "and these like silk petals" He tweaked the inner flesh of the parted lips and Odette squealed.

The guests laughed demurely, even Lord Eryan, and it took all Odette's strength to keep from closing her eyes. When the fingers withdrew and the shadow moved away she sighed deeply.

Mistress Helrose inclined her head so that her lips were at Odette's cheek. "It is a simple enough rule to remember, Odette—comply or be punished."

Odette knew Helrose spoke truly enough…and yet, she suspected that things other than disobedience might bring punishment, and that he didn't want to think about.

The Mistress turned to her brother. "Take this young lady to the room where she will be staying and feel free to give her any instruction you deem necessary."

He rose and lifted Odette about the waist from the lap of the Mistress. As Odette's feet touched the floor she guarded her eyes from the others at the table, grateful to feel the chemise fall back over her hips and burning buttocks. Yet her thighs were sodden and she worried the blush might never leave her face.

Lord Eryan took the end of one of her braids and led her from the table. In the glow of the torches she saw Yolande's triumphant grin and the apprehension in Lydene's eyes, as if she might be the next to go over Mistress Helrose's lap. Odette did not have time to gaze at them long, for Lord Eryan hastened again through the door to the hallway. It was not the dressing chamber he took her to this time, however, but a door closer to the staircase; and muted light fell over the threshold as they entered. Here were no trunks or wardrobes, though under a small oval mirror on one wall was a long table. Two heavy brass candlesticks stood here and the wicks of the candles had recently been lit. Between them lay a wreath of fresh carnations and in the center of this stood a small stone statue of Freyja. From the front of the table hung a long-handled paddle of polished wood. A brass cage identical to the ones in the courtyard hung from a large bracket in one corner. Opposite the table a heavy mattress lay on the floor, covered with a spread of light blue weave and pillowed with several cushions. To one side of the mattress hung a sconce where another candle burned, with below it another table on which sat a pitcher and bowl and, on the underlying shelf, a chamber pot. To the wall at the other side of the mattress was attached a long, smooth object encased in leather, above which dangled a set of fetters. The frame of the small single window was carved with decorative swirls and scallops, and below this a long wooden trestle had been bolted low to the wall. A folded blanket lay atop the trestle and at both ends of it was a pair of brass fetters.

Eryan released Odette's braid and went to kneel before the statue. He raised his palms in salutation and closed his eyes, and his long, dark lashes swept the crest of his sharp cheekbones. He looked so humble and tender before the image of the Goddess, nothing like the uncompromising steward who had thrown her into the cage and seemed to relish watching the Mistress spank her.

Odette stood with her hands clasped behind her, shocked to feel the heat from her punished backside radiating through the chemise. She thought for a moment of fleeing while Lord Eryan prayed—but where was she to go? And perhaps now that she had been so sorely chastised Lord Eryan would be kinder.

After a few moments he got to his feet and Odette saw that his alabaster cheeks were glazed with the faintest of color.

"You will sleep in this room each night, unless you are requested elsewhere."

Odette nodded. He took her arm and drew her toward the trestle.

"Lie down, Odette."

She obeyed and he sat down on the edge of the trestle beside her. His eyes boldly canvassed the length of her body, making her feel even more vulnerable now than when she had been locked in the cage.

"In the morning you shall be bathed…and if you behave yourself until that time I shall consider not bringing you back here until bedtime tomorrow night."

His words confused her a moment—until the next moment he took her wrists in one hand and reached for the fetters with the other. Terrified, she cried out.

"*Sshh.*"

He drew her arms over the trestle above her head and placed her wrists into the cuffs. Odette's skin dappled with cold perspiration, and she had to force herself not to scream when she heard them snap closed. He reached down and imprisoned her ankles as well. Odette's mind blanked with terror and she jerked on the metal desperately.

"Please, please do not do this!"

So frightened was she that she didn't realize he'd rolled her to her side until she felt the chemise yanked up to her waist. He spanked her several times, shocking her so that she felt her terror-seized lungs fill with air. She wept again, her buttocks stinging anew as he drew the chemise down again. He took a linen cloth from his shirt and wiped her tears away, and she felt the calming resignation return.

"The fetters do not cut your flesh, do they?"

"N-no, my lord."

"I shall stay with you until the night guard comes to his post."

He took her chin in one hand and turned her face gently left and right, examining her so intensely she forgot the fetters for a moment.

"You are very comely, Odette—a little spoiled, but that is to be expected from one just leaving their childhood in Athla." He proceeded to touch the lobes of her ears, which tickled, and the soft golden strands of hair lying over her cheekbones. He drew a forefinger down her throat, pressing the small cleft lightly. Odette's heart raced with a new fear, but she managed to stifle her protest as he edged off the trestle and knelt beside her.

He began massaging the insides of her thighs and his hands slid downward to bend her knees as much as the fetters allowed. He caressed the delicate skin over her shins and slapped her calves, inching his fingers over the tops of her feet to her soles, which he then deliberately tickled. She giggled and squirmed, terrified of a reprimand; but he only smiled and proceeded to examine her toes, startling her when he lifted each small digit and pressed his lips against them. Odette felt delirious with an unfamiliar heat, and the droplets of moisture she felt between her legs only maddened her discomfort.

He sat back down on the trestle and laid his hands on her thighs again, pressing his palms into the supple flesh, working upward until his hands were at the chemise. He pushed the hem up, making her gasp slightly, and slipped a hand under her sore buttocks. He raised her hips up from the trestle, and with the other hand he touched the exposed shining hair between her legs. It was damp, Odette knew with much shame, and she tried to look away as his fingers wove through the little nest and massaged the mound beneath. His groping hand seemed so dangerous to her, but just the same, his handling made her even damper.

"Sweet, untried maiden," he whispered.

He lowered her hips, and with both hands carefully parted the outer folds of her sex to expose the pink flesh within. Immediately the little organ the Mistress had earlier aroused began to swell and throb. He pinched the hood of it between his thumbs, sending a wave of heat throughout Odette's hips and pelvis, quickening and drawing a ravenous new hunger deep within her virginal orifice. Eryan bent over her thighs, inclining his head at her dewy fount, and flicked his tongue over the excited organ. Her hunger turned into a flame that demanded to be stoked, and her hips arched to meet his beautiful lips, the teasing tongue.

His thumbs inched down and spread the nether lips wide open. He licked the throbbing organ and probed a finger into the tight font. A current of electricity bolted through Odette's entire body. She moaned, her hips undulated, and miserable with need she forgot her bashfulness and watched as he fed on her sex and suckled the organ between his lips.

His finger moved deeper inside her until suddenly meeting a barrier that sent a wave of genuine pain through Odette's orifice. She stiffened and cried out and immediately Lord Eryan withdrew his finger. The pain eased, although the need he'd whetted remained.

She whimpered as he straightened, aware of how wet the trestle was now under her hips. He gazed on her suffering face almost sweetly.

"You shall think of this lesson tonight, Odette, this arousal provoked by a man's touch. And if you do not rebel against what you have experienced, you shall find your spirit filling with illumination."

She nodded, moaning under his gaze. He seemed less forbidding now even as she did not doubt the swiftness of his discipline whenever he deemed it was needed. His unique masculine scent and his sharp features, so exquisite in their subtle imperfections, seemed almost painfully attractive to her; and she wondered if this feeling was not part of his instruction.

He had just started to untie the cords of her bodice when the night guard came by. To Odette's added chagrin Lord Eryan did not even pause, but peeled the fabric aside to expose her breasts. He massaged these roughly, twisting the nipples with his thumbs so they swelled and hardened. Odette blushed under the guard's boyish grin and her hips arched again, though toward which man she was not sure. She had never known such consuming frustration; and she began to cry silently for it, almost resenting the resignation that gave it meaning.

At last Lord Eryan rose from the trestle and pulled the chemise up all the way to her stomach, leaving her moist sex vulnerable and pulsing in the flickering candlelight.

She heard the guard whisper, "The Mistress's new flower?"

"Odette," Lord Eryan murmured. "Do not forget to prompt her each hour."

They stepped out into the hallway and Odette could no longer decipher their conversation. Yet, she understood exactly the meaning of Eryan's instructions to the guard—that it was the man's task to return and whet her hunger as the Lord had, to keep her moist and heated and bound in frustration.

She closed her eyes and turned her mind to other things. But nothing, not thoughts of Queen Honi or her friends, not memory of seeing Yolande receive what she'd deserved, nothing curbed the passion stirred by the ruthless, handsome Lord Eryan.

Chapter Eight

ll night long the guard tormented Odette as Lord Eryan had, even after the girls who shared the room were bedded and asleep. When her whimpers and moans grew too loud he muffled her voice by tying a thick strip of cloth over her mouth. Just before sunrise he allowed her to fall asleep, and when she awoke it was to find lord Alban sitting beside her, unlocking the fetters. She cringed a moment, until she discovered her bodice had been pulled back over her breasts and the cords tied again.

"Blessed morning, Odette."

The morning light burnished his blonde hair and illuminated dimples at the sides of his mouth she had missed before. After he released her, he helped her to her feet and took her to the chamber pot. The need to relieve herself outweighed her accustomed modesty, and when she was finished he bade her sit on the floor and eat the tray of cooked peas and slices of hard bread he had brought along with a jug of virgin wine.

He stood before the trestle and gazed out the window while she ate. "Did you rest a little, flower?"

"Yes, my Lord."

"The Mistress wants to see you after you are bathed." He turned and looked down at her, his hands folded over his chest, and he reminded her of a god. Her mouth dried and she was unable to meet his eyes.

"Yes, I prefer your eyes lowered," he said, making her blush now, too. "It is not a demand the stewards make of Mistress Helrose's girls, but it is an appealing gesture."

Odette forced herself to swallow; she hadn't thought of how appealing such a simple act might appear, but his comment was flattering nonetheless.

When she was finished with the meal he told her to set the jug and tray on the floor before the altar.

"Whoever cleans this room today will take it away," he said. "Now come along with me."

As they entered the Great Hall Odette saw several other girls cleaning the tables and scrubbing the floors. Lydene was among them, and as Odette walked past she waved a quick salutation. Odette smiled but she was afraid to wave back as Lord Alban seemed in a hurry to lead her to the kitchen. No one was there as they went through but the room was immaculately clean, which told her someone had cleaned up after the preparation of the morning meal.

Odette heard Bjorn's voice raised outside as Alban took a clean length of linen from a shelf, and as she followed him out the door she glimpsed the large man standing in the yard. At his feet knelt two girls, one naked, the other in her chemise, but the faces of both were contrite and stained with tears; and it seemed all they could do not to shrink from the paddle he waved as he reprimanded them.

Lord Alban did not interfere, but took Odette through the willows to the bank of the stream, where he told her to undress. There was a well in the midst of the trees she hadn't seen before, and he cast the pail down into it as she loosened her hair and the cords of her bodice. The chemise fell easily from her shoulders. She covered her breasts and sex with her hands as she waited on the velvety grass and watched the kneeling girls through the trailing branches. Bjorn was shaking his head, exhausted for words, it seemed. He gestured for one of the girls to rise as Lord Alban clasped her arm.

"Odette, come here." Before she could obey he drew her to him and forced her arms down to her sides.

"Do not allow me to see you cover yourself again," he scolded. "Now, you are to spread your legs."

As he dipped the linen into the filled pail she saw that his endearing smile had disappeared.

"I hope you are not amused by the chastisement of the others."

She shook her head vigorously.

"There is nothing less attractive than a young lady taking amusement in the punishment of others."

He twisted the linen with both hands, squeezing out the excess water, and cleaned her face. A sharp crack sounded, followed by a poignant telltale cry. The resounding blows of wood against flesh echoed through the yard. Odette tensed with each blow of the paddle. She felt Lord Alban's hand move down below her chest with the wet cloth, startling her so that she shrieked. He stopped a moment and smoothed her hair with his fingers.

"You must accept these things," he told her softly. "Did you not see or hear the serving girls punished in the household of the king?"

"Y-yes," she said, though she did not want to admit that in the king's home she had been indifferent to it.

"It is different when one is young," he went on, sunny again even as the wails of the punished girl grew louder. "I was young once, too, and the affairs of my parents were not my concern. They loved one another and that was enough. It will be different for you, I suspect—it is a part of your life to which you naturally respond. Just do not let your curiosity show so blatantly."

She did not fully understand his meaning, but at least she knew the other girls had their own concerns and would not notice her annoyance at having to stand and let a man bathe her. He cleaned her thoroughly, paying such heed to every curve and hidden fold of her body that her face burned. By the time he drew a second pail of water with which to wash her hair, Bjorn's spanking paddle had grown silent and all that could be heard from the yard was the soft weeping of the girls.

When Lord Alban had her clean and dried he told her to throw the linens over the clothesline. As she carried them into the yard she saw the two girls, both now as naked as she was, bound one to each of the clothesline poles with ropes tied around their wrists and placed over large nails. Their toes barely reached the ground and they moved uncomfortably, making little sounds of distress. Odette fought her urge to stare and returned promptly to Lord Alban.

He slipped her chemise back on and tied her bodice, tighter than had Lord Eryan the day before, then combed out her hair and rebraid it. With a light smack on her backside he sent her ahead of him into the house. Lord Alban said something to the sniffling girls, a reproach of some kind it seemed to Odette although it was so soft she could not make it out.

Once inside he took her by the hand and led her again out into the hall. The other girls were still working; and as she struggled to keep up with Lord Alban's long strides she looked out one of the front windows and saw Yolande out on the courtyard polishing one of the cages, which had been taken down from its post and set on the tiles. Alban did not take Odette outside but turned near the door toward a curtain in a corner in the shadows, one she had not noticed before. This he threw back and gestured her inside.

They entered a long room with a low ceiling and no windows. The floor was covered with a thick tan rug. A shelf hung from one wall holding bound manuscripts; and flails, wooden paddles, fetters and other implements hung throughout. The floor was raised at the far end and there was another fireplace, cold and swept of cinders, in which hung a great black kettle. Mistress Helrose stood gazing into the kettle, her hair gathered back loosely with a ribbon that hung down the back of her simple dark-blue gown. As Odette remembered to kneel she thought the Mistress looked exquisite and seemed lost in thought.

Lord Alban stepped up beside her and had to speak her name a few times before Helrose's eyes lifted from the kettle.

"Mistress Helrose…"

The Mistress lifted her face, blinking. "Ah, you have brought our little cygnet."

She stepped down to stand beside Odette. As Odette's eyes lowered Lord Alban strode past her and she heard him take a seat on one of the benches close by.

Helrose's voice broke the silence. "Lord Eryan tells me you are a virgin."

Odette blushed and her arms crossed over her stomach automatically. Helrose reached out and stroked her temple.

"My sweet, you are no longer in the world of shame and contradiction. You are in Athla—you must forget the unnatural notions of sin instilled in the Outer Realm. Now tell me, have you experienced self-pleasure?"

Odette wanted to cover her ears and turn away from the woman, but she knew better. "No, my Mistress," she whispered.

"But you know what it is, yes?"

Odette nodded.

"And how do you come to know of self-pleasure—by accident or by instruction?"

Odette's eyes brimmed with embarrassing tears. "My guardian, Irene, from her

I first heard the word. But it was as a warning. Such pleasures, she said, are sin, as all pleasures of the flesh."

"Do you believe this?"

"No, not as they do," Odette replied, trying to formulate her thoughts into coherent words. "I do not know what I believe, except that I know the power of the Christians; and as they held the power to conquer my people, and their god judges it sin, perhaps it is so."

"Do you think your mother would agree?"

Odette frowned. "No."

"Or your father?"

"No."

"And what were they like, your mother and father?"

The tears broke slowly over Odette's cheeks. "Good, good people, my Mistress. There has never been a more loving mother and father."

"Look at me, Odette."

Odette obeyed, and was shocked by the tenderness in the Mistress's face. "The Christian conquerors did not possess the power to make you forget their love, or diminish your love for them, did they?"

"No."

"And you respect your mother and father, yes?"

"Always, my Mistress."

"Then forget the notion of sin, Odette. It is a hindrance to wisdom and real virtue, and is an insult to the memory of your parents."

The words seemed to lift from Odette a pall she'd only been half-aware she carried, so that the very air seemed clearer as she said, "I will try, my Mistress."

"Good. Now return to your silence and rise to your feet." The Mistress walked over to a long bench cushioned in gold-and-white weave. "Lie down here."

Odette did as she was instructed, although her heart beat nervously.

"I want you to lift your chemise and spread your legs."

Odette flinched. It was difficult enough to obey her, but she could not forget that Lord Alban was still in the room. She curled on the bench and bowed her frantically shaking head into her hands, hoping with all her heart the woman would see and feel compassion for her distress.

"You have just earned an afternoon of punishment, Odette. Do you care to make it last through the night?"

Odette bit her bottom lip and took a deep breath. Slowly she turned onto her back. She choked back a startled gasp to see her reflection staring, red-faced, down at her. A large round mirror of clear, polished silver was secured to the heavy beams crossing the ceiling above the bench. She looked away from her chagrined image and instead stared at the grooves of the beams around it, the knots here and there, anything that might help her not think of what she had to do. And slowly, reluctantly, she toyed with the hem of her chemise

"I am not a fool, Odette," the Mistress said sharply, making her jump. "Keep your eyes to your task!"

Odette's palms were sweating as she obeyed and lifted the hem up. Only when Odette's sex was exposed was the Mistress content and told her it was enough.

"Now take your hands and feel that little pelt covering your charms—and watch as you do."

Odette complied, raking her fingers through the dark golden curls.

"Delve down with your fingers, separate the lips."

Again Odette obeyed; she was trembling now.

"I want you now to stroke yourself, much as did Lord Eryan and the night guard."

Since her bath Odette had known a drowsing of the passion evoked the night before. She whimpered to think of it renewed, but obeyed, slipping two fingers down over the hood of the tiny organ and over the soft lips of her sex.

Helrose bent over and gently poised a fingertip over her mound, touching the organ ever so lightly. "Your clitoris, Odette, which together with what the Goddess has blessed you within here—" She patted the font of Odette's nethermouth. "—allows us to experience that which brings us into paradise without death.

"Your body was created by the sacred, Odette, every limb, every organ, every digit on your hands and feet. To know pleasure with your body and your mind is no more evil than to admire with the eyes the wildflowers and oceans and mountains created by the divine hand. It is generations of corrupted thoughts that have drawn every conceivable misery to the world in which you were born. These miseries include disease and shame at the very acts that lead to the pleasure known and sanctified by our creators. The sacred rites, Odette, perverted from their pure state into acts viewed as ugly and sinful and only to be tolerated for procreation! The same forces which claim procreation of man to be the commandment of a god are the ones who would make you feel shame to touch your body in this way."

Odette nodded, and so shocked was she by the sagacity of Helrose's words she almost forgot her uneasiness.

"Not that you should be vain," the Mistress continued, "but simply, completely, relish the woman that you were created."

Mistress Helrose smiled and moved Odette's hand in such a way as to maneuver the length of her fingers back and forth gently. Odette felt her entire sex grow hot and the clitoris bud and pulse against her fingers.

"Now, you will watch yourself in the mirror, and with your other hand trace your breasts and nipples through the bodice as you explore your nethermouth."

Odette obeyed, with only the softest of protesting whimpers. She was surprised to see how hard her nipples already were, and secretly fascinated to look fully upon her sex, to behold the tiny pale and swollen clitoris. Her nethermouth grew slick with fluids as she massaged herself. Instinctively, she began to explore with her fingers the outer folds, moving to the tender inner lips. She rubbed the mounds more firmly, so that her clitoris beat urgently, as if compelling her to some unknown end. To her great embarrassment, her hips writhed in motion to her weaving hand so that she wished with all her heart Mistress Helrose would soon let her stop, or at least move her eyes away.

"Into that little orifice, dear, gently dip your fingers."

Odette's nethermouth was still sore from the attentions it had received the night before; and now, feeling the moisture her ministrations produced, she flushed to think the men had felt it, too.

"Back and forth, carefully."

It hurt but Odette complied. Her breasts flushed brilliantly and seemed to ache for more attention, and she did not resist the urge to massage them alternatively.

"Much better, Odette."

Odette glanced down and saw that her sex seemed to have swollen, and certainly it was as flushed as her face now. The Mistress knelt beside her, and looking up into the mirror, stroked Odette's thighs.

"So smooth," Helrose murmured and bent down so that her face was at Odette's throat, frightening Odette so that she froze.

"Do not stop!" Helrose's lips were hot on Odette's flesh, and she began to suckle it in a way that created a delirious sensation that shot down through Odette's neck and into her breasts.

Frustrated as she'd never been in her life, Odette continued to stroke her breasts and work her sex. She had two fingers slipped into her vagina and worked these more intensely, prompting her nethermouth to pulse wantonly and her breasts to ache even more. The sensation the Mistress caused was spiraling down, down into her womb and her very spine, and its force banished the last trace of hesitation. She was feverish in her abandon, conquered and united with it, uncaring how her hips writhed under her rapidly stroking hand or that her mouth fell open and moans issued wantonly from her lips. She rubbed her clitoris madly now, penetrating the hungry nethermouth once, twice…and suddenly she felt an explosion of pleasure that lifted her wholly into a realm of unsurpassed ecstasy.

When she recovered she lay limp and flushed under her breathless reflection. Lord Alban stood beside Mistress Helrose, who looked upon their reflections with an approving smile. Odette gasped, mortified but accepting her captivity, and watched without moving as Helrose bent down and very lightly pinched her wet nether lips. Odette's clitoris felt as if it were burning now and yet it responded, as even her spent orifice quickened a little in anticipation of delight.

But Lord Alban wrapped his arms about Helrose's waist and, lifting her hair over her shoulder, began to nuzzle her throat. It was Helrose's turn to struggle for composure, and her muffled angry tone deterred him a little, though Odette heard him chuckle.

"You did well, my flower," Helrose said.

The next moment Lord Alban pulled her tightly against his body and with one hand tilted her face toward his. The Mistress did not resist, but wound her arms about his neck and accepted his kiss. The steward chuckled once more, and then caught her hands in his own and kissed her chin and throat most violently. Mistress Helrose moaned and tore her hands free. They flew to his jerkin and unfastened the buttons. He released her long enough to pull it over his head, and the sight of his perfectly proportioned muscles made Odette shiver with excitement.

Mistress Helrose sank to her knees and untied the lacings of his breeches. As she pulled them down over his hips Odette saw that his member was already hard and eager, a glowing limb of amber red. Odette wanted to turn her eyes but seemed helpless to look away. She watched with renewed passion as the Mistress helped Lord Alban step out of the breeches.

He reached down and pulled the ribbon from her hair so that it spilled over her shoulders. She smiled at him tenderly and grasped his manhood, kissing the head of it and drawing her tongue over the great shaft down to the wrinkled sheath at the base.

He groaned deeply and took Helrose by the arms to pull her up, tearing the gown down her shoulders so that it fell to the floor about her ankles. Mistress Helrose was beautiful, a woodland nymph sculpted in alabaster. Her pubic hair was a copse of dark curls and her buttocks were firm and white, utterly unmarked; and Odette could not help but wonder what shade of red they would turn were she suddenly to find herself thrown over Lord Alban's knee.

His hands were on her, crushing her milky buttocks and massaging them roughly. One large hand slid into the little chasm between her thighs. She moaned and struggled until he let her go, then sank to the carpet on all fours, demanding he join her. He regarded her, the power shining in his eyes, then did so. She sprang onto his lap and kissed his throat and combed her fingers through the waves of thick blonde hair across his stomach and chest. Her hand delved down to his manhood. She caressed the balls and dipped her finger down further, prodding his anus with one finger. He groaned again and grabbed her hands away, covering her mouth once more with his own as he lay back, pulling her with him.

Helrose sat astride him, nursing his mouth with her lips. She searched for his nipples, wrenching them now when she found them, twisting them until he slapped her backside. She hissed but did not fight as with his hands, he took her hips and lifted her up. He lowered her over his eager shaft, smiling lazily when she immediately bent forward.

"Not as long as I am Mistress of this household, Lord Alban!"

He whispered something then, but Odette could not hear the words. Helrose responded by leaning over and kissing his brow as she slowly raised her hips. Her nethermouth was glistening wet as she slid up and down over the length of his cock, and her breasts jutted over his mouth. He suckled and nipped as he kneaded them and slowly moved one hand to her hip while with the other he stroked her pink nethermouth. She undulated over his stroking fingers, her purr low and husky, and when he spread her legs she did not bolt but this time allowed him to press her down so that his iron-hard organ penetrated her completely.

The Mistress groaned loudly, and with his hands on her hips sat up straight and began to ride him, slowly at first, and then with growing fury, moaning as he grappled her breasts. She seemed to take much pleasure in watching the passion knit his brow, and their bodies soon glistened in sweat as a sweet musk permeated the air.

Helrose's pace accelerated and her eyelids grew heavier, until at last she stiffened and fell forward with a little helpless cry that Odette would never have imagined hearing from the mouth of a Mistress.

Helrose was still moaning when Alban rolled her onto her back, clinging to his arms and kissing the cleft of his neck as he began to drive into her. His pelvis moved vigorously, pounding her buttocks into the carpet with a soft slapping sound.

Odette's shyness surrendered to her fascination. Quietly, she sat up and watched them, captivated by the steward's grinding hips and tense rear muscles, the look of sweet despair on Helrose's face as she wound her legs about his waist. Finally, every muscle and sinew on Alban's body flexed and his own soft moan lilted through the room.

The face of the Mistress was bright and flushed as she cupped his between her hands and kissed his brow. He smiled at her, whispering something in one ear, which he kissed and then did the same to the other.

To be audience to their exchanged kisses and hushed conversation made Odette more uncomfortable than watching their lovemaking, so she lay down again and stared silently into the mirror. A minute or two later she heard Mistress Helrose get up and dress before she came to stand beside the bench.

"Come," the Mistress said, taking her hand to help her rise. Odette followed her to the bench where Lord Alban sat. He was still naked, and his beautiful, smooth skin glowed. His manhood was limp between his legs, though its size still shocked her.

She jumped when Mistress Helrose took her hand.

"Take this and cleanse Lord Alban," said the Mistress and pressed a damp cloth into Odette's palm. Odette stared at it, blushing with uncertainty. The Mistress pointed to the floor at Alban's feet and pushed her down, saying in her usual inflexible tone, "You shall cleanse him and serve him as he wishes."

Odette heard the Mistress's muffled footfalls over the carpet, the sound of the curtain as it was pushed aside and curtly drawn over the threshold again. Odette knew she was alone with Lord Alban and her heart beat so fiercely she feared she would faint.

"I shan't eat you, flower," he said. "But I shall punish you if you do not do as instructed."

Odette felt like weeping as she raised her eyes to meet his. She felt a prickling in her breast under his bold regard; and though spent he surely was, he sat as straight as a rider on a horse.

Like a god, she thought, *even with that patient smile.*

But when after several moments she had not moved, he suddenly gripped her about the waist and pulled her to her feet. He turned her and threw her over his lap, and as he tossed her chemise over her hips she fought to get away. But she could not budge at all, and he spanked her thoroughly, his palm delivering stinging blows to her sensitive flesh. Her rear bounced under the torrent of blows and her buttocks soon flamed. Her tears fell profusely, not just because of the shame and pain but for the understanding that she had brought the punishment on by misusing his patience.

When at last the spanking was over he set her again to her feet and said, "Dry your tears." His voice was languorous and comforting. "Kneel now and learn from what I show you, Odette."

She wiped her face with the back of her hands and went to her knees, watching as he took the cloth from her hand and spread his legs. With his free hand he stretched his manhood and cleansed the tip, pulling the foreskin down the softened shaft, then running the cloth over his scrotum.

"Not so difficult?"

She shook her head.

"Now, lay the cloth to the table yonder and come back."

She obeyed, and when she returned he sat her in his lap. Her heart quickened again, but when he lifted her face she found the blue of his eyes so deep and soothing that her heartbeat eased a little.

"Take it into your hand, Odette," he said and gently set her fingers about his cock. It was heated and silken to the touch, and as he guided her hand over the length of it she felt a droplet of dew seep from the small opening peeping out from the foreskin.

His masculine scent grew thick and wondrously exciting, and as his mouth drew close to her ear she trembled. His member began to swell in her hand, and as he nibbled on the lobe of her ear and licked the flesh beneath she felt her wild pulse against his tongue.

"Draw the hood back gently," he whispered.

She looked down as she obeyed and saw the head had swollen considerably. The shaft stiffened and lengthened under her inciting touch. He made a soft sound that reminded her of the breath of a sleeping stallion and lifted her face and kissed her lips. Her entire mouth felt as she'd swallowed fire, delicious fire that made her flesh tingle and her thighs ache. He cupped her breasts with his hands and manipulated them slowly, tracing her nipples lightly with the pads of his fingers so they, too, felt scorched.

"On your knees," he murmured, and her thoughts were anxious as she slipped down to the floor. But his smile reassured her and as he drew her face forward she felt no fear.

"I want you to savor it, Odette, as you did icicles or candied roots as a little girl."

She kissed the engorged head and licked the droplets of fluid. Her tongue tingled, making her smile, and when he instructed her to trace her tongue over the shaft she did so, enjoying the smooth texture of it.

"Now, grasp the base with one hand and draw it into your mouth and suckle."

She obeyed, and his cock responded quickly by swelling and hardening like stone in her mouth. He took her braids gently into his hands and guided her lips up and down so that he filled her mouth snugly. The great head she loved the most and drew her puckered lips over it slowly then quickly, lapping up the droplets of fluid with her tongue.

"Quicker," he whispered and laced the fingers of his hands behind his head as he watched her obey.

Her mouth was beginning to ache but even so she delighted in nursing his length and the almost vulnerably anxious look of his face. Her nethermouth throbbed wantonly between her legs and she could not help but wonder how it would feel to ride him as had Mistress Helrose. He groaned and set his hands over her temples, making her shiver with desire.

"I want you to take the whole of it deeply into your mouth now," he said, "and suckle harder."

She did, gratefully, and after a time felt his body tense as a burst of rich, salty fluid filled her throat. This she swallowed and, lifting her eyes, saw that the tension on his face had given way to helpless relief. When his member stilled completely she sucked the last droplet from the head.

"What a good girl you are," he said huskily, and he pulled her up onto his lap again and enfolded her in his arms. He kissed her face, her cheeks, her chin. She felt a keen and deep peace fill her soul. Another time in her life she would have never guessed anyone could know such sublime joy; but that, she knew, was a lifetime behind her.

"A treasure," Lord Alban whispered. Again he kissed her mouth, making her hot and frustrated with the tease of his tongue on hers and on the tender flesh inside her lips. She heard someone walking toward the room as he kissed her mouth again, and then someone enter through the curtain. Odette's heart sank to know her time alone with him might well be over.

It was Mistress Helrose, clad in her manly breeches and vest again and holding a leather leash in her hand.

"Did she please you, Lord Alban?"

Lord Alban grinned and lifted Odette to her feet. "Your new flower is gifted with exceptional potential," he said as he patted Odette's sore bottom and reminded her in an undertone to kneel.

The Mistress's face was unreadable as she bent down and snapped the leash to Odette's collar. The sound of it made Odette's fear return.

"Follow me, little flower."

Chapter Nine

he Great Hall was empty now and quiet. To the cool shadows of the opposite wall the Mistress proceeded, stopping between a great tapestry and a displayed battle-ax. From the wall jutted a sizable leather phallus, flanked by manacles bolted into the mortar. On the floor below was a cushion. Odette's growing apprehension made her shiver, but Mistress Helrose was indifferent and, pushing Odette to her knees to the cushion so that she tilted forward slightly, raised her wrists to the manacles.

Odette began to panic. She whimpered, fighting her tears and praying this was but a demonstration of Helrose's power.

"Hush!" The Mistress came to Odette's side and took the flail from her belt, lifting Odette's chin with the end.

"However well you pleased Lord Alban it does not excuse your earlier behavior," she said, "and this punishment has a two-fold purpose, for I expect you to think of the phallus there as a symbol of Lord Alban and all the lords and men you will serve in the future. As you kneel you will suckle it as you did Lord Alban, is this understood?"

Odette nodded, trying to hold back her tears.

"Take it into your mouth!"

Odette lowered her mouth over the phallus. She could taste the oil that had been worked into the leather so that even though it was larger than Lord Alban's manhood it fit her mouth easily. The pressure on her knees was alleviated by the cushion, but even though she was in no pain she felt unsteady and vulnerable. And just as she thought how fortunate she was for the slight measure of modesty allowed by the chemise Mistress Helrose lifted the hem.

The next moment the flail struck her buttocks, the narrow leather lash stinging her already sore flesh. Again and again the Mistress applied the uncompromising flail. It was all Odette could do to remember her task at the phallus and her heavy tears only made it more difficult. From the corner of her vision she could see as the Mistress delivered each blow, a merciless spectre of restrained disapproval.

Odette's backside flinched under the relentless lash and her muffled wails mixed with the resounding smacks of the discipline. There was no lap to hope to escape to, only this searing pain and the knowledge that if her attentions to the phallus hesitated the thrashing would be drawn out longer. Yet despite the pain, her nethermouth grew hot and aching and she was aware of moistness trickling between her tightly clenched thighs. When her tears turned to sobbing her mouth slipped finally from the phallus. The Mistress stopped, long enough to press her mouth over it again and delivered another series of thrashing blows.

At last Mistress Helrose stayed her hand and bent so her face was close to Odette's. Reaching between Odette's legs she prodded her sodden nether lips and tweaked her clitoris.

"I want you to clench those virgin lips together."

Odette blinked, but obeyed, and the Mistress told her to do it again.

"Continue to work them, thinking of what could be filling that inflamed little orifice. Do not stop suckling the phallus, for you shall be watched. Do not grow lazy in your task or your confinement shall only be lengthened."

Mistress Helrose flailed Odette's buttocks several more times, insuring they were raw before turning and leaving her alone in the manacles. Her neck grew sore after a time so that she was obliged to turn her head to one side and then the other as she suckled the length of the phallus, never forgetting to work the lips of her nethermouth. The prospect that she would be noticed, especially by the vindictive Yolande, filled her with terror. She was vexed with Lord Alban, not so much for allowing the Mistress to punish her but for spurring the yearning in her that made the punishment so frustrating.

The phallus reminded her of the shape of his cock and the contentment she'd felt as it filled her mouth, as if a component of her womanhood had just awakened. He had kindled a fire in her, one that fed upon itself; and it pleaded to be fanned and stoked until its bright blaze scorched her very soul. Odette envisioned him clearly standing behind her, stroking her impassioned sex, taking her as he'd earlier taken the Mistress, but with all the brute forcefulness she'd sensed he'd wanted to exert over Helrose.

The time passed slowly. Mistress Helrose did return after what seemed hours and gave Odette permission to rest her mouth and nethermouth. But she spanked her with her iron-hard palm this time so that Odette was again in tears when she left again. Her mouth, as sore as it was, almost craved the gorging feel of the phallus, and she wondered if this were not another subtle lesson the Mistress hoped she would absorb.

At length she was released from the manacles when Bjorn came and unlocked them. He helped her up and when she felt stable, ordered her to the kitchen. Yolande was there, along with two friends. Odette remembered vaguely that these girls, Ivana and Emleth, slept in the chamber in which she'd been fettered the night before, as did the girl beating batter in a stone bowl as she sat on a stool. Unlike Yolande and her friends this girl was dispossessed of her chemise.

Bjorn set Odette to work at the wooden table, washing and cutting vegetables. He seemed flustered again—agitated, actually—and at one point threw down his apron and ordered them all to keep working and behave, as he had to go to the butcher's.

When he was gone Odette heard a whispered "I like the color of your hair."

It was the girl on the stool, and now Odette saw how truly pretty she was, with full dusky-pink lips and large brown eyes. Her chestnut hair was bound in two braids like Odette's. She wore one of the belts with the little anus plug and the brass shield that covered her clitoris. Odette understood now that the shield served as more than mere decoration or punishment. The devices prevented the wearer from touching herself, and she sensed that the plug served only to enhance the desire to do so.

Odette smiled at her. "Thank you. You are very pretty, you know."

The girl nodded, grinning, "I'm Rystla. You are Odette?"

"Yes." Odette grew shy as she remembered Rystla had to have seen her chained to the trestle. But the girl had an inviting disposition Odette liked.

"Lydene said she thought that was your name. You know Lydene?"

Odette nodded, and heard a riffle of snickers. She glanced over her shoulder and saw Yolande and her boon companions standing at the pantry door, whispering and sharing an apple they'd taken from the large basket standing just inside the pantry.

"Pay them no heed," said Rystla, coming to stand beside her. "They are soulless creatures, though I know a certain merchant has offered a handsome price to take that one off the Mistress's hands."

Yolande's features puckered darkly.

"You know nothing, Rystla. I am wise enough to obey the perverse Mistress and her power-hungry stewards."

"Not so wise last night, Yolande. If our cook were not so obsessed with his creations, he might remember to report misdeeds to the Mistress. He does us a disservice in that way, although at least he doles punishment promptly himself."

"It was her fault I dropped the flour," Yolande said, pointing at Odette. "Her tantrum addled my wits."

"You fool no one, Yolande. You are hateful and proud and too lazy to learn your lessons. But that is to be expected from one so shallow."

Yolande did not react with the anger Odette expected, but inhaled deeply, purposefully, as if to calm the anger within. Her friends stuck their tongues out at Rystla, then Odette, but the next moment Emleth's head snapped to one side and her eyes widened.

"Someone comes!"

The girls pitched the apple outside and they hastened back to their respective tasks just as Lord Eryan entered. He strode about the room and regarded their work with a cool eye. He stopped behind Odette and she could hear the beating of his heart, swift and heavy as thunder. He inhaled as if about to utter something when Lord Bjorn walked in carrying a large sack.

Odette instantly felt the antipathy betwixt them.

"Lord Eryan," Bjorn said, "is something amiss?"

"The Mistress has requested Odette serve at her table with Uma."

Bjorn nodded and threw the sack on the butcher block. He made no reply—in fact seemed deliberately holding himself back from saying anything. And after Eryan left the cook turned and opened a cupboard, cursing under his breath.

"Come here, Odette."

She started to kneel as she came to him but he told her to remain standing.

"Put this garment on," he said, handing her an apron. "Go to the main hall and find Uma. Go with her to the cellar and fetch the beverages the Mistress has ordered for the evening. Take care to serve the Mistress's table with your best grace, and smile—always smile. I will feed you later here in the kitchen before you help Uma to clean the night's dishes."

Odette took the apron and tied it quickly about her waist. He frowned and turned her around, re-tying it to his satisfaction.

"Its just as important to perform well as to perform quickly," he muttered and, swatting her bottom with his large palm, sent her into the main hall.

Uma was a bright soul and Odette warmed to her immediately, as she had Rystla. Uma showed her the door hidden in the shadows against the back wall of the Great Hall. Through it they descended a stairway to the cellar. The earthen walls were lined with shelves loaded with vessels of wines and barrels of ale and mead, stone bottles with herbal elixirs—all creations of Mistress Helrose. The barrels were conveniently small and together the girls carried two of these upstairs, then made another trip for a bottle of dragonsblood wine and an elixir of honeysuckle and other, unknown ingredients. A steward came and opened one of the barrels, and then Odette sat down with Uma against the wall to wait for the meal to begin, As they waited Uma pulled from her bodice a sprig of catmint and offered it to Odette.

"Staves hunger and clears the mind," she whispered.

Odette chewed on it slowly. "So, where is your companion of last night?"

"Paola? Oh, one of the merchants purchased her for the week."

Odette suppressed her shock. "Is that common? I mean, for one of us to be *purchased?*"

Uma nodded. "Of course. After your Unveiling you will be available for special service as well."

Odette shuddered. "I do not think I shall care for that."

Uma smiled. "You get used to it, as all things. And it is necessary. To serve those whom our Mistress chooses demonstrates the progress of your education."

Odette was stirred with a new curiosity. "What if we fail to please—what would happen?"

Uma laid her head back on the wall. "We would be punished, of course."

"I guessed that. I meant what would befall the Mistress if we—all of her students—refused to serve?"

"She would lose her status as a teacher, of course, and be sent back to the Guild of the Instructors to be bid on herself. Someone else would be elected to act in her stead here, I am sure. Her family has a long legacy of teaching—her father before her, his mother before him."

Odette smiled at the thought of Mistress Helrose at the Guildhall. "I can imagine the Mistress caged!"

Uma bit her lips to stifle a giggle. "Yes! But I love her, you know. She is a good teacher, and I have known only the greatest security under her care."

"Have you been here long, Uma?"

Uma's eyes widened thoughtfully. "I suppose…I have lost count of the years."

"You jest!"

"No."

"I would have thought you an adept after such a length of time."

"But I am, Odette," Uma answered proudly. "I chose to remain a servant, a slave and giver of pleasure. As a priestess that is my right."

"And you are…fulfilled?"

"Yes. I have learned many things here in Mistress Helrose's household—not just the carnal, but the spiritual through the carnal. I have also been trained in other interests that are dear to me, such as herbal preparation, and I excel in the ancient dances—all things mastered for my own satisfaction. And through pleasuring the variety of men I have to serve I have learned more of finding value in differences than ever could be known in the Outer Realm. I am confident of my own opinions and thoughts and chose, at the end of my training, to remain a servant of pleasure. This is my way, just as teaching is Mistress Helrose's. I look forward to one day having but one lord and master to serve, a husband who will possess me most jealously…but I am not so rash or foolish to try and find his face on every man I see. Until fate brings him into my life I shall continue to take pleasure in giving pleasure to all those who appreciate me."

Odette considered these things carefully; and though part of her wanted to protest and make Uma believe she was but serving the interests of others she knew it was not quite that way. Then she saw the brightness in Uma's face dim a little.

"It is different, I have heard, in the Outer Realm. They say you are given no choice but to believe your body is an ugly evil."

Odette sighed. "That is a fair appraisal. Women are deemed creatures of sin and hide their bodies even as they submit to the acts that lead to procreation—necessary evils in my world, not lovemaking. And that which is called chivalry here is seen in only a woeful shade of semblance there. A man is not taught to honor or defend a woman for what she is, but for the aura of chastity she is taught to assume."

Uma frowned. "Do the priests think there is then no love but that which can be shared by men?"

Odette almost laughed. "No, no—that is considered what they refer to as a sin, a great moral wrong." She reflected a moment. "I am apt to think that in habitually trying to abstain from carnal love the priests have transferred their frustration and resentment into hatred of women."

Uma looked sad. "How regrettable! The gods gave us the capacity for pleasure for a reason. I think there is great danger of blinding oneself to the beauty of diversity in this denial of pleasure."

"The Christian priests I have encountered are not tolerant of diversity, and I have heard it is thus with other religions in Midgard."

"Religion without tolerance," sighed Uma, "is no more than self-worship."

Silence fell between them, and Odette could hear the cries of birds flying past the manor and the faint merry voices of patrons out on the courtyard. She felt tranquil sitting beside Uma, and the fear she had known when first brought to the manor seemed more distant than the mountaintops that loomed over Athla.

"Uma," she said after awhile, "what is the Unveiling? I heard the Mistress speak of it yesterday."

"Ah, that is the time when others will bid for the right of taking your maidenhood. It is a sacred time, and the moneys are rendered to the High Priestess, who uses it for the upkeep of the orphaned Midgardian children who are taken in."

Odette swallowed, her temperature rising. Despite all the things she had seen in Mistress Helrose's household, her maidenhood at least she had thought her privilege to keep or yield.

"I shall have no say in who takes my maidenhood?"

Uma touched her arm comfortingly. "No, Odette. But that is how it is. How else are you to understand that you are more than breasts and nethermouth if you do not provide that precious thing without choice? He who shall be your eternal mate will want you for what lies deeper, but in the course of the time till you meet that mate you will learn how to please him—or her, as it might be. Besides, to submit willingly is sacred to Her, for She is love incarnate through the sensual. Treasure the men you will come to serve, for all their flaws and differences, and you shall become a wise, understanding and tolerant woman, indeed."

Odette felt her lip tremble. "But what if they are cruel? What if they care not for my safety? What if—"

"You have seen much suffering amongst Midgardian women at the hands of men?"

"Not so much," Odette replied and looked down at the scanty hem of her chemise. "At least the aura of chastity would spare me from this Unveiling!"

Uma smiled tenderly. "But do you truly wish to be chaste, Odette? Prefer you not to revel in your womanhood?"

"I—I am not certain."

"Ah, well, at least remember that every teacher carefully screens the men who bid for or purchase the pleasures of their students. That is one reason our Mistress opened the courtyard to sell her beverages, so she and her stewards can better acquaint themselves with the men and women who desire her girls."

"But what of the visitors from Midgard? Are they also allowed to purchase or bid for us?"

"Yes, but remember—no one may enter Athla without a tolerant heart. Except the Darkling elves, and they come only by permit and under close observation. It is a provision set down by Freyja Herself to protect we Athlans who are Her descendants. The likelihood of intolerant men finding their way into our realm is less than that of the priests of Loki discovering the key frost."

Odette frowned. "What?"

"You do not know of the Lokian priests? The Blodsaukers, who feed on the blood and flesh and spirit of living individuals? They search always for the key frost, the doorway into Athla, for they hunger to send their emissaries here in order to harass us."

"Ooh. But why does the Goddess allow that?"

"Because though they could not tread here without great pain to their nature, they hate the Goddess and work to bring havoc to Her and all She loves. It is rumored that the Norns, on command of the Faceless Eternal, have predicted that someday the realm shall be broached by emissaries of the Blodsaukers. For every wonderful thing there is its corresponding antagonist—it is the way of the universe—and so I suppose the Blodsaukers are Freyja's antagonists, or at least their master, Loki."

Odette thought of this a little while before returning to her original concern. She had heard enough of the Darkling elves' hatred for Freyja to know why they were limited in their numbers. But she wondered still about mortal men, the Outer Realmers.

"And so there is little chance a man who hates women can enter?"

"Very little. And they are informed of our laws governing the treatment of women before the boundary sentries allow them in. An Outer Realmer who breaks the laws would regret ever entering."

Odette thought of the men who had abused the serving girl the day before. Lord Alban and the patrons had responded immediately, and she remembered the uncompromising look in the eyes of the sentries who had escorted the Outer Realmers away. She realized Uma was right, that there was little chance of any great harm coming to her. But the morals of her world still bristled against the Athlan expectations of her.

Uma must have sensed her turmoil, for her arm slipped over Odette's shoulders and she said reassuringly, "You will be fine, my sister. I feel in you the soul of one whose natural passions and thoughts attune quite easily. I predict you shall have an easier time than you imagine understanding the rationale of our lessons, and in time take great satisfaction in them."

Odette rested her head on Uma's breast and closed her eyes, grateful for the sound of Uma's heartbeat against her ear. She hoped the prediction proved true and that soon she could throw off for all time the feeling of sinfulness that still clung to her from the dour, judgmental world from which she'd come.

* * *

There were not so many guests at the Mistress's table as the night before. One of them had, however, brought a gift for Helrose, a beautiful, heavily fronded fern potted in a lovely jade cauldron. Even as she served the guests Odette noticed the blush Mistress Helrose tried to conceal.

The man who had brought the plant was one Odette knew, King Larsarian's High Archer, Edred. Handsome and dark of features, he wore a regal velvet tunic and silken breeches so that he looked quite royal himself. Odette had been speechless when he'd walked into the Great Hall, but he said nothing that would have deepened the blush on her cheeks. It was a relief, especially when once the dessert wine was poured she had to take her place kneeling alongside Uma with her brow to the floor. With her buttocks jutting out from her hemline she was grateful that her face was concealed.

Then one of the men who had been a guest the night before asked the Mistress if he might have Odette sit on his lap.

"My new flower, Holbarki?" Helrose said in an uncertain tone. "Yes, you may take her on your lap."

"Come here, Odette," he ordered, and Odette went hesitantly to his outstretched arms.

He was not handsome, this burly Holbarki with his short waves of unwashed blonde hair and heavy jowls. Still, his regard was tender as Odette sat on his knee and he lifted her chin that he might study her face, turning it this way and that as the Mistress had before.

When he grasped one of her breasts firmly she gasped, though he'd only startled her. He laughed a little and moved them up and down in his hands as if weighing them. Odette tried to keep her eyes respectfully lowered, but when his hand pressed her thigh she looked imploringly to the Mistress.

The Mistress met her eyes a second, and a second only, yet Odette detected a trace of wariness in her otherwise placid expression.

"A prize, is she not?" Helrose remarked, sounding almost bored.

Holbarki chortled and slapped Odette's hip, bringing a round of laughter from the other guests. "How much would you take for her," he said bluntly, "or in trade?"

Helrose's eyes widened, but it was her brother who responded, his face dark. "You would suggest a barter before her Unveiling? That is profane, sir."

"By what laws, Eryan?" Holbarki argued, tracing the curve of Odette's lips with his thumb. "We can pen a contract, one specifying that I make a donation myself."

An uneasy hush fell over the other guests and the stewards. At last it was the archer who said, "The mead, I think, has gone to your head, my friend."

Holbarki's jowls stiffened. "I propose an exchange, Mistress Helrose—three caskets of silver and your choice of two from amongst my other slaves."

"That is generous, Holbarki," the Mistress replied, "and though I must decline, please explain why you would offer so richly."

Holbarki shrugged. "I have a penchant for little golden-haired girls, and Midgardian accents intrigue my own customers. And though there is a long mutual alliance between our families we both know you seem to forget that when it comes time to send the invitations to the biddings for your students' Unveilings. I prefer to make my offer an outright purchase than face your indifference."

Odette saw a fleeting pained look in Helrose's eyes. "I have not meant to offend you, Holbarki. Our families' ties run long; I would never deliberately snub you."

"Not here, no—only publicly."

Odette froze at the accusation, though she did not fully understand it. Mistress Helrose regarded her friend blankly and the archer looked angry.

Lord Eryan growled, "You dare blame my sister? It is your commerce with the dark elves that has warranted her precautions."

The humor vanished from Holbarki's face. "I would never introduce one of Helrose's students to the dark elves, unless the girl specifically showed an interest in emigrating to their realm. I meant only that my usual customers would find this one's charms inviting and it has been long since I have had a properly educated slave."

The silence in the hall was heavy until at last Mistress Helrose spoke. "I can offer you this, Holbarki—bring me two of your light elvlings, that I may train them in proper service whilst you retain your others. When I deem them prepared I shall return them and you may send two others."

Holbarki laughed, but this time there was no humor in the sound. "I cannot expect an invitation for this flower?"

"No. Even were I inclined, my friend, to do so would be a breach of the conditions set down by the king's leniency to you."

Holbarki drew a long breath. "Ah, well, that we cannot have, can we?" He kissed Odette's cheek then and set her on the floor. "Off with you, pretty one," he said and gave her bottom a swift swat as she went to kneel beside Uma.

The light mood returned to the conversation at the table, but it was long before Odette could put aside the uneasy exchange.

* * *

After their late dinner Uma and Odette were put to work cleaning the kitchen. They scrubbed everything—the dirty pots and pans, the dishware and utensils—and when all the items were put away for the night Bjorn returned and put Odette to sweeping the floor. As she brought the broom from the pantry she saw him lead Uma by the hand out into the moonlit yard. And though she tried to keep her mind diligently on her work very soon a husky moan drifted in through the window over the washing basin. She smiled, hoping Uma was well satisfied, and wondered if Bjorn routinely absconded with his charges.

When she was done she sat on a little stool and waited. At last they returned, and Odette saw at once that Uma's fair face and breasts and even stomach had all taken on a deep strawberry shade and Bjorn, whose big arms encircled her waist, was humming merrily. He told Odette to go to her room, and it felt very strange to know she was allowed to walk alone through the manor.

As she passed through the Great Hall she saw Lord Alban and Lord Eryan standing together before the hearth. Their voices were low but heated, and as she hurried quietly to the door to the hallway she heard the Mistress's name spoken.

Yolande was in the bedchamber that night, sitting with her friends on the candlelight-splashed floor. Their whispering muted as soon as Odette entered.

"Lie down beside me, Odette," said Rystla from the bed. Ignoring the baleful stares of the others Odette joined her under the blankets, grateful to at last relax and let the aches wane from her muscles. Her buttocks were still sore, enough that she was obliged to lie on her side. She faced Rystla and smiled when the girl pulled the blanket over her shoulder.

For a time they said nothing, just listened to the others drone on about some new style of head covering they'd heard rumored was fashionable in the Outer Realm.

"I shall procure one of these wimples and hold my head high again," Ivana declared, "and woe to any man who asks to wed me."

"I shall wear whatever I wish," Emleth said, "and I shall never cook my husband a single meal!"

Ivana and Yolande laughed, and Odette could not help grinning at this, too.

"Are you very tired?" Rystla whispered. "I know it is hard to clean up alone."

Odette smiled again. "Ah, so Bjorn's passion for Uma is not rare?"

"Oh, no, he is quite smitten. I think he would marry her if she returned his affection."

Odette nodded sleepily. "I like her. I like you, too, Rystla."

"Thank you. But, please, keep away from *them* as much as possible," Rystla said, gesturing to the other three. "They shan't be here long, however, for our Mistress plans to hire them out to the king's mercenaries in the hope of breaking them of that haughtiness which they refuse to shed. As they have gone through little more the motions of most of their training this should not come as a shock for them."

"They are haughty," Odette agreed, glancing at the trio. "They seem to have embraced little of the dignified pride that is supposed to enhance our seith training."

"Exactly!" Rystla patted her shoulder. "Your understanding deepens already."

Odette felt surprised at herself, and as her eyes closed she saw again the phallus jutting from the wall before her mouth and felt the conflicting shame and passion being chained and exposed had brought. She sensed she was changing in outlook and objective, but whether for right or wrong she could only guess. The one thing she was certain of was that the fear of the seith training had disappeared; and she was left pondering if this surrender of fear was also right or wrong.

Rystla snuggled up close beside her and Odette, happy to have her there, laced her arms about the girl and slept deeply.

Chapter Ten

In the morning Odette discovered Lord Eryan was greatly displeased with her work in the kitchen the night before.

Lord Alban came and woke the girls and after seeing they ate breakfast led them outside to be bathed. The steward was drying Odette's hair when Lord Eryan arrived, pale and obviously angered, and demanded that Odette be handed over to his supervision.

"She is almost ready," Lord Alban said, rubbing the linen towel briskly through her damp hair. "I must dress and arrange her hair."

"I have no time for your indulgence," Eryan said, and snatched up the comb and Odette's colored cords and her collar lying on the bank. "Come, Odette, I shall braid your hair."

Odette felt Lord Alban's hands cup her shoulders gently when a hostile look passed between the two men. The other girls sitting on the bank watched worriedly, and even Yolande looked uneasy.

"Let me dress her," the steward said and bent to make a choice from the bundle of freshly laundered chemises he'd laid earlier on the roots of one of the willow trees. Lord Eryan stepped forward and grabbed Odette's arm, pulling her away from the other man roughly.

"I already have a more appropriate outfit awaiting this flower."

Lord Alban straightened and glared at Lord Eryan stonily. "I have not been informed of any change of routine for this flower."

"Your Mistress knows, and that is all you need be aware of, steward."

Lord Eryan held Odette close to him, so tightly she felt the roar of his heartbeat. She was frightened and found no consolation in the hesitation apparent in Alban's eyes.

But he looked at her mildly and said to Lord Eryan "Very well, but be assured I shall ask Mistress Helrose to give me notice the next time."

Lord Eryan turned curtly and ordered Odette to walk ahead of him. They went into the house, through the kitchen and Great Room and out to the courtyard. The clean tiles sparkled in the morning sun, the bars of the cages shone like gold. One of the serving girls Odette had seen preparing the tables now sat on her knees within one of the cages with her hands held deliberately behind her back, trying to remain still as a guard groped her dark nipples through the bars. The square beyond the courtyard was quiet, only one or two merchants worked to open their stalls. Birds squawked from the trees and a dog barked from the far streets.

Lord Eryan addressed the guard at the cage. "Veli, go break your fast."

The man nodded and gave the caged girl a departing tweak to her left nipple that made her flinch. As he trotted toward the house Eryan ordered Odette to stand and wait for him. She watched as he walked over to the table where the beverages would be set out later and picked up what looked to Odette like a belt of sorts and brought it to her.

"You shall wear this," he said and handed her the slender circlet of brass, which had strips of hanging suede on front, back, and either side. From the two side strips hung wide leather garter loops that were attached to one another by a small iron chain.

With as much grace as possible Odette stepped into the loops and pulled the belt up over her legs and hips. The loops were snug, the chain between them taut. She grew anxious, knowing she could never hope to walk quickly as long as her legs were restrained. She noticed, too, a pair of young men standing at the gates and they watched intently as Lord Eryan locked the belt at the small of her back.

She blushed and turned her eyes in time to see Lord Eryan slip the key inside his overcoat. Next he lifted one of her breasts, stretched the nipple out and clamped on it a loop of twisted bronze. It was hardly larger than a candlestick ring but the little thing bit into her flesh, making her whimper. He applied an identical loop to her other nipple. Her breasts and the aereolas about the nipples began to swell and grow pink, but, worse, the irritation unexpectedly aroused her in much the same way suckling on the phallus had. Odette fidgeted agitatedly, stilling when Lord Eryan cast her a dark look. He proceeded to affix her collar again and lock it, a little tighter than before. There was a leash of beaten gold on the table, too, but this he did not touch. Instead, he picked up the comb beside it and brushed out her hair and bound it on the crown of her head in a single horsetail that swept down the middle of her back.

The confining belt and loops intensified Odette's awareness of her nudity, but she had at least been spared the leather appendage and the clitoral sheath some of the other flowers wore.

"There, now you are dressed more befitting a girl who is too lazy to properly perform the tasks she is given."

Odette's eyes widened. She had no idea what he meant, but she dared not look straight at him.

"I inspected your work from last night in the kitchen," he continued, as if answering her unspoken question. "Our cook has a tendency to overlook the most obvious lapses, and so I have taken it upon myself to inspect the nightly work of all our girls. Very sloppy you were, Odette—the dishes will have to be scrubbed again by someone else before Bjorn begins dinner. While it might prove fairer to have you wash them, we cannot take the chance someone might have to eat off a dirty plate. So, in your laziness you have put more work on someone else."

Odette frowned, ashamed truly, but she could not help but feel there was some exaggeration in Lord Eryan's accusation.

Before she had time to think, however, he pulled her toward a bench and sitting down, yanked her across his lap. He spanked her thoroughly so that the echo of each loud smack rang through the courtyard. She whimpered as her buttocks inflamed under his palm, suppressing the pleas that came to her lips—for she knew if he heard it he would punish her all the more.

When she was quite sore he stopped. "Now, get to your knees beside me."

She did so at once, terrified that the two men at the gates might take pleasure to see her buttocks, which were doubtless glowing red.

"See there, beneath that shrub," he said, and she followed his eyes to a tiny quince tree growing nearby and the broom that had been propped against its trunk. "You are to sweep this courtyard, every inch. Do not attempt to move the tables—you would harm yourself to try—but the benches are of light wood and you may pull them away enough to do a proper job."

He did not move, just watched coldly as she fetched the broom. Without waiting she started to sweep, feeling his eyes measuring her every movement.

She was sure she was working to his satisfaction when he suddenly came up and swatted her buttocks curtly. She jumped, more angry than surprised, and seeing the knit of her brow he grasped her waist, bent her forward and spanked her again. As his hand inflamed her again her anger washed away, replaced by contrite humiliation and a new determination to perform better. The feeling did not arise merely from the desire to avoid further punishment but also the odd acknowledgment that she had been wrong to show her displeasure. When at last her bottom felt truly on fire he let her go and she put her mind fully to sweep as he expected.

When she'd gone over the entire courtyard he inspected her work. To her delight he was satisfied and told her so. But then he drew her to the pillory. She trembled, disheartened, and her eyes filled with tears.

"You did well, little flower, that is not in doubt," he said, "but the day is young and the pillory needs to be polished."

He handed her two rags, one damp with a dark oil, which he explained she was to use before buffing with the other rag.

She knelt beside the pillory in the place he indicated, which allowed all passersbys to see her reddened buttocks as she worked. The air grew warmer; her skin beneath the leather loops on her thighs itched and her breasts, swaying with her movements, felt heavy. The discomforts made her irritable, the chain holding her legs together furthered her awareness of her servitude as much as Lord Eryan's ever-watchful eyes.

When a small group of men approached the courtyard to inquire when beverages would be served Lord Eryan rose to speak with them, and she immediately longed for the reassurance even his stern presence had given. The group did not linger, but soon afterward the girls whose turn it was to clean the tables and prepare the beverages came trotting out of the manor. A steward, dressed in a white shirt and tan breeches and simple boots, followed. Odette recognized him only from the Mistress's table, but he was handsome in a way, though not so much as Lord Eryan and certainly not as Lord Alban.

As the flowers went about their tasks Lord Eryan and the steward talked for a time. They went to the cage and removed the girl—her legs were wobbly and they helped her to one of the seats, where she was allowed to stretch out. Odette noticed Lord Eryan said something to the girl that made her eyes lower and her lip quiver, but he left her to the steward's care and came to inspect Odette's work.

He was satisfied with her progress on the wood but made her clean again the hinges and locks. When her performance of that contented him he gave her a fresh damp rag and told her to clean her hands. Odette heard the steward order the girl who had been caged to go to the kitchen to get something to eat, and Odette hoped perhaps Lord Eryan would take as much pity for her. Instead, he attached the leash to the narrow iron loop on her collar.

Odette bristled, feeling like a tethered animal, but his disproving regard made her still at once.

"We are going into town, little flower."

Her mouth opened—she could not believe he was going to parade her through the very streets—but when he pulled on the leash she fell in step behind his heels and tried to take comfort in remembering that in Athla the streets were always full of naked and leashed women.

I shan't be the only immodest and humiliated soul!

The square was busy as they entered, and though Odette would have preferred keeping her eyes lowered she had to watch his every step to follow his turns. Along the way she indeed saw dozens of women paraded just as she was. None seemed embarrassed or shamed by their nudity or subservience, and the only ones among them wearing downcast faces or tears were those being reprimanded or with freshly reddened buttocks. Odette could see they were comfortable with their lives, and she felt a touch of guilt for expecting them to feel otherwise.

Lord Eryan's strides lengthened once they'd exited the square. Past the guild houses and temples he led Odette, so quickly she was forced to trot as best she could with the hobbling chain between her legs, while the bronze loops bobbed against her swaying breasts. At length he turned down an alley into a small business section of the city and continued until he reached a wide one-story cottage of dark-stained wood. The roof was shiny fluted tin and hanging on the front door was a placard on which were painted a harp, lute and drum.

The abode was cool and well lighted from the generous glass windows. The rich smells of wood and stains filled Odette's nostrils, and the faint strum of a rosewood harp lilted through the entire house. Lord Eryan wound her leash about his hand so that she stood close behind him, and though she kept her face lowered she spied harps hanging from pegs set all over the walls. Dozens of them, from breezy rosewood to pliable willow to beautiful cedar—she had never counted so many harps. In one corner leaned one giant instrument of oak. Its forepillar was taller than any man and the soundboard and neck were embossed with golden sea waves. Pegs of ivory clutched the strings that shimmered like gossamer in the soft light.

Odette heard the laughter of men here, too and, through a door to the back, the distinct sound of a paddle striking bare flesh and a fretful little wail from the punished one.

Someone approached, and Odette's humbled eyes saw a pair of beautifully sculpted naked female legs. She peeked up quickly, long enough to see the black curly mane between the girl's thighs. She was dark and voluptuous of hip, beautifully sloe-eyed. The collar at her throat was of wide leather instead of metal and her unbound and tousled black hair lent a wildness to her exotic attractions.

"Tell your master I am here," Lord Eryan said. The girl bowed low and scurried through the door in the back.

Presently the sound of spanking ended, and from the back door emerged a man wearing leather breeches and a work shirt of fine cotton with the sleeves rolled up. He was tall and muscular with long hair and an even longer beard of soft red. Even the downy hair that covered his chest was red. As he approached he clapped Lord Eryan's shoulder and eyed Odette briefly with his soft grey eyes.

"Harold," Eryan said pleasantly, "have you something I may feed this girl?"

At hearing herself referred to Odette understood Lord Eryan's expectations and lowered her eyes.

"Certainly," Harold replied, and Odette thought he must have made some signal, for the dark girl came running back and knelt at his feet.

"Fetch some cheese and bread and water for this girl," he said to her, "and a flask of ale and two cups, as well."

When she had gone Harold led them to a table in the shadows. Odette knelt at Eryan's feet as they sat down. At another table nearby two young men sipped ale from a shared flagon. They were dressed like Harold, with the addition of leather aprons; and the oil drying on their shirts plus their sweat-damp hair indicated they were taking a break from work.

One of the young men looked down at Odette boldly and winked. She blushed and hid her face against Lord Eryan's legs.

The girl came back carrying a tray with the ale and stoneware mugs and a platter with the food Harold had ordered. Lord Eryan broke the wheel of cheese into several small portions and offered these to Odette along with the little glass bottle filled with water.

"A pretty one," Harold said. "One of Helrose's new acquisitions?"

"Yes," Lord Eryan replied, "her name is Odette." His hand strayed to Odette's hair, which he stroked idly while she ate.

The two men talked for some time of personal matters and mutual friends and acquaintances. From their conversation Odette deduced they had known one another a very long time. Harold, she surmised, had been raised by Lord Eryan's own parents, brought to them as a babe after king Urls, hunting in Midgard, had found him abandoned and exposed on a hill.

"I was so proud to have a younger brother to look up to me," Eryan said tenderly, "and here you are, Harold, the king's own harp maker. Now it is my turn to be proud."

Harold laughed. "Our father outshines us both, you know. When I visited yesterday Mother was at wit's end trying to find a way to convince him to release her from that cage."

"She knows he adores her and only wishes to show her off," Eryan said, sighing. "If only all women were so eager to please."

"If they were we should be denied the amusement of sifting the gems from the silt." Harold paused a moment and his tone was more somber as he asked, "And how is our sister?"

Eryan made a disapproving grunt. "Fickle as always. Edred has her in a new dilemma. I wish he'd simply come and announce his desire. I think then perhaps she'd finally decide which path she wishes to follow."

"She is good at what she does."

"Of course. But that isn't the point. Her talents suffer for her vacillating, as does her students' training. She needs to choose her path and stick to it. I worry about her reputation for this fickleness."

"I agree," Harold said. "I fear her decision to teach was made more to please Father than anything else. But heed not what others might gossip."

There was underlying pain in Eryan's voice as he said, "The king's resentments toward me do not help her."

"He is a good ruler, our Larsarian. He has not used this old dispute to harass you, has he?"

"No."

Odette felt Lord Eryan's hand on her head again, the brush of his fingers through the length of her lifted hair. He traced the outline of her shoulders, and she felt her skin prickle warmly.

"This flower is exquisite, is she not?" The question made her blush.

"Without a doubt."

"Do you see anything familiar about her?" Lord Eryan raised her face gently so she was forced to look up at Harold.

"No, I do not think…" He frowned, studying her closely. "You—are you trying to tell me this is the queen's kinswoman, Eryan?"

Lord Eryan nodded, and the conflicting emotions in his smile were impossible for Odette to decipher.

"And Helrose knows you have her out before her Unveiling?"

"With her full consent and approval," Eryan said, his voice explicitly proud. "This flower is in particular need of a firm hand."

Harold looked worried. "Take care, brother. Remember this young lady is special in her own way. Do not disregard her own personality because she may resemble another."

Eryan's mouth twisted slightly. "I know."

Harold sighed and took a long draught of his ale. "Is she as pliant as the queen?"

"I've yet to see it. But what say we give it a test?"

Odette shuddered, but Harold drained his ale and nodded. Lord Eryan regarded Odette with a look so frightful in its strange emotions that she had difficulty swallowing the bread in her mouth. But he said nothing more until she'd finished eating.

"Hop up on the table, Odette."

She did as he ordered, her face burning at being watched by so many men.

"Now, I want you to turn toward my brother," Eryan instructed. Odette pivoted on the table, and he said "Now bring your feet up and set them on the edge and spread your thighs."

She did as he bade, her bashfulness scalding her face, and held to her ankles firmly.

"You will not fall," Eryan scolded and, as she released her ankles, "I want you to unfold the lips of that little nethermouth."

Odette wanted to obey, trying to think this was no different than obeying Lord Alban. But unlike the stewards Harold was a total stranger to her, and her old pride resented the arrogance she felt spurred Lord Eryan to demonstrate her obedience to his brother.

Lord Eryan dealt his order a second time.

She whimpered but did not move. Lord Eryan jumped up, and taking her hair into his hand, whipped the length of it against her shoulders. She growled softly, angry her own hair should be used for punishment.

"Do it now, Odette!"

Despite the threat underlying his words her own anger would not have allowed her to move now if she could have. Harold smiled slightly.

"I see you are right, brother," he said, "but she is well worth the effort it will take to train her."

"She had best learn quickly," Eryan snapped and hauled on the leash firmly so that Odette's head was tilted forcibly back on her neck.

"Thank Harold for the meal, spoiled flower."

Frightened tears sprang to Odette's eyes. "Thank you, sir."

Lord Eryan wished his brother a good day and led Odette out the front door. He walked briskly out of the alley and turned onto the street heading toward the king's castle. As they neared the castle grounds Lord Eryan crossed the avenue. Odette caught a glimpse of two of her old playmates chasing one another in the street and around a sapling that grew from a separation in the cobblestones. They did not notice as she was led right past them; and for that she felt relieved despite the rage she could feel smoldering in Lord Eryan.

Eryan strode to the structure known as the public thrashing bar. Odette had passed it many times before—two high wooden posts set with a crossbeam. Before reaching the time of her training she had seen women strung by the wrists from the several sets of fur-lined cuffs that dangled from chains bolted into the crossbeam. A sturdy stool stood on the ground below the cuffs and brass cylinders were attached to either post in which were various instruments for punishment: paddles, whips, belts and flails. On the sides of the cylinders were pegs on which hung the keys to the cuffs.

Today the thrashing bar was empty as Lord Eryan brought Odette to it, the cuffs swinging slightly in the breeze. He commanded her to stand below the middle set, then set the stool before her feet and ordered her to take his hand and step upon it. She looked up at the cuffs, so menacing despite the soft fur. In desperation she dared to look into his face and plead with her eyes for his mercy.

His face was unreadable, but he answered by lifting her atop the stood himself As he raised her arms one at a time and closed the cuffs about her wrists the little loops at her nipples quivered and her tears fell in a torrent down her face.

He kicked the stool away and she dangled from the cuffs so that her toes swayed against the grass. Lord Eryan patted the handle of his belted flail thoughtfully, then went and plucked a whip from one of the cylinders. It was made of not one but several strips of soft leather, all about the length of a man's forearm. Odette shivered as he came to her left and regarded her with the hardest of looks.

As he raised the whip her entire body flinched. The first blow sent the lashes spanking across her hip. She gasped, and understood that the ingenious design of the instrument guaranteed stinging pain without harm of breaking the flesh. Yet, this was little comfort, and when again the cords came down against her hip she could not suppress her cry.

Lord Eryan came to stand before her, his knuckles white as he clenched the handle of the whip.

"Look at me." She did so without hesitation, seeing that his dark eyebrows puckered together and his chest rose and fell rapidly from his agitation. "I shall beat the impudence from you, Odette, rid you of every last shred of vanity in that pretty head!"

He stepped back and she saw that a small crowd was gathering from the street to watch her punishment. The majority were men with their own women, but there were also a few curious youths and a vitki teacher with her male slave. They watched as Lord Eryan brought the whip smacking down. The smooth leather splayed across Odette's breasts, making her clamped nipples flare with pain. Before she had hardly caught her breath the cords descended over her stomach. Odette squirmed in the cuffs, mindlessly kicking her bound legs as hard as she could, thinking desperately that if she could break the chain she might somehow get free. The whip lashed her right hip now, the left in turn, over and over. Through her tears she saw the smiles on the young men and the mixture of fright and contentment on the faces of the women. Lord Eryan walked behind her and the cords flailed down over the tender flesh of her uppermost thighs. Again and again Lord Eryan punished her buttocks. She jostled in the cuffs, kicking and moving her smarting backside so violently it seemed she danced in the air. Beyond her own cries she heard the men cheering mildly from the crowd and Lord Eryan's labored but controlled breath.

When at last he stopped and moved to her side her cries were pitiful to her own ears. She heard the vitki say to her boy, "Remember the face of this naughty novice, Lothar, if you wish to avoid such public chastisement."

Lord Eryan stood close behind her. She had never felt so helpless in her life as she did this moment, and when she heard the welcome sound of the whip sliding back into its cylinder she sighed with relief. Lord Eryan set the stool underneath her and, positioning her feet on it, unlocked the cuffs. She tried to stand but her balance forsook her and she fell back into his arms. He lifted her about the waist and set her on the ground, and when he deemed she was fit to stand without aid took her leash tautly in hand.

Without a word he set off again, and she trotted once more behind. Her legs and buttocks were aflame and the bobbing loops on her nipples worked to chafe her tender breasts.

Upon returning to the Mistress's house Lord Eryan put her to work gathering the soiled chemises from the bedchambers, for the laundress was coming soon to take them to her washhouse. The whipping had humbled her, so much she could not even whisper to the other novices who greeted her in passing, and when Lord Alban passed her in the hallway and told her to straighten her posture she did so without thought or question. As he moved away she realized her nethermouth had warmed and moistened.

When she brought the basket of soiled garments to Lord Eryan in the Great Hall he directed her to a large, dark figure sitting on a nearby bench. Odette placed the basket down carefully at the figure's feet and knelt. A large hand smoothed the hair away from her face.

The voice of the laundress was deeper than the average man's, her accent unidentifiable. "Look up at me, little one."

The laundress was no human woman. Her body was huge and clumsy, and a head twice the size of a mortal man's topped her uneven shoulders. Her eyes were murky dark and lashless, her mouth but formless bands of tissue. It was her skin, however, scaly and yellowish and covered by short bristly hair, by which Odette deduced she belonged to the race of the trolls.

She wore a dark, shapeless fleece skirt and leather shoes. A white blouse of fleece with puffy sleeves lent an ironic charm to her formidable arms.

"You must be Odette, the queen's young kinswoman."

Odette nodded, feeling herself drawn into the troll's ink-pool eyes.

"Come, sit with me, little cygnet, child of Outer Realm."

Odette sat gingerly beside her on the bench, and the troll shadowed her like a small mountain. The laundress pushed the length of hair over Odette's shoulder and stroked the tail, and a singsong murmur rose from her pendulous bosom. Odette wondered at the feeling of complete peace in the troll's company—all the tales she'd ever heard surrounding their kind warned of their rash tempers and fondness for human flesh.

For a long time they sat quietly together, the troll plying Odette's hair between her huge fingers, singing her strange thick song. Lord Eryan strolled by once and eyed them, but he said nothing to see Odette idle, though she guessed he would have done otherwise if it were Lord Alban she sat beside. After a time he went his way, walking off with deliberately softened steps. Odette wondered if, indeed, Lord Eryan feared the laundress.

"No, he has no fear of Gleami," the troll said suddenly.

Odette shivered that her thoughts had been read, and the laundress patted her arm comfortingly.

"He fears no longer, but is respectful of Gleami. And it is well you fear your Lord Eryan—that fear will bring respect, cygnet."

It was the second time the laundress had called her *cygnet*, and Odette remembered now that the Mistress had said it once. She supposed it was a term of endearment for novices, like *flower*.

"You are your mother's child," Gleami said. "Know you not what you are?"

Odette was puzzled and shook her head slowly.

"I am sure the queen would have it that way. Ah, your hair is like gold—as your father's?"

Odette nodded, still perplexed, but in the company of this woman her questions seemed to drift into oblivion.

"My folk would slice your scalp for such a prize."

Odette shuddered in repulsion and Gleami laughed, a dry sound like a brush pulled over the bark of a tree.

"I know not your mother," Gleami continued, "but I have met your Granddame. It is She who saved me from my ravenous brothers when our hunting grounds were burned at the hands of the followers of that Paul who purported himself a disciple of the Christ."

Odette raised her voice, stifling the growing sleepiness that was moving over her. "May I speak, Lady Gleami?"

"As with Rystla and Uma, all that you wish to me, Odette."

Odette turned toward her shyly, not out of fear but from some unexplainable emotion she could not name. "You knew my Granddame? Tell me of her."

"She is heaven on earth," Gleami said, her eyelids closing a moment. "That is all you need know."

Odette sighed. "It seems so many knew my mother and her family, and yet they decline to reveal these things to me."

Gleami's eyes opened again, and there was a touch of sympathy shimmering in the black pools. "There must be a reason, think you not? I shan't speak more, for truly, I am unworthy…a better thing to leave it to your kinswoman."

"Unworthy?" Odette could not hide her surprise. "But that is foolish, Gleami. You are kind."

Now the troll laughed heartily, a sound that brought images of sweet vervain and woodland blossoms to Odette's mind.

"You are a songbird, a river of whispered eternal promises," said the laundress. "I am old and wish I were young again, but I gave my vow to the goddess to go and be Her handmaiden when my natural days are done. So I may not wait to see that day when your wings are clipped and your soul fulfilled. But young again I will be then, oh, yes, and merry with all the delights you give and receive now. Blessed balance—it awaits me, too, precious Odette!"

Odette smiled, thinking the laundress a bit mad.

Gleami smiled reproachfully. "I should punish you for that," she said. But she sighed and stretched on her seat and cast a nasty look at the basket on the floor. "Carry that with me, cygnet—my boy awaits out yonder."

Odette picked up the basket and watched Gleami rise from the bench; and she saw how slow the troll's movements were, as if every movement she made were a labor in itself. She followed Gleami to the door where a steward moved to open it for the laundress. Out on the courtyard waited Gleami's *boy,* a young man with reddish locks and a freckled face whose chapped arms and hands told of hours washing clothes. He sat at one of the courtyard tables, sipping on a glass of dandelion wine as he stroked the unbodiced breasts of the pretty flower sitting on his knee. Seeing the laundress, he kissed the girl and gave her a coin and rose to take the basket from Odette.

Gleami turned to her once again and pulled her into an embrace.

"The sweetest flowers give as much delight as they take from the attentive gardener," she said softly. "Do not let yourself wilt under the fallacies of the ignorant who shun the garden."

Odette smiled and watched as Gleami set off with her helper, and it seemed to her that the troll-woman had taken away much more than soiled laundry.

Chapter Eleven

fter Mistress Helrose had finished her evening meal and seen her guests out she called Odette to her at the cold hearth where the Mistress stood drinking a heavily aromatic wine. Her eyes lowered, Odette noticed Helrose's slippers. They were satin and embroidered with white silk thread and dusted with small sparkling jewels, and Odette wondered if they were a gift from the High Archer.

The rest of the Mistress's costume lacked any feminine adornment. She wore breeches of slate-colored leather and a long-sleeved tunic of red linen, with a brooch of knotted silver at the collar. With her hair pulled back in a tight bun her features looked sweetly boyish again.

Odette's breasts were so swollen, her nipples so sore and tender from the biting loop clamps, she'd had to clamp her teeth to conceal her anguish as she served at the table. Now as she knelt before the Mistress she yearned for the comfort of the chemise again and wondered how she could have ever resented it.

"I have spoken with Lord Eryan," Helrose said, "and he is of the opinion you need firmer training than is generally applied to a novice."

Odette heard Eryan's familiar footfalls in the room but she managed not to flinch.

"The garters are quite becoming on you," the Mistress continued, granting her a half-smile. "I think his adamancy is a service to my household, and perhaps I am a wee bit prejudiced when it comes to my brother. The request is unusual, but as he is not given to acting on personal motive I shall grant his request."

Odette fought the sudden fear that brought a dozen questions to mind and listened as the Mistress went on.

"This means, Odette, that Lord Eryan is your Master. Your *sole* Master, at least until your Unveiling. Until that time you answer to him alone. My other stewards cannot revoke his orders concerning you, and I alone can summon you from his charge."

The Mistress squatted down beside her, stroking her back gently, studying the faint welts left by the whipping in town.

"I have not made this decision as punishment, Odette. I see it as an opportunity to fulfill a potential Lord Eryan obviously sees in you. Set your heart to pleasing him and accept whatever punishments he finds necessary with grace. And never once feel sorry for yourself. It is an honor you are receiving, flower."

The tidings and the weight of their unknown consequences settled over Odette uncomfortably. She remembered the conversation between Lord Eryan and Harold, remembered the unsettling references to some issue between Eryan and the queen and king. She could not help but wonder if this plan Lord Eryan had devised was birthed from something that had nothing to do with her.

The Mistress saw her shudder and patted her cheek and told her to raise her eyes.

"Our bargain avows him to abstain from taking your maidenhood, if that is your fear. Of course, your deflowering draws nearer, so take comfort in knowing you will be very thoroughly prepared for it under his skilled hand."

Odette nodded, but in truth she feared little now but the exacting discipline of Lord Eryan.

"Now, I want you to stand and accompany me. There is one aspect of the preparation he has confided in his plans which I prefer to perform myself."

Odette stood up and followed the Mistress into the hallway. As they walked she heard the now-familiar sound of spanking from behind one of the closed bedchamber doors and the desolate cries of the recipient.

The Mistress walked the length of the hallway and ascended the staircase. The upstairs floor was carpeted and the hall divided abruptly by a facing corner. To their right Odette saw two doors on each wall, but it was to the left the Mistress took her. As they walked Odette noticed a niche equipped with black iron bars and a great padlock set low in the wall to her left. The small cell was empty but for two clay bowls, one containing a shallow bit of water.

The only other door at this end of the hallway stood at the end, and it was this one Mistress Helrose opened. The floor was strewn with carpets of intricate designs and tapestries hung on the walls. A bed with a spindled headboard stood in the center of the room. Over the silk coverlets had been thrown an old and tattered quilt, rather out of place against the other fine ornaments and furnishings. A low fire burned in the slim stone hearth and several small blown-glass lanterns sat here and there. A grey curtain concealed the corner to the left of the hearth.

Odette spied a closed door beside the hearth and jutting from another wall a phallus like the one in the Great Hall, with the familiar cuffs bolted to the wall above. There was also a small pillory, as well as a silver canister stuffed with whips and paddles and other assorted instruments of punishment.

With a delicate touch Mistress Helrose plucked the clamps from her sore nipples, then told her to sit on the bed. This Odette did, feeling at once uneasy and vulnerable to be alone with the Mistress in what was doubtless her private bedchamber.

The Mistress opened the doors of a slender cabinet and took out a small stone bottle and a silver cup. Uncorking the bottle, she poured dark liquid into the cup and offered it to Odette.

"It will calm you," she said. "Sip, not gulp, until it is gone."

The spirit was strong and as sweet, with a thick bitterness just beneath the flavor. As Odette sipped she listened to the Mistress wander about the back shadows of the room. It seemed Helrose was gone a long time; and when at last Odette dared to look for her, her head spun. Soon her limbs felt leaden and her eyelids seemed too heavy to hold up any longer. When the cup dropped from her hand and the remainder of the spirit dashed over the carpet she wept and laughed at once, though she could not understand why.

Mistress Helrose returned and Odette's heart skipped a beat. Without thinking she looked up and met Helrose's eyes. When a moment later she realized her misdeed her cheeks smarted painfully from a smile she simply could not wipe away.

However, the Mistress did not scold but rather very patiently knelt and picked the cup up and threw a linen cloth over the spill.

"Now, you lie down," she commanded Odette and helped her do so, directing her toward the cushions at the headboard. "There, yes, and onto that lovely stomach."

All Odette's strength could not keep her eyes open and she felt herself drifting swiftly toward sleep. Only dully was she aware that her arms were pulled forward and her wrists bound to two spindles with some soft, thick fabric. The Mistress unbound her hair and unlocked the belt to remove the garters.

She heard singing, tender and steady, and at first she thought it must be Queen Honi who sang before she realized that could not be.

"All 'round the green lawn
Dance on ribboned feet
All the pretty maids fit to be beat;
Wash them in milk,
Dress them in silk,
And kiss them unto dawn."

She smiled and her thoughts reeled with the melody until all was lost in a lush meadow perfumed with every flower imaginable. She glimpsed a familiar, swarthy face in the bushes, a mustache she thought she recognized. But as she approached she felt hands on her backside.

Her eyes flew open and she saw Mistress Helrose bending over her. The lady held a goatskin pouch with a long tube of leather snaking out of it. The Mistress had parted her buttocks widely and now she inserted something smooth and long into Odette's anus. Odette flinched at the unexpected invasion. Through her heavy eyes she watched as the Mistress squeezed the pouch, and the next moment Odette felt a warm pressure within her belly. Slowly but steadily the pressure built, creating a growing but inescapable discomfort.

Odette tried to roll over but the cords held her fast and when she whimpered and kicked her legs the Mistress stopped only long enough to smooth her brow and sing again, this time in the Athlan Odette did not completely understand. The words drove her into a sleep bereft of the lush meadow and handsome face.

Sometime during the night she woke. The Mistress slept beside her and the old quilt had been taken away. Drowsily, Odette moved under the blankets and discovered that a sheet had been wound about her pelvis and upper legs. The folds between her thighs were damp and she felt her face grow red in the candlelight, knowing that the Mistress had cleansed her internally, yet she was perplexed as to why. What she did know was that Mistress Helrose had not harmed her and had certainly taken measures to assure her comfort.

Helrose looked so beautiful as she slept, the harshness all gone from her fine features. At last Odette snuggled down under the blankets again and laid her arm about her waist, almost wishing she would awaken and speak. But that was inconsiderate and so Odette sighed and gazed at the Mistress's face.

Her mouth was parted a little and Odette thought how perfectly defined it was, with the firm, narrow bottom lip and the fuller, high-peaked upper. She was tempted to put her mouth over those lips, to cover the face of the Mistress with kisses of gratitude and affection, to reaffirm her devotion with caresses just as she had through resignation. How she adored the outwardly self-restrained Mistress with her guarded but eager passions! She wanted to feed on Helrose's sweet flesh, to lose herself utterly, just as she had with Lord Alban.

Odette closed her eyes and tried to forget the aching desire, but as with many thoughts that had tormented her lately it was long before this one lulled.

* * *

Odette awoke again the next morning when someone knocked on the door. She sat up as Mistress Helrose opened it and took a tray from the person outside.

"Good morning," she greeted Odette, setting the tray on one of the carpets. "I have sent for a tray for you, but if you wish you may first relieve yourself in the chamber seat there." She tipped her head toward the curtained corner; and nodding, Odette pulled the sheet closely about her and hopped over. Behind the curtain was a chair with a holed seat under which sat a chamber pot.

When Odette was done the Mistress told her to remove the sheet and sit on the carpet. As she ate the softened rye bread and honey another knock sounded.

It was Lord Eryan this time, and he strode in before the Mistress barely had voiced her permission. He regarded Odette with a hard but uninterpretable smile. She cringed and bowed her head, remembering darkly all the things Mistress Helrose had told her in the Great Hall before leading her upstairs.

However, he seemed to have other interests this morning and, taking a seat on a bench, passed to his sister the latest gossip from town. As Odette ate she listened, alarmed to hear that a party of dark elves had been spotted on the outskirts of town—or, as Eryan quipped sourly, *a confederate of suspect Darkling traders.*

"Likely waiting for Holbarki," the Mistress said. "Ah, does he never learn?"

Lord Eryan shrugged. "They have made him a wealthy man, I have no doubt."

"He would have the Darklings believe we are all as greedy as Outer Realmers," Helrose complained. Then she glanced at Odette and added quickly, "Well, some Outer Realmers."

Then she smiled, and Odette felt a flame kindle between her legs.

But Lord Eryan's sudden stern look chilled her to the marrow. "There are flaws inherent to Midgardians other than greed."

His insinuating words rankled Odette. Her mouth hardened and her eyes rose boldly.

"She is becoming this way, do you not think," Helrose said suddenly and sat down beside her to roll a lock of Odette's golden hair between her fingers.

Lord Eryan grunted and got to his feet. "As you will, sister. When she is prepared send her to me in the courtyard. I need to speak to the locksmith about fashioning a set of keys for our new steward."

He left abruptly, and Odette saw the Mistress was none too pleased by his curt behavior.

When Odette was finished eating the Mistress combed out her hair, letting it hang down full over her back this time, then fastened the belt about her again and attached the loops to her still-tender nipples.

The morning sun streaming through the windows washed the Great Hall in light. The only other flower about was Yolande, sweeping cobwebs down from the lower ceiling beams. Her face was the epitome of hostility until she glimpsed Odette. Then her eyes widened with contempt and mockery.

Odette ignored her and followed the Mistress out to the courtyard, where other girls worked to clean and prepare the tables for customers. She noticed that for once the pillory and all the cages were empty. Lord Eryan was there, too, talking to a new steward. He was hardly more than a youth, this newcomer, all plump features and soft bristle of new beard. As the Mistress approached he bowed respectfully.

"I turn her over to you now, brother," she told Lord Eryan and, taking Odette's hand, conducted her before her brother. Odette saw the reluctance in the Mistress's eyes and she hoped in earnest it would bring her reprieve.

Lord Eryan kissed his sister's cheek and she smiled wanly, but nevertheless she turned on her heel and walked away.

Odette inhaled deeply and lowered her eyes as Eryan made a displeased sound and pushed her long hair behind her shoulders.

"For the Mistress's sake I shall refrain from binding your lovely hair today, Odette. But now—on your knees, and welcome Lord Ingven with a proper kiss of his boots."

Odette did not even think as she went to her knees and kissed the soft leather. The youth laughed self-consciously and bent at the knees to stroke her head.

"Do not be easily fooled by this one," she heard Lord Eryan say. "Odette is a very spoiled flower. But I have heard she has potential, and so have I taken her under my own hand exclusively."

The youth drew his hand back, but he said in a luxuriant tone, "I understand completely, Lord Eryan."

Lord Eryan said, "Up to your feet, Odette, you have much work today."

Chapter Twelve

s she rose Odette thought of asking his permission to speak so she could ask why he had decided to forego the daily bath. But he took her hair curtly in his hand and led her through the gates of the courtyard so that they stood on the rougher stones of the public square.

A thick chain had been bolted to one of the stones, ending with a little clasp Lord Eryan fastened to her collar. He left her then, alone under the leering eyes of the merchants coming into the square to set up their stalls for the day. The chain was long enough she could sit if she wished, but she suspected Lord Eryan would be angry to return and find her doing so. Soon enough he strolled down the courtyard again carrying a wide placard and a wooden pail in which she saw a hammer and a few nails.

He nailed the placard on the gatepost behind her, and as she squinted at the Athlan rune words painted on it he told her what they meant.

"It says, dear one, *In gratitude to our many patrons we encourage all to correct the haughtiness of this maiden at their pleasure. Donations will be used for the benefit of Mid-gardian orphans.*"

Odette was speechless.

"May I speak, Lord Eryan!"

"No, you may not. But you shall stand here, sitting only when necessary, and entertain those who make offerings for the orphans. You shall treat all those who stop with the utmost respect and say nothing unless requested to speak. There will be a steward in the courtyard at all times, so you have no cause for worry. If I receive word you have displayed the least insolence I shall exercise the severest of punishments. Is this clear, Odette?"

Odette pouted and it took all her strength to refrain from stomping her feet or blurting out the plea he'd hindered her from speaking.

"Yes, my Lord," she answered at last.

But he frowned at her tone and in a swift movement cinched her wrists behind her back with one hand while with the other he spanked her soundly.

She was hopping on her feet by the time he stopped, her buttocks well-flushed. He held her to him and said firmly, "You shall behave from here on, little flower, lest you'd prefer to perform your duty out here bent over a pillory. I can bring one down, that is no problem."

Odette was crying angrily as he released her wrists, but the spanking had taken the protest from her.

"You will behave now, yes?"

"Yes, my Lord," she answered. To her surprise he kissed her brow. Setting the pail near her feet he walked back up the courtyard. She whimpered fretfully, wanting to call him back, to plead with him to have mercy.

I cannot just stand here naked and endure the ogling leers and molesting hands of strangers!

Head hanging, she cowered somewhat against the gatepost with her face to the wood. For a time no one approached, and she thought perhaps no one had noticed her...and then she felt the crack of leather against her thigh. She jumped and cried out and saw it was Lord Eryan. Terrified tears sprang to her eyes and she found herself backing into the post as if it might swallow her whole and protect her.

But there was no anger in his voice this time.

"Unless you are ill do not cower like some animal, Odette. It is unseemly and unbecoming. Are you ill?"

She stared, feeling the lie come to her tongue, but then she knew that to be caught in a lie would probably bring on the pillory or worse.

"No, Lord Eryan."

His chin lifted and he regarded her with the slightest of smiles.

"I give you only one chance to improve yourself. You are a lady, Odette, property of Mistress Helrose, novice of Freyja. You will hold your head high and accept what your punishment incurs with shameless humility. Remember those two words, Odette—they are not contradictory, but complementary."

Odette nodded and straightened as best she could, and when she could not decide what to do with her hands Lord Eryan put them straight at her sides gently.

"That is good. Remember—shameless humility."

"Yes, my Lord."

He regarded her a moment or two longer before walking away again.

Odette stared at the stones under her feet and inhaled deeply. Slowly, her heartbeat eased in its pace and she listened for any sign of approaching footsteps. For a time it seemed she stood unnoticed and she looked across the square. The merchants she'd seen earlier were set up for business and a few women walked between the stalls inspecting the goods. She watched a maid spreading linens over tables at one of the mead houses; and another girl, as naked and rosy-bottomed as herself, stood scrubbing the windows at the sausage maker's shop. Through the open door of the tanner's house she could see another young lady bent over a chair while a man whipped her soundly with a crop.

Odette smiled, though she suspected it might be deemed improper. At least she did not feel singled out for punishment. Yet, she wondered how long Lord Eryan would draw out this particular lesson. For her very life, she could not fathom what grave error she had committed to warrant Lord Eryan's personal supervision. Still, she reminded herself, he had spared her yet from the clitoral shield and anal phallus and that was something for which to be grateful.

She had no time to wonder long, however, for a gentleman and his chained woman came toward her from the square. By the gold band on the woman's left wrist Odette knew her to be the gentleman's wife. Although she tried her best, she could hardly keep her nervous hands at her sides.

The gentleman, dressed in casual black breeches and vest over a simple white shirt, read the placard aloud.

"What do you say, my kitten?" he said to his wife. "A coin to the orphans for the pleasure of punishing this girl?"

The woman's pretty face was blank as she answered, "I would say *nay*, Master Husband."

He laughed and patted her naked behind. "Very well. Nevertheless, I shall leave an offering—and, later, punish you instead."

The wife's head bowed but Odette could see the relief in her face. Tossing a coin into the pail he stretched an arm about his wife's shoulders and murmured intimately into her ear as he led her away. Odette sighed with her own silent relief.

Not long afterward a young merchant came by. He was young and tall and plump-faced and as he flipped three coins into the pail his light brown eyes pored over Odette from head to toe. His lopsided smile was so sweet he reminded her of a big puppy.

His voice was hesitant, enraptured, as he spoke. "I-I want you to dance for me."

Odette blushed and glanced helplessly toward the courtyard. She could see Lord Eryan speaking again with the new steward, the other girls setting the tables. She looked at the boy timidly.

"I do not know how, sir."

"No?" He frowned lightly. A sparkle came to his eyes. "Then kiss me."

Odette blinked and her legs seemed too heavy to move. Before she knew what next to do or say he pulled her into his brawny arms and his face bowed over her own. His lips were firmer than she would have suspected, and gently they pressed over her mouth. She felt her lips purse to meet them and then his tongue darted inside. His mouth lingered over her lips a moment and then he released her so abruptly she swayed on her feet. When she looked up his smile had broadened into a blushing grin.

"Thank you," he said and, making a little bow, ran off.

For a long time Odette was left alone, and when she could not see Lord Eryan in the courtyard she sat down on the ground on one hip so she could keep her legs pulled together. She watched the activity of the busy square—the merchants hawking their goods, the men drinking at the mead houses and showing off their women, the women free to roam on their bare feet exchanging gossip. Once she thought she spied her friends running through the throng…and realized she no longer felt panicked or ashamed for those old companions to see her tethered.

Why should I, she thought, when one day, soon or later, so many of them shall know the bondage that is service to the Goddess?

For the first time since she'd been turned over to Mistress Helrose's charge this thought aroused no anger. She was a novice of Freyja and there was nothing she could do to change it. And whether because of the Mistress's strict love or Lord

Eryan's even stricter discipline or the general atmosphere of Athla—and perhaps all of these things—her moral indignation at the laws that made her a slave were vanishing. The resignation that had lent comfort at times before was steadily integrating into her nature. The invisible but tainted skin that had been draped over her during her years in the outer world was shedding, and she sensed that just within her grasp awaited a symmetrical design so wondrous that it would banish forever the notions of sin and shame that had enslaved the Outer Realm.

Slavery without love or appreciation; punishments that chastened and bruised the soul the whole life long! Odette frowned to think of the countless mortals who had suffered under the condemnations put forth by their leaders, their priests, their loved ones only for their having yearned for the very delights that were held sacred in Athla.

A gentleman emerged from the crowded square and stood before Odette, regarding her lustily. As she started to her feet he lifted her by the arms and stood her firmly on the stones and stroked her hair savagely.

"You are a welcome sight after an exhausting morning," he said. He threw several coins, gold and silver, into the pail and ordered Odette to stand against the gatepost.

Her mouth fell open silently and she cringed, her hands flying to her breasts. He laughed softly and lifted her up again, pressing her back against the timber. He kissed her roughly, filling her mouth with the taste of mead and eager masculinity, and massaged her breasts roughly, too. Odette gasped as his mouth brushed over her throat, her heart beating so fiercely she thought certain it would stop.

And then he released her again and told her to bend at the waist and take her ankles with her hands.

"No," she said, so softly and affrighted he did not hear.

He laughed again and bent her over with the hands that had just groped her breasts so that her hair showered over her shoulders.

"Would you prefer I complain to Mistress Helrose?"

Odette shuddered and clasped her hands about her ankles. Minutes seemed to dawdle as she stood this way, and as she was bent over he touched her, caressed her skin here and there, pinching now the insides of her thighs and smacking her calves. He took his hands away then and she waited again, feeling his lusty eyes heavy upon her.

Then suddenly his hand cracked across her buttocks. She gasped and he spanked her again, then several more times with enough force that she rocked where she stood. At last, when she was weeping unrestrainedly, he relented and stood her up again and molded his hand over her buttocks, feeling the warmth he had ignited.

"I do enjoy the mischievous ones," he murmured, kissing her forehead tenderly. He patted her buttocks one last time and walked away back into the crowd.

At noontide Lord Eryan brought Odette some water to drink and a piece of cake from the kitchen. He said little, though he watched her while she ate. He patted her head when she was done and left her to entertain the two men lingering nearby, waiting to toss their coins into the pail. For the rest of the afternoon she endured the caresses and disciplines of those who came. Only once did anyone dare too much, a merchant too long at his cups. He pressed her against the gatepost and groping her harshly, ordered her to spread her thighs to him.

Odette screamed. The new steward ran to the gate and, seeing her distress, pulled the drunkard away.

"I suggest, sir," he told the befuddled man, "you go home and sleep. You should know the law shields even the most experienced of women from uncouth behavior."

The merchant's face was purplish with anger but he staggered off, cursing under his breath. Lord Ingven pulled Odette from the gatepost and smoothed her hair about her shoulders tenderly.

"Are you well, flower?"

"Yes, my Lord."

He left her then, but no other oafs approached her. When evening arrived Lord Eryan released her from the chain and herded her back to the manor, lashing her thighs and backside with his whip the entire way. Once inside the manor he took her to the bedchamber and freed her nipples from the tormenting loops. In the cool quiet of the room he removed her leash and Odette yawned and stretched so that her spent nerves again felt relaxed. Lord Eryan poured water from the pitcher and cleaned the dirt from her body and told her to rest until he came to get her again. She fell asleep on the bed so quickly it seemed no time had passed before he awakened her again, but outside the sun had already slipped behind the mountains and evening's indigo shades filtered through the window.

He combed her hair again and set it into a braid at the crown of her head, then told her to relieve herself, for it might be a time before she could do so again.

When she was finished he snapped the loops back on her nipples and, taking her braid in hand, ordered her to walk ahead of him to the Great Hall. As soon as they stepped through the hallway door Odette felt a difference in the ambiance. The other flowers sat in their usual place on the floor, but the Mistress's table had been set with her finest silver and but for the High Archer none of the guests were any that Odette recognized. Flower petals had been strewn across the floor.

But what caught Odette's eyes and made her feet freeze where she stood was the thing that had been brought in and set beside the table, a pillory she had not seen before, with wide beams and only one very large eyelet carved betwixt them instead of three. On the side of the bottom beam that faced the front door were bolted two manacles, low-set and widely spaced.

Lord Eryan's whip lashed her thighs so smartly that Odette gasped.

"To the pillory, Odette," he said.

Odette walked on, her face ashen with fright and her heart beating so wildly she could hardly hear the conversation from the table.

"Stand here," Lord Eryan said, and she watched, shivering, as he drew back the upper beam. Each half of the eyelet was covered with leather, but it was so wide that her entire torso mid-chest to pelvis could fit across it.

The next moment Lord Eryan pulled her forward and bent her at the waist so she lay prone across the bottom beam with her legs dangling. He drew her arms forward so that they fell over the front end.

Odette's temples pounded with fear. "No, please," she whispered. Lord Eryan ignored this and set the upper beam in place and locked it. Coming to the front, he clamped the manacles about her wrists.

Odette had never imagined such an engulfing sense of being trapped. With her wrists fettered her breasts hung helplessly and the loops danced at her nipples. She could see nothing behind her shoulders but the width of indifferent beam; and consumed with terror, she wept uncontrollably. Through her tears she looked to Lord Eryan, who seemed to be rummaging through the inner lining of his vest.

"Please, please let me out!"

He glanced at her coldly but said nothing, and stepping to the back of the pillory he patted her naked buttocks. She heard him walk away and Odette's panic escalated to a new height. She shrieked for help, begging for mercy from the Mistress and Lord Eryan, anyone who had mercy. Her pleas brought a riffle of amused laughter from the table and the High Archer remarked in a displeased voice that she should not be allowed to make such an unladylike commotion.

"Oh, she shan't," Lord Eryan replied. Odette heard his footsteps approach the pillory again and a moment later his shadow fell over her tearstained face.

He held a suede band in his hands. In the center of the band Odette could see that a blunt leather bit had been sewn.

"Open your mouth, Odette."

She wept harder and beseeched him again, "Oh, Lord Eryan, please let me go! I promise to be good!"

Only the widening of his intense eyes revealed his anger. He said in a voice as breezy soft as a whispering wind, "This is why you must be gagged, Odette. Now obey or I shall give my whip to our guests and ask them to correct you where I have failed."

Odette's eyes closed against the streaming tears. She felt him blot the tears away with a cloth and stroke the back of her neck.

"Open your mouth, flower," he said gently. She opened her eyes and opened her mouth slowly, her wrists battering against the restraining manacles.

He crouched and pressed the leather bit into her, buckling the band firmly at the back of her head beneath the braid. The leather of the bit filled her mouth wholly. As he rose and walked to the back of the pillory her terrified eyes darted here and there as she worried what he was doing next; and then she felt his hands grasp her buttocks and massage them roughly. His finger, oiled and smooth, plunged between them and probed into her anus.

"Do not flinch," he warned and she tried to hold still as he withdrew his finger. He handled her belt, though she could not see what he did, and then she heard a little *click*...and the next moment he spread her buttocks again, further this time. She felt him snap something at the back of her belt. Cold and slender this was and

Lord Eryan spread her buttocks a third time and directed the object between them, and pressed it against the tiny opening of her anus.

No, she thought miserably, and the next moment Lord Eryan inserted the metal phallus deep within her rectum. It filled her with its discomforting width, making her hips rock at the unexpected intrusion, and when she felt Lord Eryan move from behind her the slender phallus remained, gorging her with a new and chastening sense of ravishment.

Yet, to her added chagrin, both phallus and bit intensified the passion welling within her. Her nethermouth was dew-drenched and her clitoris fluttered. Even her breasts, swaying heavily over the floor and sore, were more stimulated.

Lord Eryan came to stand before her. A tower of pale dark masculinity he seemed and as her buttocks rocked in protest against the phallus she realized the emotion she felt for him now was more than mere anger and the tears that flowed anew sprang as much from the passion he'd whetted as the fear.

His eyes caressed her sternly.

He can do whatever he wishes and I am helpless to stop it!

Her terror accentuated to a new level. Lord Eryan's mouth hardened and he stepped behind her. The next thing she felt was the flailing descent of his whip. He whipped her a long time, inflicting such sharp strokes it was as if her buttocks had never known punishment. Her legs thrashed the air in silent protest and he lashed her calves and her thighs with the biting leather, scorching the tender flesh without wounding. With much effort she willed her legs to be still although her hips rocked as the whip spanked across her throbbing backside.

At last he stayed his hand. Odette was panting about the bit as he walked away and as her head drooped she could watch her tears spilling down her swinging breasts to puddle on the floor.

"You have a stable hand," she heard the High Archer say from the table. "I suggest your example be set into practice for all my Lady's students."

Mistress Helrose said something lost to Odette's ears, but it brought a round of laughter from the stewards and other guests. Odette felt the telling fluids flowing down her thighs and a blend of indignity and passion swelled in her breast.

Footsteps again drew near the pillory. Odette flinched but it did not prevent the hand from touching her. Large and warm and rough at once, it stroked her chastened buttocks and parted her vaginal lips. Her clitoris vibrated and her nipples hardened in their painful restraints.

A masculine voice said, "Dewed rose petals."

"Yes," Lord Eryan said huskily, making Odette wince and raise her head anxiously. He touched her with his familiar hands, stroked her thighs so lightly as to make her giggle, and then he pressed the phallus so that she felt gorged even more as he flicked her clitoris back and forth with his finger until she feared it would burst. She moaned silently and her hips strained for Lord Eryan and the satisfaction she was certain he could grant if only he would.

He walked before her again and lifted her chin so that she was forced to look at him, and she saw another man beside him. Leonine of build and darkly auburn-haired, he was extremely handsome, his hands and face bronzed by the sun. By his beige velvet uniform she knew him to be one of the border sentries. Flecks of yellow lightened his brown eyes and his smile was sublime grace.

Lord Eryan unbuckled the strap and removed the bit from Odette's mouth. He massaged her lips with his thumb and spoke to the sentry.

"I have been informed that my flower has a certain natural talent," he said, his half-mockery stroking Odette's heart. "Would you oblige me, Darmond, and test this talent?"

"It would be my pleasure."

Lord Eryan patted the sentry's shoulder and moved back into the shadows. Odette tried to look away but the sentry lifted her face just as Lord Eryan had, and the lust that shone in his regard made her quiver. She listened for the Mistress to call him away, to leave her be…and as she prayed silently the sentry bowed over and kissed her mouth.

His taste was so richly wonderful it subdued the prayer in her thoughts. Her mouth opened weakly, hungrily, and she savored his probing tongue like the first flake of winter's snow.

He withdrew slowly and stood up, tracing the curves of her mouth and face with his fingertips. Odette felt a bolt of lightning rocket through her entire body. His hands untied the cords of his breeches then and he pulled them down to draw out his stiffened member. A nest of fair curls surrounded it, his balls were long and full, his thighs firm and fairer than his hands and face. He held her face between his hands and kissed her brow once, then guided her mouth open with his thumbs.

"Suckle me, flower," he whispered.

She blanched, but knew the eyes of the others were on them; and as his member kissed her lips she whimpered but drew it in, suckling it gently, electrified by the rich taste of him. Gently, he began to thrust in and out of her nursing mouth. His hardened heat was a delight to her for all the indignity of this ravishment and eagerly she sucked it. Back and forth his hard cock moved through her taut lips, but still he held her face with the utmost tenderness. Through her heavy lids she saw his eyes had closed and his sweet mouth had parted.

Quicker he thrust, and as he did so she paid heed to the subtle reactions in his features and realized his enjoyment increased when she squeezed the organ's head just before it plummeted and as it drew back. Her sex was wet and swollen between her thighs, and her hips undulated wantonly. She had no thought of the onlookers; her mind and spirit worked only to please the handsome sentry.

The sentry gasped and plunged deeply into her mouth. His cock spasmed lightly and she felt his seed splatter the back of her throat. She swallowed it ardently, moaning at the pungent rich taste and looking up saw him smiling again.

Her thighs were wet beneath her aching orifice but as the sentry walked away she was left in the pillory, left alone with a sense of utter helplessness that buoyed her chagrin to the surface again. It wedded with her ripened passion to form a single heated, suffering consciousness. And it was a very, very long while before Lord Eryan came to release her.

Chapter Thirteen

Cu'lugh opened his eyes and stared at the heavy timber beams over the bed. Outside, the skies were overcast and heavy again. He reached under the coverlet at his side—habit, really, for he remembered immediately there awaited no softly curved limbs or silken tresses. Women, desirable women, at least, were but fruitless dreams in this realm. There were the servants, old and withered; and though it was rumored among Vanda's mercenaries that one or two healthy women survived yet in the serfs' quarters they had never accepted Cu'lugh's bribes to let him enter the gates.

He sat up and looked dismally out the window and stretched his bare arms. All his life he'd taken the sunshine for granted—until he'd arrived in his brother's fief. Here, the clouds seemed a permanent fixture, and with them a haze that grew denser with each passing day. He could understand why the crops failed to produce and even why the animals sickened from eating their rust-mottled grain.

He pitied the Saxons whose homeland this had been before Charles's invasion. Not only were they now enserfed under the Christian yoke, but those who had not been given over to Boniface as virtual slaves to build his abbeys and monasteries were dying from the same mysterious plague that had taken Thierry.

And how ironic this plague, when Charles's initial report sent home after his victory indicated this land was fecund and full of prospects. Despite the Christian arrogance Charles used to exonerate his pride and avarice, his embrace of the religion had given him some sense of integrity, at least as regarded tidings that might somehow filter down to the court of the punctilious Pope Gregory.

Cu'lugh rose from the bed and filled the chamber pot nearby. He ran his fingers through his short dark hair and smoothed his thick mustache. He dressed in the latest expensive garments Vanda had provided—a fine Italian silk tunic and suede breeches and jerkin, boots of oxen leather. Finery in which he was not truly comfortable, not after years of the wandering mercenary life. He would have preferred a gift of a girl to help warm the bed at night. But Vanda's piety did not allow for accommodation of earthy needs.

She seemed to take much pleasure in showering him with costly gifts. Soon after he'd arrived she gave him a dagger that had belonged to one of Boniface's followers. The monk had taken it from the grave of a priest, an historian in the hierarchy of the Celtic Church and suspected by Boniface's Roman peers as of being a Druid who had taken vows in order to keep alive as he could the ancient pagan rites. This dagger especially was a discomforting gift for Cu'lugh, who like many had had the sacraments forced upon him at an early age and still retained sympathy for the old pagan ways.

More profoundly, however, the giving of such an utterly pagan symbol seemed such a contradiction to Vanda's faith. She avoided looking at the pagan amulet at his neck, the chained amber teardrop given him by Thierry's mother. She smiled politely when he recalled stories from his years of service with pagan lords and chieftains; but he knew it was civility only, that the ribald tales and anecdotes disgusted her. So, he had made it a point to hide the amulet and to keep his stories to himself.

He supposed the dagger had been no more than a token of her appreciation, like all her gifts. And he would never forget that it was he who in truth was obliged. She had saved his life and nursed him back to health. And such tenderness for a man who was a stranger to her, too close to death when found to speak and inform her he was no threat, but brother of her own husband.

When he was strong again and his mind sound she had wept when he identified himself, and when he'd asked, she confirmed the thing he'd not wanted confirmed—that Thierry was, indeed, dead. He had died from the strange malady the spring of the year before, one of the first, Vanda said, to succumb.

It was not the news he'd expected to hear. Despite the suspicions of Anga, Thierry's mother, that had incited him to venture here, he had not believed them true. He loved Anga dearly, as if she were his own mother; and though he respected her more than any person he'd ever known, he thought this time her dreams and premonitions were but overwrought concern caused by the lack of couriers. As sovereign over the Saxons he'd quelled as well as brother of the lord he'd entitled, Charles had the obligation to investigate the affairs of the Saxon land and court. But his interests focused on carrying the banner of the Church and expanding the cause of Christendom. Not even Charles's vow to their dying father to protect Angla could come between the Mayor of the Palace and his obligation to the Pope.

Charles allowed Angla to keep her bequeathed residence and refrained from any attempt on her life or inheritance, but she was nothing to him save his deceased father's harlot, the woman Pepin of Herstal had loved above his other women, and certainly more than Charles's high-born mother. So Angla turned her appeal to the one son who appreciated her. And Cu'lugh, adoring her always, postponed his plans to return to Muscovy and set out to learn if Thierry was, indeed, in the peril Angla feared.

It was Angla who had strung the amulet around his neck, a globule of amber reputed by her ancestors to be a teardrop of the goddess Frigga, insisting he wear it for protection against some evil she was certain awaited in the Saxon fiefdom. As soon as he learned of Thierry's death he sent a messenger with the news to Charles's court. A month later Charles sent in reply a party of priests and mourners to insure a proper funeral rite for Thierry's remains, though these had already been buried according to the pagan custom Vanda had reluctantly allowed, for she thought it was what Thierry would have preferred.

Cu'lugh thought Charles's audacity an affront to the widow. She had priests enough about her—albeit priests different from any he'd ever encountered—and for Charles to send others to safeguard his own dignity seemed a petty display. Nevertheless, Charles's priests sanctified the oak stump in which Thierry had been buried and returned quickly to Frankland.

Charles had sent tidings to Vanda—investing her as Lady of the Saxon fief and granting her with all the powers Thierry had wielded, however reluctantly. It had made Cu'lugh smile to see the delight these tidings brought her, giving a brightness to her demeanor that her piety failed to completely hide.

It was this occasional moderation of her somber mien that convinced him to stay a while longer. It was late spring, though the shroud of bitter winter was reluctant to give over its power. The earth was muck, and the strange malady seemed to have tainted the earth and air and every living thing. Vanda's court alone seemed immune to it, and the ranks of her sturdy but corrupt mercenaries and the even more corrupt foreign merchants she'd persuaded to come dwell in her city. Vanda's will was a rough, hard gem luring Cu'lugh to seize it, to polish and make it glint softly in the hand of the holder.

Yet, for all her generosity toward him Vanda remained aloof, and none of his considerable experience with women could pinpoint the exact cause. She had been grateful that he'd come so far to inquire after his brother, and perhaps with Thierry dying in the middle of that ghastly winter and the rest of her Saxon folk dying steadily in their huts a kindred face was an unexpected godsend. Cu'lugh soon realized his sister-in-law spent too much time huddled over her financial accounts; and when not dictating new levies or demanding the latest tally on the grain supplies, Vanda was in counsel with her priest, Hrowthe.

Not a true woman's life, Cu'lugh determined, not even a life healthy for a widow. Leastways, Vanda was not some dour and death-seeking martyr as his own mother had been. She had an eye for money and Cu'lugh discovered she possessed a talent for hoarding her supplies and stocks. She ran her kingdom efficiently—the serfs lived in meager huts and the men and women were separated to prevent intercourse between the sexes. She explained she needed no new mouths to provide for; and her tactics worked, the segregation enforced by her mercenaries.

Often Vanda spoke of her dream of building a self-sufficient estate, and he presumed that when her mourning was over the rigorous ordinances she'd set over her own people would lighten. Her blue eyes flashed when she spoke of the future and her cheeks grew ruddy…and in those times he could understand how his young and pliant-hearted brother had fallen so deeply in love with her.

Lately, her affections had changed toward him—more than sisterly affection her kisses seemed, and her blue eyes held his with a tiny flame as he bowed and said goodnight. And it was becoming more and more difficult for him to take a seemly leave.

Cu'lugh was uncertain about his own strange feelings for her. She was a woman, of course, and not unattractive. He was not accustomed with a woman controlling her own purse, but that was not what troubled him. Perhaps it was the baleful impatience that showed in her relations with her servants and mercenaries.

The spinsters, who had all served her mother even before Vanda's birth, cringed in her presence. The mercenaries respected her for what she provided and that was all. He had gone into the town many times, had heard their disgust for what they called her greed and pettiness; and even the merchants complained that Lady Vanda had reneged on promises of supplies.

Cu'lugh had challenged one of these men to a duel, but the coward would not meet him on the field, claiming Cu'lugh had misunderstood a private conversation.

But it mattered not, he decided at last, for one day Vanda would be done with her mourning and ready to show the generosity she'd showered on him to all her people.

Cu'lugh sighed and walked to the window, but all he could see was the image of Vanda. He knew part of his interest in her sprang from simple bodily need. But she was unquestionably pretty, and petite under the layers of petticoats. Her hands were small, the fingers short and the palms very soft. It was these grasping little hands that had thawed him, brought him back from death's entryway. As strong as his lust was his intent to never press her.

Then, last night, over the course of dinner, she had ventured a startling proposal of marriage. She needed a strong alliance to safeguard her from those who salivated over her fief, she said, and preferred this ally to be a man she could trust. Her mouth had turned up at the corners and her eyelashes fluttered as her face grew crimson.

"My bed and half the worth of my coffers shall be my wedding gift if you consent, Cu'lugh."

He had almost laughed. He did not desire her so sorely as to yield his freedom in exchange. Despite that she had saved his life and her proud character, he simply could not see himself wed to any woman so unlike his envisioned mate.

It had been pure fancy, a childhood image that had often and unexpectedly interrupted his preoccupation, sometimes even his sleep—a dreamy vision of golden hair and pliant sweetness, delicious in its wanton desire to please him. Entreating emerald eyes that seemed to replenish his soul. When he was but a child, before he was even old enough to train as a squire, he had thought the vision a sending from the elven folk whispered about by the servants and slaves. As he grew older he reconsidered it as but a memory, perhaps the half-remembered face of one of the serving girls whose very presence had brought a glint of sunshine to the filthy, crucifix-littered room in which his mother had birthed him and attempted to suckle him on milk that dried up as she deliberately refused to eat.

But as he matured into a man and realized it was a fancy and nothing else, no woman had ever captured his steadfast affections as the nymph of his imagination.

Yet Vanda's proposition held its potentials.

Marriage. Marriage to the woman Charles had raised to the position of chieftain in her own right. The Avars and Lombards already made incursions on the land. Vanda's mercenaries had shared confidence with Cu'lugh that they feared a woman could not hold off a substantial invasion. And if Charles knew the extent of Vanda's caches he might even renege on his support. There was, of course, the religious impediment, but though Cu'lugh had his reservations about marriage, the Christian taboo against wedding a brother's wife was the least of them. And Pope Gregory certainly could be counted on for a dispensation at the right price.

In the end, his hesitation came largely from his sense there was something unnaturally cool about the Saxon princess. The taking of a woman in passion was one thing; to take her without hope of arousing any passion other than resentment was a different animal altogether.

Still, he was getting no younger. He had been hiring out his martial skills since he was sixteen. This was now his thirty-eighth year and fortune had been gracious to let him do the job he thrived on without lasting injury. But the mercenary life, as adventurous as it was, had not brought him the luxury or power, certainly not the contentment, he had sought.

The Germanic wilderness was enticing, and once the somber official Church rites for Thierry were finished Cu'lugh had felt the familiar draw to ride on. To the north lay lands still pagan, where immersing himself in his familiar habits would soften his grief for his brother. Besides, he wearied of the Church; and even here the imposing shadow of Charles hung over him, king but for the title, for even Charles's arrogance dared not let him assume publicly the power the Church had long before sworn to the mysterious Merovingian princes.

For the memory of their father Cu'lugh endured Charles and overlooked his ever-increasing penchant for usury. If not for his pride he might have even accepted Charles's offer of one of the many daughters from amongst the numerous vassals obliged to the Frankish ruler. Cu'lugh could not deny that kind of power held its own seduction. But he was averse to living as the indebted fief lord to his avaricious brother.

In truth, he longed to live stripped of the capricious tenets of Christianity, and marriage to Vanda would forever mute that dream. Once, shortly after his father died, he had spent an entire night at cups with Thierry. His younger brother had regaled him with a tale of adventure the younger swore to having experienced.

He had visited a fabled realm where men and women still lived by the pagan ways, under the tenets of the Great Balance. There, Thierry declared, he had been shown the greatest hospitality by the king and enjoyed himself so thoroughly he had dragged himself away only when he dreamed of their father's death. It had been an intriguing tale that had made Anga truly smile, a thing she hadn't done in a long time. It saddened Cu'lugh to know it was but a tale produced from drink, for the Christian faith was nothing to him but rules that seemed designed to wring the very humanity from its followers. He'd successfully concealed his feelings from Charles, though his powerful brother had witnessed in his childhood the same as Cu'lugh their father's leading the troops of the Pope to quell the lands of his loyal allies, some even kinsmen, with the excuse the native tribes were hostile to Christ.

Thus were the Pope's mercenaries paid handsomely with the wealth of these chieftains and their tribes, and the coffers of the Mayor of the Palace swelled so abundantly that Pepin grew arrogant. He began killing the descendants of Merovech, those whom the Catholic Church had acknowledged as the hereditary kings of the Franks generations before.

But it was the sordid character the Church gave the old gods and the relations between men and women that most repulsed Cu'lugh. The bribes of the Church flowed into the coffers of the new Frankish lords, so that for political interests the old faiths were transformed into superstitions, the gods into myths, the goddesses into demons.

And where was the gentle Christ the priests of the new religion spoke of?

It was not until Cu'lugh had sailed to E'rin, the land of his mother's relations, and was introduced to the histories and records kept by the Celtic Church fathers that he understood that the religion of the Romans was the religion not of the Christ but of the saints, and in particular of Paul of Tarsus.

At least, the very least, the priests he'd known in Frankland did not destroy the relics of the old gods, not like Boniface and his crusaders. Fanatics like Boniface Cu'lugh had learned to recognize and avoid. But the priests who served Vanda, those peculiar counselors that surrounded her too often to be healthy, these were men of an even more disturbing mold.

Boniface had been schooled by those in England who, in perfect resentment of the Celtic Church, had repudiated learning history and the sciences of the past and accepted only those mediocre teachings that satisfied the agenda of the Church in Rome. Vanda told him that in the temple she'd had built for her priests were scrolls and texts from antiquity, records and information from a time before the first pharaoh had ruled Egypt, information written on scrolls between wooden spindles in human blood that were said to be the words of a great Mesopotamian wizard-king.

Cu'lugh did not doubt it—the priests, he'd discovered, knew how to read the Oghams, the holy leaves of the Druids, and could recite the songs of the ancient Frankish bards. They knew the writings of the old Hebrews by heart, as well as the doctrines of those who worshipped Allah. For all their learning, however, in their stoic righteousness they looked down on mankind with a passionless commitment as pervasive, or more so, than even Boniface's fiery fanaticism.

In the entourage of the clergy Charles had sent to consecrate Thierry's burial place had been a cook and her little boy. As Cu'lugh helped packed the woman's belongings when they were ready to depart he saw her stoop and hug the boy. One of the strange priests emerged from the twilight shadows and made a disproving sound. When Cu'lugh eyed him the priest spoke.

"Every embrace a mother gives her child is but another mockery of fleeting security doled out to a vulnerable soul."

The influence of these passionless men on Vanda only added to the hesitation of wedding her. These men, she admitted, had enlightened her to the need for making a complete break with the old gods. There were no festivities allowed the Saxon serfs, no marriages permitted. Even those couples already married were separated by a towering fence between the quarters of the men and women. Their labors were overseen by the mercenaries. Even pious Charles would have been shocked by the consummate joylessness of their lives, the starvation and prevalent illness.

It angered Cu'lugh to think what arguments the priests had implemented to make Vanda blind to her people, and he had often wondered if the Pope even knew of their fraternity. Was their order so old not even the sanctions of Rome guided them?

But they were safe from the Pope's interest, that was doubtless, for he was far away; and as long as Charles was content with Vanda's leadership the Pope would not uncover the priests' secrets.

Vanda evidently found solace in the company of the brothers, especially their leader, the one called Hrowthe. They had given her comfort after Thierry died, she told him, when the Frankish companions of her husband had vanished and the plague seemed to laugh in the very faces of the Saxons. Cu'lugh knew it was inappropriate, too like Charles, to criticize those who had aided Thierry's widow even as he suspected their agenda was not as selfless as Vanda was likely led to believe. What kind of man of faith or decency could position himself as a woman's counselor and fail to help her see that overwork and lack of shelter and food was killing her people as surely as the malady—a malady that curiously seemed to have little taste for the lives of mercenaries, merchants or priests.

Vanda was a woman, and even as she proudly held claim by her Burgundian lineage, it was her Saxon side that concerned the people she ruled. Cu'lugh knew of her father, the chieftain Rulf, who had successfully defied the Franks and broken that yoke. He had liberated his people, for a time at least, when other German tribes bowed to the demands of their Christian masters. It was a proud heritage, one surely even the necessity of politics could not disregard entirely.

There was strength in Vanda, inherited and individual—Cu'lugh saw it and knew from observation the mercenaries and merchants saw it as well and reacted to it. A strong and purposeful woman she was, and though she seemed at times to loathe her femininity there was hope in her strength if she but tempered it with compassion. The priests about her had failed in this; and perhaps it would take more than spiritual guidance to unveil the compassion he was certain was innate to all women.

Cu'lugh poured water from the pitcher on the windowsill into a goblet and drained it. The marbled glass smelled of the dried rue Vanda allowed her servants to burn in the kitchen—the old spinsters thought burning rue and or mugwort would keep the eyes of the mercenaries from their mistress. But it was not the incense that guarded Vanda's chaste body, Cu'lugh knew, though never would he speak of it to her. It was her contempt for men and the carnal thoughts she perceived in their every glance.

Yet, she had offered him marriage and a place in her bed. Mayhap she had a desire for children stronger than even her aversion to the act that produced them. He could not be sure. In the end it mattered not what she sought but that she would have her way whether it was through his aid or that of another man. And she was wealthy and pretty, and once wed there was still a chance she might come to take pleasure in lovemaking as well as achieving whatever result she sought afterward.

Thierry had been one of the gentlest of men and likely bedded Vanda only as her faith allowed. Cu'lugh would have no compunction to take a wife eagerly and inspire her to the heights of pleasure in which he had practiced so many long years.

Cu'lugh pictured Vanda moaning huskily at his ear, her small hips rocking under his pelvis. He gazed out the window, smiling to himself when he saw several men, some holding axes, standing about the tiny grove of rotted trunks. Vanda had pronounced the trees past saving and wanted the feathery, moldy timber out of sight. Cu'lugh noticed that all of these serfs looked past their prime, except for a single youth who was tall and gaunt and crippled in one leg. An armed mercenary stood guard as was Vanda's edict, in case any tried to run away. Not much chance for that, really, for the high timber fence that surrounded the town, built, Vanda said, during the hunting party Thierry had taken just before coming home and falling ill. She had not trusted Fate to keep the serfs from the danger of marauders, she explained.

But it seemed more an imprisonment than a defense to Cu'lugh, though this he kept to himself like his other observations made during the time he'd spent in Vanda's household. And he recalled now a conversation he'd had with the priest Hrowthe one evening in Vanda's anteroom when she had gone to speak with her captain of the guard. The mercenary had reported that one of the Saxon women had tried to climb the segregation fence in order to see her husband, whom she feared ill.

"It is not surprising," Cu'lugh had remarked. "I can think of nothing so unnatural as to separate families."

The priest smiled complacently at these words and patted him on the shoulder as one might an ignorant child.

"It is our duty to prohibit the carnal act, my son. If God decides procreation is needed here He will provide the means."

The words had left Cu'lugh chilled. He wondered now if Hrowthe knew of Vanda's proposal of marriage. If so, was the priest laboring to dissuade her at least from the *carnal* potential that marriage invited?

Cu'lugh was jolted from his thoughts by a knock at the door.

"Enter, it is open."

He turned from the window as the door opened slowly. A drape of grey fabric rustled over the threshold and the haggard-looking Hrowthe entered. His eyes were without luster, but deep within the almost colorless orbs Cu'lugh felt a hidden vitality, something that struck him as unseemly...unnatural...

"Enter, Father Hrowthe. The servants have not yet brought a meal, but do share with me when they come."

It was a pointed suggestion and Cu'lugh watched with some amusement as the priest's narrow, pale lips turned up at the corners in a gesture resembling a smile. He had never seen the priest accept even a mannerly portion from Vanda's table. She said that Hrowthe dined only with the other priests in their temple.

But as Cu'lugh studied the priest's painfully sallow, fleshless face he thought it seemed ages since the man had taken a single morsel.

"There is an important matter I need speak of with you, Sir Cu'lugh," the priest said. Unlike his fragile features and limbs Hrowthe's voice was rich and melodic.

"Yes."

"It is that I have this morning conversed with Lady Vanda, and she tells me you have broached the subject of marriage."

Cu'lugh felt a brow lift, not knowing if this were but a trick of the priest's or a misunderstanding. "Has she? I have thought of it, yes. You cannot blame me, can you, Father? Even through your stoic ideals you can still see her with a man's eyes, can you not?"

"That matters not," Hrowthe said, his tone gentle. "As her confessor and friend, she has asked me to remind you that she still intends to apportion half her holdings to you and invest you as her champion. Now, I have little understanding of chivalry, but it seems a reasonable custom…and quite complimentary."

Cu'lugh mused a moment. "A gracious bequest," he agreed slowly, "but quite unneeded—if we are to wed, that is. I shall be lord here, and as her husband warrant her my unbridled protection and honor."

The crack of a smile parted one corner of Hrowthe's parched mouth. "Lord? I am afraid your good brother does not see it that way."

Cu'lugh was silent a moment, realizing Vanda must have been contemplating and negotiating this proposition long before broaching it with him. "Vanda has contacted him about this?"

"It behooves her interests to do so. A woman is more vulnerable than a man, is she not? We received word this morning from Charles. Along with his accord with the proposal he sent his wish that Lady Vanda should retain full sovereign power if the Pope gives his blessing."

The sigh Cu'lugh released held a familiar bitterness. "Ah, and what else does my good brother say?"

"That his decision is no reflection on your mother's claim to her status as your father's wife."

"Only on my claim of legitimacy, yes?"

Hrowthe nodded hesitantly. "You have never taken communion since your initial Confirmation into the Church. It is well known you were but a child then. I imagine, Sir Cu'lugh, Charles knows it will be easier to get the Pope's approval of this marriage if His Holiness knows Lady Vanda will hold title of vassal lord…or lady, as you will. Unless, of course, you were to prove yourself stripped of all pagan sympathies."

"I care not for the approval of either the Pope or my brother," Cu'lugh said, but he knew the same was probably not true of Vanda.

"Lady Vanda is willing to disregard any of these requirements," Hrowthe went on. "She will confer upon you, before the witnesses of her army, full power of Lord of this land."

Cu'lugh felt uneasy. He trusted Vanda's integrity, but he could hardly see her bequeathing so much before men she had confided she felt only contempt for, saw only as necessary evils to fortify her kingdom.

He studied the priest's pale face. "Is it truly marriage Lady Vanda seeks? I wonder if you have counseled otherwise?"

Another brush of a smile passed over Hrowthe's face. "I am but a messenger, sir. The Lady awaits you in her rooms."

Cu'lugh turned to the window and watched as the Saxons cut and piled the wasted trees. At last he said, "Why do I sense your feelings on this matter stream deeper than that, Father?"

"Although the state of marriage is often but an excuse for interdependence, I comprehend that Lady Vanda needs the figure of a husband to protect her interests in the eyes of the Church. A marriage of convenience to her, whatever her personal reasons, and it is her wellbeing I consider foremost. It shall prove a defense against those forces that might seek to overthrow her just because she is a woman. I should hope, however, you shan't enter the agreement with any notions other than these. Take what proper things you may from an alliance such as this, the only acceptable reason for marriage in this fleeting and unreliable life."

Cu'lugh stared at the priest, hardly believing what he'd just heard. But there was no mockery in Hrowthe's face, no hint of some trick. The priest believed exactly what he said, and this frightened Cu'lugh for Vanda's sake.

If Hrowthe saw Cu'lugh's horror he made no comment but went on. "Charles will not try to stop you, this you know, not with the favor Boniface demonstrates toward Vanda. Already Charles's inquiries into the affairs of this fief have ceased. He is satisfied with her management and, besides, his principle interests lie in quelling the other pagan tribes and the infidels. His own Christian chivalry will prevent any interference once Vanda is your legal wife."

Cu'lugh felt more uneasy than ever, and as Hrowthe moved toward the window and looked out at the Saxons he thought of asking the priest to leave. Hrowthe squinted against the sunshine and pressed his lips together as if he were in great thought—or pain.

"Two objectives I strive for, Sir Cu'lugh, only two. The first is to see every last sordid remnant of the pagan world stripped from this kingdom, to know mankind cleansed of the sins that bind them to the temporal flaws, those deficiencies of nature that keep them from taking their rightful heritage. This does not sound pious, I know, but I believe with all my heart it is God's plan that mankind stand as gods themselves, independent of one another completely, to be perfect, immortal, safe from illness and war and death. To be as *He* is in the everlasting realm where He dwells.

"And God knows that this cannot transpire unless mankind embraces what is correct and responsible and repudiates forever all the falsehoods that compel men and women to cling to this world—love, lust, pleasure, sentimentality. All deceptions of this world, all things which, when we accept them, bring suffering, despair."

Cu'lugh shook his head. "You do not believe paradise can be known by simply accepting your humanity and tolerating differences?"

Hrowthe smiled indulgently. "And where was all the tolerance before He made His disappointment known? In the hands of pagans bent on destroying themselves over an ideal of chivalry and femininity. You have read some of our ancient texts, those passed down in diluted form through the Scriptures you were taught as a child. You know that God Eternal is more than the god of the Hebrews or even the father of Jesus. He has attempted to redeem mankind before, to bring it back unto its true heritage. He cleansed the written memory by destroying the pagan records and histories of their civilizations, He has instilled His countenance into the hearts of men who would reach out and extend what He showed them to their respective peoples. Boniface is one such as this, as are all the saints as you know them.

"But He must take care not to show Himself too brightly, for the human animal is weak after the generations dedicated to paganism. These men must know a little and no more, for His strategy is the same—that all the respective and slightly different paths shall one day meet. And there, at that divine spot, shall mankind understand completely all the pious tenets contain but a single, resounding truth."

Cu'lugh sat on the edge of the bed, his heart swelling with impatience and the desire to trip the priest on his own dogma.

"I am acquainted somewhat with the history of your brotherhood, Father," he said. "I have read the documents you left in Lady Vanda's rooms. The resounding truth? *'For the laziness of women, who had depended on the exaltation and protection of men, and for men's lust of these women and the pride they claimed in protecting them, the Eternal raised His hand against the lesser gods, the corrupters of truth, and destroyed the civilizations of earth. But for His beloved children, mankind, the Eternal conceived new and varying tenets in which to educate the races and lead them eventually to Truth. Despite their different rites and the manifold names given the Eternal, once the peoples immerse themselves in their respective vision of Him, shall then the veil He has put over His face for their protection be brought down and they shall stand with Him, their Father, and He shall make them free of one another and their mortal desires and the limitations these desires bring; and all men and women shall be liberated and redeemed and live as He in His realm of self-sustained and everlasting serenity. "*

Cu'lugh paused, smiling mirthlessly. "You truly believe all this, do you not? That men and women are equal in all ways and have enslaved each other by a mutual, grasping dependence? I do not seek to tell others their religion, Father Hrowthe, but I see a flaw in such an assertion. It speaks with the same arrogant contentions as the priestesses of those old tribes who believed men useless but for seeding their wombs. Despite their claims of superiority, they were conquered. By whom? Men. Not because we are wiser, not because we heed the words of chivalry, but because we are physically hardier and more naturally suited to the arts of battle.

"I have known many women, of all temperaments and dispositions; and it is my firm belief that by nature and spirit men and women are complementarily different one from the other. You would believe women have sought to enslave men by promoting a false guise of vulnerability. Nay, I cannot see that. I have lived a man's life, Father, and know that men are aggressive animals by nature. It is that very aggressiveness which necessitates we do protect our women.

"And I see, too, how men of our society blatantly ignore the advice of women, who often have better understanding of the muddles and discord we create. Yet, we fail again and again to consider their counsel or even ask for it, marking them down as carriers of this concept of sin. If we but sought and heeded their counsel, I think we would regain the character we have lost. That perfect world could again be known. Then should all the races and tribes enjoy the simple act of living. Men would enjoy women as they are meant to be enjoyed, taking delight in them as more than just bearers of the grief and guilt we have sired through reckless acts and excuse with self-serving dogmas."

Hrowthe regarded him a few moments. "A well-spoken dream, my son. One that can never be realized. No man can be truly happy who takes delight in possessing anything, certainly not another human being. Men are as guilty as women—we took delight and pride in the laziness of those who relied upon us. But in answer to your speculation, look upon Lady Vanda, the woman you consider to wed. Does she need a man to fulfill her? To shield her person? No, she cares not for these things, only for the prosperity of her kingdom, the salvation of her people."

Cu'lugh smiled now. "Are you sure this is all she seeks, Father?"

The priest stared at him—unblinking, desiccated orbs his eyes were, lifeless as his manhood, filled with a lusterless light that stemmed from his impotent heart. And yet Cu'lugh pitied him, somehow.

He said impulsively, gently, "It is sublime weakness, I feel, Father, for one as learned as you to hide cowardice behind religion."

"Cowardice?" Hrowthe said in a voice almost as fragile as his appearance. "Nay, it is rational to know paradise can be opened by simple repudiation of the mortal desires! One day we shall all stand liberated before the Eternal One, sustained by the Truth. Weak I was ages ago, when my homeland village was destroyed by the careless touch of this world's elements. I was spared the fate my family suffered, saved by a priest of my brotherhood. Later, I was honored to be chosen an apostle of God's plans and knowledge. I have seen His suffering in that despicable place where He lies chained by the demon gods. Long have I waited for Him to release Himself, yet I know it is a sacrifice He has chosen to give mankind the time to accept its liberation through Him.

"And I shall continue to wait, as long as it takes, for mankind to accept the conditions of salvation, to desire the release from fleeting fleshly desires, to embrace self-sustenance in order to be one with the Eternal."

Cu'lugh frowned. He had not read about this sacrifice in the scriptures he'd studied. "The pagan gods chained God Eternal? If He is the one true god and concerns Himself with mankind's salvation, it seems He has made a mistake. Tribes grow ever more increasingly intolerant of each other. This is His will through the varying faiths He has created? Then better I be godless and retain my pagan chivalry than avow any of His tenets. For I have no desire to war over gods or make women and children suffer for those I honor."

A foul stench had arisen from the depths of Hrowthe's emaciated stomach, and now Cu'lugh understood the reason for the scent of the herbs on his breath. He had tried to cover the smell. Perhaps the result of his deliberate starvation. Cu'lugh backed up and saw the mockery that bleached the priest's already pale mouth.

"I expect," Hrowthe said, "that you would seek to extend your faith in the pagan notion of chivalry into marriage."

Cu'lugh replied stiffly, "If, indeed, I marry, I shall abide no interference by the Church into the affairs of my household."

"You have a heart for challenge," Hrowthe said and there was something hesitant in the lightness that came to his tone. "It may be, Sir Cu'lugh, that Lady Vanda wishes a token demonstration of your loyalty before deciding to wed."

Cu'lugh stifled a wearied yawn. He wanted nothing more than to go outdoors and breathe what fresh air the miserable weather allowed. "Do I sense correctly this has something to do with your second objective, Father?" he asked.

Hrowthe nodded. "Vanda seeks more than anything in this world the return of her sister from the wicked place wherein she dwells. For misdirected intentions your brother took the girl there, surely unaware of the evil into which he was thrusting her. It is likely he had heard some gossip from amongst his less-honorable knights and deemed the place a safer haven than the Burgundian household to which he first delivered her."

Cu'lugh's attention quickened at mention of his brother. "Thierry took this girl away? Why?"

"For her safety, sir. As she is the daughter of chieftain Rulf by his harlot there is always a danger that the heathen forces would use her illegitimate heritage as a banner to lay siege to a Christian domain. Thus, to protect her sister and Lord Thierry's interests, Lady Vanda made arrangements for the child to be raised by allies in Burgundy."

"But that makes no sense," Cu'lugh said. "I have seen the remnants of Rulf's tribe—they are but a sickly and starved people. They could not carry out an uprising on their best days."

Hrowthe shrugged. "The likelihood of that is slight, yes, but there is a danger the pagans to whom she was so regrettably delivered would be strong and willing enough to attack...and murder whoever holds title here."

"Has Vanda taken this up with her military leaders?"

"They are but greedy men, loyal to whomever offers the highest pay. Their treachery could easily be bought with the right incentive."

Cu'lugh crossed his arms and looked at the priest hard. "I cannot believe Thierry would knowingly jeopardize the people put under his protection."

"He was...naive," Hrowthe said. "Your brother had a kind heart, sir, too kind. He did not even inform Lady Vanda of what he had done until it was too late. It is known that the people of this land I speak of are less than hospitable to the godly. Lady Vanda wants her sister back, but she is in an unconscionable position, for her very piety prohibits her from reclaiming her sister herself."

Cu'lugh smiled warily. "And so I am her fitting hero to champion this cause? I know well Vanda's piety, but what if the girl prefers life amongst a pagan folk?"

"Whether or not," Hrowthe said, "this is as Vanda wishes." He stepped in front of Cu'lugh and laid his hands gently on Cu'lugh's shoulders. The urgency in his face diminished the haggard look. "Give her sister back to her," he urged mildly, "and spare her—protect her—from further worry."

Cu'lugh felt a stab of guilt. "I have to be assured this is as she wishes, not just some concern bred by another's contempt of the pagans who shelter this girl."

Hrowthe showed no response to the insinuation. "She is in her library this very morning, having found little rest last night. Speak with her yourself, my lord."

Cu'lugh nodded, angered still but silently impressed by the true concern for Vanda he felt in the passionless priest.

"Very well," Hrowthe said, bowing to Cu'lugh, "I have said my piece and will leave you to your conscience, Cu'lugh."

Cu'lugh watched him go out the door, thinking how drawn and sickly the man was from the unknown denials and torment he'd obviously inflicted on himself for a very long time. Whatever these penances were they had taken a dreadful toll on his body.

But Cu'lugh knew Hrowthe cared not, for to concern himself with that necessitated a concern with the body's needs and desires, and to care for these things might tempt him to love the world he'd divorced.

Two concerns banished his worry over the priest: Vanda's proposal of marriage—*her* proposal, no matter what misgivings led others to conclude he had brought the subject up—and the familiar hunger in his loins he would have to quiet once again before going to her rooms.

Chapter Fourteen

anda greeted him with her congenial smile, but weariness was evident in her face. She kept turning her eyes to the neat little piles of parchment on the table before the couch she sat on. Demands, she said, from her mercenaries, who had grown discontent waiting for the customary share of the possessions her patrol had seized from a band of Avars passing through weeks before.

The Avars were legendary vagabonds, too quarrelsome to make efficient raiders but accomplished at pilfering crops. Vanda's scouts—an unknown brigade Cu'lugh had never seen—had spotted the Avars ransacking, or trying to ransack, the early wheat crops that struggled to grow along the northern border. The invaders had been quickly dispatched, and the patrol had brought everything of value they'd found on the bodies back to Lady Vanda. At the time she had made a promise through her captain that she would use the treasure to purchase new grain from Frankland and wine from Burgundy. But she had grown preoccupied with other matters and forgotten her promise. The mercenaries were complaining— loudly so—and, in Cu'lugh's opinion, rightly.

But her anger distressed him. Her little hands were balled into tight fists on her lap, the veins on the back standing up. Her face was flushed an unhealthy deep crimson.

She does not understand the needs of others, he thought. *How can she, when those unnatural priests prate against the immorality of human needs day and night?*

"They demand ale and women, Cu'lugh," she said breathlessly. "Ale and women! My fields lie barren, and the plants do not sleep but rot in the earth! Our fruit trees slump on their very roots and even our bees have forsaken their hives! Yet ever they whine in this persistent obsession with the flesh! Oh, strong backs I direly need, and, yes, I shall consider purchasing what women I need to till and work the soil once it is fecund again. But if they expect me to let them rut with my property they are more fools than sinners!"

He sat on the couch beside her, mulling over a response. He felt ice suddenly under his shirt and realized with mild surprise that it was the amulet that lay against his chest.

"Vanda," he said slowly, "these are not unreasonable requests to meet, especially if it keeps the loyalty of the mercenaries. Remember, we cannot forever veil from Charles that Thierry's knights deserted you or that this malady has reduced by half the male populace of your people. You need these men to protect your position. The conquerors and crusaders might ravage the tribes and bind them to the cross, but it is the fief lords who must have understanding to insure the survival of those conquered."

She looked at him directly, her face almost the color of blood. But her eyes grew pale with her fury, like those of children he'd seen on the verge of a mindless tantrum.

Then, suddenly, she laughed, a rare thing for Vanda. Her dark red lips spread out in a fragile smile and she touched his arm affectionately. The tips of her small fingers pressed like cool glass through the padding of his jerkin.

"My Cu'lugh would know, yes, mercenary that he was. Very well, wine and ale will be sent for and the boots my captain requested, as if water from the mountain streams could not quench their thirst and flax strapping protect their dainty feet. But there shall be no women but those I bring in, and only those as chaste as my serving women. I shall tolerate no strumpets."

He grinned. "You will never rebuild the bloodlines without women, my dear. Buy the slave women and let some of the men have land on which to settle with the ones they wed. Think of it as carrying out God's order to be fruitful and multiply."

She sighed, but continued good-naturedly, "But why promote even a necessary sin, as my mother pointed out, when this land can prosper with it outlawed?"

"The Saxon women you have are all dying, dear, or old and barren. Unless you retain a work force you cannot keep up the levies to Charles. He is not shy to fight for what he thinks is his. Not even the most battle-experienced mercenary is likely to fight in defense of a lord, or lady, who expects them to live like monks. They must have a compelling and lasting reason to take up the sword."

She tossed her head, shaking the pretty dark curls over her shoulders, an innocent gesture surely; but he couldn't help but notice the peep of white breast above her bodice the movement offered.

"I shall send for the drink and the grain—the boots, too. But if I must resort to marrying these men off I shall have to persuade Boniface to release some of his holy women from their vows. For never again shall I condone the pageantry of flesh that existed here before my father died."

"Holy women," Cu'lugh said, trying to stifle his laugh, "Vanda, these men need real women, not brides of an impotent image of God. They are used to women willing and desirous, not those who would shrink from the act that makes children."

Her small mouth pinched unattractively a moment; then she smiled again. "I prefer to think God originally intended for procreation to come about by other methods. A blessing bestowed by grace, not the carnal act."

"This sounds like a tale from one of Hrowthe's texts," Cu'lugh scoffed. "Why, not even the Church is so fundamentally hateful toward physical love. Tell me true—you do not put all your faith in his priesthood's lore?"

"I cannot say," she answered. "I get bored listening to their history lessons, hearing them go on about the annals of mankind before the supposed fall from grace. However, these records do seem to explain things that were either overlooked or forgotten by the Hebrew and Christian historians. But whatever the history of this world, what I consider is that ultimately this state of sin shall be cleansed from the world, all the obscene pagan infatuations of love and lust eliminated. And then there shall be no need of physical love, no need for women to think they must primp and play the helpless strumpet, for they will be men's equals in every way. We will no longer delude ourselves we are weaker, and therefore will not seek the state of marriage—and certainly not the false belief that we need that lewd act which lazy women have too long used to secure the protection of a man and, in the end, sentence themselves to whoredom and slavery."

Cu'lugh was speechless, but she saw the horror in his face and sighed wearily and patted his hand. "I am unfair, yes? Discount my words as the complaints of one tired and overwrought."

He was too relieved to comment and saw that the crimson was fading a little. "I have come to inquire as to your most private thoughts regarding your sister and this land to which I am told Thierry delivered her."

Vanda's head tilted slightly over her left shoulder and she looked wistful. "I have heard many tales of the wickedness that prevails in that land, but I do not put all my faith in tales alone. I know only that Thierry was lured through concern for Odette to take her to that place. That is depravity, is it not—temptation through ideas harmless, lies brazen? I will not lie to you, dear Cu'lugh, I want Odette home."

He glanced uneasily at the discarded piles of parchment. "But what of her choice, Vanda? If she is happy there—"

"Happiness in Gomorrah!" The sudden outburst renewed the flame in her face. "If you do not wish to fetch her back to me, I understand. Hrowthe and his brethren have told me it is a land shrouded in mystery and protected from God's reckoning by mankind's love affair with secrecy. There are none of my men as solid of mind as you, and certainly I cannot trust any Saxon man to return. The priests would surely meet death in that place. But, perhaps, in time, I can find someone..."

Her voice drifted and she turned her face away, her eyes closing tightly. Cu'lugh felt the hammer of guilt swing into his chest.

"Vanda, look at me," he whispered. She did so, her lips trembling, her eyes glistening, though there were no tears in her proud regard.

"I shall bring her back. Fret no more. I shall ride to this land and fetch Odette, whatever the cost."

For once she was speechless.

"For us," he said, the resonance of the hammer's strike twisting into a knot. "I do not undertake this lightly. I hope you can understand that."

Her blue eyes shone like a wolf's gazing at the full moon. "Oh, dearest, return her to me and half my kingdom I shall share. Oh, so little for so much!" She laced her arms about his neck, slowly, carefully, as one unfamiliar with affection. But he could feel her shudder, and it made her seem so womanly, so needful, that his hesitation dimmed into joy.

"I will bestow upon you my everlasting gratitude," she whispered and nuzzled his neck with her face. She kissed his neck and, shyly, loosened the cords of his jerkin at his collarbone and kissed his chest, too.

At once Cu'lugh felt an urgent stirring in his loins and he clasped his arms about her, circling his hands over the smooth width of her back. He massaged her hips and then her buttocks, surprised at the ampleness of them—buttocks used to sitting and contemplation as she pored over documents and talked with her priestly advisors and financiers. He envisioned all the delicious ways he would firm these precious muscles once they were married, and how he would savor all the other lovely assets that waited beneath her voluminous gown and petticoats.

But as rousing as was her sudden passion he would not take advantage of her innocence. He banked his desire, thinking only on this vow he'd made. She saw him to the door and kissed him again, so that the fragrance she wore doused his clothes and his heated skin. Before he left she whispered more promises into his ear, things sweeter than even the most precious perfume.

* * *

Hrowthe turned from his observation point in the corridor down from Lady Vanda's door and proceeded to a portal at the end of the wing. The overcast sky protected his eyes as he stepped outside and moved across the spongy grounds toward the new part of the village, where stood the modest huts built especially for those who served the brotherhood. The roof of the timber temple rose above every other structure, and presently he could hear the melancholy song of the wind as it blew through the eaves and beams. A pair of guards stood at the end of the street, and as they saw him both bowed slightly. Although their faces betrayed nothing Hrowthe felt the surge in their heartbeats, the loathing in their ignorant hearts.

He forgot them as soon as he'd entered the Temple. In the unlit stillness of the anteroom he walked to the table that stood in the center of the dirt floor and closed his eyes, inhaling deeply of the comforting smell of uncomplaining earth. From the back of the temple the scent of something else touched the air, a familiar smell so rich and tempting his jaws ached and his desiccated tongue spasmed. He had not expected it, and instinct compelled him to savor it a moment; and when he opened his eyes again after a time his predator's eyes caught a droplet red and crystallized on the edge of the table. It was tiny, unnoticeable to mortal eyes, but his stomach panged to see it.

But it was the mortal emotion of anger his mind sought out from the needless pathos he'd put away so long ago. And he found it, buried beneath so many layers of discipline and self-denial. He drew it out of that dark and forgotten place and mantled it deliberately, so as to lend weight to the reproach he must give whoever had surrendered to temptation during his absence.

In the archaic language Loki used and from which their holy vows had been made he summoned the brethren. Out of the shallow hidden plots many scraped their way; others drew out of the recesses and comforting shadows. In their grey and dirtied robes they came to stand before him, their sunken eyes expectant and reverent.

Hrowthe's emaciated hands balled, and he pounded the table with one of these fists so that their decrepit eyes widened.

"Bring me the corpse," he said at last and saw the shudder that passed among their number. But they said nothing and one of them turned with an almost humanly sheepish manner and disappeared into the remote shadows. Moments later he dragged the body into the anteroom. The stiffened flesh plowed softly over the ground, the heels through the flimsy shroud tracing the earth in its wake.

It was an old woman, Hrowthe saw through the ripped cloth about the corpse's face. Its hair the young Blodsauker clenched in his soiled hand as he came to stand before Hrowthe. The white hair was yellowed from the sickness she'd suffered before death, but against the soiled, hardened flesh of her thief it looked like shining straw.

"You fed less than a fortnight ago," Hrowthe said as the youth lifted the body and laid it across the table.

One of the others laid his palm on Hrowthe's shoulder. It was Rathra, who had witnessed almost as many decades as he had.

"He is a novice, my brother. We must remember."

Hrowthe smiled at the boy, pitying him, actually, for the gorging to which the brotherhood was dedicated had not yet bloated his stomach or greyed his flesh or even filmed his eyes.

"The flesh of the dead imparts little from the cache of aggregate memories to our cause," he said in his most angry tone. "Such gluttony serves the taker's whims, not the pious purpose for which you were initiated."

There was a noise from behind the youth, the illusion of a sigh. Hrowthe looked up and saw that the restless noise had come from the novice Owhyt, one of those who had been initiated at the same time as the youth. He leaned against the wall, as if unable to support himself, and his appearance was much changed from the night before when Hrowthe had seen him. He was as startlingly pale as the most ancient amongst them, and his flesh was parched and peeling about his chin as if he'd tossed and turned all day under the earth.

"Dreams in your slumber, Owhyt?"

Owhyt shook his head slowly, painfully. "Our Lord summoned me. He-He wished to feed."

Hrowthe frowned but did not voice his shock. He had thought Loki's requests were rare, and perhaps it was so, yet Hrowthe did not question the Lord's affairs. He had made comment to Hrowthe that He preferred the offerings of the older brothers for His vision feasts, as their richly attenuated reserve of human memories more easily allowed for penetration into the matters He wished to observe.

"You have been given a great honor, Owhyt."

Owhyt stared at his feet, looking very boyish despite his stark complexion. "I am not so certain."

"Not certain? How is that, Owhyt?"

The young priest searched Hrowthe's face. "Our Lord initiated us with our vow to gorge for the sake of the great future sacrifice—to fill our veins with generations of wisdom from those whose veins we rend, so that when that expected day comes we shall tear our flesh and let that wisdom pour upon the roots of Yggdrasil. It was not to be this way, Father—to consume simply to assuage His perverse appetite!"

Hrowthe flew from the stool so quickly as to scatter the others in his wake. He stood before the shocked Owhyt, pressing his hardened features into the novice's.

"Sacrilege," Hrowthe roared. He felt the spasms of his own desiccated organs, the grains of dried blood sifting through his tissues and arteries. "Do you not believe that Ragnarok will come? Do you prefer to think humanity will continue forever under the great evil of hope?"

Owhyt gaped and said slowly, "I believe it shall come, Father. But-but I fear it shall be at the expense of a sacrifice which has nothing to do with us."

"What foul influence has clouded your thinking, boy? Have you listened to the boastings of the shallow mercenaries? The regrets and sorrows of the ignorant serfs?"

Owhyt hesitated, but under Hrowthe's coaxing glare he continued. "His lips were coated with fresh blood when He took me, Father. I could see lying in the shadows the body of another of our brethren. There was no aura of existence left to the body, Father Hrowthe—none at all."

Hrowthe heard a murmur from the others, and he shook his head and silenced them with a curt wave of his hand.

"You were mistaken, Owhyt," he said at last. "An error, no less, no more."

"I-I have taken enough human blood to know the smell of a glutted stomach when I am near it! We are the ones He commanded to feed, and not for any pleasure save the stocking of it for that inevitable day. But He takes for His pleasure, to stave the hunger which we here have suffered just to cleanse ourselves for this rite you say He wishes!"

The dread in Hrowthe erupted, dashing away years of practiced restraint. He struck the boy's face so hard that it slammed against the wall and he heard the lifeless bone shatter under the white flesh.

"Hrowthe," Rathra warned, "do not let the humanity of this village corrupt your sensibilities!"

Hrowthe backed slowly away from Owhyt, staring at him as if he were some creature he had never encountered.

"You are mistaken," he repeated to the young priest, whose eyes seemed to blink toward the true death. "It was an honor you were given, to lend Him the Sight. Our sacrifice alone shall stir the roots of Yggdrasil and commence the twilight of the gods. If you have doubts of our Lord's words I can prove it by showing those priests He warns us all to avoid. You know whom I mean? Yes, the Berserkers. In a land not too far to the east dwells yet a small pagan tribe where the priests of Odin carry out their rites. I could take you there, leave you at the front gates that you may know the truth. And they would prove Loki's words true by killing you completely, releasing you from this case of humanity you dwell in through their savage, painful rites. I have seen it with my own eyes, boy, the unspeakable things they do.

"And their revenge does not stop when the animation of our bodies ceases, for by their curses they will send you to Valhalla, home of their patron, and there you can expect to be hunted every day and slaughtered every nightfall—nothing but sport for the amusement of Odin's wicked sons."

Owhyt looked at him fearfully, but there was something rebellious in that fear. He held the broken jawbone in place with his palm as he rose from the ground, trembling as the ligaments of his mouth moved to speak.

"And if I find all these things, Father, does it prove any more than I already suspect? Or shall I come to understand that the pagans were right in saying *Loki tempered his lies with truth so as make them believable?*"

Hrowthe was too stunned to move now and the old adage, one he had thought lost to the ages, stole his anger away. He could say nothing and watched as the young one turned and slunk into the safe recesses of the room.

There was uneasiness in the faces of the others and this, at least, Hrowthe was prepared to address, for if he was anything it was a crusader for his Lord. He spread his arms in benediction.

"The time is approaching to give honor to Him, our Lord and Father," he said. "Tonight, the building of the Harp shall commence. And when that offering is made, brothers, you shall feel Loki's blessings for that we give in His honor. You shall see that our actions, as always, have been inspired in the name of sanctity."

Several of them murmured their assent and a couple even knelt and touched the consecrated earth of the temple floor. In the shadows Hrowthe saw Owhyt, and the ghost of tears that could no longer fall upon his cheeks; and Hrowthe felt the fanatic's hope rekindle in the boy's inert heart.

It was not until Hrowthe found sanctuary in the temple earth, however, that his own impious doubts quieted.

Chapter Fifteen

After a night spent in the pillory Odette was more anxious than ever to please Lord Eryan. Perhaps it was the cruel and abiding desire he'd aroused that night, or maybe the humiliation she'd come to endure without complaint or question. But his agitation with her eased over the course of the next several days, even as he put more duties upon her.

She was charged with cleaning his room after her morning bath and whatever other chores he selected for her. Often he took her along on his errands in town. She still had to assist Uma in bringing up the beverages each evening and to serve meekly at Mistress Helrose's table. If Lord Eryan had been pleased with her during the day she was allowed to sleep on a pallet on the floor of his room; his dissatisfaction brought a night behind the bars of the uncomfortable cell in the wall upstairs.

No matter which fate her behavior fetched at night Lord Eryan would tantalize her beforehand. He would either order her to lie across his bed or over his lap and would then tantalize her sex. Forbidden to protest or complain, Odette endured his skilled and tormenting hands as he worked her until she was wet and heated and her hips strained to the point of orgasm. Never did he allow her satisfaction, and when she whimpered for it he spanked her. Each night she slept in utter frustration, and the one time she dared to relieve herself her relieved sigh awoke him. He was furious and whipped her severely with his flail, locking her in the cage for the remainder of the night with her hands tied behind her back until past noon the next day.

As he grew content with her progress, however, his possessiveness of her became more and more apparent. If Lord Eryan found her obliged to speak with or listen to another steward he immediately found some task to send her to. He questioned her relentlessly about any man who stopped her in the street or on the courtyard. But it was toward Mistress Helrose his jealousy proved most intense, and every other morning, when he was obligated to take her to Helrose's den for special lessons, his attitude was its most coldly impatient.

During these lessons alone with Mistress Helrose Odette was educated in the fundamentals of the seith training—proper dedications to Freyja, the days most sacred to Her, the flowers and animals for which She had particular favor. Odette studied the various herbs used for healing, for divination, for magics and those used in flavoring and cooking. On occasion Helrose shared with her some of the recipes of the beverages that were served to customers and at her table.

There were many lessons in the sensual arts.

"Grace is as important as the acts of pleasure themselves," the Mistress instructed during all these sessions, "for uncouth, hasty gratification is but a mechanical gesture."

She coached Odette in recitations of the Athlan love ballads and songs, on how to speak demurely but articulately, on how to conduct herself while others inspected and caressed her. There were instructions on how to focus attention on the one Odette was bade to please, how to put away wasteful and mundane thoughts and gaze upon her possessor as if he or she were the only other being in all the world.

Augmenting Odette's study of the arts of pleasure were instructions on how to defend herself against those unworthy of her skills. By Athlan law, Helrose explained, all women were exempt from serving the inebriated and those released from the king's Hold for abuse of women. Nor need she accept the attentions of anyone—even her husband—when there was mockery or verbal abuse or defamation demonstrated. Needless to say, anyone suspected of an inclination toward physical savagery was to be avoided.

"If you are approached by or apprehended by any boor such as these I've described, it is allowed and encouraged you to do whatever you must to put yourself away from them, whether by screaming, kicking or calling for aid. Pretend unconsciousness, if necessary. If you are correct in your suspicions or charges, all these things are sanctioned and the person who seeks to abuse you shall be brought to the king's law. There have been occasions when a woman was mistaken in her suspicion, and that chivalry forgives. But be aware—intentionally false accusations are punishable by at least a year's sentence in the private hall of the king's guards, where the prisoner is not allowed out of their compound either day or night until the term of punishment is completed."

Finally, Mistress Helrose introduced Odette to the techniques of wyrding, the important practices that helped to transform reality. The first of these lessons involved the proper way to inhale and exhale and, by complete relaxation, to touch the world beyond the temporal. Repetition of movement, such as drumming the floor with the fingers or sliding a damp fingertip over the lip of a crystal goblet, helped Odette's mind course from her ordinary thoughts into those buried deep within her consciousness. Her preferred method was to ring the crystal goblet, to follow the lilting melody as it took her. Soon her mind's eye would fly through the rooms of the house, to peer at the activities of others, to hear their conversations and, once in a while, even their unspoken thoughts.

One morning she even escaped the walls of the manor altogether and soared free through the ethers surrounding the city. Over the fecund Athlan fields she flew, the river and the waterfalls from the distant mountains. It was over one of these rushing cascades that she felt a profound desire to dive straight into the foaming water. The next moment she plummeted, to be engulfed by a washing coolness that stole her breath away. She gasped, unable to breathe. The next moment she was blinking and saw she was in the safe, dry den. The Mistress was sitting cross-legged beside her in the lantern light, and as Helrose patted the sweat from her brow

Odette realized that her crossed legs and her fingers on the goblet had grown numb.

One morning Mistress Helrose unlocked the collar from her throat.

"The time for your testing has come," she said. "For you to transcend the safety of the temporal and journey into your fate."

The Mistress unbound her hair and led her to a heavy wooden bench. A length of thick, dark cloth lay there, which Helrose wound over Odette's eyes, tying it at the back of her head so she was quite blind.

"Now, kneel on the floor, but do not sit on your heels."

This Odette did, her heart beating faster. Her hair tickled her buttocks as she knelt, and she felt the Mistress string heavy cords about her ankles. These she tied to the legs of the bench, drawing them taut, though not painfully so. Next, Helrose tied Odette's hands behind her waist.

Odette felt a sensation as if she were falling over and cried out. Helrose gently patted her shoulder.

"You are safe, Odette, I will be with you.

This was a relief, and yet Odette felt awkward, on the verge of swaying too much one way or the other. She was aware of the Mistress kneeling or sitting beside her and felt Helrose's breath close to her cheek.

"Odette, I want you to tell me at once if you begin to feel ill," the Mistress said. "Other than for that, you are to say nothing—and do not even think of complaining. I shall chastise you slightly, enough to help you seek the dimension beyond. Transcend your discomfort. If you complain the ministrations will only fall harsher and quicker. Can you remember?"

Odette nodded, annoyed a little by the hair tickling her shoulders and face.

"You will, in your bonds, go beyond yourself, Odette, in a quest to find your fate. Search for that which attracts your individual character and all those qualities that comprise your soul. Think of this—only this—in your quest."

She heard Mistress Helrose rise and move away a little and felt a moment's panic. Then it seemed hours passed while she remained blinded and bound with her knees aching. The strokes of Helrose's flail were delivered lightly across her breasts and backside, almost irritating in their lazy descent.

At last her thoughts began to drift. She thought of Lord Eryan, of his fearsome coolness as he'd awakened her that morning and then of the beauty of his flawless pale face and the fleeting images of his supple naked flesh she had espied now and then as she knelt before his bed while he changed clothing. Her sex quickened at these images and she thought she moaned, though she could not be certain. The renewed passion brought more images, now of Lord Alban, and a longing to suckle him again and to feel his manhood inside her. His scent she smelled again as if she were sitting on his lap and her mouth tingled with the taste of his seed.

Odette's nether mouth grew insatiably wet, and she began to pant, envisioning Lord Eryan ravishing her maidenhood as she knelt to suckle Alban...

Suddenly the tip of Helrose's flail singed her buttocks. The strike was only slightly harder than those last dealt, but it stung enough to warn her to move past her ripe lust. She felt bereft as her mind shifted away; but remembering the Mistress's warning, she dared not complain—certainly not utter the truth that she'd forgotten exactly what it was Helrose wanted her to seek.

The flail struck her again, even more sharply, then on and on rhythmically, making her long to move away from it. When at last she made a whine of irritation her head was raised up by the roots of her hair. Her lips were pried open and a bit of wide leather inserted into her mouth, the strap of which was tied to the back of her head.

The Mistress, however, did not sound angry as she said, "If you become ill, Odette, you must now nod twice."

She proceeded to flail Odette in the same rhythmic way until Odette's buttocks tingled with pain.

Yet strangely, as utterly helpless and chafed as she knew herself to be, Odette felt a growing drowsiness settle over her. After a time the hateful, spanking flail seemed but a minor and faraway agitation. She envisioned herself straddling Lord Eryan's lap and kissing his mouth. It seemed more than an image, as if she actually felt the smooth head of his manhood brushing her drenched font.

The distant lashes of the flail drove her on, toward an utter and lonesome darkness. She thought of Lord Eryan but could not find her way back to him. Frightened, she called out his name—and then she saw a shadow move before her.

Tumbling toward her was a configuration of oblique light, resounding with a drone of indistinguishable sound that she felt as well as heard. She felt a force strike her from within the light. The invisible energy dug through the pores of her flesh, piercing her skin with a thousand heated needles. Her skull and bones contracted, her muscles and tissues spasmed. Her cries sounded inhuman to her pounding ears and her vision filled with earthly scenes.

She knew she was moving, and when her vision cleared she saw far below a green valley. She sailed quickly onward to make out the details of the landscape. From there she flew into the hazy atmosphere of a great wasteland. She recognized it without even seeing the details, though she had forgotten it somehow. Then again, she had been so young when Thierry brought her through it.

Her course did not falter and soon she saw fields on the horizon. As she left the Wasteland she recognized this place, too—the grey mountaintops and deep valley, the sunken grottos everywhere, the forest. Her flight slowed, and very dimly she was aware Helrose had stayed her hand. Odette blinked and saw the sharper, manmade outlines ahead.

She heard voices and began to circle the place from whence they lifted. She saw faces, weary and hollow-eyed, a few familiar. The people labored in a corrupted field behind a village of drab abodes. They did not see her as she passed, nor know that she saw their suffering faces and the unmistakable signs of starvation. It was a village of the wretched—not a single healthy and able-bodied man amongst them. No children, either. The women were stick-thin caricatures of the fairer sex, clad in filthy flaxen rags; and their scarred and disfigured faces bore testimony of unspeakable abuse.

As Odette steered from the pitiful faces she saw the field and inner valley were encompassed by a great timber fence with four watchtowers. From the looming parapets Odette heard virile voices laughing and arguing.

She glided past these men and saw they were all armed and ruddy with health. Moving on, she crossed the barrier between the workers' area and the town, and she saw down on a street another soldier carrying a loaf of bread under one arm. She wanted to alight and snatch the loaf from him and take it to the workers, but something invisible barred her from acting. Saddened, she turned and sought the portal of light that had led her to this place.

At that moment her eyes fell upon a sight that made her heavy heart clench. After all these years, and despite the additions of towers and turrets, a new garrison quarters and refurbished domed roof over the main court, Odette recognized her father's Hall at once. She circled it, viewing the high, sterile stone ramparts that now separated it from the village. The circular walls of her mother's garden still stood, but the flowers and herbs, the rose bushes and even the pear tree had all died long ago.

Soldiers in unidentifiable livery guarded the ways leading to the old and new quarters alike. Atop the entry were set enormous wooden crucifixes. For a time she searched for a familiar face, but none of the companions of Thierry did she see amongst these men.

From the Hall she went on, soaring over the older part, searching for the banners of the smiths, the rune masters, the traders and merchants. But there was nothing anymore to designate these crafters had even once walked the streets. The blacksmith's shop was empty; beside it stood a new building. From the door hung a sign with the insignia of the guild, but the shutters were closed tightly so she could not see within. Farther on, where once had stood the pillared temple of Friggi, the ground was littered with broken and scorched shards of the precious black marble of which it had been built. The only sign of human presence among the ruins was a crucifix planted in the devastated grounds.

Onward Odette went, to the Well of Idun that had provided her people with a convenient source of water. But the opening had been covered over with rough timbers. The Arch of Thor on the eastern side of the village had been vandalized, the stones dismantled and most of them evidently carried away. Someone had constructed a small stone wall where it had stood, and Odette saw it had been etched with lettering she recognized as crude Latin and, here and there, an attempt to write a curse in the runes of her people.

Odette lifted her wings and turned away. But soon she beheld a sight that appalled her almost as much as the sickly and neglected Saxons. The Grove of Freyja had been sanctified by her father before she was born, but all that remained was a devastated ruin of ugly, blackened stumps. Even the wild pool where she and her mother had often brought offerings of flowers and greenery had dried up. Odette gasped—she could not help it—and she knew a mourning deeper even than that she'd known when her mother and father had died that fateful morn…

But it was the enslavement and despair of her folk that sorrowed her most as she flew swiftly away from it all.

And then the oblique light swallowed her again. Her eyes smarted from the startling shadows, and yet she made out something new—a lone figure, a rider garbed much like the Franks who had invaded her homeland. She could not see his face, but she felt his intentions—a strong, unrelenting quest for adventure and advancement and respect that had always eluded him. As Odette was pushed closer she saw his face clearly—the brutally handsome features and intense dark eyes. Those eyes turned and scanned the space where she hovered, and though he did not see her he reined his horse to a stop and stared through that space, the hair raised on his arms and his heart longing.

"My nymph..."

Odette knew the voice but from where? She felt cold with perspiration and the shadows blinded her and pulled her back into the light. Her skin was afire and her muscles and organs spasmed painfully. Her bones cracked back into familiar alignment and her lungs seized in her transforming breast...

Chapter Sixteen

Her name was being spoken frantically by a familiar voice, and she felt something cool and wet on her face. Her lungs continued struggling for air. For a moment she glimpsed Mistress Helrose's face before her, her brow crumpled and her eyes shining with worried tears. Odette tried to speak but had no breath.

Helrose's face vanished and a drape of silent blackness enclosed Odette. For a long time it seemed she floated in this place that made her emotions and thoughts drowse. But at length she heard a voice nearby. The blackness ebbed and her eyelids fluttered. Slowly, her vision focused so that she saw a small oval face before her, framed in a halo of shining flaxen hair.

Odette's wrist was lifted by a warm hand. Looking down, she saw she was on her feet, and that it was the young boy's hand that clasped her. He tugged her urgently.

"Come, Odette, the Mistress needs you."

Odette glanced around, seeing sunlight pour through the many windows, making the polished white walls and the silver trim and pearl festoons sparkle so vividly her eyes burned.

This is not Mistress Helrose's den, she thought.

The boy looked desperate and she nodded, touching her brow unconsciously, noticing for the first time the gown she wore, a thing of clinging white fabric woven with soft-hued stripes of different shades.

"Come, Odette!"

"Yes, yes," she said and followed him through a door nearby. They entered a new corridor, this one awash in sunlight as well and the walls adorned with silver and gold mirrors framed with mother-of-pearl and little statues set within niches and on gleaming maple shelves.

They reached another door, one of an amber wood, and the boy opened it and stood aside for her to enter. Odette stepped over the threshold onto a black-and-pink-ticked marble floor within was so lustrous she could see her reflection. A great hearth governed the wall facing the door, in which burned a low fire, and about the other walls stood row upon row of cradles. They were empty, though clean blankets had been folded and laid within each.

The silence in this room was so deep her footsteps were heavy to her ears and the air was sweet—not like the essence of flowers or perfume or incense but something that imbued the entire room with an overwhelming tranquility. She saw there were no windows here, only a few beeswax candles burning in brass holders set on small tables. The walls were like none she'd ever seen, seeming as if they'd been plastered in living tissue. And as Odette regarded them it appeared to her they expanded slowly and then, just as slowly, rebounded.

The boy made a small noise at her side and led her on toward the high back of a chair facing away from them. A woman garbed in a gown of black gossamer sat in the chair, leaning over the floor to stare at something Odette could not see. Her black, coarse hair was piled high on her head and her visible neck was long and unusually thin, so that it looked too fragile to hold up her head and the weighty hair.

"It gets cold," the woman said in a voice so despondent that the sound of it touched Odette's heart with sadness.

Just then a gust of wind blew in from the corridor and the door sucked closed with a loud bang. Odette heard what sounded like a lock turn, though she could see nothing but the brass handle shake. The wind was not gone, but raged through the room, extinguishing the sweetness from the air and the fire in the hearth. Every candle save one blew out...and this single candle flickered over a particular cradle, but it remained, trembling under the wind's wrath as wax dripped onto the blanket below.

The fair boy hugged Odette's arm. She started to move her other arm to protect him when something ice cold grasped her other wrist. Gasping, she saw the woman's sickly blue face peering at her, horribly disfigured with sorrow and with a mouth cemented in the countenance of grief.

The woman's eyes were lusterless, sickly blue orbs and now Odette made out in the shadow the contours of her gown more truly than in the light. Like a layer of black ash it covered her flesh, and when the woman took a breath Odette watched with horror as a scrap of the bodice crumbled and fell to the floor.

The wind died down then, but the temperature of the room plummeted. Odette's breath was thick in the air and her limbs ached and felt heavy. The boy's hand slipped from her grasp and he slumped to her feet. She bent down and saw he was unconscious, his little hands frozen to the hem of her gown.

Odette's voice shivered as she looked at the woman. "What have you done? He will die!"

The grotesque head shook on the frail support of the neck, sickening Odette with the fear it would simply fall from the sinews.

"I have not done this, my child," she answered, and Odette winced to see the corners of her mouth crumble as she spoke. "Worry not for us, Odette, but for the next Babe due. His lungs shall never quicken without protection."

Odette, not understanding, looked at the cradles. They sparkled with ice, every one, and the blankets had vanished.

"I do not understand what you mean, madam! There are no babes here!"

No sooner had she spoken than Odette heard a high-pitched, plaintive cry from behind her. Turning, she saw one of the cradles swaying lightly, as if someone had disturbed it. Odette's uncertain fear grew and she knelt to touch the shoulder of the sleeping boy. He did not stir and so she shook him as briskly as her numbing muscles allowed.

"Wake up!"

But he moved not and she saw that his chest did not rise or fall. Angry and horrified, Odette stood up. Her skin was white and shimmering with cold and she could no longer tell if she breathed or not. But she ignored her own worries and the fearsome woman and took a straining step toward the swaying cradle.

When she peered in her heart rate quickened, for within the frozen wooden bed lay a rosy, precious infant, beating the freezing air with its tiny fists. Naked and unprotected it was, its sweet flesh covered over with goose bumps and its little limbs shivering.

She looked to the woman. "What shall we do? It freezes in here and my touch will only chill it quicker!"

The woman's long hands went to her skirts and she pulled the hem up so that the threads broke and crumbled like tiny bits of black glass to the floor. She pulled something from the folds, however, something that caught the glint of the surviving candle. Odette watched as she laid it on the floor and, using what seemed the last reserve of her tormented body, kicked it across the floor to Odette.

Odette stooped, hearing her bones crackle. She stared, dismayed to see the thing was a small sickle.

"What? You will have me kill a babe? No!"

The woman's strength gave out and she fell to her knees, supporting herself on her thin hands. Odette heard her teeth rattle as she said, "If you seek to save it, bundle it in your hair."

Odette blinked, uncertain. But then she grasped what the woman wanted and lifted her hair over one shoulder. Strangely, the unbound strands were warm to her fingers. Lifting the sickle in one hand she beheld it reluctantly. But then she heard the babe's cry soften and, looking, saw its little fists fall limply to its sides. Only its knees rocked once or twice in its dying struggle.

Odette caught her hair in her left hand and lifted the heavy length of it, stretching it out as tautly as she could. With her right hand she raised the sickle and set the blade against her hair. She began to scissor through the golden drape, her frozen joints snapping in protest. But at last the sharp metal separated the final strands and the golden mass fell free in her left hand. She dropped the sickle and bent over the cradle. She swaddled the babe in the warm drape of hair, covering it from head to toe.

At once the infant's cheeks began to take color again. Its eyes opened and it began to coo contentedly.

As Odette looked at it the lush sweetness filled the room again. It consumed her senses with a joy indescribable. She began to weep, but so profound was this wonderful delirium that she only half-noticed how warm the tears felt.

Then, as the candles blazed again, Odette's eyes stung; and with the warming temperature, her muscles tingled. She saw from the corner of her eye movement and, turning, saw the boy rise from the floor. He blinked, the life returning to his fair complexion. He helped the fearsome woman to her feet and her gown suddenly transformed into a resplendent velvet blue shade and the ice crystals that had formed on it transformed into brilliant diamonds. Arm-in-arm the woman and the boy walked to the renewed fire in the hearth and when they looked at Odette she saw the disfigurement of the woman's face had softened a little.

The hinges of the door creaked and it opened as if never locked. Another woman entered, beautiful and mahogany-skinned, with eyes of dewy brown. A slender golden circlet crowned her black kinky hair. Her arms were covered with bands of gold and copper and carven ivory, and her gown of softest animal skins swept past her naked feet as she joined the others. She kissed the fearsome one's hollow cheek and they embraced, and the boy wrapped his arms about the newcomer's hips and sighed sweetly.

"Who has rekindled the living fires, Hela," she asked.

"Odette," spoke the fearsome one. Now both women looked at Odette and their tender eyes were penetrating.

"The swan-maiden's daughter, with all her self-recriminations?"

The disfigured one nodded, and Odette cringed, fearful once again that too-slender neck could not support her head. The two women sat down on a bench and Odette heard the babe breathe deeply, peaceably. When she looked again into the cradle its face was abloom with life.

There was a knock at the door and a servant girl with a freckled face and waves of deep-red hair came in and bowed. She was naked but for a garland of flowers about her head, but she gave no hint of embarrassment as she knelt before the one named Hela.

"The babe lies there," Hela told her, gesturing to the cradle. "This one a victim of illness unattended. Take it to the nursery quickly—I feel others coming presently. Several. But worry not, they shall be warm now—the fire has been relit, and the exit door of the nursery you shall find has returned to the room."

The girl came to Odette and bowed to her. She lifted the babe in the swaddling of hair and carried it out the door.

"When the exit door vanishes the ice-wind comes," explained the boy, and he looked at Odette with the most amazing iridescent eyes. "No child may know the solace betwixt lives without an exit door, and the ice-wind blows out the guiding light to Hela's domain."

Odette studied his face, unable to grasp his meaning.

"Swan-maiden's child."

It was the dark beauty who spoke; and Odette raised her eyes, wondering why the woman had chosen to address her with that appellation.

"Now you are disfigured as Hela," she said, and were it not for the tenderness beaming in her face Odette would have thought it an inappropriate remark to speak before her friend. Then she thought of what she'd done, remembering the beauty of her hair; and she felt sad she had been forced to cut it off. She looked uneasily at the sickle where it had fallen.

To her surprise the grain of the wooden handle was stretching and tiny green sprouts poked through. The sprouts grew quickly into a vine that twined over the blade. Odette saw diminutive crimson buds emerge over the greenery. Astonished, she leaped back, her fear overwhelming now of this place she did not know.

"Where am I?" she asked, touching the ends of her shorn hair. "Why do you call me the swan-maiden's child?"

"What do you prefer, my child?" the dark beauty asked gently. "You are blood of my sister's line, a reflection of my own self—our own Self. I think with some rest you shall understand."

"Understand? Am I dreaming? Is this just part of Mistress Helrose's test?" Odette blinked hard, hoping to awaken, to slide at least back through that tumbling light...

"Dreams are for mortal things," said Hela, and there was a certain comfort in her fathomless eyes. Odette saw that her skin moved in the same smooth way as the tissuey walls, and a rosy tinge glowed now beneath the surface of her blue complexion. Odette looked at the walls again and stared at the veins of the texture. She noticed that behind the rise and fall of the tissue there was a mild but constant motion, a pulsing, of sorts.

Like a beating heart!

Her flesh tingled and she stepped back from the women clumsily.

"No dreams here," Hela repeated. Her head lowered and tears fell over her bodice. "Ah, my own father has turned me into a monster before the eyes of mankind, Odette, for I loved the Eternal Father more."

She turned to her friend and embraced her. As their lips touched their arms intertwined lovingly. A tiny pink spark popped where their mouths met and suddenly the skin of their faces seemed to melt. The skin melded and their arms and legs sealed fast together. As Odette gaped their torsos merged and in a blinding moment they stood now a single glowing figure of rose and blue and mahogany flesh.

The face that looked down at Odette seemed the face of all women—dark and fair, olive and bronze, a perfect composite of diverse features and attributes. It was not so much this transformation that now held Odette spellbound, but the indescribable power shimmering in the regal, rainbow eyes.

Odette screamed and staggered back into the arms of the boy. She turned to him and covered his eyes with her hands. She looked back cautiously and watched as the Woman now sat on a throne that had appeared. A thick vine, heavy with waxen red flowers, emerged from her womb and meandered over her limbs and her face and even into her flowing tresses of shimmering rainbow colors.

"And look there, at my son and father and beloved," said the All-woman, "the essence of virility that the Evil One murdered. Not enough He must die again and again for evil, but now that eternal enemy has found the way to obliterate My true self forever from the world."

The boy's warm lips pressed against Odette's palms, and he gazed into her face with a look that penetrated her soul at once for its outward innocence and the virility she could see lying hidden within.

"Come, Odette, it is time you returned," he said.

Odette's shock had addled her reasoning. She nodded mutely and her legs moved by a will not her own. He led her to the door, and only after they had crossed the threshold did she dare look back. Now she saw the disfigured one, Hela, reposing again before the blazing hearth. Hela's neck turned painfully and in her tragic eyes was heavy, unfathomable patience.

The boy took Odette through the corridors, where the warmth of the sunlight filled her with a great desire for sleep. She did not know she'd staggered until the boy labored to help her rise.

"You must move," she heard him say.

Odette felt swoony and used the panes of a window to steady herself. Beyond lay a grassy field where half a dozen children romped and played. She smiled to watch them, until she saw in the distance a rock cavern. Two men stood just within the recess. At least, she thought they were men...until the sunlight reflected on their skin and made them both shade their eyes with their hands and turn away. So pale they were, she saw, paler than the dead. As they moved farther inside the cavern she saw a naked youth. The two watched as he lifted his scrotum in one thin hand. His other hand lifted high, and the sunlight glinted on the blade of the knife he held. He smiled at the others as if seeking their approval; and the mindless grins that came to their lips sickened Odette. Then, at their nods, the youth stretched his scrotum out and brought the blade against the hairy seam between his legs.

"Tell me this is not needed," Odette gasped.

She watched as the youth sliced through his flesh and the blood splattered down his legs and over his hands. The scrotum fell from his red-drenched grasp to lie limply on the cavern floor. The other two went to their knees and raised their arms heavenward and they began to sing some dreadful dirge even as their faces burnt with a fanatical light.

The fair-haired boy came to the pane and looked out. His face grew sober. "No, what he did, he did for himself." He sighed and shook his head. "I tried to tell him, but he did not want to listen."

Odette felt ill, and she looked worriedly at the children...and her heart faltered to see that they had changed into statues, cold and grey and captured in the transformation with the shock of it set forever in their faces.

She snapped her eyes shut against the horrid sight and the boy dragged her away from the window.

"It is time." His whisper echoed in the corridor.

She heard a door open and he prodded her through it. She turned just as his small hands released her and looked down at him. His smile was richer than the fecund earth and his iridescent eyes balm to her rattled nerves.

"The spurning of life is what makes a weakling," he said, his voice manly and deep. "Help drive back to darkness the foolish cravens who seek to debase the sacred Marriage Bed, Odette."

Odette felt herself bathed in a warmth much more powerful than had been the frigid wind that pervaded the nursery. She closed her eyes, allowing it to fill her, intoxicate her, caress her very soul and spirit; and when she looked again the white door had closed.

Someone called her name. She turned to the direction from which the voice emanated and the light whirlwinded toward her, scooping her away with such force her lungs lurched and air filled them as if it had been an eternity since her last breath.

"Ah, sweeting, I feared you gone forever!"

Odette's eyelids fluttered and the earthy light of the den banished the mist. Mistress Helrose was looking down at her, smiling so radiantly she did not seem to notice the tear falling down over the corner of her mouth. Odette tried to sit up but she swooned back to the floor where the Mistress had laid her. Footsteps approached and she saw from the corner of her eye Lord Eryan looking down.

The already minimal color of his fair complexion had bleached even more, but as he crouched beside her she saw relief in his eyes and a tender smile on his lips. He took the damp cloth from his sister and touched it to Odette's brow and cheeks and throat.

"You lie there a time," he said quietly and she nodded willing compliance. He looked at Mistress Helrose and said, "She will be fine. Let her sleep a while."

Mistress Helrose's face contorted. "No, I should stay here—"

"No." His voice, hushed though it was, was as stern as ever he'd spoken to Odette. He folded the cloth evenly and laid it across Odette's brow. "Rest, Odette. We shall be close."

He got to his feet and pulled Helrose away. When they were out of sight Odette wondered vaguely where the Mistress had taken the gag and cords and cloth used to cover her eyes.

But she soon forgot about those things. It was all over with, Helrose's test, and the dreadful images of the vision but things best left to think of when she was not so tired. She closed her eyes and heard the Mistress whispering with her brother. Their voices sounded angry and Odette regretted this; but she had not the strength now to open her eyes, let alone to ask permission to tell them there was no reason for anger.

"I did not think," the Mistress said in a voice deep with self-reproach. "I am a fool! She is not like the others and could have too easily been whisked back to Vanaheim before she even knew what was happening. I should have remembered!"

"Shh," Lord Eryan whispered reproachfully. "You are too hard on yourself. If there is fault, it is mine. I have overworked her these last days."

"No, it is not that." The Mistress sounded peevish, but Lord Eryan silenced her with another "Ssshh!"

"Come, let her sleep. And you, you shall explain to me this talk of Vanaheim."

Odette heard them walk away, but she did not hear the door close; in fact, she heard nothing else for a long while.

Chapter Seventeen

hen, after a dreamless sleep, Odette awoke in Lord Eryan's bed it was well past nightfall; but she could not hear his familiar deep breathing as he slept nor any sign anyone else was in the room. By the light of the lantern on the nightstand she saw a basket filled with ripe quinces and pears; and as she cleaned the room daily, she knew it was against his fastidious nature to bring or have food in his room. She smiled, grateful and touched by his thoughtfulness.

She was, however, too weary to think of eating and closed her eyes and settled under the coverlet. Images from all the things she had seen in the vision came flooding back unexpectedly. The sweet, flaxen-haired boy with the iridescent eyes, the strengthening words he'd given before her spirit returned to her body. But that was little comfort against the distressing suffering she'd witnessed in her homeland—her starving, enthralled folk and the desecration of her village and its sacred places. Could this be a true revelation? The question made her shudder. What possible aid could she yield them if it were so?

Then there were the other disturbing sights—discoveries that seemed to have so little to do with her: the youth castrating himself; the children turned to statues; the image of the Goddess Hela, too real to dismiss comfortably; the infant wailing for warmth; the dark, beautiful woman and the regal figure created when she melded with Hela; the two men watching as the youth castrated himself. What possible connotation had these images for her?

But, then, the All-woman had called her *Swan-maiden's child*, and this perplexed her; for it had been ages since she'd even thought of the silly fable surrounding her mother.

She did not like it, or Helrose's distressed reaction when she came out of the wyrding vision. What had she learnt but this lingering unease for her father's people?

Still, the image that haunted Odette most was that of the rider. Unlike the phantoms of Hela's Abode, he seemed all too real, and unlike the Saxons, who had not sensed her presence, he had perceived her. Of this Odette had no doubt, nor that she knew him, although she had never laid eyes on him.

She crawled deep down under the warm coverlet and hoped Lord Eryan would return and take her mind from these things with his stern voice. After a while she drowsed. In her dreams the rider appeared, now traveling away from her down a dusty, winding road. She ran after the horse but a tree fell across her way and the trunk swelled into a high and ambling fence she could not cross. She ran left to right and to left again searching for the end of it, but the roots and canopy extended for miles. At last she crawled laboriously up the trunk. By the time she could see over it the very dust had settled from his passing and her heart felt as if were shattering.

Then she felt the ground quake and something pulled her hair. She screamed as she was hauled backward down the rough bark to the ground.

"Odette!"

Her eyes flew open and she looked up into Lord Eryan's face. Even in the darkness she could see the glowing paleness of his face, the deep and penetrating eyes. She sat up, weeping, and she clung to him like a child. She was relieved to have him there, happy to call him *Master*. Yet, despite her affection for him and deep gratitude her heart yearned for the Rider. Eryan's features seemed to melt away and she thought for a moment she was gazing into the handsome, swarthy face from her visions and she wept harder, knowing she would never love Eryan the way he needed.

He held her close and stroked her hair until again she fell asleep.

After bathing her the next morning Lord Eryan informed Odette that the Mistress had decided it would be a while before she would be summoned for any more lessons. While he garbed her again in the familiar collar and restraining garter belt with the clitoris shield, he was generous enough to take off the anal phallus. Arranging her hair in a tight braid pinned at the crown of her head, he sent her off to the courtyard to help in the morning preparations for the customers.

The sun was hot that day, making her very uncomfortable in the brass belt and chained garters. It was all she could do not to snap at the other girls, who seemed to be always running in the way of her broom as they scurried to set up the tables. They were not at fault, she knew, only her own foul mood. Only Lydene could she truly criticize. The girl had earlier in the week been released of her own garters and belt, and Odette had discovered the depth of her laziness. She was haphazard in her efforts, content to leave what she'd overlooked for the other flowers to straighten or clean.

Lord Ingven was too pressed that morning to take note. Merchants ran to the courtyard and announced that a man had been apprehended for attempting to maim a woman. The man, they reported, had only recently been let out of the king's Hold for one such attempt; and now he was to be taken directly to the royal lawn for public execution.

The streets and squares were bustling with angry citizens, and Ingven walked back and forth between the courtyard and the gatepost to ensure none of the commotion broached the Mistress's property. Odette noted several of the other flowers gazing after him lustily.

When at last the furor had died down he expressed disappointment in their work, though Odette sensed this was not quite the truth. Rather, she suspected, he was still edgy from the tumult. He announced loudly that if he caught any of them failing further in their chores he would punish every one of them. When all had returned to work with renewed vigor and downcast eyes, he came to where Odette stood with her broom. He wiped the sweat from his brow with the back of his hand

and said quietly, "You have done well, I notice. And as Lord Eryan is detained in town this morning and left you in my supervision, you shall help serve this morning."

The sun was behind him, and Odette had to squint to see him. At once she saw the lust in his regard and her knees felt as if they had turned to sand. She blushed and managed to nod, and he sent her along with another flower to bring ale and other refreshments up from the cellar. When they returned the first customers were just beginning to wander in. Odette was not surprised to see Lydene bent over one of the tables receiving a spanking with Lord Ingven's thick belt. Odette bit her lips to keep from smiling as she watched Lydene straining to keep still as the leather rained fast and hard down over her buttocks. And when her bottom cheeks were glowing red the steward carried her to one of the cages and locked her in.

Then, true to his word, Lord Ingven spanked the others who had been present during Lydene's act of laziness. Only Odette and her companion were spared, and for this Odette was grateful even as her sex swelled wetly when she watched the flexing of the muscular arm that wielded the belt.

The steward gave Odette the task of collecting in a box the coins paid by the patrons. For those with tabs she was given a tin box filled with colored threads, which she had to spin about wooden spools etched on one end with a certain rune that represented the customer's name. Lord Ingven pointed out to her those customers who were not to be charged—the Mistress's personal friends and those who supplied goods for the household in exchange for free beverages.

One of these men was the merchant Holbarki who had tried to barter Mistress Helrose for her. Odette could not shake off her dislike of him. He had done nothing to her, and so she decided her feeling was but another instance of her bad mood. He sat by himself as he quaffed down his mead, counting out piles of copper and silver pieces and chortling loudly at the jokes of others sitting about. He seemed to make the other customers uneasy, Odette thought, and even Lord Ingven seemed to distance himself from the man.

She was standing near the serving table fingering the pretty threads for the tabs when she heard Holbarki call her name.

"Yes, you, little flower with the golden hair! Come here, Odette."

Holbarki had finished his drink and turned on the bench so he straddled it with his heavy legs. Odette stared numbly as he patted his meaty right thigh, and when he waved her to come to him she looked to where Lord Ingven stood under one of the willow trees. He appeared lost in his thoughts until Holbarki spoke her name a third time, now impatiently.

Lord Ingven came and took the box from her hands. "Appease the old dog for a time and he'll be on his way."

Odette had to swallow the protest that rose to her throat but she obeyed and walked to Holbarki's table. He laughed and pulled her down on his lap, and the stench of his body made her turn her face. But he did not notice as he kissed first her shoulder and then, drawing her arm out, kissed down to her wrist. Odette struggled to remember that someday she would have to serve men in a capacity much more intimate than this and that it would not be her place to judge but to respect and entertain.

And until I am Unveiled he cannot expect to indulge many liberties!

But just as the thought passed through her mind Holbarki pressed her against his corpulent torso. At once Odette tried to turn her head away, but he grasped her chin and turned her face toward him. His complexion was pasty, his jowls and chin dark with uneven stubble, and unhealthy bags weighted his eyes. Although these eyes were a lively shade of blue there was no depth beyond the color, no hint of intellect or even circumspection.

"You have the look of a frightened rabbit," he said thickly and pulled the ends of her hair teasingly. "Is this not nice, to sit with a real man?"

Odette had to bite back the remark that came immediately to mind. He chuckled absently and lifted one of her breasts with a large clumsy hand. Flicking the loop there he rolled the nipple between his finger and thumb and pulled it out from the loop. This irritated Odette mercilessly. She sought something else to dwell upon as she bore his touch; and as he began to torment the other breast and to massage her thighs she thought of the handsome, clean stewards desperately.

But when he turned her face again and planted a kiss to her lips the anger drove her grace clean away. She growled without thought or intention. He laughed again, his dull eyes betraying no comprehension of her loathing for him. He held her tighter, so tight she could hardly breathe enough to smell him now, and she felt his hand slip down between her thighs. He pinched the flesh there and she jumped.

She growled again and his hand came about her head to cover her mouth. She watched, outraged and helpless, as he pried her legs apart with the other, slobbering over her cheek one moment, laughing at her smoldering glare the next.

When his fingers touched the shield over her clitoris she thrashed her head violently and sank her teeth into the flesh of the hand over her mouth.

He yelled, shocked and angry, and jerked his hand away. She stared at him expectantly, praying the foul man would be done with her now and creep away to whatever filthy lair he'd emerged from. But he did nothing but slap her thigh.

"Spoiled vixen!"

Instead of releasing her Holbarki clamped the end of her braid in one hand, pulling her head back painfully on her neck, and bellowed for the steward.

Lord Ingven was fully roused from his inner thoughts as he scrambled to the table. "What is it? Something wrong, sir?"

"This flower bites," Holbarki said, yet even as the words seethed from between his teeth, the fingers of the hand between her thighs brushed through her pubic hair.

The steward's eyes widened and he looked at Odette for a single shocked moment.

"She will be punished immediately, sir!" He snatched Odette's wrist, much to her relief.

"No. I demand to have her services for the rest of the day," Holbarki said, and Odette's chest swelled with panic. She tried to wrest herself from him then, which only made him hold her tighter.

"I mean this as no offense, sir," he went on, "but I think she has suffered for lack of a mature man's supervision. Give her to me and I shall teach her what befalls a flower who scorns her betters."

Lord Ingven frowned. "I apologize for her behavior, sir, and I know Mistress Helrose will see to it you are adequately compensated; but you would have to consult Lord Eryan before taking this flower."

"Are you afraid to make a decision without his consent? Are you not in charge of these girls?"

"I am."

"Then you know you owe it to Mistress Helrose's reputation to make amends, yes? I would hope that you do not hold my past against me, sir, for though I have been censured by certain parties, it is established that I've never harmed any woman."

"No, sir, I would never have suggested that." Ingven regarded Odette thoughtfully. "But, she is a maiden yet."

"I shan't compromise her chastity, this I vow," Holbarki stated. "I seek only to give a naughty girl a lesson in respect, which evidently her *master* has failed to instill. I shall see to it she is escorted safely home by nightfall."

Odette whimpered and struggled to get loose from the merchant. But her struggle only brought a disappointed furrow to Ingven's brow.

"This is your promise, sir?"

"If I say it, I mean it."

The steward at last sighed and said to Odette, "You will attend this man, Odette, or I shall have no choice but to report this incident to Lord Eryan."

Strong words, but Odette knew he was seeking only to do the right thing. And even if she wanted to protest as Holbarki released her hair and pinched her nipples smartly she knew by the way Ingven watched that nothing she could say would change his mind. She had brought this consequence on herself and she felt close to weeping for it. Why had she not simply endured Holbarki's touch? He would not have sought to take her chastity on the Mistress's own property after being specifically forbidden to do so. Now she had no choice but to accompany him, terrified that he would break his vow to the steward at the first convenient moment.

How she longed for Lord Eryan. Holbarki possessed none of his stern composure, and so much better was Eryan's painful, swift and sure punishments than this uncertain terror!

Chapter Eighteen

olbarki tethered Odette with a short leather leash that obliged her to hobble when combined with the chain between her legs. As they walked through the crowded streets she searched desperately everywhere for sign of Lord Eryan, but she did not see him or hear his voice.

Down the main thoroughfare Holbarki took her, past the king's castle and the rows of temples and guild houses, into the eastern section of town where the smiths' private houses stood and the temple of Thor. Leading off from the main thoroughfare was a dirt path that led up a small hill. Odette followed the merchant up the path and was amazed to see tables set all about, cluttered with items of every imaginable use: riding gear, household wares, farmer's tools. One table was strewn with blankets and other clothing items, all heaped in untidy piles. A tall wooden pole was set in the ground to her left, studded with at least a half-dozen iron rods from which hung everything from hammers to tunics to whips.

The house that stood atop the hill was bereft of maintenance, the only neglected building Odette had seen in all her time in Athla. Two short, dark girls ran through the door as Holbarki approached. They carried boxes stuffed full of doorknobs, nails and other things. Only the barest of nods did they give Holbarki as they passed, and he acknowledged the trifling gesture with a benign smile and led Odette into the house.

The front room was large and cluttered, but bright for the flood of light through the dusty windows from which the curtains had been drawn; and cheerful talk flowed among the tables set up all about. The smell of food, old and freshly cooked both, clung to the stagnant air. The tables were all covered over with things better maintained than the neglected items outside. Woven mats of exotic designs stretched across one while on another stood an assembly of footstools fashioned of solid ivory. Many tables glittered with objects of gold and other precious metals, vases and lanterns, statues and jewelry, boxes and puzzles. The walls were hardly visible for the animal skins, tapestries and rugs, though here and there Odette found a niche filled with some small precious object.

Men browsed through the items, though it seemed they'd come more to exchange conversation than to purchase; and another dark, naked girl carried a silver tray through their midst, offering tiny glasses of wine and mead.

One of the men, his pretty brown-haired woman on a leash by his side, approached Holbarki. "What have you here, friend? I thought you purchased only elven girls?"

Odette's curiosity was whetted now, and she stared at the serving girl. She noticed a faint but swirling aura to the girl's burnished skin, distinctly different from the pulsing colorful auras produced by humans. The girl's eyebrows were pronounced and more arched than that of human women as well. Her succulent lips Odette quite envied, and her torso was shorter than the average mortal female, as were her limbs. Her voluptuous breasts and hips were flawlessly proportioned.

The girl suddenly jerked her attention away from the customer she served. She threw a savage glare at Odette, who flushed and heard Holbarki laugh good-naturedly.

"Do not be offended, Theli. This little bird has probably never set eyes on an elf. She is from the Outer Realm—a gift from Mistress Helrose, at least for today. Our friends from the north wind shall be arriving later. Do you not agree they will be most interested in seeing this fair one?"

Odette was surprised by the familiarity with which Holbarki spoke to the girl, but more by the phrase he'd used. She had been in Athla long enough to know that *from the north wind* referred to the light elves.

The patron cleared his throat uneasily. "Best be careful, friend. Do not forget that levy last year almost put you out the kingdom's gates."

"I have no intention of bartering her to the Darklings," Holbarki said, absentmindedly patting Odette's head. "I want to gauge the reactions of the light elves only. At least then I shall know how much to offer Mistress Helrose in the future."

The leashed woman stepped from one foot to another and her master smiled down at her tenderly. "You are tired? We shall go." He looked at Holbarki. "You know, Helrose is aware that the Darklings come to the boundaries to trade with you. She will never barter on account of this. No self-respecting individual would, my friend. Why not wait and prove yourself washed of last year's escapade?"

Holbarki shrugged. "If not this flower, there are others. And I know for certain there is one amongst her flowers who has routinely rejected her education, one who has vowed to leave Athla altogether if given the chance. Helrose has said to me already she is at wit's end about the girl and tempted to give her freedom. That one would make an ideal recruit for the Darklings. Certainly, I will never again introduce a girl to the Darklings, but there is no law against accepting a commission for submitting the name of a possible volunteer."

This unguarded conversation intrigued Odette more and more and some of her fears waned a little. She listened intently as the patron said "It is regrettable when a young lady proves more lazy or proud than willing to learn. If this girl rejects our ways, it is best she go to the Darkling world, unless she would rather face the Wastelands. The civilized have nothing to fear of that wretched place, of course, blessed be the Lady."

This last statement Odette understood. The Darkling elves—descendants of Loki—were allowed guarded visits into Athla in honor of one of their ancestresses who had been a daughter of Freyja. They could not enter the boundaries but by special permit and even then their numbers were held in check. Because the Darklings despised Freyja and the tenets of The Great Balance they were held in suspicion. Their hatred of Athlans did limit their own desire for contact, though they came occasionally to barter; and they had attempted on several occasions to recruit citizens to work in their mines by promising salvation from what they termed "false hope."

Humans were the only ones who ever accepted their canon—a dismal doctrine that maintained pleasure and hope and love were only misleading delusions. In their realm, the Darklings promised, their recruits would find salvation from this false hope by knowing oblivion of the senses and of optimism. The means by which this was effected remained the Darklings' secret, but Athlan law sought to protect all by making it illegal to mingle with the recruiters. Only a few had ever been known to succumb to the Darkling propaganda, and only from among those born outside the boundaries. Odette understood now the commerce practices that had incurred Holbarki's legal problems must have stemmed from introducing some angry or disillusioned soul to these Darkling recruiters.

It was almost incomprehensible to Odette that a man raised in the chivalric codes of Athla could end up as unethical as many of the Midgardian men who had touched her life. At last she understood her innate repulsion for Holbarki. It had nothing to do with his want of hygiene or even his ill-mannered behavior. Her fear had turned a new direction and more urgently than ever she wanted to be out of his company.

Holbarki's business apparently hadn't suffered much from his stay in the Hold. As the patron departed with his woman Odette felt a twinge of apprehension, but Holbarki seemed to have forgotten her as he conversed with his other potential customers; and so she wandered from table to table and looked through the paraphernalia. As the elven girl passed her she felt a stab of jealousy. The girl's breasts were large as well as exquisite and her flesh like polished gold. Compared to such exotic beauty Odette felt plain and undesirable.

After awhile the customers began to leave. The last of them was a pair of young men who stood talking by the doorway. Holbarki, who had been guzzling the last of the wine from the elf girl's tray, cast his eyes Odette's way. They widened and he grinned and, putting the glass down, sauntered over and took her by the arm.

"Almost forgot you, lovely."

He led her to the back of the room. There, between two great tapestries hanging on the wall were the only implements of discipline she'd seen in the entire place: a narrow trestle bolted to the wall several inches above the floor, and high above it a pair of brass cuffs set into the wall.

"Come, sweeting," he said, and lifted her by the waist and set her feet on the trestle. "Look pretty for me, with no tears, and I'll give a trinket to take home with you."

After he had snapped her wrists into the cuffs above her head her weight rested solely on the balls of her feet. She felt stretched and unsteady. Holbarki unwove her braid then so that her hair fell in thick rivulets over either shoulder. He pinched her cheeks smartly so they flushed, and then her nipples. Lastly, he slapped either side of each of her breasts and the sides of her buttocks so these areas of flesh were all rosy.

"Radiant," he murmured when he was finished. He pinched her thigh and sauntered off to the front of the room.

Odette was quickly aware of the encompassing quiet of this shadowy part of the room. As she wondered how long Holbarki would leave her displayed or if he'd just forget her again she felt like a helpless ornament.

After a long time the solitude was broached when the elven girl she'd stared at before walked by. She carried a folded blanket over one arm and this she deposited carelessly on a table past the tapestry to Odette's left. There was a certain disgruntled look on the girl's face, a frown that Odette could not quite decipher. When she returned she stopped and looked up into Odette's face. It was her turn to stare now, and her hard azure eyes made Odette turn hers away uncomfortably.

Suddenly, the girl reached out and touched Odette's belly with a forefinger. With her fingertip she stroked Odette all the way up to her right breast, and this she seized and kneaded roughly, pulling the loop this way and that, tugging it out and twisting the nipple until Odette cried out. Apparently satisfied with this, she parted Odette's nether lips with her hands and inspected the soft flesh beneath. The little shield she snapped up and she touched the clitoris. It beat wildly as she patted it this way and that and Odette felt a bolt of electricity shoot through her pelvis. It took all her effort to keep from arching hungrily toward the malicious girl.

At last the girl put the shield back in place and took her hands away; she pouted irritably.

"My master says he would barter me for you," she said. "I hope your Mistress consents."

She walked briskly away then. Odette's passion waned to but an irritable simmer but she was angry the girl had tormented her. Yet she could not stop thinking of that touch or of the girl's admission. She yearned to experience the very humiliations and punishments that to Odette had often seemed the most unbearable of indignities.

Odette grew restless as her shoulders ached. She did not fear Holbarki's taking her maidenhood—no, his attentions were hardly drawn to his own girls, let alone the property of another. His passion was for monetary gain, not women. The most ambitious threat he posed was the possibility he might sell the right of taking her maidenhood, and that she doubted he would attempt yet.

Odette shuffled her toes over the trestle to keep them from growing numb and mused over the conversation between Holbarki and the patron. She pondered over which of Mistress Helrose's flowers Holbarki referred to when he said there was one she was tempted to free. Whoever the girl was Odette was sure the Mistress would warn her to stay away from the Darklings.

She heard someone enter the house and soon she heard Holbarki speaking with another man. She figured it must be one of his light elf friends he was expecting. They could come and go freely in Athla and their artists had a penchant for Athlan trinkets, which, obviously, Holbarki could supply easily enough.

Two silhouettes approached from the front of the room.

"My finest stirrups are on a table in the back," she heard Holbarki say, "in front of the tapestries."

She watched as the merchant stepped out of sight and the other figure advanced. It was a man, so focused in his purpose he seemed unaware of everything else. An Outer Realm soldier, she guessed by his worn boots and scuffed scale mail and the much-used scabbard at his back. He was sweaty and unshaven, his mustache thick and dark as his short hair. He was stalwart but not overly tall, his neck was thick but smoothly attractive under the stubbled chin. Evidently weary from travel he showed none of the eagerness most visitors to Athla came in with, nor the satisfaction of having prevailed against the hardships of the Wasteland to enter the fabled borders. No, this Outer Realmer's demeanor was like none she'd ever beheld before. She could not read the look but she was sure of it, so glaring was it behind his weariness.

As if this were but a stop on some journey he'd rather have over, Odette thought.

The warrior's almond-shaped eyes glittered like dark coals as he examined the stirrups displayed; his face was grim, preoccupied. Odette breathed shallowly, hoping he would find whatever it was he needed and go away. The elf girl's attentions had been one thing; she did not want to endure a man's touch without the protection of Lord Eryan or one of the stewards she knew.

For several minutes he browsed through the collection, his tanned brow creased; and even in her frightened impatience Odette could not take her eyes from him. He was different from the men of Athla with the animal-like energy that radiated from his very being. Not even the Athlan soldiers exuded such an aura of raw power...and it stirred something very deep in her sex that bade her to plead for but one glance from his beautiful eyes.

She chastised herself silently. Certainly, she should be glad this Outer Realm warrior had other concerns. Surely, he was no more than a barbarian who had stumbled out of the Wastelands and been allowed to enter the borders simply because of his personal tolerance, not because he'd quested to find Athla. Otherwise, she told herself, he would be overjoyed to be in the realm and probably already have his own serving girl on a chain by his side.

But her sex was wet and throbbing. She closed her eyes and tried to think of nothing as she waited for him to leave.

Holbarki's voice piped close by. "Find what you need, good sir?" Odette heard the man mumble something indistinct and the merchant went on. "You have come to the right place. Unlike many merchants in this realm I understand the practical needs of the Midgardians. You need something, I will do my utmost to make it available hastily. You do not need to dally about while I craft the thing from raw materials or imbue it with magical incantations or artistic fancies."

"No?" The soldier sounded bored, and Odette opened her eyes just enough to peek out and saw the dissatisfaction on his face.

"My own mother is from the Outer Realm," Holbarki explained. "She told me time and again the more common-sense habits of her people as compared to the

Athlan folk. With their lax lifestyles, they have no conception of necessity. The blacksmiths, for example, save you be one of the street sentries or a member of the army or royal guard, would put you on a waiting list."

The soldier's mouth turned up in a smile. "Well, perhaps your king pays highly to promote such an enthusiasm to join his army."

Holbarki laughed overmuch; and by the hardening of the soldier's smile Odette knew he saw clear through the merchant's ingratiating polish.

"I am sorry, but I do not find...what I need. Where may I find the closest ironworks?"

Holbarki darkened, but his gloss did not fade. "There is Reir and his son, just down the avenue, the red stone house." Seeing the soldier nod he added, "I see by the fashion of your mail you favor Celtic work. I have just a few days ago received a cargo of horse blankets from friends in Brittany you may be interested in."

The soldier's brows rose. "Celt? From which tribe?"

"A tribe friendly with the Frisians, who give them aid against Boniface's crusading monks."

The soldier's face grew thoughtful again. He rubbed the back of his neck and glanced about, and in that moment he discovered Odette. At once his somberness fled. A heated, almost dazed smile softened his mouth and he gazed at her with an intensity that made her tremble. She lowered her eyes instantly, and as she endured the blush that scorched her entire face she prayed he would look away again.

Instead, he walked over to the trestle and raised his fingertips to the ends of her hair over her left shoulder. Her heart beat so rapidly that her ears rung.

"I was shocked—pleasantly, that is—when I entered your realm and found the women running about unencumbered by wasteful apparel," he said to Holbarki, "and when the guide who led me in explained that this is custom, well, I thought for a few moments I had passed into the realm of the fey."

Odette felt stifled with heat as his dark eyes canvassed her flesh. And though she sought to turn her face away, those same penetrating eyes drained her will.

"She is quite real, as are all our lovelies," said Holbarki. "However, this little flower has been displayed for viewing pleasure alone. She belongs to Mistress Helrose, one of our most esteemed priestesses, and has not yet been Unveiled."

The soldier threw him a questioning glance. "Unveiled?"

"This girl is a virgin novice of Freyja and will not receive her official status until the ceremony of the Unveiling, in which the privilege of deflowering her goes to the one who offers the highest donation to the sacred order."

Odette was chagrined that her fate was spoken of so casually, especially before the ears of this brutal soldier. A moment later he touched her collarbone and Odette whimpered at the heat of his fingers. Both men laughed softly and she tugged angrily at the manacles and drew her legs so tightly together her knees dug into one another.

As if in tardy answer to her prayer a clamor issued suddenly from the front of the house. Holbarki turned and the soldier withdrew his hand reluctantly from Odette.

"I will see who that is," Holbarki said, just before a voice thundered through the room.

"Trader!" The newcomer spoke with a thick accent and his tone of impatience boomed against the walls.

The soldier's brow creased as footsteps tramped loudly toward the back of the room. Odette saw several figures—small, slim men all—geared in heavy chain mail and gauntlets and helmets, though they carried no weapons but for empty scabbards and sheaths. Their darkly tinted faces were sharp-featured and their eyes large and blazing black. The armor of the one leading was stained with old gore, his iron-plated boots mucked over. He halted before Holbarki and for once the merchant's pretentious demeanor seemed frail.

"My friends," he said warily. "I was not expecting you."

"We are in need of supplies," the leader responded. His huge eyes lifted to Odette and the fine jaw tightened with utter disapproval. "You still retain these lurid examples of decadence?"

At once the soldier's face hardened, and he stepped between the Darklings and Odette with his feet widely apart, his hand rising to the hilt of his sword.

The Darkling leader's lips turned up in a baleful smile. "A defender, of course. These trifling creatures have a talent for seducing the common sense from even the most stalwart amongst their kind."

Holbarki tittered. "Loic, let us go speak alone," he said and laid a hand on the leader's shoulder.

"Outside," the Darkling grunted, "where the stench is not so pervasive."

The soldier's knuckles whitened over the hilt and he held his stance adamantly as Holbarki accompanied the band outside.

When the door had fallen shut Odette swallowed hard. His defense of her could have been no more proper or chivalrous had he been born and raised in Athla. She hated that she'd so misjudged him. After several long moments he drew his hand down from the hilt and turned and looked at her. He said nothing, but his scrutiny felt as if it alone could ravish her, weaken the metal that bound her and make her fall into his expectant embrace. So many secrets she gleaned just behind those beautiful dark eyes, some sweet and others painful, and defining them all a proud and uncompromising will.

Odette strained in the manacles, wanting his burning gaze to turn away, to stop making her pulse race like a butterfly confined.

Holbarki came back and cold sweat broke out over her flesh as the soldier turned reluctantly away. The merchant seemed shaken as they returned to the front of the room to speak. Odette heard them converse for a long while, though their words she could not catch. Finally, she heard the door swing open and close again, and Holbarki trotted to her. She could see his hands trembling as he released her to stand on the floor.

"I'm afraid I'll have to send you home now,"

Through the grimed windows as he led her forward she saw that daylight was relenting to coming twilight.

"Stay here till I come back," he said, and disappeared through a door. He returned a minute later accompanied by a filthy youth with a bowl of disheveled sandy hair.

"I was just sitting to eat," the boy whined. He regarded Odette sullenly and wiped his mouth with the back of his hand.

Holbarki's mouth pursed. "Just take her home, for the love of Thor, and send the girls to eat when you get back and close down for the day. I have to go into town."

The youth snatched Odette's hand and stepped to the door. "Into town? I thought the light ones were expected."

Holbarki snorted. "Their ministers have closed their own borders."

The youth shrugged and pulled Odette out the door. Never had the air smelled so fresh to her as outside Holbarki's cluttered abode. The evening air was cool and made her shiver, but she was so glad to be going home she hardly noticed. Down the dirt path her escort stomped, and onward to the street. The street was almost empty now, the torches in the temples just being lit by the respective priests and priestesses. Across the city the youth yanked Odette, making her bare soles slap the pavement in an uneven, painful gait, grumbling about the chain that limited her strides.

"What a foolish thing—only a mad man would want to hear someone shuffling at their back with every step!"

Odette flushed angrily and only her training kept her from kicking the bumpkin's backside and telling him she would prefer to walk home alone than be escorted by a cockless boy. She could not help but think of the soldier back at Holbarki's who had defended her and admired her and glazed her flesh with raw heat with his touch.

Just as they passed the castle grounds she saw a silhouette marching toward them from the direction of the western square. The youth did not notice, but as he came nearer Odette recognized the face and her heart quickened happily to see the rage that paled it to a glowing white.

"You," Lord Eryan thundered, pointing at the youth so that he stopped in his hateful tracks. "Remove your hands from my property!"

The bumpkin stammered, "Sir, I-I was just returning your girl. I swear it!"

Lord Eryan took Odette's hand and pulled her to his side. He looked her over, gently turning her this way and that as he scrutinized her completely. The youth cringed on his feet, whiter than even Eryan now.

"Inform Holbarki that he is forbidden from entering the property of Mistress Helrose. And if I discover he has taken liberties with this girl I shall not await justice by petition of the king's judgment but will take matters into my own hands."

The youth nodded earnestly. "Yes, yes...but I swear, there were no liberties taken."

Lord Eryan's raised his hand as if he would strike the boy, but he stayed his arm and snarled softly, "I shall believe whatever my slave reports, not the babbling of some sniveling half-man. Now go and deliver my message."

The boy turned at once and fled. Lord Eryan turned Odette by her shoulders and examined her again. The anger in his face was so dreadful she cringed as the youth had.

But the next moment he embraced her tenderly, securely; and her arms went about his neck and she breathed easily at last.

"I do not blame you, Odette," he said softly. "This was but another contrivance on Holbarki's part. If I had not had business to attend in town today it would never have happened."

He escorted her back then to the clean and familiar manor. Dinner was just being served as they entered the house. Mistress Helrose left her guests to meet them and, obviously aware of what had transpired, bade Odette sit with the other flowers to eat. As Odette took a place on the floor beside Rystla she managed to put aside the remaining irritation for Holbarki.

But when the meal was completed Mistress Helrose ordered a steward to bring Lord Ingven in from the courtyard. She upbraided him lengthily in her cool, articulate voice for allowing the merchant to take Odette without either Eryan's consent or her own. He was contrite, quick and earnest in apology to the Mistress and to Lord Eryan. As the Mistress dismissed him she cautioned him against any future blunders lest he wished to lose his place in her household.

Odette almost pitied Ingven's shame. But he took it all honorably and sank to his knees by Helrose's chair and kissed her hand, thanking her for giving him another chance and apologizing again. When he rose at last he approached the hearth and bowed to one knee before Odette.

"I regret my neglect to thee, flower. Please forgive any harm this has wrought and know I shall never again neglect my service to any woman."

He rose and went out again and the room echoed with silence.

Later, in Lord Eryan's room, Mistress Helrose questioned Odette over what Holbarki had done; and she was satisfied when Odette assured the man had taken no liberties.

"Holbarki took advantage of my friendship," Helrose said as she stood behind Odette, whom she had directed to the pallet on the floor. She smoothed Odette's hair with her long fingers. "Once you have been Unveiled, certainly you shall have to accompany any who wish to taste your pleasures in town. But it is an integral part of your training that while you are prompted with desire your maidenhood remain intact. Your Unveiling, of course, draws close."

Lord Eryan stood with his back against a wall, sipping an elixir of flowery bouquet. "Are you certain of this, sister?"

Odette could not see the Mistress's face but she felt the coolness that crept over her. "Yes. Tomorrow, in fact, I wish you to distribute the announcements."

Lord Eryan stared at Odette languidly. "Is there to be the regular announcement at the temple as well?"

"Certainly—why wouldn't there be?" Mistress Helrose walked to him. "Eryan, it is my decision. For you have I given much. Do not question me about this."

A sad, ghostly smile touched his lips. "Think you I have forfeited my self-restraint?"

Odette saw the affection on Helrose's face. "No, never that." She kissed his cheek then smiled at Odette before she walked out the door, leaving them alone.

"Time for sleep," Eryan said and he knelt beside Odette as she crawled under the blanket. He brushed the hair from her face and gazed at her a time. His sadness pained her, and she sensed he wanted to say something. But he kept his words to himself and shortly he left her alone to sleep.

"I love you both," she whispered aloud. It was true. As well, she loved almost everyone in the Mistress's household. And she longed to comfort Lord Eryan. But that was not to be. No, he was a steward, self-restrained and responsible, and she but the novice and she could only wait and hope he would share his burden.

She thought of what Helrose had said of her upcoming Unveiling. No fear did it instill in her now, no sense of shame, no doubt of morality. She was content in being the woman she was learning to be. She had survived and passed the trials, and she looked excitedly to her future. Gone forever was the girl nurtured by ideals shallow and intolerant. As an innocent child in Honi's household she had known security without price, taking it without thought of giving anything in return. The lessons in Mistress Helrose's care had prepared her to give as well as receive. Demanding was life for women of Athla, but every demand had its corresponding expectation: honor for respect, chivalry for vulnerability, adoration for submission. A mutual exchange between men and women that defined, fulfilled and exalted their differences.

She turned on the pallet and sighed, content for the first time in all her life. Mind and spirit—soul, as well—and her body embraced the relentless passion the lessons inflamed.

As she drifted to sleep she thought of the soldier again, with his penetrating dark eyes and roughly handsome features. She sighed regretfully, for soon she would belong to all those who sought her pleasures, and it was improper and selfish indeed to dwell on the attractions of a single man.

Chapter Nineteen

he first thing Cu'lugh did on arriving in Athla was to find a stable and suitable blacksmith to attend his horse. The journey through the Wasteland had been more wearing than the priest Hrowthe had forewarned, and his horse had thrown two shoes.

The guide who had led him into the city showed him the way to the trader's slovenly abode, the only place available for immediate obtainment of riding gear. But Cu'lugh had come away without the horseshoes and without the new stirrups he'd needed for some time. He reminded himself stridently that he was pledged to Vanda and could not linger, not for the moment, anyway. However, his quest would take much less time than he'd expected…he had pressed the trader to reveal the identity of the girl on the wall.

Clearly, some divine intervention had led him to stop first at the trader's—God, Jesus, whoever—and so there was naught to do now but get a good night's sleep and try to thank fate that he would shortly be back again with Vanda. Once rested, he could devise a plan. For the time being, though, he had to forget the girl.

The guide had also given him directions to an inn that served Gaelic ale and he sought it now, walking the long distance to the quieting northern district of the city. Set amongst the picturesque private homes that dotted either side of the street, the inn was a large white building painted in the Italian style with a wide ambling portico. As Cu'lugh approached the portico he was splashed by the children wading in the water from the Well of Nana in the center of the street. It was late but there they played in the twilight-sparkled waters as their mothers sat watching from the rim, throwing in an occasional coin and gossiping with one another. Cu'lugh had been shocked by their scantily provocative clothing, yet the men seemed only too proud to watch, too, or lead other women by leashes attached to princely collars upon their throats.

Except for the pool there was little activity on the street. He heard voices from within houses and caught the scents of food through the windows. He turned into the portico and discovered that halfway through it enlarged into a spacious area decked with wrought iron chairs and tables set with vases filled with hyacinths and sprigs of herbs. Two narrow wooden benches sat to either side of the wide center. The legs of these had been bolted solidly to the stones and six cushions were affixed along the tops of each. Flanking each cushion were fetters. Four girls knelt before one of these tables, their chins propped on a cushion while their wrists were fettered securely. These pretty faces were every one suffused with frustration, their eyes lowered or closed in shame. Their uplifted buttocks were rosy all, lightly welted here and there. Cu'lugh paused to look upon the astonishing scene.

One of the girls glared at him, her pouting lips only making her restraint all the more lovely. A young man emerged from the inn carrying a polished wooden paddle. The girls whimpered when they saw him, and as he stepped behind them and raised the paddle their hips began to dart from side to side and their buttocks to brace. To each firm backside he delivered a sound spanking, the sound of which resounded throughout the portico, dimming the cries of the chagrined receivers.

The sight spurred in Cu'lugh a most urgent desire. He watched without interference, savoring the sight even as he wondered what they had done to deserve such a public chastisement. He did not truly care, either, only that their distress was delightful to witness, a spectacle he enjoyed.

A small voice from his distant youth carped that he should turn away—the voice of propriety, or at least propriety as he'd been taught it in the hypocritical household of his father. Sin, it hissed, for women to go about unclothed. Base for men to take pride in that nakedness. And sin unmitigated to know a moment's pleasure in the doling of punishment to wicked flesh.

Cu'lugh laughed to himself, remembering the duplicity of those who had created the voice. Holy men, in the household of his two-faced father. They despised women and the carnal act. But the impotent priests had never been above accepting gifts and property in exchange for an indulgence of his father's countless liaisons.

Two or three other men passed by, nodding in greeting to Cu'lugh, giving approving smiles to the youth with the paddle. The women who trotted after them on their golden and leather leashes did not show horror or even flinch at the punishment taking place before them. It occurred to Cu'lugh they had probably known their own share of such chastening and would likely experience more in the future.

At last the youth stopped his paddle and took a seat at one of the tables. Cu'lugh glanced once more at the line of tearful faces and reddened bottoms before walking on to the inn door.

The delicious smell of cooked beef and spices accosted him as he entered. From a room behind the foyer he heard voices. A dark-bearded innkeeper greeted him pleasantly, a fellow as clean and well-mannered as most of the Athlans he had so far encountered—hardly the band of vulgar barbarians that Hrowthe had made them out to be. Cu'lugh requested and paid for two nights' lodging, and as he took the key the innkeeper asked if a girl should be sent up for the length of his sojourn.

"It is an amenity, of course," the innkeeper added. "I do not offer young men, however, though I know where young priests can be contracted or bought."

"No!" Cu'lugh had said it more brusquely than he'd meant. He cleared his throat. "But you have young ladies?"

"Certainly, sir, as you require. And anything else you may need, do not hesitate to inquire. Our cook, I would dare to say, is the best this side of the city."

The thought of enjoying one of the little Athlan girls was tempting. Cu'lugh considered the offer momentarily, knowing it would be the final chance to indulge in sensual pleasures before he married Vanda.

But as her name crossed his thoughts he saw not her but the girl bound on the wall of the trader's house.

Fortune had been kind to him—or cruel, depending on how he looked at it—to have led him straight to the very girl he'd come to find. She possessed none of Vanda's aloof and fierce beauty, yet the naked Odette was stunning with her graceful figure and long golden hair. Her legs were perfectly shaped, exquisitely curved. How he'd wanted to touch those legs, caress the silky skin. Her face was pretty in its own way for its childlike features. And for all her lovely abashment as she hung helpless from the cuffs he had seen an ember of passion barely veiled in her innocent green eyes. It had called out to be kindled—and he would have offered the trader handsomely to keep his silence to the girl's Mistress that he might not just kindle that passion but stoke it hot as the flames of a pyre. And that she resembled—no looked *exactly* like—the vision that had haunted him all his life only deepened his desire to an excruciating level.

If only she had not been who she was.

He declined the innkeeper's offer, and the man summoned a serving wench to take him to his room. She was pretty but her face seemed to vanish each time she smiled his way, her features fading before his eyes into those of Odette. He could not rationalize it but that she was so much like his vision; never before had a woman managed to captivate his thoughts so utterly that he could not be stirred by another pretty face. He gave her a coin for her service and caught a flicker of confusion in her eyes as she retreated back downstairs.

The room was immaculate, with a bed wide and firmly sprung. There was a wardrobe provided and two high-backed chairs, a large trunk where he set the pouch of coins from his belt. A pitcher of water and a bowl for washing had been set on a table by the wall to the right of the door, as well as a bottle of perfumed oil, a razor and strop and other amenities. From the frame of the window hung a basket of lilies and a trailing vine. Cu'lugh threw his scabbard on the bed and went to the window.

A woman with a belly swollen with child crossed the street below. She was garbed in a robe of black—shimmering, revealing gauze—and a collar of spangled black ribbon. An immense dog marched beside her, his eyes darting this way and that dutifully, as if the animal had been trained to protect the woman. From the other end of the street a man strode toward them, his arms outstretched. The woman hurried toward him, embracing him over her belly. The dog's tail lifted and flicked eagerly. Together the three crossed the street and disappeared into the long shadows.

Cu'lugh yawned and stretched. The effects of the strenuous ride through the Wasteland were settling into his limbs. Grabbing the pouch, he lay on the bed and poured the contents over the coverlet. Coins and jewels, a small fortune. His fortune—all he owned besides his gear and sword; the horse he had purchased from Vanda. The money and gold she had insisted he take along lay in a safe box he'd rented at the public stable. Those things he intended to return; it had only been to appease her he'd agreed to take them in the first place. Never had he accepted the monies of a woman, but there had been a measure of good sense in her contention that there might prove to be obstacles in getting Odette out of Athla. He had learned that very often the seemingly most difficult obstacle proved surpassable with a common bribe.

He closed his eyes and rested, not really sleeping, his vision filled with scenes encountered recently. Of the haze of the Wasteland suddenly parting before him and the snow-jagged mountains rising before his eyes. Of a little path that had brought him through these into the vast, sprawling green valley of Athla. So beautiful it was, and then the city with its roofs and turrets gleaming gold and silver in the sunlight. The sentries had met him with the tidings that he would never have found the path in had he lacked the capability of embracing all that he would find therein.

It had captivated him to enter the gates and see the women roaming about, unconcerned with their total subjugation. It was a restraint unlike the one that condemned the women of his world to bear suspicion and injustice for their alleged inheritance of Eve's sin. They had to conceal their bodies beneath layers of fabric, to serve and labor and procreate in shame and without expectation, allowed to hope for a place in heaven only by virtue of the conflicting acceptance and hatred of the sex to which they had been born.

In Athla it seemed to Cu'lugh their enthrallment was based on appreciation instead of aversion. Even from the young girls who had been spanked in the portico he perceived not unhappiness but only a fleeting frustration and embarrassment in their bonds. It was not for him to say if the Athlans were sinful; and perhaps, he considered, many of the women obtained a sense of security in enduring what they did here.

And what of Odette? If she had found that, too, who was he to take it from her? *I am a man obligated elsewhere.*

He owed Vanda his life—oh, yes—and he'd made his vow. He tried to envision her as he had whilst he'd lived under her roof, her demure glances and comely face, her striking blue eyes. The images were gracious, but he felt nothing. She had incited his passion because she was a woman, and there had been no relief of that passion to be had. Now he was surrounded by available women, and he did not care if he had her or not. Yet, he now had no desire to take delight in the lovelies at his service, either.

Not even the desperation he knew Vanda had surely endured all this time over Odette's safety diminished the potent desire that had come over him. It was Odette he wanted and no one else. And he was angered to think of the ridiculousness of it, how unlike himself he was acting. Many women he had taken pleasure in—they were always delightful in some way or other; they all had their qualities and talents. Why should he not enjoy one of the Athlan girls? He had little time for regret; life was too short for that.

I am possessed by a malady, surely, to want what should not be had.

Despite the rational thought a part of him argued there was something more, and again he saw Odette hanging on the wall before him. How he wanted to make her thighs writhe beneath his bolting passion, if but to relieve himself of this madness.

Cu'lugh wondered darkly where she was that very moment. He had not known until the trader told him that Odette was related to the Athlan queen. With that kinship her keeper undoubtedly kept an even closer eye on her than on her sister novices. And in that guarded sanctuary, wherever it was, what eyes were drinking their fill of Odette's succulent limbs and sweet face now? Envious, his frustrated thoughts drifted into a mazy half-dream. He saw himself in a shadowy house, come to take Odette from the manacles with which she was fettered. The point of his sword lay across a man's throat as he ordered that Odette be released. The man grimaced and fumbled through his vest for the key.

"*You* have the key," Odette's voice said from behind him. "You always have had."

The skies were darker when consciousness snapped back. He was sweating and his manhood had stiffened under his breeches. Getting up from the bed he unlaced them and lowered his member into the bowl and doused it with the water from the pitcher. When at last his desire had diminished to but a dull ache in his loins he dried with a linen cloth and purposely put his thoughts to other bodily needs.

The tables downstairs were crowded with hungry patrons. Cu'lugh took a seat in the back of the room, close to where a minstrel sat on a stool with his lute. The melody of his song was catching but Cu'lugh did not recognize the language, though many others in the room sang along.

He ordered the honeyed capons, which his serving girl declared was the cook's specialty, and a jug of ale. When the food came Cu'lugh ate ravenously and drank more than he'd intended. The ale mellowed his mood and even the chafing thoughts of Odette dulled a little.

As he finished off the jug and listened to the minstrel, he sighted a serving girl who reminded him much of Vanda. He thought back on the vow he'd made, of the cheer it had brought to Vanda's pretty face. As he prepared to set out from her land he had paused and kissed her hand before mounting his horse and reassured her again. How pale the blue washed in her eyes, but there was a flicker of immodesty across her lips. Her small fingers laced around the back of his neck and she had kissed his mouth with none of the matronly decorum of before.

"Promise not to fall into the temptation of that horrid land, my love. Come back and fall into my arms instead of abiding whoredom's embrace."

Her gaze had been hard, desperate, imploring…and yet her passion had seemed directed to something besides him, as if she were pleading with more than just one man.

He had nodded and kissed her again and then rode off toward the Wasteland wondering over the mysterious display of passion. So much had she promised and so disappointed now would she be to know the full extent of his temptation.

As he drained his tankard he saw on the other side of the room a man at a table with one of the little serving girls on his lap. He lavished kisses on her throat, stroking her breasts as he did. The girl squirmed and giggled bashfully. And near a table in a dim corner stood a pair of noblemen. One of them held a serving girl with her fair hands above her head whilst his companion stroked her glistening sex. She moaned huskily but no one else seemed to notice. Cu'lugh's manhood surged and he tried to imagine the tightness of the girl's hot orifice, or that of any of the other delicious creatures flitting around the room.

All he could see was a tremulous face peering down through the veil of gold.

Cu'lugh's slammed his fist down on the table, bringing the attention of several of the other patrons. He did not care. Damned Hrowthe, by whose mysterious talent for far-seeing Vanda had believed her sister was to be found in the king's household. He had planned to make the king's acquaintance and offer his mercenary experience to procure access to the property and then to those entrusted with guarding the girl. All his adult life Cu'lugh had acted with foresight, methodically planning the details of dealing with the situations that came before him. He disliked haste and more so the unseen. Of course, catastrophe had come before but he had dealt with it by his wits. Not until he had unexpectedly laid eyes on Odette had composure ever eluded him; and he feared secretly his wits would be next to go.

As he wondered how a single pretty face could so jeopardize his very constitution, he looked at the empty plate on the table before him. A meal that sufficed, but one he had not truly tasted.

Like marriage without love.

He sighed. Why should he regret now? He was frustrated, that was all. Why, Vanda was beautiful and what he could teach her in the marriage bed was enough to enliven any marriage of convenience. He was too old to quest after ideals of love. Besides, from what he had seen in the world only a fool would trust another human being entirely, and romantic love was based in large part on just that kind of trust. Thierry's mother had given her love and trust to his father only to be discounted as his court harlot. And Thierry had loved only to discover the object of his adoration loved him in but the most pious and provincial of ways.

He would marry Vanda and enjoy what he was offered from the arrangement. As he had no intention of attempting to separate her from her piety and interests, they would both be content.

Even the most practical and potentially beneficial alliances had their requisites, and this one required of him only the meeting of a promise.

He bade the nearest serving girl to bring another ale. While she filled his cup he quite consciously ogled her wide hips and muscled legs. Not his preference in women, but she was comely and he was easily tantalized by her large, deep-rose nipples that showed over her short bodice. Her eyes widened when he thrust a coin into her hand, and Cu'lugh grinned as she scampered away, her black tresses flying, to show the amused innkeeper what she'd been given.

A few minutes later her face blurred altogether from memory. He was almost thankful for the pain of his spent muscles, and the thought of sleep called him to finish his ale and return to his room. As he reached for the mug a strong current blasted through the room from the front of the house; and raising his eyes, he saw a woman enter the dining chamber. Garbed in a green cape, she walked tall and proud and pulled a chain behind her. Attached to the end of this chain was a collar that encircled the throat of a young man. Cu'lugh gaped. Except for his breeches of soft beige velvet the youth was naked, and he crawled bear-like on hands and feet as the woman took a seat an available table.

She snapped her fingers and the youth squatted at her feet. His eyes lowered submissively—contentedly, even. The serving girl who came running up showed no concern for such an astonishing spectacle.

Cu'lugh frowned and imbibed the last trickle of his drink. He could not take his eyes from them. When the girl had taken her order the woman eyed Cu'lugh. She smiled, and he managed to nod uneasily. When his serving girl returned he asked her who the woman was.

The girl glanced at the blonde. "Ah, that is Mistress Oni, sir."

"Mistress?" The word reminded Cu'lugh of the information the trader had shared. "A priestess of your faith?"

"Yes, sir."

Cu'lugh looked at the woman again, saw how she stroked the youth's hair with her long nails. She was poised—almost cruelly so—and beautiful, not a woman to be taken lightly. But she was more than that. She was a priestess, as was this Helrose; and he had not yet met a religious type whose sentiments or at least superstitions could not be played upon. Cu'lugh breathed easily, satisfied that his addled wits had decided to obey his will again. A solution to the problem at hand evolved in his mind.

"Do you think by chance she may then know where I may find the other Mistress, Helrose?"

"I am certain she does, sir. We all know Mistress Helrose."

"Yes?" he said happily. "Please do tell me, sweeting."

The girl readily gave him the directions. He committed them to memory and thanked her and put another coin into her hand. Setting the tankard down, he walked toward the door. As he passed Mistress Oni he smiled congenially, noticing, as she did not, the jealous furrow that creased the youth's brow.

Chapter Twenty

he wind had grown cool and brisk, knocking the last of the ale's effects from Cu'lugh's brain as he made his way through the dark streets. The western side of town was a distant walk and few souls did he pass but for an occasional street sentry. One of these men stopped him and asked where he was headed.

"To Mistress Helrose's manor," Cu'lugh answered.

The sentry smiled. "Ah, she has the sweetest girls. You are an Outer Realmer? Mind that you abstain from too much drink. It is improper to forget one's manners, especially in the company of ladies or children."

"Certainly," Cu'lugh answered, "that is only responsible."

The sentry let him pass and soon he reached the western square. The windows of the taverns were flooded with light from within and laughter and conversation floated out into the night air. Up ahead he saw the gates the serving girl had described. A guard stood before them, and as Cu'lugh approached he straightened expectantly.

"May I help you, sir?"

Cu'lugh glanced casually at the property behind the man. Discreetly, he took note of a second guard in the courtyard, of the manor's heavy door and of the woods that encompassed the entire property. His ears registered the faint sound of running water from the back of the grounds and of men's voices from inside the house.

"Mistress Helrose," he said. "I wish to speak with her."

"Does the Lady know—" The guard's words were interrupted by a ripple of laughter from the courtyard, and Cu'lugh saw a shadow skitter through the shadows. The other guard dashed after it, murmuring something huskily. And then Cu'lugh heard a giggle, distinctly feminine.

The guard pursed his mouth. "Wait here."

He retreated into the shadows and spoke with someone. As Cu'lugh waited his discerning eyes made out in the shadows a palisade of poles holding what appeared to be cages. As he studied them he was sure of it; and in one of them he saw the unmistakable figure of a girl. She sat with her back against the bars, huddled under a quilt or blanket. He could not even distinguish if she was awake or asleep, only that the fabric covering her moved in relaxed rhythm with her breathing.

He was staring at the captivating image when the guard marched back, now accompanied by another man, likely the guard Cu'lugh had watched dart into the shadows. He was a head taller than the other; and on second look Cu'lugh realized by the cut of his silk shirt and his high leather boots the man was not likely a common private guard. By the insignia of the bow and crossed arrows on the breast of his laced vest Cu'lugh guessed he was one of the royal archers.

"What is your name," he demanded.

Unwilling to show deference to any peer, Cu'lugh waited a moment before answering. "Forgive me, but I have come to speak with Mistress Helrose."

"Are you known to Mistress Helrose?" the archer demanded.

"No. It is a personal matter. She is Mistress here, is she not?"

The archer stiffened and his hand went to the hilt of the dagger at his waist. "You have not even the decency to give your name, sir. Mistress she may be, but my Lady she most assuredly is. And you shall reveal your name if you wish to request an audience with her."

Cu'lugh breathed slowly and decided to incline his head. "Well done. I am Cu'lugh, from the tribes of the Franks in the Outer Realm."

The archer frowned and was about to reply when someone emerged from the shadows. Draped in indigo cloth brooched at one shoulder, she had features like a combination of honey and steel, and her hazel eyes were unfathomable as she stepped round the firm-footed archer to regard Cu'lugh.

"I am Mistress Helrose. What is your business with me, Sir...Cu'lugh?"

He marveled at the crispness of her voice, considering he suspected the carefree giggle he'd heard only moments before had issued from the same uncompromising lips.

He glanced indifferently at the men. "I have come to ask of the girl, Odette, who was today in the keeping of a trader to the eastern district of the city."

A tiny flicker shone in the Mistress's eyes. "What of her?"

"I wish to make an offer for her."

"You are a visitor, yes? An Outer Realmer?"

Cu'lugh nodded.

She stared at him for several moments and the stony expression of her eyes seemed to become somewhat hazy. "Cu'lugh," she said, her voice suddenly lush and dreamy. "*Hound of the god Lugh.* You are a Celt."

Cu'lugh nodded, not sure if she was experiencing a vision or simply testing his honesty. "I have been told that Celtic blood runs through my veins."

"Ah," she said, her voice but a tender hiss, "you carry a rich Celtic legacy. Your mother scorned her pagan heritage, Merovingian as well as Celt...and yet in memoriam for the Celtic grandsire who loved her she gave her son a name to please his spirit. One to be proud of, one worthy to defend, and more so, to honor by your actions. So, are you as the hound of the god, loyal and single-minded toward all that touches you as sacred?"

Cu'lugh wondered exactly how much of him this woman thought she glimpsed. Whether her visions were untainted or not by her own perceptions, there seemed no malice behind her interest. Still, he had to know how much she thought she at least guessed before he moved on with his plan.

He smiled innocuously. "Do you not know by your spirits?"

She blinked and her eyes focused again. "I know only what the spirits and the gods deem I should know. However, I do sense a practiced sense of purpose in you, Cu'lugh, and a noble conscience that has waited long to be acknowledged."

Cu'lugh bided in silence to allow her to satisfy his interest, and at length she said, "This innate integrity in you is invaluable, good sir. And though you were worthy enough to be given welcome into our land, I am quite particular about whom I allow to offer for the pleasures of my flowers—and especially my maidens. Only those I name on the formal invitations are allowed to bid for a deflowering."

Cu'lugh cleared his throat. "What I have to offer has special worth to your gods, Mistress Helrose."

The Mistress sighed. "My customs are rites in themselves, good sir. I cannot break custom on a whim."

Cu'lugh felt his chest tighten impatiently.

"I must have Odette," he replied, gruffer than intended.

"She is not available to the public yet," Helrose said stiffly. "Her Unveiling is planned in a few days. He who wins the right to deflower her has the right to retain her for up to thirteen days and nights. After that you are welcome to bid for her pleasures."

"That is not good enough!" Cu'lugh's temples pounded, and at that moment he knew keeping his vow to Vanda was but a thin veneer for his true reason for coming here. He wanted nothing but the helpless beauty who had struggled so hard in her bonds to keep her passion hidden from his eyes. For the first time in his adult life he was near to losing his self-possession utterly, and for what? A mere virgin, not even experienced in the arts of lovemaking, as he had always preferred in his women, without wealth and denied of title, at least in the world to which he was accustomed. She was no one but a pretty face with nothing of value to offer. And yet that pretty face compelled him, drove him on, and he did not care.

He said hotly, "Excuse my forwardness, but I am prepared to offer whatever it takes to have her."

"You have mettle, I give you that, Cu'lugh," Helrose said. "And I have other girls prepared and ready to meet the needs of a fine gentleman, for however long you would like. Pray, come in and sit at my table, and I shall be happy to have them brought round for your review."

He shook his head and glanced at the girl in the cage. "Doubtless you have a fine collection. But it is Odette alone I seek—*whom I shall have!*"

The archer bristled and took a step forward. The glaze of the starlight revealed the angry lines in his face, the lift of his dagger from its sheath. "She has told you the girl is not available."

The guard in turn drew the sword at his belt. Cu'lugh inhaled deeply, letting go the instinct to draw his own weapon. He had no doubt he could hold his own against the two of them, but any fray would cost his welcome in Athla. Instead, he reached to his collarbone and pulled from his jerkin the chain that hung about his neck, raising the amulet so the heavens glinted in the murky depths of the amber.

"I will give it to you in exchange for the right to claim the girl."

The archer grunted, but Helrose stepped forward and reached to touch the amulet. As the pad of her finger touched the stone it softly vibrated. A gentle radiance birthed in the center of it, like a milky rose. Helrose's eyes widened and she drew her hand back; and as Cu'lugh released the chain the amber singed his chest ever so slightly.

When he looked into Helrose's face he saw tears in her eyes.

"Take it to Freyja's Temple, Cu'lugh," she said, her voice quivering. "Give it to the priestess there. I shall come and speak with her on the morrow. If this, indeed, proves to be the true Tear of Friggi I shall bring the girl to you myself."

The archer scowled. "This is rash, my Lady!"

"It is my decision," she said firmly. "And that of the High Priestess. Lord Cu'lugh, let her know where you stay, that I may find you and give you the verdict. Be forewarned, however, before you enter the Temple. If this is a hoax, a trick of any kind, it would behoove you to leave this land now, lest by our king's laws you come to regret having ever entered."

Cu'lugh inclined his head. "How may I find the Temple?"

"It stands in the very center of our land, directly across from the king's residence. Of green marble it is built and can only be entered through the rose arbor."

Cu'lugh felt a cold twinge, though he knew not what had summoned it. He was relieved, content, and bowed to Helrose.

"Thank you, Mistress Helrose," he said. She made a dismissive gesture with her hand and turned away curtly, leaving the archer and guard to eye him steadily. But they kept their silence as he headed off.

Only as he walked back through the public square did he realize the angry wind had not blown once since he'd stepped onto the manor grounds.

* * *

The temple was just as the Mistress had described, a great marble structure with no walls, only columns and an arched roof. The entrance arbor was covered with roses—white and red—that sheltered the inclining red brick path to the floor of the sanctuary. Cu'lugh barely caught a glimpse of the feline outline that darted before him at the entry and listened as it meandered on padded feet outside. The passageway was dark, but not utterly, and he discerned the glimmer of moonlight as he stepped up to the Temple floor. Tiles of green covered it completely, and these were strewn with rose petals. The ceiling was invisible for the trellis that tapestried it, thickly blooming with magnificent pink roses.

Through the columns he looked out over the city, the rambling wilderness to the north, the fertile farmland in the west. To the east he sighted great stones covered with ivy; in the south, fields lush and tailored with night-blooming flowers. Surrounding all of Athla were the mountains, their moonlight silhouettes taking on the semblance of benign and slumbering guardians.

In the middle of the petal-strewn floor sat a brazier of monstrous proportions.

A pair of alabaster cat statues, each as tall as a man and twice as wide, flanked it. The face of one peered out toward the north, the other to the south. From the crosspiece of the brazier hung a large black cauldron from which billowed the thick smoke of incense.

He moved around the brazier to the cat facing the north. To his surprise he discovered a throne of gold there. Upon it sat a woman. She wore nothing, not a seductive collar or even the winsome masculine apparel of Athlan Mistresses. Upon her lap sat a cat, a living cat. It appeared asleep to Cu'lugh, and its black fur gleamed like a reflection of the pure color of night against the woman's translucent flesh. So pale she was he could see her veins glowing blue just under the surface, especially those in her large white breasts. She was a voluptuous woman and her head was bowed so far over her shoulder he could not see her face under her mop of ebony curls. He approached the throne with a respectful step and she was so still he could not even tell if she was breathing.

Cu'lugh was trying to think of a proper way to announce himself when suddenly the woman lifted her head. He beheld her face and immediately his stomach filled with ice water, for upon the single head were three faces. What was more astounding was that the faces were so eerily different. The one that faced the left shoulder was young, a child's face. Its eyes remained closed and he could even see her long eyelashes trimmed with the speckle of sleep. The one facing the right shoulder was ancient, lined and furrowed, and its dim black eyes seemed to gaze at nothing in particular, though the mouth moved silently.

The center face peered forward. Her features were more beautiful than any he'd ever seen, and the irony of this touched him as a sublime cruelty.

He could not speak, but he heard the word *monster!* echo in his thoughts.

The doe eyes of the center face blinked and the smile that came to her lips paralyzed him.

It was the Crone who spoke first, in a raspy voice. "Who is it, Mother?"

"'Tis a warrior, my dame, the warrior prince Cu'lugh."

"Prince," murmured the Child drowsily. "But he has never called himself by that title."

"Yet that he is," continued the Beauty, "if that he chooses to be."

"Of course," cackled the Crone, "what makes you think he will? He who has shunned the opportunity upon opportunity to rise above the mercenary position."

Cu'lugh stepped back a pace, undecided if he should stay or simply retreat completely from the deformed and discomforting woman. In the silence the Crone's eyes shut and she began to snore lightly.

"Speak, Cu'lugh," commanded the Beauty. "You have waited long enough to look upon Me."

His skin crept coldly, and at last he forced the tremble out of his voice. "I would speak to the High Priestess—is this you, Lady?"

The face of the Beauty glowed proudly. "As I have been before and shall be always." The words clung to the rose-perfumed air. "State your cause, warrior."

Cu'lugh's palms were covered with sweat. "To bring a gift to you, for the

Temple, that I may prove myself worthy of deflowering a certain novice dedicated to Freyja."

The sweet face dimpled sadly. "There is nothing you possess by which you may have anything of mine, mercenary."

Cu'lugh inhaled sharply, and he drew the chain forth again and unclasped it from his neck. "Tell me what this is, then, Priestess," he said and tossed it onto her ivory thighs just beside the cat. It awakened with a hiss and glowered at him with its huge yellow eyes.

Slowly, she lifted the chain and, holding the stone skyward, examined it. The Child's mouth pursed as she did this and he saw the Crone's eyebrows arch.

"The Teardrop of Friggi," said the Beauty in a lulling voice. "Gone so long from Us. A grand token, indeed, though not one brought with faith."

Cu'lugh's patience was ebbing but he controlled his tone. "Whether I believe or not, if this be a relic, as I have heard, is it not worth one girl? I could take it back...and gone it would be again."

The cat's ears folded back and its fur bristled. The High Priestess stroked it soothingly so that it turned on her lap and lay back down.

"As you will, warrior. But whether you leave it or not it shall not get you Odette."

Cu'lugh went cold, and now he realized that what he spoke to was neither human nor Athlan, but something else entirely. He glanced at the tiles at his feet, angry for the dampening humility he felt. All his reason told him to flee the Temple and leave Athla for good. But that was the logic of the craven, the cautious forbearing instilled by the Christian indoctrination he had long known flawed.

He fell to his knees and bowed his head to Her feet. "What may I give then, my Lady? What have I good enough for thee?"

She was silent a little while and he heard the cat yowl again but he did not look up. At last she replied, "No possession, Cu'lugh, shall get her. Were you to take her hostage this night your heart would stop before you could touch her. This fate have I deemed, for there is something you may give, though it you cannot hold nor would you wish to if you saw it."

His eyes closed, and he felt himself sway with the tides of the landscape and the movement of the heavens above.

"Tell me, Mistress, for I know all I have are but petty things."

Her voice was so faint he knew not if she spoke or it was the breeze teasing his ear. "That very thing, sweet one, that very thing... Relent thy pettiness that seeks attainments through the godless. For you have searched for me since before your birth and here now I stand before you. Destroy your *own* monster if you wish to know the grace you've always had within your grasp."

He felt her pain, then, and knew he had spurred it—a pain birthed from the human capacity for cruelty and hidden from its sins by exoneration of righteousness. He looked at her through his tear-swollen eyes. She rose to her feet with the cat clutched to her breast, suckling as a kitten on the teat of its mother. A current spun about her waist and a spark inflamed on her breast. The spark ignited over her flesh quickly, consuming her entirely in blue fire. And as he stood, not sure whether to offer aid or to bow, the three faces merged into one.

The Goddess hovered over him and Her countenance shimmered with the beauties of all races of women and her demeanor radiated with the virtues achievable by all; and as she spoke again, her voice trembled with a power so fragile it inflamed his loins despite his awe.

"O man of my eternal Husband and Beloved, if thou would live fulfilled thou must defend me unto thy dying breath."

Her radiance blinded him; and he fell on his face, caring not for the pain but that he might please Her and take away Her suffering.

"I relent my monster," he said, "and accept this responsibility."

Fire touched his shoulder. It seared through his flesh and sped into his blood. The surge shot through his heart with such strength that he was lifted and thrown back on the tiles. The earth roared beneath the Temple foundation and the mountains trembled. He rolled over and the flames needled through his chest. Through the columns he saw the clouds billow over the sky and the fragile stars wink out. The moon burst forth and careened toward earth, and as its aura kissed the world the entire heavens exploded in a radiance of blinding rosy light.

Cu'lugh felt the scorching fire die down, and when he sat up he was bathed in perspiration. On the throne the High Priestess reclined, petting the cat as it toyed with the amulet. He pulled himself up to his feet and bowed before her, his emotions too disquieted for coherent reflection.

But the Crone said sadly, "Love is more powerful than faith, warrior. It has built faith, you know."

He looked at her, touched by the sadness in her rheumy eyes. The Child's eyes opened for the first time, and he saw within the rainbow orbs reflections of the vineyards in which he had played with Thierry as a small boy.

"The hearts of the jealous and avaricious know no heroes," she said, yawning. "Why would you seek to build sand castles on the unsound clay?"

But the Beauty shushed her, saying, "You speak too much, my darling." And she eyed Cu'lugh again. "Go now, hound of Lugh. Leave the token for my daughters to know we have spoken. And if by morn you find your monsters driven out then shall you have what you seek."

He nodded mutely, wanting to kneel again and kiss her feet, but she stopped him with her words. "And remember, 'tis easy to take responsibility within the fields of ease, another to wield it amongst the thorns."

Cu'lugh nodded, though this time as one led to do so. He did not comprehend yet what this last meant.

But as he departed from the Temple he saw again the rose-blasted heavens. And he vowed he would discover the meaning to her cryptic words, even if it meant his very life.

Chapter Twenty-One

uarrelsome voices awakened Odette at dawn. She turned over onto her side and heard the familiar inflections of Lord Eryan's voice. But there was a feminine voice, too, sharp and shrill; and he cautioned the speaker to lower her tone lest all the household be alarmed.

Odette opened her drowsy eyes and saw it was, indeed, Lord Eryan returned. But she was shocked to see Yolande standing there, dressed in loose breeches and heavy boots and a man's crimson shirt, her hair pulled back untidily and bound with a strip of cloth. Her face was inflamed, not by blushing chagrin but by pure anger. Lord Eryan looked tired and his eyes were reddened, as if he had been weeping.

Yolande stomped forward and Odette snapped her eyes shut.

"Freedom," Yolande said, "is long past due. When can I expect to leave? And with coin in my hand, for I expect payment for all I have suffered, doubt that not!"

Lord Eryan sighed. "You are being given that life you've droned on about for all these years. You can either leave now, as I see you are impatient to do, and face the penalty of the law for wandering the streets without license of your freedom or you can wait until legal arrangements are made. Then may you offer whatever skills you feel you possess to anyone willing to pay for them. Unless, of course, you are so eager for this freedom that you'd prefer to simply run into the Wastelands."

"I am no fool, Eryan." Odette gasped at the girl's rude tone.

"Those are the choices," he said. "If you are set to live as you have dreamed, I will make arrangements with the king. We cannot allow you to leave now if you wish to avoid the scrutiny of the street sentries."

Yolande growled and stalked up and down the floor.

"I have waited long to cover myself from ogling eyes such as yours. I can wait until your sister signs the necessary papers."

"She said it is so, so it shall be. Stay in your old room tonight, the others will never know what has happened. Come downstairs at noon and I am sure Helrose will have all the necessary documents signed. And I will also have time then to write out a notice to forward to your family."

"I care not to console their conscience," Yolande said bitterly. "They brought me here, they can find where I will choose to go, if that is what they wish."

"They expected you back over three years ago, Yolande," Eryan said tenderly. "They have shown much patience for your pride. If you must be independent, why not be responsible as well and let them know what has transpired?"

Yolande snorted. "So they can interfere?"

"Because they love you."

"Love?" Yolande laughed. "Love is all I have heard about. And where did it get my sister or myself? Love, in all its masks and fickle notions, is but a bondage that I prefer to live without. I am of age by the laws of my homeland and will not assuage the guilt of those who brought me to this vile land. No offense, Lord Eryan."

"Were you less offensive we would have tried another ten years to teach you. But Helrose is wearied from it…and if you do not mind, I am weary now."

"Very well," Yolande said, and Odette heard her move to the door. "I am still obliged to you for intervening on my behalf. And just as I do not forget my enemies, I do not forget those who have offered their aid. I look forward to the acquaintance you suggested last week."

"Shh," Lord Eryan cautioned under his breath. Odette trembled as he moved to open the door. She heard him whisper something and Yolande make some hushed reply. Once the door had quietly closed she felt him walk to the bed. For a long while he remained there, hardly moving, though his breathing was deep; and she felt his eyes caress her through the coverlet. This time, however, she sensed anger in that ravishing gaze, though not at her, she was certain. It filled her with fear and she knew no relief of the fear until at last he moved away.

All that morning Odette thought she perceived an inexplicable expectancy somehow embracing the entire household. Mistress Helrose was gone without giving information when she might return. If anyone knew where she was they kept their secrets from their wards. The rest of the flowers seemed as uneasy over this as Odette.

Lord Eryan had let Odette sleep late and when at last she awakened handed her over to one of the other stewards with word she was to be kept inside that day. She was glad for this, given what had happened the day before, but her imagination played with her, leading her to carelessness. She was polishing the Mistress's table when she knocked over a glass vase. It rolled over the edge before she could catch it, shattering into dozens of shards. The steward overseeing her was incensed. Just as he propped her over his knee and commenced to dole out punishment Mistress Helrose returned.

When the steward had well reddened Odette's buttocks the Mistress ordered her to her room to rest.

"And mind you, young lady, I mean the room you shared with the other flowers."

Odette nodded, wiping the tears from her cheeks, and sought out the room in the corridor. Lying down on the bed, she crawled under the blanket and rubbed her sore backside. She wondered what the Mistress was thinking by discharging her from her usual tasks, and what Lord Eryan would say when he was informed.

After some time the door opened and Helrose walked in. Odette lifted her head and waited for a command.

* * *

Cu'lugh had not found sleep until past dawn. He was dreaming that he sat astride his mount, in pursuit of a bird of unidentifiable plumage. He carried a net he'd found in a graveyard somewhere and tried again and again to capture the bird when it dove.

"What you do forfeits your future, mercenary."

He reined the horse at once and, turning about, looked down to see Vanda standing beside the beast. Her uplifted face held a smile, and her lips were redder than the lovely gown she wore, more tempting than any mouth he'd ever seen. A glimpse of one white shoulder showed through her black tresses and as her arms reached up toward him one firm breast slipped from her bodice. He felt the net slip from his hands, but he cared not and stooped to possess that divine mouth.

She kissed his ear and whispered again, *"Come back to me before the talons take your eyes!"*

Something sailed past him then, brushing his face. Bolting upright he saw the bird soar overhead. It encircled his head, squawking; and he heard Vanda speak soothingly to it.

A drum struck up from a distance. So sudden was the sound that the bird shattered and dissipated before his eyes. Cu'lugh peered around to find the source of the irritating thunder, noticing the churlish scowl that ruined Vanda's beauty. His anger grew and he vowed to slay whoever was responsible.

He awoke, sure that Vanda had turned away—and realized where he was. The light through the window stung his eyes and the rapping at the door abruptly ceased. He mumbled in peevish gratitude and turned over.

Moments later the rapping started again, this time more urgently. He groaned and sat on the edge of the bed. He had gone to bed without removing his breeches, and now rose and answered the door grudgingly.

It was one of the innkeeper's serving girls, a deeply bronze-skinned girl with black hair cut squarely across her brow and over her shoulders. Her plump cheeks dimpled sunnily as she smiled, but the gesture struck Cu'lugh's sour mood as almost a mockery.

His voice was thick. "'Tis better it be a fire or worse to wake me up. "

Her sunny expression dimmed at once and he felt a stab of regret. She was but a servant, after all.

"I apologize sincerely, sir. But there is a visitor for you outside. I think a visitor you would wish to see."

"For me?" He frowned deeply. "Are you certain of this?"

She nodded so earnestly the ends of her hair bobbed over her shoulders. "Mistress Helrose, sir."

Cu'lugh was surprised. He had not expected to see her so soon. Perhaps she'd come with an apology for her haughty attitude. The thought made him grin.

"Tell her I'll be down promptly."

The girl bowed and pranced off toward the stairway, making the bells of her brass ankle cuff jingle. Cu'lugh closed the door and relieved himself in the chamber pot. Then, pulling on his jerkin and boots he went out.

The downstairs was quiet. Only a couple of serving girls were at work, sweeping the floor of the dining hall under the supervision of the same youth he'd seen in the portico the day before. The youth stood beside a window holding a thick strap of leather in one hand that he struck rhythmically across the palm of the other while he kept an eye on the girls.

Cu'lugh entered the portico and saw the girl who had come to his room cleaning the tables. A thin brunette was fettered at one of the punishment tables. Her eyes were heavy and she looked ready to fall asleep, but when he glanced down she gave a little gasp.

He stepped out of the portico onto the bright walkway that edged the street and down a ways he saw Helrose's proud, straight figure. She was dressed, rather flatteringly, in dark leather riding pants and a vest of crimson suede. Her boot soles echoed crisply as she paced. Her auburn hair was pulled back into a tight bun, lending her a far severer look than the night before.

Hardly the giggling girl running through the courtyard from her lover!

Bemused, Cu'lugh walked toward her. Clasped in Helrose's right hand was something small and shiny that she slapped lightly, thoughtlessly, across her thigh with each stride. As Cu'lugh drew nearer he noticed farther up the way two sturdy-limbed young men standing beneath the heavy branches of an ash tree. Betwixt them they carried a large brass spherical cage with a squat rim of black iron welded to the base. Behind the gleaming bars Cu'lugh saw Odette.

She was naked but for a collar and a garland of flowers on her head. Cu'lugh realized he had halted and that he was staring. His loins ached at the sight of her crouched and bowed submissively in the cage, her long hair showering over her arms like a veil of spun gold. The dimensions of the cage did not allow her to stand or lie down, and she knelt on her fair knees, clinging endearingly to the bars with her thighs pressed close together.

She raised her head a moment to peek out timidly through the golden veil. Her eyes were wide with anxiety, like huge emeralds, and her quivering mouth pouted. Then she caught sight of him and crimson flushed her cheeks. She bowed her head again, and Cu'lugh could not stop gazing at her.

A frightened caged bird, he thought and felt Helrose beside him.

"Lovely, isn't she?"

Cu'lugh forced himself to cease staring like an enraptured boy. He regarded Helrose pleasantly, but he noted how she clenched the thing she held so tightly her knuckles paled.

"Yes," he answered.

"Shall I have her brought in now?"

Cu'lugh felt suddenly awkward with the situation. He had wanted this deeply, but a part of him had truly thought it hopeless. It would also take time for him to feel comfortable with the frank Athlan attitude toward situations that in his world were considered indelicate and sinful.

"Your gift was accepted by the High Priestess," Helrose told him, as if confirming a doubt on his part, "and I always keep my promises, sir."

Cu'lugh nodded, and Helrose gestured to the young men. Immediately, they came forward with the cage, carrying it gingerly, and as they passed by a breeze stirred and swept Odette's hair from her face. Her brow, Cu'lugh saw, was crumpled and her eyes brimming red with tears. He hastened forward and led the young men through the portico to the inn and opened the door, directing them to the proper door upstairs.

The serving girls paused at their work as the young men ascended the steps. Just as Helrose entered the inn the attendant youth stepped toward her and bowed deeply, reverently; and Cu'lugh saw the Mistress pause a second and lay her palm on his head. She uttered soft words Cu'lugh could not hear, but he knew it was some blessing she had imparted.

"Do not stare," the boy reprimanded the serving girls as Helrose and Cu'lugh followed the young men. The girls obeyed at once and returned to their work.

Catching up with the escorts, Cu'lugh opened the door to his room and waited until they and Helrose had entered before joining them.

"Where would you have them lower the cage?" the Mistress asked. "Or is there a hook you'd prefer it hung from?"

Cu'lugh glanced around the room and finally pointed to the floor between the window and the foot of the bed. As the bearers lowered the cage Odette sank to her hands and knees inside so her backside was directed away from his eyes. He loved the way her hair spilled forward to cover her arms and cascade over her swaying breasts when she lowered her head, and he wondered if the gesture was one of obeisance or a graceful attempt to conceal herself.

The Mistress bade the escorts wait for her outside, and when they were gone she asked Cu'lugh to shut the door.

"Thank you." She opened her hand; a key lay in her palm. "This is the key for her cage."

The room seemed suddenly sweltering as Cu'lugh took it.

"Customarily, I am present on the rite of reception," Helrose continued, "occasions that usually transpire in my home, though there have been exceptions. Thus, I thought it best to bring the cage here."

"I suppose I would be a stranger amongst your people," Cu'lugh said.

"That is not it, no. It is only that I have broken my usual custom concerning the Unveiling rite. And my brother, who had taken on the responsibility as Odette's personal overseer, has exacting views on our rites. Besides, he has grown very attached to our little Odette, and I wanted to avoid a possible scene."

Cu'lugh felt a jealous twinge. "Personal overseer?"

She smiled gently. "Yes. Sometimes a flower needs special supervision. Thus was it for Odette, and I must avow my brother succeeded in quelling the disdainful obstinacy she displayed when first she came to us. Odette has since developed exemplary humility and a satisfactory desire to please."

Cu'lugh knew it was inappropriate to question Helrose's practices; without her counsel he would never have sought out the High Priestess. And yet he was incensed to think this brother had been allowed to train Odette, to touch her in whatever manner necessary for her training.

"You must have spoken with the High Priestess early."

"It is my routine to break my night's fast each morning at the Temple. I still have old friends who serve there." Her eyes shifted to the cage, and she bit her bottom lip. "I have to remind you of the laws against abuse," she continued, and as she met his eyes her poise seemed strained. "No wound may be inflicted, no brutal punches, no burns. Verbal abuse is forbidden. She must be allowed time for adequate sleep, and it is your responsibility to insure she is kept clean and out of danger. You cannot share her with criminals or known abusers. Likewise, unseemly work, such as cleaning the streets or the filth of animals or sewers, is by law allocated to criminals alone. And, certainly, she may not be taken beyond the Athlan borders."

This last reminder cut into Cu'lugh's conscience and he peered over to the window, fearful that in his eyes she would see his guilt and know the vow made to Vanda.

"She must be returned at the end of thirteen days and nights, at which time you may arrange to extend her services, if that is your pleasure, or obtain the services of other girls."

Cu'lugh cleared his throat. "How does one go about obtaining a girl permanently?"

"That can only be arranged if there is the desire for marriage, which I only consent to if there is a mutual love expressed between the man and my flower."

He looked at her again, smiling amicably. "'Twas only curiosity."

Helrose nodded and regarded Odette silently several moments.

"The amulet you gave up," she said, "its magics are shrouded in time. Nevertheless, it is a priceless relic we thought forever lost. I must thank the gods for directing you to Athla, Lord Cu'lugh." She paused and inhaled deeply, and her face beamed with forced aplomb. "I shall leave you in the faith you shall act as a firm and honorable master to my little cygnet."

"I will," he said, thinking again of the last promise he'd made a woman.

Helrose held his eyes a moment and he blinked fearfully, expecting her mind to sift through his memories again. Instead, she turned and left, closing the door firmly but softly behind her.

Cu'lugh sighed, knowing a relief unimaginable. Glancing at the cage he saw Odette had raised her face and stared desperately at the shut door. Her eyes were two large emeralds clinging to hope, her mouth like a rosebud shuddering against the indifferent breeze. Never had he laid eyes on a more delightful vision. So many women had he pursued in his lifetime, almost as many had he bedded; and not even Vanda's fierce beauty surpassed this nymph in the gilded cage.

Odette's eyes swept fearfully from the door to him, widening anxiously to discover he was regarding her. At once she bent her head, pulled her hair down thickly over her breasts and clamped her legs as if by doing so she could elude the scrutiny of the world.

Cu'lugh's passion mounted like an aching hunger, and the knowledge that

Odette could not escape the cage only worked to season and sear the desire.

Burnished, blushing angel, he mused, *like the vision from my childhood.*

The nape of Cu'lugh's neck crawled. He forced himself to look away from her now and striding to the window looked out, hoping to effectively banish the superstitious, ridiculous déjà vu that vied to possess him.

I should just fetch my horse, ride with her now into the fields and find a path that leads through the mountain passes out of Athla. Return, unscathed, to the real world.

And as he searched for logical means to fulfill this plan he realized he would have to obtain clothes for her, to conceal from those who might see him ride out the little novice he carried—and to hide her tempting naked charms from his own eyes. Perhaps a gag he would keep ready, too, in case she grew vocally affrighted once out of the city. If she cried out his plans would be ruined by the king's men. Cu'lugh searched his internal map of the city desperately, recalling the clothiers' shops he'd passed by on the streets.

Through the glass panes of one such shop he had spotted a woman trying on a gown, a flimsy thing of spun silver thread that had clung to her arms and graceful breasts and hips. The fabric had reminded him more of a shining spider's web than of cloth—the gown entirely more of a decoration than a garment. A man had sat on a stool nearby as she dressed, regarding her thoughtfully as she turned this way and that. A naked shopgirl stood holding a variety of jeweled chains for the woman to try on as well.

An image of Odette formed in Cu'lugh's mind, draped in the silver gossamer gown, her legs wrapped with the lacings of silver sandals. The image whetted his hunger anew so that it was merciless, ravenous.

Anger broiled just under his passion; and he did not know if this was directed at himself, his weakness or at whatever fate had seduced his reason away. What a fool he had become, surely, to waste a fortune on this girl who was nothing outside Athla but a bastard without title. Her sister had title and wealth and offered an auspicious union, a union made in the world he knew and understood. With Vanda as his ally he would have the power and affluence he had dreamed of having. As well, the knowledge how deep a thorn he would be in Charles's side once wedded to Vanda enhanced that rational desire. Even the possibility of a cool marriage bed was worth the attainment of these offerings.

He inhaled sharply, knowing it would never be—for he would never know happiness to think he had committed the sacrilege of spurning the reflection of the one image which had so comforted him all his life.

He turned his head enough to survey the cage and its little occupant. Odette appeared not to have budged, but she was trembling now more than ever. He rolled the key between his palm and fingers thoughtfully. No, he had not thought of the image before setting eyes on her, and so this passion was not some act of self-delusion. Coincidence, that she resembled the image. And yet he knew that no amoral desire, no quest for power, not even the profound obligation to Vanda excused using this flesh-and-blood girl, either.

I have always been amoral and always shall be. To hell with obligations; Vanda deserves a husband who will give her happiness in marriage.

"Superstition," he grumbled. The unintended words brought no visible reaction from his captive.

Obviously, she is under no spell or glamour, he decided, though the thought offered little comfort. He knew better than to indulge the fancy that to Odette he was anything more than the man who had won the right to take her maidenhood.

Cu'lugh stepped to the cage and regarded the trembling prisoner intently. More compelling even than this overwhelming desire for her was the compulsion to take her with all the unabashed force and impenitent delight for which she'd been prepared. It grated against all the ethics of society as he knew it. But for all the civilized approaches he'd facilitated with each separate chase he had come away with only a fleeting satisfaction. Perhaps his dissatisfaction had sprung from the fact he had no interest in the woman besides for the fleeting moment; perhaps there had been something integral missing in each carnal encounter—and perhaps it was both these things.

He laid a hand on the cage to find the bars still warm from the trek through the sun-drenched street. Slowly, he extended his arm inside and touched the hair shading Odette's face. She twitched and gasped. Cu'lugh smiled and pinched off one of the fragile blooms from the garland. He rolled the waxy petals between his fingers and savored the heady perfume they imparted.

"Look at me—raise your head," he commanded.

Odette's eyes fluttered through the veil of hair and he could see her lips press together. But she obeyed, pulling the hair back and lifting her face to him. Her terror was as wild as the precious orchid he'd pinched. He loved her lips, so unlike the wantonly full lips he had often pursued to kiss before. Delicately scalloped they were, softest pink, seductive in their very innocent appeal.

Cu'lugh's heart jolted as he pressed the key into the lock and turned it. Opening the door, he extended a hand to her and said, "Come."

Chapter Twenty-Two

he laid her hand in his reluctantly and he helped her out of the cage. Her eyes darted to the door again, and she was breathing rapidly. He feared for a moment she would bolt and wondered what he would do, but the next moment she went to her knees and kissed his boots.

"I am to acknowledge that I am for you, Lord Cu'lugh," she said in a voice at once articulate and timid.

"Yes," he murmured, nodding.

She pressed her brow to the floor beside him and extended her arms so that her palms lay upturned against the wood. Her back was a smooth inverted arch and her shapely buttocks glowed with the slightest of blushes.

A vision of submission, he thought contentedly and for a time said nothing as he savored the sight of her.

But he wanted to see her eyes again and said "Look at me."

She looked straight at him. No guile whatsoever did he find in the emerald depths, no resentment, no corruption. Simply the rapt but nervous desire to please.

"You have haunted my every moment, little girl," he said and flung her hair back gently over her shoulder. Kneeling, he surveyed her breasts. Full and fair they were, with nipples like two tiny, dusky gems. Her stomach was flat, her hips wide but not heavy. Then came those legs, those long and shapely legs. And between them, a thick triangle of soft brown hair. The hair appeared to have been brushed and as he gazed Odette's hips moved slightly and he heard her make an almost inaudible, frustrated little moan.

Cu'lugh stood up and, taking her hair in one hand, pulled her to her feet. He held her wrists to the small of her back, delighting in the shudder this sent through her.

"I want to kiss you," he whispered and pulled her against him and lowered his mouth to her exposed throat. He grazed her flesh with alternate lightness and harshness, until he could see goose bumps rise on her quivering limbs. Holding her wrists firmly he journeyed his mouth down her collarbone, her shoulder, back across her throat. He clasped her left breast suddenly and kissed the cresting fair mound and darted his tongue over the nipple. It swelled under his taunting tongue, and opening his mouth he nursed it gently. He moved onto the other breast, teasing the nipple as the first, then suckling it, too. When again he kissed her throat he looked down her back to see her pinned hands clenching and unclenching over her swaying buttocks.

Drawing slightly away Cu'lugh assessed her firm belly and made circles over it with his fingertips. Enchanting little goose bumps sprang up over her flesh, and releasing her wrists, he placed a hand at either side of her waist. How lithe she seemed cupped in his hands, and he slid them down her hips and over her thighs, relishing the firm suppleness of her. He knelt to massage her legs, kissing her delectable calves so lightly that she giggled.

He looked up at the thatch between her legs and parted the hair gently and then the lips so that she shuddered.

"Spread your legs," Cu'lugh whispered.

She obeyed and he unfolded her vulva lips. Her little inner lips were scarlet, tightly folded and when gingerly he unfolded them she gasped. Her fount was tight, glistening wet and he saw her tiny clitoris swelling beneath its hood.

His desire for her was urgent now. He rose to his feet and unpinned the garland from her head and threw it to the windowsill. Then, sweeping her up into his arms, he carried her to the bed and laid her down. Her hair spilled out beneath her in a fan of golden waves. She did not meet his eyes, but he minded not, for it added to his pleasure to know that it was he who caused her little hands to clench nervously at her sides. It seemed all she could do not to either raise her knees or clench her legs together.

Kneeling on the bed with his legs on either side of her he leaned over and hungrily kissed her mouth. His tongue parted her trembling lips, and as he explored the honeyed insides of her mouth she moaned and undulated. He withdrew and gazed down at her again, massaging her breasts with one hand, stroking her cheek with the other. Her eyes fluttered and met his a moment, just long enough for him to catch the torrent of emotions going through her mind.

"So fair," he sighed and climbed off the bed so he could remove his boots and untie his breeches. Though neither disillusioned nor vain of his looks, Cu'lugh knew he was well endowed below the hips, and now as the great shaft of his manhood was exposed Odette's eyes widened with much distress. He smiled and, returning to the bed, leaned over her with his elbows pressed to the mattress and gently kissed her mouth again. Then, he scooped her breasts into his hands to feed on them a time and flick his tongue harshly over and around her hardened nipples.

He raised one knee and carefully parted her legs. Her sex was hot and damp to his searching hand and with a thumb he pressed her clitoris. Odette's hips jerked and a gush of fluid spread out over her thighs, but when he glanced into her face again he was dismayed to see a tear roll down her cheekbone. He brushed it away with his lips and kissed her brow.

"I do not want you to be afraid of loving me, Odette," he whispered. "No, never that."

Taking a pillow from beside her head he lifted and propped her buttocks. He spread her legs a little further and lowered the tip of his hardened shaft against the virgin mouth. Like a tautly folded lily it felt to him and when Odette moaned faintly a wild ache bloomed in the depths of his scrotum. He kissed her ear tenderly and tasted her lips again and his manhood invaded her untried font.

Odette cried out under his penetration. Cu'lugh gathered her to him and plunged onward with merciful care. Her muscles were heavenly tight and with each considered thrust her hands seized about his back a little more tightly. Quicker, deeper he thrust, feeling much like a pike splintering maiden timber, and it was not long before all thought fled and his senses swept into a vortex of pulsing, thoughtless pleasure and when his jism burst forth his heart stopped and his soul soared to a rapture consummate.

When Cu'lugh's heart began to beat again he felt Odette's flesh burning against his own. Opening his eyes, he found her staring into his face. Her eyes were wide and her face wet and he kissed the tears away and, turning over onto his side, pulled her into his arms. She was shaking, but not hard, and between her thighs he saw the bloody fluid of her claimed maidenhood. He shuddered with an immense sense of contentment. Not only was Odette the first virgin he had deflowered, he knew inexplicably he would never again have cause to see the mythic beauty of his visions. Odette had supplanted her, and the memory of this time with the woman of flesh would give far more solace than even the vision.

"You have pleased me wholly," he whispered into her ear. Odette laid her head on his shoulder. He watched the flush recede a bit from her cheeks and shyly she wound her arms over his chest and timidly looked into his face.

"May I speak, my Lord?"

The humble petition sent new warmth through Cu'lugh's spent loins.

"I find it graceful you ask—and, yes, you may."

She cleared her throat and said "My Mistress said that you donated a great relic to the Temple for me. I-I am very honored."

He kissed the crown of her head.

"I have little need for such things as relics, but it held personal value." The room was quiet except for the rise and fall of their breathing. Cu'lugh realized his discomfort was gone—in fact he'd never felt more relaxed in the company of another as now. "It was all I could offer to convince your Mistress of my worth. I do not regret it."

Odette raised her head and licked her lips hesitantly. "May I speak, my Lord?"

"All you wish until I say otherwise." He smiled.

Her eyes lowered a moment. "I am glad it was you who Unveiled me."

Cu'lugh's heart swelled. "You are sweet, but I think you would be gracious to whomever won the privilege."

Odette frowned. "But I mean it, my Lord."

"Why do you say that?" He smoothed her cheek with his fingers, wanting to smother the tremble from her lips with kisses. "I am but a mercenary, an Outer Realmer—no refined gentleman as are the lords of Athla."

She shrugged. "I thought of you last night. Even as I fell to sleep I saw your face. I remembered the vitality you imparted the merchant's tawdry abode after you left. The look in your eyes when you defended me…it seemed as if you were meant to be there at my defense."

"You are a romantic young girl, that is all."

Her eyes bored into his, two deep, verdant pools. "I am a slave, my Lord, and have no cause or need to hold romantic ideas."

He was touched by her honesty. "No, I suppose not." A lock of gold fell over her temple and this he kissed and folded behind her ear. "So, I believe you, that you are glad of it. That is an honor to me, Odette."

She nodded and he was thoughtful a moment. With care he said, "And what do you think your mother would say—to know you are a slave of passion here in this realm?"

"She would be most proud," Odette answered without hesitation. "She was content to be my father's passion slave."

"And this was in the Outer Realm?"

"Yes, it was a lovely place." Odette was smiling now and Cu'lugh saw tears mist over the verdant pools. "I had a happy home with my mother and father. They loved one another greatly."

"How did you come to be here," he asked in a guarded tone.

"My sister's husband brought me here from a Burgundian estate to which my sister had sent me years before. Thierry—that is her husband—had been appointed vassal lord after the Franks quelled our tribe, and I suppose my sister thought me safer in Burgundy."

"Did your sister's husband tell you why he brought you to Athla?"

Odette shook her head. "No, save to say he knew the king here, and that King Larsarian could offer sounder protection than anyone else."

Cu'lugh's brow lifted. "That he knew the king? Are you certain of this?"

Odette nodded and laid her head against him again. He saw then a shadow of sadness in her face.

"Your mother and father are dead."

Odette nodded and closed her eyes, and her eyelashes, he noted, were wet.

"I am sorry," he said softly. "And I should not have mentioned them if it gives you pain."

She smiled wryly. "Do not apologize, my Lord. It eases the pain of their deaths to remember how happy was our household then. I was loved and I loved them and they adored each other. They died together, you know, in their marriage bed. On the very morn the Franks lay siege, as if the Gods were showing mercy to take them together."

Cu'lugh felt a cold blade cut through his insides. "The morning of the attack? Are you certain?"

"Oh, yes. Oh, yes, I came to their room in the early morn and found that they were dead. The menfolk came and removed them to a death-pallet in the Great Hall. Very shortly thereupon the Franks attacked our village."

Cu'lugh could hardly breathe. Somewhere in this revelation he sensed some treachery, as vicious as Charles's campaign of terror, as malignant as the plague that he knew firsthand had swept through Odette's homeland. He could not point in which direction it clearly lay, but he knew it was there, waiting with deadly purpose.

He cupped her chin with his fingers and turned her face so she would look at him.

"Your sister," he said slowly, "did the two of you love one another?"

Odette reflected a moment and replied, "I wanted to love her—she was, after all, my sister. But she kept to her private rooms so much I hardly ever laid eyes on her until Mother and Father died. My father said she grieved overmuch the passing of her own mother, and that she could not forgive him for marrying mine. I suppose to look upon my mother reminded her of her own."

"But she sent you away to protect you?"

"I was young, but, yes, she explained it was for my own well-being. She reminded me that she was of Frankish descent through her mother, and so could expect more civility from Charles Martel for that where I could not."

Cu'lugh opened his mouth, eager to press for more details that he expected would enlighten his growing suspicions. But Odette's voice seemed so pained to speak of it he dared not.

Instead, he asked with a true interest, "Your mother, was she all golden hair with skin all milk and roses as you?"

This brought a blushing smile to Odette's face. "No, my Lord. She was fair, far more than I, with hair and eyes like the night. And she was beautiful."

"She could not have been more so than you," he said, and Odette's blush deepened and she shook her head.

"You flatter, my Lord."

"Why, have you never realized you are beautiful?"

"I am not beautiful, my Lord," she answered flatly.

He lifted an eyebrow and said with deliberate firmness, "You speak true when you say I am your Lord. And I say you are beautiful and will not abide contradiction, young lady."

This made Odette's eyes widen, and though she bit her bottom lip abashedly, he perceived a part of her took pleasure in the compliment.

"Tell me, my sweet, are you happy to belong to Mistress Helrose—to serve as a passion slave?"

"I have for a time now, my Lord."

"Is it difficult?"

"Yes, my Lord," she replied and as he listened expectantly, continued, "In the beginning of my training I did not understand why it was expected I should yield. Not only my body but my will. I resented it. But that is natural, I have since discovered, for all new novices."

"I suppose the household in Burgundy you spoke of—it was a Christian family?"

"Yes, my Lord."

"Did their ideas of morality differ vastly from that of your parents and Saxon folk?"

"Yes," she said tightly, "and my foster parents possessed a gift for guilt that transcended even the practices of the monks left by Boniface to reconstruct our Saxon homeland. In time, I came to look upon my Saxon upbringing with suspicion, as if there was something fundamentally perverse about our customs. I heard it said enough by my foster parents that we were conquered on account of our sin and as well for it. Not only did my foster parents speak of the inherent sinfulness of our people but claimed by my every act and gesture to see it incarnate thrice-fold."

Cu'lugh grunted with repulsion. It still shocked him how cruel some people could be.

"If you hear it enough when you are young it is easy to begin believing it. And such a perception surely made it more difficult for you to accept what you found in Athla."

"Oh, yes. The ethics of Athla are those held by my mother and father—all my folk when once my father parted ways with the tribe's forced capitulation under the Christianized Franks." She paused a moment. "I dwelt in the castle for a time after Thierry brought me here. Like other children I was given freedom to enjoy myself more than anything else, and so I paid little heed to what went on between the adults. All that changed suddenly the morning when I was told I'd reached the age when I must be educated as every other young girl of the land."

"Do you ever resent the education? Of having to serve men, of having to bow to the will of your Mistress?"

"For a time, my Lord, yes. But I have learned the value of what they are teaching me."

"And it does not make you feel debased?"

"No, my Lord. The young men here receive their own education—how to treat the women who are at their pleasure without cruelty and to take responsibility for protecting and defending we who serve them. There is debasement in the Outer Realm, where a woman's compliance is expected without expectation of respect. Under the banner of shame they serve as inferiors, with the name of *iniquity* branded upon their gender."

"Heirs of Eve," Cu'lugh said sadly. "Yes, I've heard that claim all my life."

Odette looked at him curiously. "And what is your opinion, my Lord? Are we inheritors of corruption?"

"No, not at all."

"And what of these Athlan customs—surely, they conflict with all you have known as well."

He laughed lightly. "Yes, it does. But I am not in the Outer Realm now, am I?"

A broad smile brightened Odette's face. "Do you plan to stay, my Lord?"

He was silent, struggling with the image of Vanda that suddenly intruded on his contentment. "Yes, for a time. How long I cannot say."

She nestled back down in the crook of his arm. "Tell me of your childhood, my Lord," she said huskily. "Was it happy?"

Cu'lugh stared at her, pleasantly surprised. Of all the women he'd ever been with she was the first to ask such a personal question. Many had made overtures of interest; the more honest simply inquired about his future plans, his titles, any holdings he might have and, of course, whether he had been included in his father's estate. Not a one had ever shown an interest in his childhood or his happiness, and in turn he had never taken the chance to yield any personal secrets.

Odette was not so shallow, and thus he found himself relating to her the years of his childhood—of his noble, pious father, his mad and even more pious mother. He told her of Angla, whom he could not have loved more had he been born of her womb. He described his elder brothers and his father's other wives, sanctimonious and petty creatures every one. Odette's eyes never left him as he revealed these things. She laughed at the amusing anecdotes and her face pinched at the grievous secrets he'd never shared with anyone before. It seemed truly she understood his pain, or at least sympathized without judgment; and as he spoke it seemed a great weight had been unbuckled from his waist. After a time the very air smelled fresher and everything in the room appeared sharper to his eyes, more vivid with color and texture.

"My father could not abide me," he said at length, "and so I set out to disappoint him. Looking back I know that this was in part more than just rebellion, that I wanted his attention. Later, I continued because the mercenary life offered me the chance of fulfilling the dream of holding my own kingdom and of being sovereign on my own terms."

"Were you an amoral mercenary," she asked slowly, the word *mercenary* sounding distasteful.

"No, I do not think so. My companions and I took the old vows of our respective tribal heritages. We did not offer our skills to greedy lords and noblemen. We sought to serve meritorious men only. Also, we declined to serve those who sought to press their gods upon others." He looked at her steadily. "I want you to know, Odette, I am a Frank. We were taught young the Saxon language, my brothers and I, though I must say this far north I was surprised to be greeted in the language."

"They have their own," Odette said in a confiding tone, "though I do not know it well myself."

He hugged her and gave her a lingering kiss to the brow. "I never joined the cause of Charles or of the Church, nor do I intend to ever do so."

She inhaled drowsily and drew the back of her fingers down his cheek affectionately. "I believe you, my Lord."

Relieved and grateful, Cu'lugh pulled her atop him and embraced her. As his lips swept over her throat again he said, "You are a rare girl, Odette, more precious than you can imagine."

His manhood swelled with renewed life. But even as her beaming smile would have surpassed the sun he could see her eyelids were heavy. He laid her down beside him again and told her to rest. There were days enough to enjoy her, and she was worthy of patience. For now it was delight enough to lie beside her. As he watched her drift to sleep he suffered for the desire to take her again and marveled at his control to refrain.

Truly was she was rare and precious. He had known brief infatuations; he had experienced spurned affection. This was the only time he had known both ardor and affection for a woman. Odette held no interest in his wealth or status, of this he had no doubt. She enjoyed listening to him, of knowing of his life. And she—well, she held a fascination that extended beyond the wonderful Freyjan training. He had no qualms with those, of course, and welcomed the long-denied penchants the delicious Athlan ways had roused in him. That Odette was happily surrendered to her fate validated his welcome.

Quietly, Cu'lugh withdrew from the bed, determined now to do his part to refine and clarify her surrender, to give it the meaning and respect it so gracefully begged. Imparting a kiss to her cheek, he ventured into town.

Chapter Twenty-Three

The familiar sound of spanked flesh brought Odette's hand immediately to her bottom. Slowly, she grew aware it was not her buttocks that were receiving the punishment and listened with interest to the sharp, clean blows that resounded from downstairs. The receiver was blubbering in apology, the giver silent; and several minutes passed before the spanking ended. Odette heard a masculine voice order the recipient to go out to the portico and await him.

Odette sat up and peered about. She was surprised to find herself alone. She glanced at the cage, its intimidating door left ajar, and at the possessions of her new Lord that lay on one of the tables. Her vagina ached dully, and when she pulled back the coverlet she saw a small stain of blood on the bed sheets and the insides of her thighs. She went to the table where sat the pitcher of water and poured some of it into the basin, taking a clean cloth from the stack to wash with. Her vulva lips were tender but the warm water eventually abated the pain. When she was clean again there remained the slightest prickling high within her vagina.

Uncertain what her Lord's reaction would be to find her up, Odette returned to bed. She gazed at the drapes on the window as she nestled down on the pillow, but it was not the curtains she saw. Thoughts of her Lord possessed her. She blushed happily to recall his touch and the wondrous blend of pain and fear and pleasure he'd wrought in taking her maidenhood. She retraced the contours of his firm muscles, the headiness of his masculine scent, the smoldering glint of his dark eyes. Every word he had spoken was branded on her memory—all those endearing and tragic events of his life...and the sense of unworthiness of love that imbued what he had revealed. He did not realize he perceived himself this way; but the sense was there, a driving and dormant component of his character.

Yet, it was not the most vital of his components. Cu'lugh was stalwart and loyal to his friends and family. Whatever loveless relationships he had pursued were none of Odette's affair; still, she could see he was tired of shallow associations. His soul pressed him to venture to new horizons, and it was this affinity with his true self that Odette guessed had unconsciously goaded him to seek more than the fleeting adventures of the mercenary life and come to Athla. No matter what mistake it was he had alluded to that had brought him, the fact was some fate had led him down the path that had led him here. And even though he had no faith in the relic he'd donated to the Temple he had been in possession of it.

Mistress Helrose was in tears as she told Odette that morning her Unveiling had been won by the very special donation. Odette's breath was taken away by the news; but she listened, knowing it was right and meet, a thing sacred. The Mistress went on to elucidate that the donor was a gentleman who had seen Odette at the establishment of the trader Holbarki. Odette knew at once who it was—the man whose stirring brute handsomeness had haunted her night—and her passion fled in the face of the ardor she now knew beyond doubt he held for her.

It was one thing to imagine sensuality; another to feel its anxious breath bearing over one's repose. Odette had taken it for granted that her Unveiling would occur in Helrose's manor, her home and haven. Secretly, she had hoped her deflowering would come at the hands of Lord Alban or Lord Eryan, but of course that was selfish. Not once had it crossed her mind it could be a stranger to the Mistress, let alone an Outer Realmer.

"All shall be well, my child," Helrose had promised. *"He is a worthy man. And I have no doubt he shall treat you with honor."*

Mistress Helrose prepared Odette herself and had the cage brought in. Before Odette stepped in Helrose had dried her frightened tears with a handkerchief and blessed her in the old tongue. The journey through town had not devastated Odette as she had expected—nothing like the mortification she'd felt when Lord Eryan first led her through the city. Yet her helplessness had been visible to everyone and—worse—to the man who awaited. More keenly vulnerable she felt than when hung in Holbarki's house, and when she saw the soldier from the street she prayed Freyja would hide her with Her magic.

Not the lengthiest spanking nor the most frustrating display had made her heart feel a rush as did the look in his eyes that morning. No polished gentleman or aloof steward was this Lord Cu'lugh.

She hugged herself, smiling so hard her cheeks ached, and knew now that she preferred him to any of the men she'd known. He reminded her of the men of her homeland with his demand to have his way, and yet he was respectful of women. She could never visualize him working as a steward. Not that he didn't possess the qualifications, but that he simply would never bow to the instructions of a Mistress. Lord Cu'lugh might have his own household of serving girls and without doubt he would inspire their adoration as much as their respect.

He was nothing like the Christian men from her childhood, either. Her Lord was no ravager of pagans as was Charles Martel. Yet, he was from Midgard, and if he returned there would be vulnerable to the handicaps other men faced. Unless he relinquished whatever loyalties tied him there he would age and die just the same as other men and women.

He was so vital, more so than almost any Athlan man, the king excepted. Something animalistic burnt brightly in his heart and soul; and yet even this animalistic vitality, this extraordinary passion for life would, in time, falter and wilt under the great delusion that pervaded Midgard. Like all the others he would assume life was a short and innately miserable journey. Generations had conditioned the consciousness of their descendants to believe this misery was ordained by the divine or was a lesson demanded by the governing soul. And so the Midgardians were born and lived, suffered and died before even achieving what happiness life had to offer.

Odette sighed sadly. Lord Eryan's words had remained with her: *Things are different here in Athla, Odette, than in Midgard.* She'd come to understand the Athlan way of looking at things—their esteem for life's joys, their regard for youth, their understanding that the soul learned more by savoring life than by plowing through obstacle after obstacle. And she had come to realize that the Athlans did not age as the Midgardians did. They were not prone to illness. Never was there worry that one more birth might mean an insufficiency of the food resources. They were not obsessed with the future, either, for they relished too much the moment's pleasures.

She rued the great delusion of the Outer Realm and wondered how many generations would suffer under its misguided falsehoods before reaching the state where they'd had enough? The priests of the new gods—the alleged Father of Christ or Allah—certainly labored to promote it with their assertions that the world was fundamentally evil and that an infatuation with earthly life led directly to eternal punishment. And what had their devout convictions brought mankind? Nothing but cruelty and greed and war for the sake of religion. Their respective jealous gods exonerated acts of wickedness perpetrated for the sake of achieving heaven, and thus had wickedness found its way into every aspect of the follower's life.

Odette shivered to think of these things; but she could not put them from her mind as there was always the chance her Lord might return to Midgard. The thought of him aging without necessity troubled her deeply. And yet, in part, it was his heritage that made him so endearing.

She perceived in this proud mercenary a man who truly understood her own suffering during her years in Midgard. For all her love of the Athlans, as much as she felt a part of them now, they might recognize that suffering but could never understand the experience. And though she had no qualms about this and no interest in ever stepping foot in Midgard again, there was a bond she shared with Lord Cu'lugh no man of Athla could ever appreciate.

The time would come when she would be with other men. No longer did she know fear of the Athlan men, nor trepidation to pleasure them or give her devotion when required. She could not, however, allow her fondness of her present Lord to blind her to the respective attributes and qualities of those who would come. Her training allowed for Cu'lugh to be her world and every thought for now, but the same training expected the same grace to be extended to the next Lord who entered her life.

Nor was there any grace to what she felt now—only selfish desire that Cu'lugh would find her as unforgettable as she found him.

Odette closed her eyes and determined she had failed somehow in acquiring the selflessness Mistress Helrose and Lord Eryan had worked so hard to instill. She did not wish to be strong-headed and wondered if it was a part of the experience of the first ravishment to feel so fervently, so selfishly about the master? Even if that were so she saw the madness of it would only lead to pain for her and embarrassment for Lord Cu'lugh if she failed to control herself. Obsessive love had no place in the life of a priestess of Freyja, not even that of a novice.

Odette cherished the Goddess Who had taken pity on her, Who led Thierry to bring her from Burgundy and into Athla. Goddess of fecund pleasures and unconditional love was Freyja, divine embodiment of all the graces of the living universe. Everything worth experiencing and remembering issued from Her hands.

"Ah, Mother," she whispered, closing her eyes, "help me to be as Thee—to love instead of seek love! To show grace instead of demand. And to give pleasure wherever I am needed!"

An hour or so later Odette awoke again to the sound of the door handle turning. She waited hopefully and when she saw it was, indeed, Lord Cu'lugh her heart fluttered happily. She watched as he came in and set something to the floor. He turned and smiled at her and sat down on the bedside.

"Hello. I had hoped to find you awake."

Odette was about to reply that she was accustomed to being awakened at the whims of her Mistress and the stewards when she realized it had been a time since he'd given her permission to speak. Also, Mistress Helrose had warned her that some masters and mistresses took it as a slight to have a flower mention her overseers, and Odette did not want Cu'lugh to feel slighted.

She loved the way the flesh wrinkled slightly at the corners of his almond-shaped chestnut eyes. How very handsome he was! With his short-cropped dark hair and mustache and the fine but swarthy features he had a martial bearing about him that made the king's soldiers seem like young boys in comparison.

"We are going out," he said and kissed her mouth. His lips scalded her, the taste of him made her feel lightheaded. He pulled her up to sit and she looked at the floor. It was a basket he had brought, covered with a cloth of deep blue. Beside it lay a brown velvet pouch. She guessed by the smells that made her mouth water that the basket contained food.

"Are you hungry?" At the nod of her head he said, "Good. I have some food for our little trip."

He found a comb amongst his personal items on the little vanity table. "Perhaps this you should do," he said and offered her the comb. "I am not accustomed— and would not wish to pull that beautiful hair."

Odette blushed at the compliment and combed her hair until it was smooth and fell softly over her shoulders. He gazed as if fascinated and touched a lock over her breast. The warmth of his fingers sent a tingle through her stomach.

"Let us go," he said and threw the pouch over one shoulder and lifted the basket.

"Walk before me," he commanded. She proceeded timidly, acutely aware of the masculine voices sounding through the inn. Several patrons were gathered at the tables downstairs, and seeing her descend the staircase a couple of them eyed her boldly. For a moment she was paralyzed, but Lord Cu'lugh stepped beside her, and giving the basket over to her to carry he took her hand and led her past the men and through the front door.

As they walked through the portico Odette saw two girls kneeling and bound over a narrow cushioned bench. Their breasts swayed behind the fetters that bound them and their buttocks, propped by stools under their bellies, were swollen and well flushed from recent chastisement. They were both very attractive and Odette felt a deep pang of worry that her Lord would stop to admire them. But he strode on without pausing, leading Odette across the street toward the east.

The streets were crowded and noisy with passersby but eventually Lord Cu'lugh turned onto a path that led to a shaded clearing. A tall pole stood near the entryway, and atop it was a placard painted with the Athlan runes that designated these were public grounds. The grass was thick here, by the looks of it probably shorn once a week by grazing sheep. There were stone tables set about, draped with oilcloth and flanked with ironwork benches.

Children darted past everywhere, playing hide-and-seek behind the shrubs and trees and carrying little poles to fish with. Odette saw a brook up ahead as they contined through the park. A couple sat on the bank, a man garbed in simple, genteel fashion, a woman naked but for the braided cord of silver at her throat. Between them sat a toddler with a head of soft red curls and a dimpled smile. The child laughed happily as the man and woman took turns handing him coins to toss into the water.

Odette did not realize she'd stopped to watch the little family until her Lord called out her name. Immediately, she hurried to the table where he had set the basket and pouch. She fell to her knees at his feet and kissed his boots penitently.

He bent and ran his fingers through her hair, sending another tingle coursing through her spine.

"You may sit on the bench beside me and speak freely till I say otherwise."

She nodded and took a seat quietly. Lord Cu'lugh laid out from the basket a round of cheese and a huge bunch of grapes, a plate of smoked meats and a loaf of dark bread. A jug of water he'd also brought.

"I drew this from a well here in town, the one they call the Well of Idun."

"Its waters are reputed to have rejuvenating effects," Odette told him. She smiled shyly, for rejuvenation she needed not—she had never felt more alive in her life.

Over their meal they talked of many things. Odette learned Cu'lugh's favored dishes and of the ballads he knew by heart. He described the lands he had visited and his own homeland. She enjoyed his easy way of speaking and amusing recollections. And he listened attentively as she answered his questions and told him more of herself than ever she'd revealed to any in Athla besides the queen.

"Once you have attained your priestess training," he asked after a time, "and are free to choose your path in life, what think you it shall be?"

She mused a second or two and said, "I think I would like to practice wortery as Mistress Helrose does. I'd like to create my own elixirs, especially perfumes."

"You do not need perfume," he said, his gaze sweeping over her so boldly that she quivered. "Your own scent is enticing as it is."

Odette's cheeks inflamed. "Thank you, my Lord. But I would like to make and offer exotic fragrances to those men and women seeking such things. And I have enjoyed the experience I have had so far under the Mistress's instruction.

Beverages, too, are interesting to brew, and I have in my mind some concoctions I'd like to attempt. Some spiritless versions for those who like to keep their heads clear."

Lord Cu'lugh propped an elbow on the table, resting his chin in his hand as he held her eyes.

"You have an artist's soul, Odette. A commendable ambition."

His gaze was penetrating, as if by sheer will he tried to disrobe her soul.

Her voice sounded frail to her ears. "My Lord, I know you have a Celtic name. May I ask its meaning?"

"Hound of Lugh. Lugh was one of the fertility gods worshipped by my mother's ancestors. Why she gave me a pagan name I have reason to wonder, yet I am proud it is mine. You can be proud of your own name, as well. *Odette—girl of Od*, the enigmatic husband of Freyja and secret identity of Odin. Your father was dedicated to Him?"

Odette nodded. "Yes, and my mother dedicated to Freyja."

"Your father was a fortunate man."

Odette smiled appreciatively. Lord Cu'lugh gaze grew even more penetrating so that she could hardly breathe. Averting her eyes, she fidgeted with an errant length of wicker on the basket, hoping he realize how self-conscious he made her.

"I want you to look at me," he said huskily, startling her terribly. "You are lovely, do you know that?"

Odette shrugged shyly as she met his eyes. But there was no anger in them, only that smoldering, discomforting steadiness.

He bent forward then and kissed her. Her mouth seared beneath his ravishing tongue. As he released her he smiled and picked up the pouch and basket.

"Come, Odette," he said, standing up.

She followed him through the grounds, passing the family sitting on the bank and children laughing and running through the copse. Further along they came to a grove, and Cu'lugh proceeded down a narrow pathway here. The voices of the children faded as they broached deeper into the shade. The songs of wild birds rang through the canopies and the babble of the winding brook echoed nearby. When the sparkling water came into view again Cu'lugh stopped and lowered the pouch to the moss-carpeted bank.

The brook was wider and deeper here and farther upstream a pair of swans glided side-by-side over the surface of the water. Their long, graceful necks inclined one upon the other, and they seemed as oblivious to the rest of the world as the family back in the park.

"Swans mate for life," Cu'lugh whispered. Odette, turned to watch the birds, felt his hands drift up her shoulders. He pulled her back into his muscular embrace so that her naked buttocks pressed against his loins.

"Tilt your head back, Odette," he commanded, and as she did his mouth draped over her face. His bottom lip crushed her upper one, and the electric sensation it brought coursed through Odette's mouth and face. Her knees weakened but he held her up. Slowly, his mouth drifted toward her throat and lingered over the spot he'd awakened before. A paralyzing pleasure swept over Odette, and her helplessness drew a delighted growl from him that sent a wave of chills over her scorched flesh.

Several long heated moments later he pressed her gently to her knees onto the grass. She watched through heavy lids as he stripped off his boots and then his clothing and threw the items aside. His great shaft was erect and in the bright outdoor illumination she saw how truly endowed he was. He lay down on the bank, looking like a god to her. Taking her wrists Cu'lugh drew her to him so that the crest of her pubis pressed against his manhood.

"Kiss me," he whispered, pulling her forward. His mouth engulfed her with virile sweetness and her nethermouth grew ravenous and wet. In his massaging hands her breasts flamed and her nipples hardened into two cones. His hands roved down her back and he gathered her buttocks into his palms. He plumped and pressed them, gently then roughly, and gingerly he parted them and plunged a finger into the little mouth of her anus. Odette stiffened as he probed her rectum with gentle strokes that to her surprise caused her clitoris to billow hotly under its hood.

He touched her vagina and by his triumphant smile Odette knew she was drenched. With a little laugh he extended her arms out from her body and suckled her swaying breasts so that they flared. She wriggled shamelessly, her clitoris pounding against his dauntless manhood and when she looked down his face was sublime with fearsome authority.

"Oh, my Lord and Master," she cooed.

He released her arms then and grasping her hips firmly raised her up so that she hovered above his scarlet member.

It shall run me through, she thought in terror.

The next instant he brought her down, impaling her and gorging her utterly. She whimpered, but Lord Cu'lugh seemed oblivious to her fear she would be wounded.

He captured her wrists at her back. "You are fine, Odette. A perfect fit, see? Now you shall ride me."

She obeyed reluctantly and it was as if a stave of living steel had been inserted into her. His organ rubbed and teased some drowsy core deep inside her. As she rode this core awakened and she felt a frantic need ignite. Mystified by this overpowering feeling she slowed a bit and looked at him with confusion.

"Faster, young lady," he reprimanded and when she pouted he spanked her briskly. Horrified, she rode faster, her knees now bouncing on the ground at his sides. She remembered Mistress Helrose's lessons on focusing her attention on the man's pleasure. She constricted her nether muscles and forced away all thought but that of gratifying him. In her effort her own sensations were pushed with merciless clarity to a new height. Odette moaned and her wet orifice rose and dove over his manhood eagerly. Her entire body was rampant with needy desire, as if it had been transformed into a well of raw sensation.

The stern glint in her master's eyes impelled Odette's pace. Suddenly her clitoris spasmed, and as her eyes fell shut the whole of her orifice flooded with heavenly convulsions.

Lord Cu'lugh pulled her down and covered her mouth with a savage kiss. His pelvis rocked furiously so that his cock crushed her still-throbbing core. Holding her against him as his seed exploded inside her, he moaned softly at her ear.

Odette knew a contentment no conscious thought could define. She lavished his dear face with gentle kisses.

"You are mine," he whispered. He embraced her to him firmly and his even voice was thick with passion. "I would rather die than let another possess you!"

Odette kissed the firm throat at her lips and as he rolled over she cupped his face in her palms and kissed his mouth again and pulled his face to her breasts. He lay there contentedly, and she felt his breathing against her skin. They lay a long while, with only the songs of the birds and the lapping of the brook intruding on their silence.

When at length Lord Cu'lugh moved and raised her up, there was a gleam in his eyes that quickened Odette's heart.

"Come with me."

She followed him a little ways down the bank of the brook, and there he took her by the hand and escorted her into the cool water. She watched as he squatted and splashed himself clean, even his head and face. She smiled, amused, to see the water drip in long currents through the hair on his chest, belly and thighs and that dark nest about his manhood. His balls shrank considerably and his flaccid manhood sparkled pink.

"You wash while I fetch something," he said and stepped out onto the bank again. While she cleaned herself he trotted over to the spot where they had made love. She was lying on her back and letting the water ripple through her hair when he came back. When she was done he extended his hand. She took it and stepped out, and he held out the blue cloth from the basket to drape over her.

Her skin quickly covered over with faint goose bumps as he patted her skin dry and, worrying if he were not chilly, she asked, "My Lord—"

"Do not speak," he said, and though this surprised Odette she did not attempt to question him.

He lifted the pouch from the moss and opened it.

"Stand perfectly still, Odette."

He went to one knee beside her and took something from the pouch. It was a belt of slender braided bronze looped with suede garters—leather circlets held together by a thick iron chain—very much like the one Lord Eryan had put on her.

"Lift your feet," he said and guided her legs through the belt and into the garters. He locked the belt snugly in place at the small of her back. The tiny key he returned to the pouch. Odette moved her legs a little, finding the iron chain quite a bit tauter than the one she was used to. She bit her bottom lip nervously and saw Lord Cu'lugh draw forth what looked like some kind of delicate bronze breastplate. The two suede ribbons of it he tied over her shoulders and her breasts he placed into the bronze shell cups. They cinched and uplifted her breasts just as the bodice of her old chemise, but the cups had been designed so that her nipples jutted over the scalloped rims.

For her nipples he had brought clamps with silver bells. These tormented her greatly and she whimpered at the bite of them, but the disproving look he gave silenced her at once. A wide leather collar with a brass chain loop he locked upon her throat.

The adornments were designed to heighten and reinforce the sense of servility in the wearer. Odette knew that in time she would get used to the irritation of the clamps, and in her heart she was flattered that he wished to showcase her so provocatively.

I should be grateful there is no phallus, she reproached herself. She saw Lord Cu'lugh take from the pouch something that looked like a long hairpin with a pearl on the bend. Although she had no idea what it was her heart pounded with a new fear.

"Spread your legs, sweet."

As soon as she'd complied he parted her nether lips with his left hand. With his right Lord Cu'lugh tweaked her clitoris between his thumb and forefinger. Odette gasped and tried to keep her legs still. Gently he insured the hood was drawn down and slid the clip over the length of the tiny organ. It aroused under the metal, an arousal only intensified by its confinement.

This controlled arousal seemed almost brutal to Odette and she whimpered crossly for the first time.

He looked up at her firmly. "It will only pinch mildly, and after a time you will grow accustomed to it. And you shan't think to remove it, lest you wish to arouse my greatest disapproval."

Odette knew she shouldn't speak but her indignation took over. "But *why*, my Lord?"

"The lady who makes these promised that it will keep your passion incited. And that is how I want you always—with no relief but at my discretion."

She pouted darkly and stomped her foot. At once he threw her forward over his bent thigh and spanked her smartly several times. Her sex heated as much as her buttocks, but it was her face that pained most. As he set her back upright he shook a finger in her face.

"That is but a warning, young lady. I am not afraid to punish you as ardently as love you."

The words made Odette's breast swell. Her eyes lowered and she saw the pearl gleaming within the damp thatch between her legs.

Lord Cu'lugh drew from the pouch a pair of suede boots dyed a deep lilac shade and a pair of long silken gloves of the same color. The gloves extended over Odette's elbows and encased her hands and arms perfectly. She was obliged to sit to draw the boots on and lace them up. As she stood she was surprised how well they fit.

Lord Cu'lugh's smiling eyes pored over her. "Do the boots fit?"

"Perfectly, my Lord."

Odette stretched her arms to admire the soft feel of the gloves. Timidly, she looked down at the lovely boots. Sublime display of his ownership this was, to sleeve and subdue her limbs and tantalize her nipples and clitoris in tormenting, pretty devices.

"How do you feel now?"

Odette's voice trembled. "At your mercy, my Lord."

"Perfect," he said and she lowered her head instinctively as he rose.

"This is how I want you," he said and tilted her chin up so that she had to meet his eyes. The fierce, dark flame of his gaze sent a flare of desire through her thighs. But as she watched him dress she sensed that it would be long before he allowed her full relief of her passion. She did not mind; in fact, she welcomed this, and in gratitude of his loving mastery she went to her knees and kissed his boots again.

With a tender laugh he pulled her up and drew her into an embrace. His arms were constraining and resolute brassards; his kiss the firebrand that soldered the last trailing threads of self-doubt. He ordered her to walk before him out of the grounds, smacking her bottom every few steps. She wept as she made her way, not for the sting his firm hand delivered but for the ache to be in his arms again.

On the way home she could not contain herself any longer. She turned on the walkway and threw her arms about his neck. He laughed sweetly, showering her with a dozen impassioned kisses. Upon releasing her he smacked her bottom again and took her hand and led the way up the street at a leisurely pace to accommodate the iron chain between her legs. Odette was proud to walk at his side, intoxicated with a happiness that made her forget all else but him.

Chapter Twenty-Four

nly Hrowthe's invitation could have coaxed Vanda into stepping into the Temple of the Blodsauker priests. It was a loathsome place they had constructed with her beneficence, using property and labor in her own village. A simple, four-story, single-spired plank church of rough cedar and lime mortar, its ugliness chafed even Vanda's sense of simplicity. Only a handful of windows, and these haphazardly placed, detailed the dull exterior. Next to the unsettling structure the rustic buildings of tiered and split logs and quaint thatched roofs, all built in her father's time, looked attractive.

But she had needed the alliance of all of Hrowthe's brethren, and if it took an eyesore to content them she would swallow her repulsion for a while. One day she would have all the strong backs she needed to build the gilded castle of her dreams and be at liberty to choose and exclude who passed through the gates. She would gladly provide the brethren their gloomy Temple in exchange for the service of overseeing her human vassals.

The strange glass orb affixed at the summit of the spire did fascinate Vanda and often she stood gazing at it. Hrowthe said the brethren had found it lying in a pasture in a distant northern realm, a gift left by a dark star that struck the earth. She knew the priests would gaze at the orb and scry, delving into the mysteries of their human frailties and confronting the temptations of their emaciated mortal shells. Hrowthe explained that should a brother gaze into it long enough he would connect with God.

Vanda hardly shared their zealous fervor, but when she studied the orb for a while a feeling of serenity would settle over her, allowing her perspective into her life and into the hearts of those around her. Along with these insights the orb helped to temper her anger and impatience with those she discovered had tried to deceive her. She could return to her Hall and conceive just the exact and just reward to dole to her abusers. And the offenders would never see their reckoning coming, for their superstition averted their eyes from the orb.

Vanda had little patience with the mentality of the Saxon serfs and her mercenaries, who loved superstition as a child loved games; but she had discovered that her Lombard and Florentine artisans shunned the Temple just as adamantly. She had seen them cross the street just to avoid walking on the same side where the Temple stood. It shocked her, for she had paid highly to commission them, seducing them away from foreign courts and lords with promises of gold and silver. She had deemed their refinement would accentuate the ambiance of worldliness needed to raise her estate from its decadent pagan heritage.

At least the shadow of the orb kept the populace from her streets at night. She could not afford to trust those used to comfort not to bribe the mercenaries into letting them into the quarters of her female serfs. So, she soothed her disillusionment by knowing the orb served a practical use.

Now, as she ascended the steps to the Temple doors the hair on her arms raised under the crushed-velvet sleeves of her gown. Vanda had come with a pouch of gold to pay the artisans hired for the Brethren. Out of the corner of her eye she noticed the Saxon crone who carried the pouch had stopped in her tracks to make a sign against evil.

"It is a house of God," Vanda reproached her.

The crone's encrusted eyes spanned the Temple from base to the orbed spire.

"I shall not go further."

Vanda seethed. Only her respect for Hrowthe kept her from kicking the crone hard enough to hurl her down the stairs. She, too, loathed the thought of entering this dismal place—its dreariness reminded her of the isolation she'd had no choice but to indulge to avoid her stepmother not so many years ago. However, Hrowthe himself had requested she come, to see with her own eyes the object that had been commenced and finished in the month since Cu'lugh set out to Athla. Vanda's impatience to see her sister was consoled by the knowledge that at least Odette's homecoming gift would be waiting.

For a fleeting single moment a smile had touched her old friend's lips as he beseeched her to come in person. She could hardly keep the amusement from her face as he promised in fervent tones that she need not stay long.

"There is no need to beg for my presence, Father. I shall come see the Harp."

She was still sometimes amazed at her fondness for her old advisor. Men rarely deserved respect, let alone trust; Hrowthe had won both from her. What had commenced as an association to aid and promote one another's private interests had over the years turned to something much deeper. Vanda did not seek out his views as once she did and of this she was proud, for utter independence, especially from men, was her single purpose in life. She had proved her capability in handling her own policies and setting her own laws, of governing her vassals and inferiors.

Yet, though their association had started out as a practical one, she would never forget it was he who had understood the dynamics of her hatred for her father and her father's whore. Whilst her husband lived and she held the title of comptroller of his fief, it had been Hrowthe who instilled her with self-confidence and taught her to conceal her true purposes behind the mask of fastidiousness. Thierry's Frankish knights and counselors had frowned on her every levy and enactment, claiming she was parsimonious and inhuman toward her own enserfed race. And, without doubt, she could not have suffered her marriage as long as she had without Hrowthe's assurances of the future.

Vanda knew that she and Hrowthe stood together on the brink of a most auspicious event in their respective schemes. Together had they formed the path, though differently would they benefit. She hardly needed him now, but she wanted him near for however long he wished to hold the cherished space he'd so long occupied. And though it went against their religion of independence without illusion and hope, she sensed the Brethren depended on Hrowthe to guide their otherwise hollow intellects. She could see their reliance upon him even if they could not.

But the truth was that Hrowthe's temperate piety and intellect whetted and polished their fanaticism. This was a double-fold blessing, in Vanda's mind, as it insured their loyalty to her and as well provided the homage from his peers she felt Hrowthe well deserved, though his humility would never allow him to actually desire such a thing.

He could not prevent her from cherishing him. And so she came to see this sacred instrument, this wondrous Harp that was to be used to demonstrate the Blodsauker's loyalty to God, and which would eliminate the last obstacle to Vanda's aims.

She glared at the crone but managed to curb her ire.

"Then stay here," she told the woman and snatched the purse from the withered hands and thrust it into her girdle. The knocker on the door was so large she had to use both hands to lift it. As she carefully lowered it the echo inside resounded like a stone thrown down a great shaft. She gave the crone a last look, hoping that her own example would shame the woman's cowardice; but to her shock the woman had turned away and was hobbling down the street in the direction of the women's quarters, muttering "Fool!"

Vanda willed herself to be gracious until nightfall; then would she order the crone's feet cut off.

The massive door groaned on its hinges as it was pulled open. A young priest Vanda recognized welcomed her inside. He was young and ethereally thin, his limbs and face practically hairless, his arms unnaturally long and feminine due to the effect of the self-mutilation he'd performed upon avowing his intention of joining the brotherhood. Castration was not a requisite for membership, but the boy's sacrifice, Hrowthe had said, was one worthy of emulation.

"Lady Vanda, we are honored by your visit."

The anteroom was barren, drearier even than the outer aspect of the Temple. There were tables and chairs set about the clean-swept earthen floor, and within recesses along one entire wall Vanda saw row upon row of neatly piled scrolls and manuscripts and texts. The other walls were bare. A small brazier, crackling with offerings of yew sprigs, sat near a dark doorway in the back of the room, and the pervading damp cold of the place told her it had only recently been kindled. There was a consciously restrained feeling in the room, something she suspected the Brethren had tried to sterilize with the yew.

"Father Hrowthe waits for you in here."

Vanda followed the boy to the door of the sanctuary. As soon as he opened it a waft of freezing air struck Vanda's face. Yet the room was glaringly bright, and as she proceeded in she understood why—the spire supporting the orb stood above this section of the Temple. A staircase wound about the tower supporting the spire, and Vanda saw doors here and there at various levels of it. She imagined there were hidden chambers on the other floors where the priests could sleep or mediate, perhaps more libraries. If the spire needed maintenance or the orb needed cleaning they would need a way to get up.

The sanctuary itself was empty but for a rough dais built in the center of the room and that which stood upon it, the Harp.

It was a colossal instrument. The forepillar was a thick column of granite rising from a soundboard of ebony marble. Vanda did not recognize the red and grey material used for the sloping neck, but it was polished to a high sheen and reminded her not so much of wood but rather the Saxons' descriptions of dragon leather. The strings of the instrument were pure silver and pegged invisibly within the soundboard and the neck. From the rear of the soundboard a black cord trailed loosely across the length of the neck and plunged into the ornamental boss at the top of the forepillar. About a quarter way down from the boss were two apertures—deep, black, perfectly bored cavities, side-by-side—and from the very center of the forepillar jutted a sculpted protrusion. At first Vanda thought it but a decoration until she drew nearer the dais and realized it was a double-headed phallus carved in the likeness of twinned serpents' heads. The black eyes and mouths were hewn deeply into the granite. Below the phallus was another pair of deep cavities.

She wondered why the priests would have placed such a disgusting object on their sacred instrument. Then, as she stepped up on the dais to inspect it better a small, black, reptilian head darted out from one of the mouths of the phallus. Vanda pursed her mouth in disgust as the creature's tongue flicked the air. Its lidless eyes were two tiny, muck-gray, visionless pools.

Vanda laughed suddenly, and the serpent shuddered angrily, its mouth gaping wide to bare its slender but dull fangs. She had wondered if the priests could give what they'd promised; for all Hrowthe's assurances she had doubted the strength of his priests' resolve to create a sacred object that would satisfy their respective designs. She did not yet grasp the full workings of the Harp, but it was apparent they had put much more labor into its creation than she'd even imagined.

Coldly beautiful instrument of justice!

"The venom of these creatures," she said. "I hope it does not work too hastily."

"It contains no poison."

It was Hrowthe; and she wheeled, her cheeks aching in her effort not to show her joy too clearly. He joined her on the dais and laid an arm about her shoulders.

"Their purpose is not to bring death."

Vanda furrowed her brow. "But she will die, yes?"

Hrowthe nodded once. "When she has served her purpose to Loki, my dear, you are allowed that privilege."

Vanda ran her fingertips over the cool granite. "I still cannot imagine how my father's bastard would benefit any sanctified rite."

"Perhaps your personal objectives in this matter blind you to the truth that lies before you."

"I hope that is not a reproach," she said lightly. "I understand that the worth of a sacrifice is defined by its irony—and I know all too well the decadence which courses in the bloodline of Silfr."

Hrowthe smiled indulgently. "You are a dauntless and beneficent woman, Vanda, and our Lord's gratitude is boundless. When our rite is completed, have assurance your wrongs shall know vindication."

She sighed and squeezed the frail hand resting on her shoulder. "Yes, I have no doubt. And the treasure of the Nibelungen shall be used to help recreate this world. My rule shall be one decent and moral; I have no tolerance for sin in my kingdom or weakness. It shall be the dignified world for us all, sterilized of the false sentiments and dependencies for which we have all suffered."

There came a commotion from the anteroom. Vanda and Hrowthe turned to see one of Vanda's eunuch serving boys coming through the door. He bowed, his face red and breathless.

"What is this, Lunor?"

"Riders have come, Lady Vanda, riders from the north section."

Vanda's heart sped more anxiously than she would have thought. "Sir Cu'lugh, returned to us?"

"No, my Lady—they are dark elves."

"Dark elves," Hrowthe said, and his eyes grew distant and narrow as they did whenever he fell into a vision. "There is strange news."

She warmed with impatience. "If this is but another attempt of their Prince to sue for a marriage agreement, I shall have his riders put to death—one way or the other."

Hrowthe blinked back to himself and looked at her steadily. "No, be not so hasty—this is an offering you should not ignore."

"I have already obliged too many men. I have no intention of sharing my desmesne with any of them and certainly not the Darkling Prince—that I already know."

"But they do not know it," he replied, "and this time they arrive with news advantageous to us."

She looked at him thoughtfully and her affection for him softened her anger. "You know this?"

"I had suspicions, and so I have kept the Darklings busy—in case your plans went awry." He took her hand between his hard, cold palms. "It is never wise to carry all your coins in one purse."

She felt her heart drop. "But Cu'lugh has not been gone so long. We can wait."

Hrowthe waited a moment or two before replying. "If that is as you wish, of course."

Vanda bristled at his condescending tone. "He did give his word."

"The word of the fickle godless, my child, just like your husband."

"I shall have no more husbands!" She was infuriated that Hrowthe would still treat her as a child who needed a reminder of a lesson.

But he had a point. Thierry had never truly broken his word; he'd remained faithful to her till the last. It was only that after years of being the passive, worshipful husband she had envisioned when she'd agreed to marriage the man had suddenly, fatally, decided to garb himself in the cloak of pagan chivalry with all its false notions of men's obligations, responsibilities and rights. It was this she suspected had sent him flying off without word to remove Odette from Burgundy.

Until the moment Hrowthe discovered Thierry's whereabouts and revealed the purpose of his disappearance Vanda had not once considered disposing of the man. Over the years she had developed a fondness for him, much like she had felt for a wolf-pup she'd found as a child. Never had she had to—or even wanted to— resort to beating her husband as she had the pup, for unlike the animal Thierry willingly adored her and conceded to his proper station. In the end, her father had taken the wolf from her, complaining she abused the creature…and it was her father's bastard who had seduced Thierry's sanity away.

Perhaps it was this that still agitated her—the unreliability of that submissiveness. What foul spirit he had allowed to possess him she would never know. He had paid for his betrayal when her men buried him alive in the roots of an oak stump in her father's shattered grove. His actions reaffirmed the axiom first demonstrated by her father's actions: that the wound created by betrayal was long in healing, and not even death could sufficiently ameliorate the scar.

"Women are not frail creatures needing coddling," she murmured, and now it was Hrowthe's turn to look chagrined. While his hardened features could scarcely twist with the animation of fully revealed regret Vanda knew him well enough to recognize it.

"You are right, woman of faith," he said and inclined his head as she stepped from the dais.

Why, she lamented as she left the sanctuary, *why could not Thierry have remained so respectful?*

* * *

Lady Vanda's hall was the most silent abode Loic had ever entered. The Darkling realm never knew a moment's quiet—their industrious nature did not allow for even rest or sleep without interruption of argument or conflict. Thus did the recruitment of human workers serve two purposes. Mining the gray, snowless mountains the humans labored to find the Treasure, that magic gold that would invest the Darklings with the full power of their chaotic heritage. But, just as importantly, the regret of the fickle, frail race added to the resounding strife and misery saturating the realm's ethers. Silenced never were the precious lamentations of those who had voluntarily given up hope and life in exchange for the incontestable assurance of equality and the knowledge that no other human could govern them. As much to ensure that treasured desolation as to enforce their toil did the barbed steel whips of the Darkling overseers flail night and day. It was a fair exchange jealously protected by the Darkling magistrates.

Loic had made too many ventures into Athla, however, for the health of his constitution. His Prince might not have sympathy, and that was as it should be. But the more time Loic spent trading in Athla the less he could contain the urge to lash out where he could amongst their decadent number. The obsession with life the Athlans courted! And the perverse displays of affection, the remorseless parade of flesh and reciprocating dependent relationships! He could not fault his companions for waiting outside now while he spoke with Lady Vanda. The stench of human frailty lingered in the floors, the beams, the walls.

At least the brooding atmosphere of Vanda's hall was an improvement over Athla. The ethers, too, were comfortably thick enough to defy the sun. The only perturbation to his composure was the sight of the Blodsauker priest who sat by the Lady's side.

"Send the priest away, my Lady," he demanded, inspecting the glass vessel her servant had filled with the sweet drink called wine.

Hrowthe's animated features stretched in the gesture denoting amusement. "It was I who hired you to venture into Athla, sir, and the lady knows of this."

"My words are for her ears alone, priest." Loic kept his eyes on the mortal face studying him from the end of the table. Tight-lipped and restrained this woman was, her attempt to hide her eagerness commendable but futile under the scrutiny of a Darkling mind. She impressed him as no other human had—pure in her loathing for all those things most detestable in the human race and appropriately conscious of her status, therefore rightfully arrogant. Her features were soft and attractive in that short-lived human way, and this she knew, though, unfortunately, she had strayed from purity by taking pride in the fact. Yet, he sensed she knew this habit was self-defeating, that to cherish her own femininity made her vulnerable to grieving it once aged and destroyed. She endeavored to correct her tendencies, dreaming and working for the day she ruled without the slightest need to be comforted by a man's approval or desire.

Lady Vanda sighed now, so quietly no mortal would have ever detected the sound. "I do not tolerate ingratitude to my counselor, Sir Loic. Do tell us what news you gathered under his wage?"

"He claimed my service was for your benefit and so must I insist he leave us." Loic grinned and emptied his glass. "You both know my race well enough to know you are perfectly safe from any carnal designs, my Lady."

Hrowthe stood up and the hem of his robes rustled slightly as he stepped to the door. Vanda looked at him, frowning uncertainly. Loic heard the Blodsauker's haughty thoughts touch her mind, a way of communication the priest's kind used often. *"We must hear his news, my Lady."*

When the priest was gone and they were alone Vanda's hostility infused the very air. Loic felt her love of the Blodsauker, an emotion she did not deal out easily; and though he did not understand the emotions of humans he knew enough to be aware when he'd succeeded in insulting them.

Unfortunate flaw for one so otherwise perfect, he thought, *and mayhap rectifiable someday.*

For the moment, however, Loic realized he would have to use the tact and humility her social class expected from perceived underlings were he to penetrate her barriers and interest her in the true reason for his visit.

"Forgive me," he said. "I forget you are close to the…priest."

"It is difficult for you to say the word, isn't it?" she said. "Why is that? They are pious servants of your great Sire, after all. For that should you not offer your utmost respect?"

"That is a story for another time, my Lady." Loic set the glass down and dabbed a finger idly around the vessel's rim. A light silvery note hung for a moment or two on the air. "My companions and I traveled swiftly to bring the news most precious to you."

Vanda's blue eyes flickered. "News—from Athla?"

He nodded. "Your priest was correct, your sister dwells there. Unfortunately, she has been initiated into the decadent rites of the whore-goddess so loved in that place."

"You have seen Odette," Vanda said carefully. "How did you recognize her?"

"Her name and parentage are used quite loosely by some."

"I sent a man to fetch her. Now I may rest assured he will not come back empty-handed."

Loic licked his lips slowly. "I know of this man—it was he the priest directed me to follow into Athla. I must be honest, he has no intention of leaving any time soon."

"What do you mean? Has he met obstacles?"

Loic stretched out his forearms on the table and eyed her squarely. "He has taken your sister as his love captive."

Vanda's face flared with crimson. "No! He has sworn to me!"

"We kept clear watch on his comings and goings, and learned from the proprietor of the place where he sojourns that Lord Cu'lugh was brought the girl by Helrose, a priestess of Freyja, that he might deflower her. On discovering this we took rooms ourselves for the length of time the Athlan law allowed us stay. For two days and nights we observed his activities. Indeed, we witnessed your sister in his ownership. This knight revels in the Athlan debauchery, my Lady. He is not…not what you believed."

Vanda scanned the table before her and her fingernails gouged into the wooden armrests of her seat.

"Did you hear no hint he plans to return with her?"

Loic shook his head, patiently waiting for the full impact of the news to register in her proud heart.

"So, he has fallen into temptation," she seethed. "Where are those chivalrous manners he so proudly assumed?"

"It may be he considers reveling in both of you," Loic offered slyly.

"He will have *nothing* now, not after dallying with the whore!" Vanda breathed deeply, purposefully, composing herself so that only her heated cobalt eyes betrayed her fury.

"That is harsh," she conceded. "As far as Cu'lugh is concerned, I did have my misgivings. His sympathy for the pagan ways tarnishes any claim of nobility, tarnishing the piety his mother and father endeavored to instill. I must thank you for your honesty, Sir Loic—and for your thoughtfulness in sparing me humiliation before my counselor."

She had recaptured her aloofness impressively, and Loic said, "I would never give a Blodsauker excuse to reproach his betters."

Her wrath was temporarily diverted. "You dark elves loathe the brotherhood dedicated to your great progenitor, don't you? I cannot understand that antipathy for those who seek to wreak His desires. Are you not grateful they work to sacrifice themselves for that day when they shall rend their veins open upon the roots of the world tree and usher in Ragnarok? Do you not care to see sin banished from this realm?"

Loic smiled at her innocence. "We tolerate the creatures, for they do serve the cause of our great Sire. But that they must be coerced into service under the delusion they work to serve the good of their race sickens us."

"The human race?"

"You are superior to most of your kind, dear lady—if you were otherwise I would not be at your table."

"You would not have the Blodsaukers aid the race of man? Why not?"

"Its core is fundamentally base and sentimental."

Vanda was momentarily speechless. At last she retorted, "The Blodsaukers, as I have witnessed, seem to have thrown off such fickle traits. What makes you certain the rest of mankind cannot embrace their philosophies, their fealty to abstinence and independence? Already the sin-loathing religions begotten of your Sire's influence sway powerful leaders and help construct great governments. Surely that tells you that neither is the rest of mankind hopeless."

"Those who follow these dogmas will have their chance to fight for the righteous cause when Ragnarok begins, with each follower allowed to see our Sire as his or her religion has been prompted to envision Him. You must understand, my Lady, when that time comes the Blodsaukers will discover the necessary deceit used to recruit them to the cause. I have no doubt the shock of it will be too much for some of their altruistic hearts to bear. Those individuals will surely renounce Loki and come to question if there was any wisdom in abhorring the carnal gods they so long worked against."

Vanda's cheeks bloomed angrily, though her eyes were curious. "What necessary deceit is it you speak of?"

"Do you believe truly, Lady, that Loki instructed his priests to gorge on the blood and flesh of their mortal kinsmen, roaming through the generations forever on the hunt, for the sole advantage of their petty race? That the collective memories and learned experiences of mankind is what will usher in the end of the world? Man is a trifling, petty creature, almost none worthy of the air they breathe. Yet, it serves well for the Blodsaukers to devour them, for the racial consciousness collected does offer the power of far-seeing. The desire to help their race, directed to purifying this world, is honorable. But that pity and the endless effort to lift their fellow men, these very sympathies which had to be appealed to in order to recruit them—it is these sympathies that demonstrate their essential flaws.

"They seek Ragnarok on the premise it will bring to mortal man liberation from sickness and death and want. This is not the purpose of Ragnarok. The purpose is to purify the earth for us—Loki's children. To wipe away all remnants of evil from this once-perfect world by ending once and for all time every brazen or subtle act of reverence for the immoral goddess. Ah, the genders shall be eliminated, yes, the Blodsaukers are right in this. The world shall be made chaste and all hope and misconceptions and yearnings wiped away from human consciousness. The old visions of fundamental gender differences will be stripped away wholly, and those unwilling to accept the new reality eradicated. No mortal shall be allowed life who nurses the romantic lies which defiled the primordial order my race brought this world. No more pretty illusions to maintain their hope, not a one."

Vanda stared at Loic and he felt her fascination.

"You would have me believe the priests do as they do for purposes other than what they believe? If this is true…then what *will* initiate Ragnarok?"

"A sacrifice." Loic saw the understanding illuminate her eyes. "But one made by all that will disquiet the pagan deities and spirits utterly, made in the form of a mockery of a much-cherished icon. An example, if you will, to spite their insatiable romance and carnality."

She flinched as if she'd been pricked. "*No*," she whispered, her eyes widening with dismay and delight. "And the Blodsaukers have no idea—not a one of them?"

Loic shook his head. "For all the functional knowledge at their command, they are proudly ascetic creatures. This characteristic is one of the requisites for their order, though one that has been kept from them. For their pride and asceticism inspire the practice of denial sought by Loki. I have witnessed as He has suckled the human essence from their undead veins. It is a matter they keep private, never sharing the truth with one another. They fear doubt would spread amongst their brothers if they divulge what they have been led to believe is a unique offering."

A fleeting look of sadness crossed Vanda's face as she thought of her counselor.

"But the sacrifice will usher in Ragnarok?"

"Yes."

Vanda took a balancing breath, but Loic knew her elation and how she worked to suppress any show of that elation. She pleated her napkin slowly to steady her hands.

"I-I cannot be faulted for wanting my own flesh and blood out of that kingdom of sin."

"What Christian authority should fault you? If it is enough for them, pious children of Loki, then who is to speak otherwise?"

"What of that which I was promised, the treasure that will afford me to build my demesne? Will your race seek to eliminate me, a mortal human, when all this begins?"

"I would not have disclosed all this to you were such the case." Loic rose and walked around the table to stand next to her, looking down at her with the dark, glistening eyes he knew appeared to her large and all the more formidable for the ancient spirit that her human instinct detected behind the childlike directness.

"You are special, Lady Vanda. Our Sire must have seen potential in you, else he would have turned to another source to see the Harp adequately havened. And that you can separate yourself from the human flaw of family loyalty speaks much to your character. Be assured that my Prince, direct descendant of our Sire and overseer of our realm until His return, wishes you as an ally for your outstanding virtues. Nevertheless, we must act shrewdly as well as quickly, and as we know your mercenaries could never find their way into Athla my Prince is willing to give the full aid you need in seeing our mutual desires fulfilled. But he has a request to make in return."

She shivered, and Loic heard the word *marriage* ring in her thoughts and he laid a strengthening hand on her shoulder.

"Be assured our interests are pure, my lady. You have set into motion the process that will lead to attainment of our mutual goals. But neither I nor my kin have the desire to witness the necessary spectacle, mockery to the foul Goddess though it may be. You must be the one to prevent any interference that may arise, whether such threat issues from human mercy or the rage of the Blodsaukers should the inevitable moment of their understanding arrive prematurely. We ask that you ensure none of this transpires, to see the offering is allowed to run its full and unseemly course. Do this, and you will have our enduring gratitude. Our armies will be at your hand to defend your land, title, chastity, the treasure you were promised—all, once the petty gods go to battle against our freed Sire."

A cold smile touched Vanda's lips. "That is no dread bargain, good sir. Tell your Prince I agree to this—it shall be a pleasure."

Loic bowed. "And our honor. I must return to my Prince to tell him the good tidings, that he may enlist a host to succor the cause."

Chapter Twenty-Five

anda's mind was a myriad of charged, delicious, reckoning images that filled Loic with satisfaction.

"Soon," he continued, "you shall have the justice you have long awaited. Your alliance is most valued, and we know how repellent it shall be for you to witness the sacrifice. But in assuring its completion you set into motion the righting of your world. When that righting is completed, then, too, may my race throw off the semblances we must don to enter the world still claimed by the gods. We will be liberated and shed of those forced guises. Never again will my race be forced to bear limitations in this realm. Together, you and we shall reclaim this world into the bosom of righteousness."

He felt Vanda's regained assurance. No betrayal could deflect this woman's designs—no, and Loic suspected that once the sacrifice was made even her tiny flaws of devotion to her counselor and the enjoyment of her own beauty would vanish. Then would she be perfect to rule beside his Prince in the Darkling world—the perfect example of purged weaknesses to the survivors of her race.

"Please excuse me now, Lady. I have dwelt too long in the company of humans and must return home with my companions who wait outside."

She nodded silently and started to rise.

"I can see my way out, Lady."

He bowed again and left the room. The clinging essences of humanity in the Hall were beginning to affect Loic's ability to maintain his semblance and he quickly strode through the corridors. But after a time he perceived heavy footfalls at his heel. He paused and turned, scanning the empty floor with the true Darkling vision guised beneath his counterfeit eyes.

A glint of passive white light slammed into his face with such force he was knocked back into the wall. He roared and clawed at the attacker, but what he touched was nothing of earth—no mortal, snoopy servant, no undead priest. The light he raked possessed substance not of the physical realm. Loic bared his teeth at it even as he was astonished by what drew back and formed, widening and taking texture and shape.

A tall, golden-skinned man with streaming golden hair loomed before Loic. The shade's right hand shot out and seized Loic's throat, while the left raised a battle-ax above the Darkling's brow. The wide metal blade looked material enough with its glinting sharp edge. Loic's skin prickled and he saw the shade's mouth move as if it would speak.

Loic shut his eyes and commanded the fear, which he'd never experienced before this moment, to still in his breast. Even so, his voice shook as some weakling human's. "Return to Odin's abode, chieftain, or to Freyja's palace—wherever it is you indulge your fancies! No longer have you potency in this dominion!"

Loic felt something scrape his forehead, and it pressed urgently, as if seeking to enter his skull. The voice that responded to his was as raspy as the Wasteland winds, and its resonance blasted cold against Loic's face. *Leave my home! Leave my children be!*

Loic forced himself to breathe. Opening his eyes, he saw the warrior's right hand lay over his heart. The fingertips pressed harder on his chest, and the arctic chill of the grasping fingers seized his heart. It jumped, and his head throbbed with blinding pain. Desperately he attempted to push the shade away, but it drew the power of unseen ethers to its cause. Loic felt as a helpless child against it, and as he battered at it he felt the coldness creep into his pores and begin to shrink his semblance. Bones and marrow, sinews and muscles cramped under the pressure; his entire false body felt as if it were about to implode. Blood trickled from his eyes and his tongue heaved forward between teeth that were rapidly losing density.

It seeks to destroy this semblance I wear!

Loic gasped for the shade's mercy. For a Darkling to be divested in Midgard meant instant death, and death in this realm would enthrall him to the will of the humans' diverse and petty gods.

Suddenly, though, the shade released his grasp as suddenly as he had attacked. Loic's eyes and tongue snapped back into place. His skin seared as the pores closed once again and every organ vibrated under the dozens of fractured bones the shade had delivered. Tears of pain sprang to his bruised, aching eyes, and as Loic shook them away he saw the shade's golden countenance dim. The face sank into the invisible air. For a moment the gleam of the battle-ax hung on the air, but then it, too, snuffed out.

Loic sucked back the cry of pain that arose and pushed away from the wall. As he began to walk again he realized the crotch of his breeches was soaked with urine.

He pondered the shade's impotent display and the thought of that impotence eased his humiliation a little. His relief was short-lived, for in a moment something else stirred in the shadows up ahead. He froze and felt for his dagger when he saw a figure move toward him.

It was the Blodsauker, Hrowthe. He approached Loic in his soundless way, the furrows of his face drawn into a look of compassion. Probably just a reflection of what the creature would have felt in his old mortality, yet the gesture repulsed Loic. The creature's listless hand rose in a consoling way and Loic jumped back. The Blodsauker came no closer, but in the silence Loic felt Hrowthe's insolent thoughts.

"I do not need your pity or mercy or any other of your leftover human sentiments," he growled.

Hrowthe's pity did not diminish. "You perceive, but you will never understand the human soul, not even those who live in ignorance."

Loic smiled maliciously. "Do not be so hasty to cast the name of 'ignorant' on these shades, priest. I know Loki's true aims, and what fate awaits you and your brotherhood once your purpose is fulfilled."

Without another utterance Loic marched out of Vanda's Hall, only too happy to leave the priest to contemplate the meaning of these words.

* * *

Vanda felt Hrowthe's unease, but he revealed nothing of his personal concerns to her as they conversed. It was as well, for her thoughts were elsewhere and for the moment his prying into her conference with the Darkling was more irritating than helpful. She did tell him the Prince's offer if but to hurry him on.

For several long and irritating moments he was thoughtful. At last he said, "Did he ask to see the mantle?"

Vanda pulled her shawl about her shivering shoulders. The chill from the other parts of the Hall had managed to seep into her private rooms. The trespassing cold only aggravated her growing impatience to have all this over with. Too many years had she waited—why had not the Darklings offered this before? Could they not sense her need sooner?

Hrowthe should have seen their interest earlier instead of keeping silent and forcing me to trust that amoral lecher, Cu'lugh!

And that Hrowthe would now dare to ask her the question he just had tried her affection sorely.

"No," she replied crossly. "Why do you ask this? How dare you! No one has been allowed to see or touch it but you."

Looking at him, truly looking at him, Vanda felt she had never seen a more weary face, as if the mere waiting between the moments of time was suffering to him. His thoughts were closed to her now, as adamantly as she had succeeded in shutting off her thoughts at last to the prying Darkling.

"Then I shall leave you to your sanctuary, my dear."

When he was gone she felt a fleeting stab of remorse, and knowing she had wounded him by deliberate distance further vexed her mood.

All on account of one perfidious knight!

Vanda crossed her arms and pinched them cruelly. She had been enchanted somehow by Cu'lugh. He'd fogged her common sense with charm and corrupted the purity of her motives. Motives that necessitated playing on his chivalry, his frustrated lust, the debt of his life.

But she had been weak, too, and no matter what innocent betrayal she would have to feign before others she could not deceive herself. A place in her private guard had she planned to offer him so that his bold, desiring eyes were always close at hand, all the while keeping him bound with maidenly reluctance. Marry him? Never. The offer of that particular kind of alliance and the repulsive sensual insinuations that went with it had been necessary lures and nothing else. Yet, even as she'd never lost sight of this she had allowed his desire to inflate her vanity. She had looked forward to seeing him again, of seeing the admiration shining always in his dark eyes.

Equally with every ounce of her self-reproach did she despise his fickle desire. How dare any man play upon her frailties of character just to seek base satisfaction with the likes of whores such as Odette?

From Hrowthe Vanda knew of the ways of Athla—how the women there practiced the deceiving submissiveness and self-serving adoration Silfr had used to steal Vanda's father. No real man could be fooled by this kind of woman, Vanda firmly believed; honorable men looked for strong, independent women. Only a woman such as this, as she herself was, could humble men of their pride and the animal urges instilled and conditioned by the wiles of the submissive women. With more conviction than even the Blodsaukers, Vanda concluded it was these seemingly yielding females who sought to enslave men.

Whores who seek to have men fight over them in order to validate their vanity! Craven strumpets who pretend delicacy to obtain the protection of men!

It was this conviction that angered Vanda the most with Cu'lugh. As unforgivable as his treachery was the knowledge that he had let himself be allured by one trained in the craft of deception. It made him deserving of death. And that Cu'lugh had insulted her by committing this sin with Odette, whom he already knew to be a whore's daughter, warranted torture more slowly delivered than even that meted out to Thierry.

Vanda's eyes flashed across the room and she realized that she shook as much from the cold as her wrath, for the fire in the brazier had dwindled and only a single, tiny red ember glowed in the ashes.

"I am no coarse-minded servant to be insensitive to this," she seethed. She threw two handfuls of charcoal on the brazier and heard a gust of evening wind sing across the rafters. She glanced at the window and saw the moonless night creeping swiftly through the crimson twilight sky, and as she stirred the growing flame she imagined a great fire outside beneath those cantankerous elements. She saw herself winding a spit over it, and there within the heart of the flames rolled the bound traitor. Deep under her icy skin a flame kindled, lit by a new image added to that one; and it raged higher than the thought of Cu'lugh's screams—the horrified face of his whore watching on as the flesh slowly roasted from his bones.

Someone knocked on the door, interrupting the sweet image. Vanda's muscles tightened in her fury, sinews at her neck cinching so tautly that black dots swam before her eyes. She grasped the poker from beside the brazier and strode across the floor.

She flung open the door to find that the intruder was Pauline, the oldest of her servants, who had held her position from the time Vanda's mother was a child. Pauline wore a heavy, tattered overcoat, so well padded that Vanda could hardly see the hunch of her back. In the old crone's knobby hands was a tray of food. She did not seem to notice her mistress's shaking rage as she shuffled into the room, but muttered in her croaking, familiar way about Vanda's culinary preferences.

"Heart of roe roasted in tissue of gold," the crone tut-tutted as she set the tray on a table. "When you were a child it was all I could do to coax you into opening your mouth to taste a good roasted hen's liver."

As Pauline turned, her ancient eyes squinted at Vanda and she drew the overcoat tightly over her shoulders.

"Your room is chilly, child. This is a day I thought to never see."

"You dare accuse me of miserliness!" Vanda bit into the inner flesh of one cheek, tasted a trickle of salty blood, and she wondered if perhaps Pauline's advancing age had addled her wits, or maybe she had just grown too comfortable in her long-held position. Whatever ailed the hag, she was dangerously close to going too far.

Yet she went on, incautiously. "My child, we both know you do not hesitate to keep the strings of your purse drawn tightly when it comes to your servants...and open it quickly and freely for your own comforts."

Vanda drew herself straight as an iron pole.

"Tell me you do not mean that."

Pauline's head bobbed on her wiry neck. "I would prefer to say you are the babe I used to hold on my lap or the carefree little girl I taught to chain daisies."

Vanda saw a tear glisten at the corner of Pauline's eye and as the old woman blinked it fell slowly across a leathery cheek.

"I do not know what happened to that child, Vanda, yet I know she is in there...somewhere." She touched Vanda's breast and Vanda flinched. "It is not wicked to indulge oneself if life has allowed us such a liberty. But to expect others to endure hardship when you can provide more is selfish. And as meagerly as you expect your servants to live, whom I grieve for is your own people. You watch the numbers of your Saxon folk declining fast, yet you confiscate their food and make them dwell in deplorable, wretched sties. They are forced to eat decayed roots and the leaves of the ruined grass. You have the assets to feed them but you do not. Not even your own mother, as selfish as often she was, was so uncharitable to those in need. Her memory you claim was offended by your father, yet I do not remember him eating from silver plates and donning silk and brocade while his people starved and wasted away."

Vanda was shaking even more than before, but now her blood seemed to boil in her veins.

"You have been tainted by heathen gossip!"

Pauline's mouth pursed, as one trying to hold back a poor response. She looked down at the tray and ran a finger down the smooth edge of the white cloth under the porcelain plates and saucers.

"Look here, girl, I have brought what you wished as I have for over twenty years. A roe's heart simmered in wine. How far did your man have to go to find that single deer to slay? Here, a loaf baked from a dainty grain it took your traders months to bargain for. Scallions sautéed in wine—scallions from the serfs' allotment, wine that you refuse to even buy for your army. A bowl of broth with lamb's meat here...when the Saxons have not even the bones of carrion to suckle on!"

Vanda felt foam at the back of her throat as she said, "They are Saxons, woman. *Pagan* Saxons I might remind you."

"I am no priest, but I know they are not the enemies of your faith! And as any people, but especially as *your* people, they should be shown decency. God has favored you, girl, and it is not too late to earn that favor."

Vanda's hands fisted over her breast. "I have shown you hospitality all my life, and this ingratitude is all I merit?"

The old woman stiffened; her wrinkled face hardened. "I deserve to freeze whilst you stay warm and comfortable in these forbidding rooms, Vanda, for once I hated these folk with a passion to rival that martyrdom-seeker Boniface. My heart was narrow, foolish. But since that time I have watched while able-bodied men were sold away or forced to work without rest so they grew old before their time. I have seen babes and children torn from their mothers' arms, sent away to never see their families again. I looked on as the sickly women you allowed to remain were starved of their vitality. Families separated, marriages annulled at your decision; your *own* people so heavily levied that many have been forced out of the squalid shacks in their quarters. And why all this? For the same reason the fairer, younger women were sent to serve Boniface's impotent followers—to spare you a moment's thought that these Saxon families might have the chance for the happiness you spurn!"

"You are mad, old one, and wanton of tongue!"

Pauline's faded lips turned up in a sad smile. "What wisdom has directed your actions, Vanda? What foul thing have these people committed to deserve this fate? You refuse to curtail the levies even when there is nothing left to glean but dung and blood! The crops produce no more; the herds are sterile. Yours is the shrewdest mind I've ever known, my child, and I know that by your keen investments and alliances you prosper brightly.

"There is still a heart in your breast, I know it—hiding somewhere behind that wall of thorns and venom you've cultivated to protect it. You have nothing to prove to your mother, Vanda."

These last words pierced Vanda's last shred of restraint. She kicked the table on which the tray was set. "*You have pressed too far!*"

Pauline's old hands reached gently toward her, but Vanda jerked back from her touch, the foam now drying every bit of moisture in her mouth. Even then, as a scorpion bent to sting, the crone would not shut up.

"Your mother died because she rejected life, child. Do not do as she did, do not hate as I did. You are shrewd enough to give more of yourself than any man I have met. For the sake of heaven and your own soul, give yourself to your people!"

"They are not my people!"

"Then why rule them, my dear, why? Is it you fear losing your power?"

Bloody dots grimed Vanda's vision and she shook her head until they dissolved. And when she turned to Pauline again she could feel the ghastly red glow that burnished her cheeks, the inhuman grin that made Pauline gasp and stumble to fall on her backside.

"Power," she seethed, "power grappled from the men who would have seen me either a whore like Silfr or a boot-licking dog, as Charles believes me. I have extinguished the last hope of these pagans who held my father a hero for his devotion to a temptress. And one day, much sooner than you'd imagine, old one, I shall extinguish the hope of the Christian nobility as well."

Pauline rose to her feet, but she was trembling, her face dark and fearful. "But why? Tell me, child—why?"

Vanda began to shake again, from an ancient anger far colder than the snow that had girdled the land that winter. "Were it not for the over-zealous elements of the Christian Church, I think my father would have never questioned his original conversion to my mother's faith; and were it not for his pagan sensibilities he would not have taken that whore to wife! I am stronger than Christian arrogance, stronger than pagan lust—I shall have everything I wish, with the labor of those I've conquered, with no god to which to answer, no man to play the politics of romance, no self-serving display of feminine guile to bind me and steal my independence!"

Pauline's voice was soft and miserable. "You could never forgive them, not a one of them, for slighting your memory of your mother. And what did she for you, Vanda? Knowingly starve herself and leave you that she might join God. No wonder you hated Silfr so, who wanted to love you."

"No!" Vanda's grasped the poker so tightly she felt the knuckle of her fourth finger break. But in her anger the pain was a remote, inconsequential thing. "My mother alone loved me!"

Tears glistened in Pauline's eyes and she wiped them away with the back of her trembling, bony wrist. "She loved her vision of God more, child. I would never have spoken this, but that I know your aims have been birthed from a false hope of love. Ah, child, you were loved by your father, pagan that he was, and Silfr, and these Saxons who are your folk!"

Vanda heard the panting of her own breath beyond the sea of blood that tinged her vision. She'd been more tolerant this evening than ever in her life, but her dignity would allow no more abuse. She put aside the temptation to simply strike the crone with the poker and dropped it to the floor. It clattered sharply over the wood and Vanda went to the door, hearing Pauline hobble after her.

"Are you well, child? I do not mean to—"

The crone's next words were silenced when Vanda suddenly pitched her away with both hands. Pauline slammed against the table. She stared, stunned and speechless as Vanda threw open the door.

"Guardsman!"

At once she heard movement from the end of the torchlit hall, and two towering masculine figures advanced hastily toward her.

"Madam, did you summon?"

Vanda drew aside to let them in, and she watched as Pauline backed away instinctively.

"Take her to the boundaries of the land," Vanda ordered. "Find a great oak, like one of those the Saxons favored to carve with the image of Thor's hammer. Lash her to it very well, so that she cannot escape—after you have stripped her every last garment."

The mercenary guards looked at one another, and Vanda saw the uncertain exchange that passed between them.

"Madam?"

"You have ears, you heard me. Take her away."

Only one of them moved and Pauline shrieked and tried to flee, but as she backed away he seized one of her arms.

His companion spoke gravely, "What has she done, Lady, to deserve this?"

The one that had obeyed dragged Pauline flailing and kicking to the door. And when her foot collided with the man's knee Vanda stayed the retaliatory fist that seemed to lift of its own accord.

"Do nothing to hasten her fate!"

"You would not dare this, Vanda," Pauline crooned in her weeping voice. "Not this much!"

Vanda's fury had lulled to contemptuous amusement. "You have shown your affection for the pagans—you will now meet death in the garb of their sluts."

Vanda nodded, and as the guard started to pull Pauline out of the room the woman shrieked again and scratched his face. He growled and yanked her free arm behind her and with a cruel kick to her calf, pitched her over the threshold.

The other hesitated still, and said gravely to Vanda, "This is your old nurse, my lady—what crime could she have committed to merit this?"

Vanda regarded him coolly. "There is a Lombard smith in my town who possesses tools used to remove the tongues of boars and oxen. Need I summon him to silence your curiosity?"

The mercenary's mouth hardened. "There would be none to help you in that," he said, but she saw the tinge of doubt in his eyes. He bowed curtly and went after his companion and together they dragged Pauline away.

Vanda eased shut the door and went to stand by the brazier. A strong yellow flame had taken hold now and she rubbed her hands before it. As she gazed into the obedient fire she saw the image of Cu'lugh again, and her satisfaction in cowing the guard dispelled the last of her self-reproach. Cu'lugh would pay for his abuse sooner or later, that she vowed to herself. She heard the savage wind outside beat against the roof but she ignored it. A mindless element it was, as ineffective against her willpower as the foot-crushed bramble or even the enchantment of a heathen warrior.

She stood straight and removed her shawl. She threw it over a chair and went to look at the food overturned on the floor. The scallions, broth and bread she did not touch, but had it returned to the kitchen to be thrown out come morning. The roe's heart she had sent to the billet where the two guardsmen slept, for them to eat upon their return.

Chapter Twenty-Six

f anyone had asked Odette what she wanted out of life she would have smiled and answered only that the gods allow her to know from time to time the contentment she knew presently.

Lord Cu'lugh had become such an integral part of her life she could think of no greater or sweeter task than serving him. The sun was never truly brilliant without his smile, the night without stars lest in his arms she dreamed.

It was selfish, she knew, this consuming passion for one man. And yet it did not adversely affect her responsibility to him. Through her adoration she had come to fully appreciate the lessons of love her Mistress and Lord Eryan had taught, all the exercises in purposefully delayed and titillated pleasure she'd been introduced to in Helrose's house. Her Master was teaching her other things as well; and through his patience coupled with his determination, she had become adept at all he wanted and filled with a delirious, uncertain anxiety. What was more, he listened without judgment and often asked her opinion, which seemed truly important to him.

He was not always easy to accommodate, being very cross when first waking up in the mornings. He sometimes made quips about the male love-slaves that bordered on the intolerant. And often Odette found herself frustrated in her love when her Master would sit at a table and sip ale all afternoon, striking up conversations with other men and making her sit at his feet or showing her off as he pleased. This, of course, she'd been trained for, and yet being around him kept her in a constant state of excitement, the kind of excitement that made her yearn so with passion that she often found herself squirming against his leg like a cat in heat. He would smile at these times and caution her to behave until *he* bade her to squirm, and she would sulk and work hard to forget the throbbing heat between her gartered thighs, the firm hand that stroked her shoulders and hair, the bed that beckoned in his room.

On her fifth day in his custody Lord Cu'lugh announced they were going to visit Mistress Helrose. It was morning and they were eating downstairs. Odette had been allowed to sit on the bench while she'd eaten but now she was kneeling as Lord Cu'lugh finished. His announcement shocked her; she searched her mind, desperate to know how she had displeased him.

"You look startled, little one," he said and leaned down and stroked her hair that he'd brushed before they came down so that, as he preferred, it would cascade over her shoulders when she looked up from the floor. His smile was tender. "Do you fear I am taking you back?"

She nodded.

"That is not it. I plan to keep you on another day or two." He grinned and she understood he was teasing her, yet it was a jest without comfort. Despite his reassurance she felt uneasy going back to Helrose's house this soon, even if just for a visit.

"You would like to visit your friends there, wouldn't you?"

She nodded again, hesitantly, though indeed it would be pleasant to see Uma and Rystla again.

"Good," he said huskily and bent down and kissed her mouth.

His taste calmed Odette's panic, but still she wondered about his personal reason for making a visit to Mistress Helrose. If she asked he might well tell her—at least he would not lie, at most tell her to mind her curiosity. She decided not to chance his displeasure and would wait until he was ready to disclose his reason.

Before leaving the inn Lord Cu'lugh brought out a new pair of gloves for her to wear. Made of sturdy leather, these items served a practical use along with the high boots that padded her knees and shins—for that morning he attached an iron chain to her collar and led her on hands and knees all the way through town.

As they entered the gates of Helrose's property Odette heard Lord Alban's voice from the courtyard. She kept her face lowered as she crawled after her Master, for she could feel the painful blush on her face, though she was uncertain if the color rose from her constraint or from the pride she knew to be the property of such a virile man.

"Would you care for a table, sir?" Lord Alban said. "I'll have one of our flowers find a..." He paused and knelt down and Odette gasped in surprise.

"Why this is our little Odette," Alban mused. He tousled her hair affectionately before standing again. "Still our timid flower. I hope she is not so timid in her duties, sir."

"Not at all," Cu'lugh said brightly. "But, then, I think I bring out the best effort in all women."

Odette's face pinched at his almost callous remark, but she knew it was only his kind of humor.

"Ah, you are most fortunate in this bright flower, good sir," Alban said. "May I offer you a bottle of our most celebrated elixir to celebrate your fortune in being named her Unveiler? There is, after all, usually a small feast given at the time of the designation."

Odette glanced up at Lord Alban long enough to see his striking face. But the old desire for him was not there anymore; and compared to her swarthy Master, Alban's fair good looks seemed lusterless to her.

"That would be well appreciated," Master Cu'lugh answered, "but I seek an audience with Mistress Helrose first."

Alban asked soberly, "Is there a problem, sir?"

"Nothing with Odette's behavior. But it is an important matter."

Alban smiled his endearing smile. "The Mistress is within the house. Explain to whomever opens the door that Lord Alban has given his recommendation for you to see her."

"Thank you," Cu'lugh said. "Favor me by allowing Odette to stay outside and visit what friends may speak with her."

Lord Alban agreed readily and took the leash Cu'lugh handed him. Her Master looked down at Odette and warned her to behave. She watched as he walked to the manor and then Lord Alban led her to one of the tables and wrapped her leash lightly about the seat beside it. The heat of the tiles poured through her boots and gloves, but it was the steward's scrutiny that made her tremble. He knelt beside her and drew his palm down the length of her back and kneaded her buttocks. His other hand brushed the metal of the shield that thrust her breasts high. With a delighted murmur he pulled on the nipple clamps until she whimpered.

Her thighs grew hot and damp as he inspected all her accoutrements. She understood his lust, his admiration, but despite the passion he incited it was not his ministrations her languid stirrings craved but those of Lord Cu'lugh.

All about passed Helrose's flowers, the girls she knew, all engrossed in their work and not daring to look up. Lord Alban's hand moved down her buttocks and pinched her nether lips. Lightly his finger plunged into her vagina, which he bored with a steady, easy stroke. Odette felt her lubrication spill out over his hand and she turned her face away even as her hips began to sway in harmony with his strokes.

"You are still taut," he whispered, his voice so deep that her whole spine tingled under the sound. He lifted her chin forward with one hand as with the other he slapped her nether lips with the fan of his fingers. Odette's clitoris pounded under the clip and the bell clamps crushed her hardening nipples.

He did not torment her long, however—nothing like the lengthy sessions she endured under Lord Cu'lugh's touch. As Lord Alban withdrew it occurred to her that he was likely intruding on her Master's prerogatives. If he was aware of this as well, he said nothing but grazed her brow with his lips and untied her leash from the bench.

"Stand, Odette," he told her and as she rose he patted the bench to indicate she should sit there.

She felt strange. Lord Alban walked off and she saw there were only a few customers come in so far. The flowers finished with their chores sat together under one of the cage poles. They were talking quietly amongst themselves and were oblivious to the fact Alban had disappeared. Odette glanced around nervously, wary that some other steward might come by and demand what she was doing sitting like a free woman or runaway.

A young man from another table winked at her and she looked anxiously for Lord Alban.

He returned in a short while and Uma was at his side. She was dusted all over with flour, even her hair, which was coiled in a braid at the top of her head. Odette suspected she had been serving Lord Bjorn personally again. As soon as Uma saw her she ran over and embraced Odette in her long arms.

When Lord Alban turned away to talk to the patrons Odette took Uma's hands and pulled her down on the seat next to her. "You look happy as always!"

"I am." Uma eyed her with a knowing smile. "As happy as you these days?"

"Oh, I am happy, yes. My Lord is so…so—oh, he is just magnificent!"

Uma chortled. "*Magnificent?* Ah, listen how you gush! I am happy to hear it. When we were told you had been taken away to meet your Unveiler—well, we did not know what to think. As always, our Mistress explains only what she is in the mood to explain."

"Are you well, Uma?"

"My contentment remains constant. But things have been so different of late, as if the gods reeled the heavenly orbs on their sides just to give everything a new flavor."

"I know you care not for gossip, but now you have my interest piqued."

Uma glanced about cautiously. "I can tell you a little. The Mistress has done the most extraordinary thing—two days ago she gave Yolande her freedom."

"Freedom?"

"Yes, but more than that, she has given her a position as a Lady. Yolande is now one of our new stewards. It is a very disquieting change. Yolande is curt and cruel, and yet that hateful nature seems to have vanished now that she is clothed and holds power over the rest of us."

"But Yolande was so…disagreeable." It was not quite the word Odette was searching for but close enough.

"Yes. And I think it grieved Mistress Helrose deeply to know she was unsuccessful in at least helping Yolande understand the value of tolerance. Lord Bjorn confessed to me that the Mistress was desperate and after all these years finally concluded Yolande is undeniably, forcibly beyond training. I also think that, as well as she knows the girl, this position she offered is Helrose's attempt to keep Yolande from abusing her freedom and finding herself meeting the king's royal judgment for vandalism. She pledged to set the whole city on fire when first she arrived. After her Unveiling she swore to have revenge on the man who took her maidenhead, in a most painful way, I might add. Another time she tricked one of our stewards into the cage upstairs outside Mistress Helrose's room—pretended illness. When he came in to see about her she knocked him in the head with the water bowl several times till he passed out. Then she took his key and clothes and locked him in the cage."

"You jest!" Odette gasped.

Uma covered her face with her hand but her body rocked with laughter. "She garbed herself in the clothes that she might look like a man and slipped out through a window. She made her way into the streets by climbing the fence…might have even succeeded in passing herself off as a man to the sentries, too, had she remembered to button the shirt."

Odette giggled so hard her side ached.

"Thus far Yolande has not abused her status," Uma continued, "but acted with surprising reserve. Why, she hardly seems the same girl now that she goes about in her leather breeches and shirt—properly buttoned, of course—and that paddle tethered at her hip. Not that this sits well with the other flowers, and a few of them have tested Yolande quite purposely. But not once so far has she met their tests with anything but the most controlled efficiency. I am quite proud of her."

Odette's good humor drained away to think of having to take orders from Yolande once her time with Lord Cu'lugh was finished. For the first time she realized how very short that time was, and a deep sadness settled over her.

"Oh, do not fret so," Uma reproached lightly, "Yolande is a problem and all problems need a remedy. This arrangement will spare Mistress Helrose from any further heartache; and, as you know, we cannot choose our stewards any more than our lovers. That is a constant in our lives which gives us security and allows us to appreciate one another."

Uma's words, as true and innocuous as they were, only deepened Odette's misery. And yet she knew, as she'd always known, selfishness had no place in the life of a novice.

"Yes, you are correct." She tried to feign a smile and said, "Is there more?"

"Well, there was some argument between Mistress Helrose and Lord Eryan, a terrible argument, the afternoon after you were taken away. We all overheard it from downstairs. It became so violent the stewards forced open Helrose's door. That is when Lord Eryan stormed out of the manor. He has only been back once or twice late at night, I am told. I believe he is angry with the Mistress for letting you go without a formal Unveiling."

Odette frowned. "A violent argument?"

"Not physically violent, no," Uma assured her. "But they were screaming at one another, terrible things. And since then Helrose's High Archer has practically moved in. It is he who gives me the orders at the dinner table, not the Mistress. I find this very strange, though, indeed, the Mistress has a calm about her now that suits her. I dare propose she is prepared to yield her power over to him utterly."

Odette was shocked. "No, not Mistress Helrose."

Uma nodded. "She practically inherited the position, you know. The other brother is a musician with no interest in keeping the family tradition and Eryan— well, he has his darker traits. I am of the opinion that Mistress Helrose chose the role to keep the status firmly in the family. If she weds and gives over her power, her master-husband would have full reign here, and she would belong to him more completely than even we now belong to her."

"But Mistress Helrose is accomplished at her position. She seemed fulfilled to me."

Uma shrugged. "She was well trained, not only as a novice but as a daughter. And if this is the role she desires then I hope she finds much happiness, and especially if there is to be a marriage."

Marriage. The word with all its connotation of permanence and fealty and shared lifelong dreams made her again think of her limited time with Lord Cu'lugh. Soon she would have to leave him and await the next man to please, and try to look at him with the same eagerness and adoration as when she lifted her eyes to Cu'lugh's...

Odette knew she should simply be grateful to know there was a home to come back to when it was over, a place where she was wanted and loved.

Selfish and ungrateful…to have found the security I've always needed just to grieve now!

She knew that somehow she would have to dispossess herself of the passion for Lord Cu'lugh. But how? For a moment she considered asking Uma's advice, but that would be too much. She'd learned enough already in her studies to know that she simply had to accept the inevitable. It was her faith, she was sure, that was lacking. She would have to pray and pray with pure intention that Freyja would show the way to release herself from this obsession.

One of the serving girls came by and set two glasses of rosewater and apple juice on the table, with chips of ice from the cellar. Uma and Odette grinned at one another, and when Odette looked up she saw Lord Alban looking across at them from under the shade of a tree. His arms were folded over his chest but he smiled.

"Ah, your Lord has impressed even the stewards," said Uma and her mouth twisted as she eyed the glass. "I have never been allowed to sit with the customers, let alone be served. I do not think I care for it."

Odette frowned. "This drink?"

"The privilege," Uma corrected. "I much prefer to serve."

"I do, too, but as my Lord undoubtedly had this sent to the table, let us not insult his consideration."

Uma grinned and took a sip. "I am glad you are happy with your Unveiler. They are magnificent in their own individual ways, all real men."

Odette's heart beat frantically and before she could stop herself she blurted, "Are they, Uma? I fear I shall not be able to forget him easily."

Uma patted her arm and her eyes were sympathetic. "It is to be expected—he is your first."

"I think it is more than that. I fancy myself in love with Lord Cu'lugh."

"What are his feelings? Has he expressed them?"

"He says I am all he wants me to be. I-I know he is fond of me—he says I delight him as no other ever has."

"That is wonderful, Odette."

"I am selfish, Uma! This passion for him cannot bode well for either of us. My thoughts are to please him and take pleasure in that, but it is more, agonizingly more! An ache that is never soothed. I cannot imagine serving another; in fact, I do not wish to now."

Uma's mouth drew in a troubled look and she was about to speak when her eyes moved past Odette's shoulder.

"Is that your Lord?"

Odette followed her gaze to the end of the courtyard before the manor, and indeed it was Lord Cu'lugh coming toward the table. He was frowning slightly and his eyes had a distant gleam about them; but when he saw Odette he smiled in the merry, assured way Odette had come to cherish.

He pulled her hair aside and browsed his mouth over her throat. "Did you miss me, little flower?"

Odette's skin felt smothered by the musky heat of his aroma and her clitoris beat again. "Yes, my Lord."

Cu'lugh looked to Uma. "You must be one of Odette's friends she has told me about. I would guess…pretty Uma?"

"Yes, sir."

"I am sorry I need to curtail your conversation, but I have some affairs to attend to, and Odette has some chores."

Uma nodded graciously. She pressed her cheek to Odette's ear and whispered, "Remember, a heart never broken blindly breaks those of others."

Odette smiled weakly, not sure what to make of the advice, and kissed Uma's face. Lord Cu'lugh lifted her leash and immediately she sank to her hands and knees again. She almost crooned as he stroked her hair gently, pouted when the next moment he gave her buttocks a sound slap.

"Follow at my side," he said and he walked her back through the gates that opened to the public square.

As she crept on her knees beside him Odette wondered what it was that he had spoken about with the Mistress. He had the look of a man lost in thought. She feared this an indication he had tired of her and, too genteel to return her early, had asked the Mistress to have another flower ready when the thirteen days had passed.

But he cannot be too tired of me to have me on his leash.

Cu'lugh had shown no disappointment when he'd come out of the house; for that matter, he could have just as easily left her at the inn. For all she knew his reasons for visiting Helrose might have had nothing to do with her. Again she felt stained by selfishness and was glad to know Cu'lugh had work for her planned. Work would surely place her thoughts in a more constructive direction.

He stopped by one of the merchant stalls set up on the square and purchased from the proprietor a large wicker basket.

"You may rise to carry this," he said to Odette and she carried the basket on her hip the rest of the way to the inn.

Upon returning to his room Lord Cu'lugh removed the leash and bade Odette to rest on the bed. He filled the basin on the table with water and washed his hands and mustache, and then taking a razor from the table shaved the stubble from his face. Odette felt a sublime thrill to watch him in this mundane but particularly masculine activity. When he was finished he patted the loose stubble away with a damp rag and raked a comb through his hair.

He turned then and held his arms out. "Do I look presentable?"

She could not help but smile with curiosity at his cheerful tone. "Yes, my Lord, very much."

"This evening I shall show you how to polish my boots," he said, catching a quick last look in the mirror. "But I must make haste for now, sweet one."

Odette cleared her voice and ventured, "May I speak, my Lord?"

With his consent she asked where he was going.

He smoothed her face with his hand. "To speak with someone. It is not a girl, if that is what you fear."

She blushed shamefully but felt tears of relief in her eyes.

"We shall have a talk later, Odette, a very important talk. Right now, however, I want you to gather the dirty laundry into the basket to take to one of the public washhouses. I know you will have a wait while the clothes dry, and I had best not hear of you speaking with another man during that wait."

Her eyes widened. Was he trying to comfort the insecurity he sensed in her with a demonstration of jealousy? No, she remembered, he had already said he could not abide the thought of another man having her. As her heart surged she wondered if just perhaps there had been more to that first declaration than simple passion.

"Yes, my Lord," she answered at last and moved to fetch the dirty laundry from the little heap near the headboard of the bed. He came to her as she stooped on one knee and laid his hands upon her shoulders.

"I spoke perhaps too strongly," he said softly. "I give you permission to speak when spoken to; but please, do not take part in unneeded conversations with other men. This is all I require."

She looked up at him and nodded obediently, and her fears were honeyed by the tenderness in his voice.

He smiled and pulled his fingers through a wave of her hair. "I shall return as soon as I can," he said. "Behave yourself. Oh, here—" He stepped to the table again and slid some coins off and put them inside a little pouch which he cinched by the strings. He hung the pouch over her neck.

"I would not have you penniless," he said and kissed her waiting lips. "Good-bye."

"Good-bye, my lord," she whispered.

When he had gone the room seemed suddenly huge and cruelly silent. At least Odette had found a measure of comfort in his demonstrative words. But she chided herself for responding to them and for letting him sense her fear he might be off talking with other women. As if it were her right to question where he went or with whom he spent his time. No, that was wrong, terribly wrong. That he was possessive of her was his right as her owner, but it certainly did not entitle her to behave as if he were her husband.

She sighed and set her mind to the task at hand, curious still why he had worried so about his appearance before setting out.

Chapter Twenty-Seven

ollowing his request for a meeting with King Larsarian, Cu'lugh was welcomed into the castle by a burly man-at-arms and turned over to a young page dressed in breeches and shirt of dark red velvet. As they passed through the sunlit rooms Cu'lugh had trouble keeping up with the boy, as every room seemed flooded with life—throngs of musicians and minstrels, little groups of dancing girls chained together with silver cords, legions of cats in tailored garments. There was even an assembly of children practicing a song in the room where at last he spotted his young escort waiting at the foot of a wide staircase. As Cu'lugh ascended he was nearly stampeded by a team of half-clad and whimpering serving girls who came rushing down under the snapping command of an older male servant.

"They have been allowed to watch the rehearsals and preparations," the page explained when Cu'lugh caught up. "The day after the morrow is the queen's birthday."

"Ah," Cu'lugh murmured, remembering that Queen Honi was Odette's kinswoman. "That is cause for celebration."

The page smiled doubtfully. "If she behaves, that is. She earned the king's displeasure and has been locked in her rooms but for to receive her punishments at his table each morning and night."

"You jest," Cu'lugh said. Athla certainly had its pleasant customs, but he was surprised to learn even the king's wife subject to the same strictures as the common women.

"No," the boy answered as they reached the landing. He motioned Cu'lugh to the hallway to the right. "Queen Honi sought to give her opinion on a state matter without permission or consultation. It will do her well to know there is a proper way to address her husband."

Cu'lugh did not reply, but silently he applauded the king's firmness. The boy led him to an ornately carved double door at the end of the hall and stopped to knock. Moments later the doors were opened by a squire, dressed in a staid gray ensemble. The man seemed to be on post in the foyer between the double doors and the single, silver-gilded door just beyond.

"An Outer Realmer knight wishes to speak with the king," said the boy.

The man nodded and, turning, went into the room beyond the gilded door. He returned shortly, holding the door open and gesturing Cu'lugh inside.

But Cu'lugh entered alone and the door was shut gently behind him. The room was very warm from the fire burning in a small fireplace. Shelves lined the walls, laden with scrolls and manuscripts; and behind one of them a voice rose in greeting.

"I am to be found…somewhere in here."

Cu'lugh walked around the shelf and almost collided with a fat stripped cat lying in the small alcove he'd entered.

"Step over him."

Cu'lugh complied carefully and approached the heavy desk beyond. The man who had spoken wore a tired smile.

"I am Larsarian," he said and gestured to a cushioned bench nearby. Cu'lugh bowed respectfully and, taking the seat, saw that the man had the aura of kingliness to him. Lean and tall and fair of beard and soft, curling hair, he wore a black surcoat embroidered down the front with two ranks of minute filigree bees.

Strewn over the king's table was an array of wide, smooth stones, etched and reddened by runes from a style of writing with which Cu'lugh was unfamiliar.

"I am Cu'lugh, of the Franks."

The king rose and stepped to a heavy trestle adjoined to a wall by the desk. Several cruets and pitchers sat on it along with a copper platter holding an array of small stone cups. He filled two of these and offered one to Cu'lugh.

"May you never thirst," Larsarian said.

"Nor yourself, sire."

The king returned to his seat and Cu'lugh sipped the drink—fine mead with a hint of meadowsweet for flavor.

"What need or request brings you to me, Sir Cu'lugh?"

"I would like to offer myself into your service, sire."

No hint of surprise showed in the king's face. "You are interested in staying in Athla as a permanent citizen?"

Cu'lugh nodded.

"Tell me your skills."

"I am well experienced with the sword and pike and hand-to-hand combat," Cu'lugh said and was aware that, unlike most other lieges he'd approached, he felt no necessity to boast of his accomplishments or embellish his feats to the man before him. Bragging was considered a manly grace in many places he had traveled to but something about this king discouraged such custom.

"Are you experienced with the bow?"

"It is not my preferred arm, but I have a keen eye."

"Whom have you served?"

Cu'lugh recounted his years in the service of the various kings and chieftains of E'rin, sometimes as a paid solider, other times as messenger. There was the Frisian landowner Moki for whom he had trained squires in all forms of combat. For a few years he had served as a bodyguard to the sickly son of an Andalusian chieftain. After the boy succumbed, he had gone again to Frisia, and there helped defend the borders of a small tribe against the vandalism of Boniface and his crusaders. And in Muscovy he had fought in skirmishes for Donnar Bull-Loin against the pillaging forces of the chieftain's brother.

"A mercenary soldier," Larsarian commented.

"As the need called for," Cu'lugh answered. "But I chose my sides conscientiously, I trust. I do not offer myself to petty or avaricious lords."

"That must be a difficult road to follow in the Outer Realm. From what I know it seems the leaders there have become eager to quarrel for the pettiest of excuses, without heed to the suffering their choices place on women and children."

There was a baiting quality in Larsarian's voice, as if he were testing Cu'lugh's reaction. But Cu'lugh had no argument with the observation.

"Very true, sire. Political and religious dicta have overshadowed the more reasonable concerns of everyday living. These issues have complicated and aggravated even the oldest rivalries."

One of Larsarian's fair brows rose. "We have little use for intolerance here. In fact, we have not known battle for almost forty human years, when last our armies met an invading host of giants from the caverns from over the eastern mountains. My warriors must keep prepared, however—that is a necessity for any strong defense. But service to Athla precludes anyone who savors the taste of the battlelust. Our army is maintained in the event of attack for defense, and that alone. We Athlans treasure peace, Sir Cu'lugh, and the right to maintain our customs. If you have visions of pillage and plunder and taking down as many men as you can slaughter for the pure joy of it, you would be greatly disappointed."

Cu'lugh swirled the mead in the small cup gently. "My desire is to dwell in Athla, sire. I am ready to embrace your customs as mine."

Larsarian brought his hands together over his chest and laced his long fingers together. "You have no wife or children awaiting your return in the Outer Realm?"

"No. My family, the only family important to me, are dead, but for my father's mother; and she has made it known my happiness is what she expects me to pursue. I think I have found that happiness here."

Larsarian was silent a moment. "It is easy to find happiness, here, Cu'lugh, but for those from the Outer Realm it is more difficult to maintain that happiness. To have lasting contentment here one must yield the concepts that were learned and instilled beyond our borders. For, here, happiness is eternally viable, with no need for ambition other than pursuing that happiness and certainly no sanction for harboring the petty emotions that often develop from ambitions. It is a life some men cannot accept for too long. By that I mean Outer Realmers, for they have been conditioned to think they need suffering to know success and have a very limited number of years in which to do both before death takes them away. To appreciate Athla, Cu'lugh, you must be prepared to embrace now the pleasures most men and women seek in the afterlife. We endure because we have accepted and prize this. War and suffering, death and old age rarely make their way into our realm; and when we are vulnerable it will be in the face of a force of a magnitude beyond the grasp of mortal knowledge. And for that reason, too, we are selective in granting permanent citizen status—a man must be willing to defend our traditions to the death if the need arises."

Cu'lugh weighed these words carefully. He had already guessed the Athlans, for all their mortal qualities, were somehow longer-lived than Midgardians. He cared not to live forever, though, if that was what the king was alluding to. As for the other things, he had experienced enough of bloodshed and pettiness to fill three life times.

"I am prepared to accept the requirements, sire."

Larsarian frowned and stroked the end of his beard. "The giants I spoke of, they ravaged our beautiful city when they attacked. Few of us perished before they were annihilated—we were fortunate for Freyja's protection—yet what they destroyed took long to rebuild. Especially as we did not once lose our grace or the dignity of our culture during that time. We rebuilt without taking hostages from Midgard to labor for us, without our loss griping our men into melancholy…and we did not turn our refined, beautiful women into beasts of burden or targets to bear our anger at the devastation. Do you understand what I mean by this, Cu'lugh?"

Cu'lugh looked at the king squarely. "If by that you mean your women serve as slaves but not workhorses or rugs to wipe one's feet on, yes." At Larsarian's nod he continued, "I find the tradition is one beautiful and sound."

"And so you would protect our traditions—fight to your death to defend them and our women and children?" Cu'lugh avowed it adamantly, and Larsarian continued. "But are you prepared to accept them completely? To embrace them without reservation, to give up all notion that the naked body and the carnal act are sins, as you have been trained? To understand and accept our ideal of harmonized balance between men and women and the natural acceptance of the body as a temple of the gods themselves? That the acceptance of the bodily desires and the intimate relations between men and women are sacred things—and that the satisfaction one takes in a lover is in itself a marriage of the divine principles of male and female, which together are the Eternal?"

Cu'lugh had not guessed the easy Athlan customs extended to their very religion, but now he understood those customs were not reflections of amorality or indulgence. Their ways were their culture, their politics, their religion—complete and interconnected. Ambition—the self-motivated, selfish kind Larsarian had spoken of— jeopardized the equilibrium of their entire society, while brutality insulted it and intolerance negated it.

At another time in his life Cu'lugh would have laughed at their ideals. He would have discounted them as but a pompous antithesis to the Christian dictums. That was before he'd looked into the face of his former ambitions and seen them for the delusive fantasies they were. Power would achieve him nothing but to gall those who had belittled him. Wealth was a means to survival; but he had survived before without money or friends or even the assurance he would live through the night. There was not a single joy wealth could provide that he hadn't already proved attainable by but sheer determination.

There was only one ambition left for him to achieve: to possess completely and in sanctity a woman more noble in her subservience than all the fickle, prim ladies of wealth and privilege he'd known before.

"I am quite prepared," he said at last, "and I am willing to lay down my life to uphold the principles of Athla."

Larsarian exhaled deeply and brushed his fingertips over a couple of the rune stones. "And you have no interest in farming or establishing a business?"

Cu'lugh shook his head. "Aside from a fondness for music, my skills are honed for the warrior's trade alone."

"Very well, Sir Cu'lugh. You could offer your services to my standing army, with opportunity for knighthood and all its privileges after a year's service. My warriors are allowed free indulgence with all the women of the city and handmaidens of my household, the wedded ones excepted, and allowed to build homes where they might anywhere in Athla.

"We are also in need of a few new street sentries. The duties are simple—to patrol the streets and keep the peace, to break up any possible discord and such similar responsibilities. Ours is a peaceful community altogether, but we must maintain visible guardians of stability to insure the safety of our citizens. Sentries answer to the Brotherhood of Od, in which I sit as one of the high counselors, and to the High Priestess of the Temple of Freyja. Though she consults my opinion often, she is in truth the final judge of suspected lawbreakers, determining guilt and innocence and all issues of punishment. As such, all matters of sentry membership rely on her final verdict. Our sentries are, however, required to live in the city, though homes are built for them at the expense of the royal purse. As with the warriors, the sentries are entitled to amuse themselves with any unwed women, even the handmaidens, when they visit."

Cu'lugh had not forgotten the High Priestess. Her unworldly faces, the eyes of the middle face that had seemed bent on pilfering his every secret and weighing them on some mysterious balance. Her questions, allusions and warnings he had thought for a time but a test of his sincerity; now he felt perhaps there had been more behind them than he'd understood. He was content to let time help him discover their full meaning. For now he still owed the High Priestess for accepting his offer and his word, and could think of no more opportune way to demonstrate his gratitude than pledging himself to protect her city.

"I would prefer the position of sentry."

Larsarian said steadily, "To have been able to find Athla you must have been worthy before the gods, and to come here and offer yourself you obviously seek more than a holiday. I have been king for some time and have developed, I believe, a good feel for the men I meet. Athla would be fortunate to have you as a citizen, sir, and therefore do not feel pressed to make a hasty choice."

Cu'lugh shook his head. "I am not given to making hasty choices. I enjoy this city and would be proud to serve as sentry."

Larsarian nodded slowly. "Then I shall submit your name to the council tonight. If we vote for your recommendation, it will be given over to the High Priestess for final decision. It is not wise to guess how long her decision may take, but tell me where you reside that I may deliver to you council's decision by tomorrow evening."

"I am staying at an inn in the northern district, the only inn in that vicinity."

Larsarian smiled. "I know it. Then it shall be done, Cu'lugh."

Cu'lugh knew the conversation was over, but there was another matter he felt he should take up with the king.

"Sire, there is something else."

"Yes?"

"I have a woman in my possession, one who is a relation of your queen."

"And who is this relation?"

"The student of Mistress Helrose, Odette."

Larsarian grinned. "Our little Odette? You are her Unveiler?"

"Yes. And my desire to keep her is quite...my own."

Larsarian touched his beard again, his eyes wide with interest. "Does Odette return this ardor?"

"I think she does."

"You would have her to wife?"

"Yes."

"Love is the most valuable of commodities, my friend. If she consents, I hope you will invite us to the handfasting—my Honi would be rather distressed to be left out."

Cu'lugh smiled now, reluctant to go further, but felt prompted to disclose himself completely to the man as he dared never do with Odette. "It is for Odette I came to Athla."

The amenity in Larsarian's face hardened to stone. "What is this you mean?"

"My brother, Thierry, brought Odette here. It is for his wife I offered my services in fetching her back."

"Thierry." Larsarian's voice was chilled. "You are Thierry's brother?"

Cu'lugh nodded, prepared for the sternest of incriminations, which he knew he deserved.

"Thierry wanted her here," the king said sternly. "He said her life was in danger. He is a dear friend. Why does he not come himself?"

"My brother died several months ago, sire."

The king was silent for several moments, but his sadness was evident. "I shall mourn Thierry. He was an honest man." Larsarian scrutinized Cu'lugh. "By telling me this, I know you share his integrity. Even so, you understand that Odette is an Athlan now?"

"Yes. I would have her no other way." Cu'lugh swallowed back the regret that weighed the back of his neck. He should have told Odette his reason for coming to Athla the first day he had her. "Her sister acts under the misconceptions of her religion. I felt obligated to her and so agreed to aid her, but for deep motives as well which had nothing to do with Odette. Now, here and knowing Odette as I do, I could never take her back. Nor could I live happily without her."

"Does Odette know why you came?"

Cu'lugh shook his head.

"She must be told, Cu'lugh, whatever your reasons for failing to disclose this to her, whether for her protection or your own interests as they were before. As much as men are inclined to protect their women, a woman cannot be truly satisfied without total divulgence of what dwells within her man's heart. Believe me when I say that these precious creatures have a gift for gleaning secrets, sooner or late, and know when they have been deceived. If you love her, you will tell her your purpose for coming."

"I do love her…almost more than I care to admit. And I shall tell her as soon as possible."

"There is no problem then. Unless there is more of consequence of which she has not been informed?"

"No, but that Thierry is dead."

"If Odette loves you, you will know beyond doubt by her reaction to your disclosure." Larsarian offered a hopeful smile. "Odette has a most loving heart, Cu'lugh; and as she seems to have inherited the best qualities of both her mother and father, that is quite a testimony to her heritage."

"Her mother," Cu'lugh asked curiously, "she was from Athla?"

"No, Silfr was not born here," said the king and a troubled wrinkle pressed his brow. "Do you know if the mantle went with Silfr when she died? Thierry was told it did."

"Mantle?"

"Yes, the swanmaiden's mantle."

Cu'lugh blinked. "I-I did not know Silfr possessed one."

Larsarian stared at him, bewildered. "You do not know, do you? Silfr was a daughter of Freyja, sired by one of Her warrior guests in Her palace in Vanaheim."

It was a second or two before Cu'lugh could speak. "All my family knew was that she was found in the forest by the chieftain Rulf as he went out to hunt one day."

Cu'lugh's stomach hardened so tightly he could hardly breathe; and he remembered the tiny, pinched face peering into his own that bitter day when he'd at last left his expired steed to find a place of shelter. A relentless force that scavenged his mind and rifled his memories as if they were bones and sinews of the carcass he'd left behind. It had raked through every thought he'd ever possessed. And when at length it uncovered the vision of the golden-haired girl it had drawn away instinctively before the image could blind its prying eyes.

Vanda!

The realization almost smothered him. Vanda had seen the vision; she had glimpsed the image of the girl he had long ago discarded as but an impossible phantasm of his spirit. And he knew how much Vanda had hated her stepmother by the spiteful words she had offered.

"I know nothing of the mantle," he admitted, discomforted. "I should think it was buried with her, or that Rulf destroyed it if he feared her escaping him."

"Silfr adored her master husband," Larsarian replied. "That much the High Priestess saw in her dreams. The mantle, I pray, was destroyed with Silfr's earthly remains."

"I do not understand, sire."

"If it were intact after she died, its powers would have transferred to her eldest living daughter," Larsarian said, "and that would be Odette. The man who possesses the mantle, possesses the woman. When a man retains the mantle the swanmaiden is bound to serve him by its magic. Possession would insure ravishment, but afterward the man would be faced with a weighty decision: to keep the mantle and assure his possession of the woman or destroy it, if he wishes to know her love not one bound alone by it. However, you have nothing to fear on this if she professes love when you do not have the mantle."

"Whoever possesses it—a woman even?"

Larsarian's eyes were discerning. "The answer to that I do not know. Do you suspect someone in Midgard of having it? If this is so, Odette has no choice but to remain in Athla forever if she is to be safeguarded from being enslaved outside the boundaries."

Cu'lugh tried to calm his fears. He knew Odette was safe here, even if by some mockery of fate Vanda had the mantle in her possession and had deciphered his thoughts when she'd found him in the forest. Vanda had no use for those things she considered relics of superstition any more than, he realized now, she had for her sister's happiness. If she had come across this mantle she surely would have destroyed it.

But another possibility crossed Cu'lugh's mind, one that comforted him somewhat.

"If anyone besides Odette were to don this mantle, what would be the outcome?"

"If a man, he would fall dead. As for a woman, I have never heard."

Cu'lugh knew that he had little to be concerned of either way. He could not care less now for Vanda's reaction when she realized he would never return. She had entered his mind and stolen his secrets without ever confessing her pillage. For all her theatrical assertions and concerns, he was certain now that sisterly devotion had never been a part of her desire to have her sister back. But Odette would never be in jeopardy, for he would never let her leave Athla.

"It is a pointless issue, sire," he said at last, rising to his feet. "Odette will remain out of harm's way, I will see to it."

King Larsarian stood up. "I am happy to hear it. But protect her heart as well—tell her the truth, Cu'lugh."

"I shall, sire." Cu'lugh thanked the king for his audience and bowed again. As he made his way out of the castle his heart swelled with a joy to pale even the solace of the old vision.

Because the vision came to life, he reminded himself.

Chapter Twenty-Eight

he public laundry Odette found was an open area paved with red bricks. Washtubs stood about the edges, along with numerous buckets for the bringing of water from the nearby waterwheel supplied by an inlet of the river. To rinse cleaned laundry a great shallow copper pool had been raised in the center, into which a fluted pipe carried water from the waterwheel supplied by an inlet of the river. The water slowly drained through a silver grate at the bottom of the pool and emptied into another fluted pipe. This pipe carried the dirty water to the sewer built under the city. And on the grassy bank leading to the waterwheel stood several poles with wooden crossbars between which were strung cords for the hanging and drying of wet laundry.

As Odette approached she saw seven or eight other women working at the pool. More sat on the log benches under shade trees beyond the lines, catching up on conversation while their laundry dried, and a few small children played nearby. When her garments were clean and she moved to the rinsing pool the girl to her right began to talk. She was a pretty girl, though her braids were a mess and she didn't seem concerned about the smudges of grime on her face. Her attention was hardly on her task at all as she inundated Odette with information about another novice in her household who had recently been returned from her Unveiler. Odette was shocked by the girl's coarse language and tried to ignore her, but she didn't seem to notice this as she continued with her gossip.

"She wasn't ready and she knew it," the girl complained in a delighted tone. With the back of her wet wrist she crammed one of her braids over a shoulder. "It was no secret she always feigned her passion!"

Odette sighed and tried to think of other things. Still the girl went on, relentlessly describing with much malice what sounded like an endless host of flaws in the other apprentice. Just as Odette considered moving to another place at the pool one of the other women standing there dashed water into the girl's face.

"Every week you are sent here, Jamye, and every week we have to listen to this. I am about ready to make a report to your Mistress for your gossip."

Jamye's face darkened. "And why do I not go to your husband and tell him of your rudeness, Ericka?"

The other women began to talk at once in Ericka's defense. Odette quickly squeezed the excess water from her garments and collected them in her basket. The other women had at last silenced Jamye's gossip as she lifted her clean laundry and headed to the drying lines.

A familiar somber, pale face stared at her from the across the street. Odette's stomach felt as if weighted with stones. Although there was little reason to think it, she feared he would make a scene; but as the minutes crawled on Lord Eryan did not move, remaining like a statue behind the passersby on the street. Odette forced herself to work, but his icy stare followed; and as she draped the clothes over the line she felt his mind attempting to invade her own. Her thoughts shuffled like a farmer flinging stones in a garden. At last she snapped her face toward him deliberately. She knew her features betrayed her anger, but she was glad to see his astonishment.

She willed an invisible wall between herself and him, and when it was satisfactory her thoughts again flowed unimpeded. His pale brow was crumpled with his own anger now; and though she had no interest in his thoughts she recognized the cold promise set on his face, a promise to make her regret this show of willfulness.

Odette closed her eyes and breathed strongly on the invisible wall, imbuing it with the single thought: *move away!*

He did turn then and left with the long, proud strides she knew so well.

She did not see him the rest of the afternoon, but as she sat on the bench waiting for the clothing to dry she thought of him. His unspoken promise held no power to intimidate her, she was surprised to discover. She felt sorry for him, knowing now his wounds were much deeper than she'd ever suspected. And she could never lust for him in the same way again, not just because her heart belonged to another now but that she realized it had not been his student he'd seen as he'd instructed her, not her desires he had worked to arouse and make wanton, but the desires of Queen Honi.

A sad understanding fell over her with her realization, for if Eryan, with all his experience, knew a love spurned, then the consequences of her own selfish love would surely rebound with even direr consequences.

She wiped away the tear that sprang to her eye and put her thoughts to the night ahead, of the pleasure she would provide her Master...pleasure with devotion and bereft of expectations. As was meet, as was fated.

So fleeting these rapturous moments of life! Perhaps in the afterlife we are allowed to plunge and drench our unfulfilled souls.

It was a desperate hope, she knew, but it was all she had for comfort. She sat down under one of the dense maples on the bank and tried to be grateful for the shafts of sunlight that filtered through the branches and speckled warmly over her skin and to remember how fortunate she was in health and security and all the dear ones—Honi and the king, Helrose, Uma, Alban—the friends whose company she would again enjoy one way or another.

When the garments were dry Odette folded them into the basket. Her muscles were a little stiff as she carried the basket through the streets. The curtailing chain forced her to walk at a steady little march, and slowly her melancholy washed away beneath the awareness of her senses: the agitating, hungry beat of her clitoris under the clip and the jingling of the nipple clamps over the scalloped breast cups. The admonishing rhythm of it all reminded her of who she was and of her inner strength. She was renewed, she was herself—strong by virtue of her own embrace of submissiveness—and she would treasure what she was without regret and those whom she loved no matter what weakness fate tempted.

A bold street sentry pinched her buttocks as she passed by, and a pair of priestesses accosted her and demanded to know if she was headed home like a decent young lady. She nodded silently, careful to keep her eyes lowered, and when one of them swatted her buttocks she felt an impulsive need to put the basket down and bow low before the holy women.

"You are well trained," said one. "May the Goddess see your faithful compliance and reward you kindly." Then both women made the gesture of blessing over her shoulders and went on their way.

Odette lifted the basket into her arms again and turned onto the street leading to the inn. She saw a man standing outside his house with one foot propped up on a stool as he delivered a severe spanking to the girl bent over his thigh. Odette wondered idly what infraction the girl had committed. She could see coming down the street another young woman running at high speed from another man brandishing a belt. The passersby laughed at this spectacle, and just before the girl passed Odette the man caught the end of her flying hair. He scooped her up over one shoulder and carried her away, his promises of punishment drowning the girl's pleas.

Odette smiled, not meaning to, but moments later she felt a hand clasp her left arm. She was swung about harshly and found herself looking into Lord Eryan's eyes. Her knees that had genuflected to the priestesses felt heavy and disjointed. Desperately, she hugged the basket, the only barrier between them.

"My spoiled brat." His voice was calm, with no trace of reproach or malice, but just the same they both knew he had no right to accost her when she belonged presently to another man.

"Good afternoon, Lord Eryan."

"The last time I found you on the street I was on my way to save you from that swine, Holbarki."

Odette flushed. Indeed, she was grateful to him for that—but why this reproachful tone?

"Yes, Lord Eryan," she answered.

"What? Is that not *my* Lord Eryan?" His mouth drew up caustically at one corner. "My sister has lost her control completely under the influence of her archer. You should be home, Odette, you are aware of that?"

Odette glanced down the street and saw the roof of the inn's portico, the patrons coming and going from the entranceway. She did not see Lord Cu'lugh, but she was tempted to wrest from the hand at her arm and hobble as fast as she could to find him.

"I must go, Lord Eryan, my Master expects me—"

"Your *Master?* Your misdirected loyalty, your unsettled heart—do you not see how you confirm what I tell you? There is only one master for you, Odette. I was going to bid on your Unveiling. No matter what the cost, I would have had you. I am the one you should be with, not this barbarian stranger. My sister has lost her good sense in this personal dilemma over her own direction. But I can rectify her wrong to you, and shall most eagerly."

"No!" Odette was shocked by the loudness of her voice. Nevertheless, she went on. "Lord Eryan, I am not free to go with you now! It is forbidden. Why do you do this? Please, let me go!"

The street sentry who had pinched her before walked by and cast Lord Eryan a suspicious look. With a low growl Lord Eryan released her. His eyes bored through her with a frightful intensity as she made her way along the street.

Like a weight lifted was her relief, but before she got to the borders of the inn's property a commotion across the street drew the attention of the pedestrians. Odette stopped and saw a man had fallen from a ladder within his own yard. The sentry came running to his aid along with half a dozen other men. As she resumed walking she heard heavy footfalls advancing on her heels. Heaving the basket on one hip, she trotted as rapidly as she could toward the entrance of the portico.

As she entered she saw ahead some men dallying about one of the punishment platforms, where presently two naked serving girls were bound. Odette trotted toward them, sure that with these men near Lord Eryan would forget his pursuit. A moment later, however, she heard the footfalls again, and before she could turn her hair was wrenched and her head pulled back. She spun about with an angry hiss that brought an amused titter from the other men.

She struck with her free hand at Lord Eryan but he would not release her hair.

"Come with me, Odette," he said.

"Leave me be," she whispered. "Go, return to the manor! I am not Honi!"

He flinched as if she'd slapped him, his face a mask of sharply chiseled hoarfrost.

"No, no, you are not," he said thickly. "For you are mine."

Odette glanced around at the amused men, wondering how much harm she would bring Eryan if she were to openly charge him with infringement on another's property.

"Can you leave me, please?" she whispered again. "I belong to another for now!"

He grabbed her free wrist. "That contract is invalid," he said, and pulled her toward the entrance so roughly the basket fell from her other arm. It overturned on the tiles, spilling the clean clothes everywhere.

"Oh, see what you've done," she said, but the next moment his hand clamped over her free wrist. The soles of her feet skidded over the tiles as he pulled her to him. Odette shrieked and tried to wrestle from his grasp. Eryan muttered darkly and, hoisting her by the waist, slung her over his shoulder as she'd seen the man in the street do his woman. He turned and had started out of the portico when she heard a familiar voice from behind her.

"Take your hands off my slave."

She raised her head and could see his muscled legs walking toward Eryan.

One of the men spoke up. "Your slave? Let go the girl, brigand!"

217

The lot of them surrounded Eryan now, but it was Cu'lugh who took her from Eryan's shoulder and set her on her feet. She gazed up into his face, so brutally angry that even in her relief it frightened her.

Eryan turned and glared at Cu'lugh defiantly. Cu'lugh's hands were clenched in ready fists at his hips, and she watched Eryan's eyes move from man to man, calculating his chances in challenging them all.

"Go," Lord Cu'lugh ordered him, "and do not let me see you approach her again."

Eryan was slow to respond, glaring at his rival for several dreadfully silent moments. At last he turned and marched down the walk into the shadows of sunset on the street.

"Our apologies, sir," said one of the men. "Had we realized she was owned we would have told him to take off."

"Or thrown him out ourselves," another added.

"All is well," Cu'lugh said and, stooping down, gathered the spilled garments into the basket. As he rose his eyes settled on Odette with a strange heaviness that disquieted her not much less than Eryan's obsessed stare.

"Take this upstairs, young lady, then return to me at once."

"Yes, sir."

She hurried into the inn and once in his room set the basket on the floor beside the bed. As she turned to leave she saw a half-dozen lit candles had been set about on the tables. Rose petals were scattered over the coverlet, and in a small brass bowl on the windowsill she saw a small cake of candied mayapple root as was used for incense...love incense.

Odette's breast swelled and her heart sank at once. Lord Cu'lugh had planned this special welcoming for her and the encounter with her former teacher had ruined it. As she returned downstairs she wondered if Lord Cu'lugh was angry with her—and received the answer as soon as she returned outside.

His heated voice was implacable. "Did I not tell you not to speak with other men, Odette?"

Her eyes filled with frustrated tears. "Yes, my Master, but—"

"Why did you not raise your voice, protest where these men could hear? You know that is your right as my property."

She could hardly speak without weeping, "I know, my Master, but that man is High Steward in the house of my Mistress. I-I felt obliged to speak respectfully."

Lord Cu'lugh sighed and set his hands on his hips. "High Steward? Then he has more than enough knowledge of the laws not to attempt such an outrage. He was wrong, Odette—you are mine, and you should have shown respect for that by protesting your ownership."

Odette nodded, too ashamed to reply. He seized her hand suddenly, not hurting her, but still his anger was so great it permeated the very air. She followed him humbly and in tears as he walked into the inn.

He did not go upstairs right away, but made his way to the dining room and pulled out a bench from one of the tables. At once he threw her over his lap so that her arms and legs dangled over the floor on either side. He stretched out his palm just over her buttocks and the heat of it made her hips dance in dreadful anticipation.

"How dare you disobey me," he said so loudly she knew every patron in the room could hear. "Do you think I give you instructions just to hear the sound of my own voice?"

Odette sought desperately for an answer, but not fast enough. He raised his hand and spanked her several times so that her buttocks were splayed with fire.

"Well?"

"No, my Master, no," she sobbed.

He spanked her again, this time much harder and longer. Odette's buttocks scorched and she was sure they glowed red before the patrons. Humiliated, she closed her eyes, but his spanking palm bore down even harder and she heard him say over the resounding sound "You will keep your eyes open!"

Through her tears she endured the punishment, and with each fast, precise spank her hips bounced helplessly over his legs and her uplifted breasts jiggled wantonly between her arms so that the bells jingled discordantly on her nipples. She saw two men watching from the next table, their approving looks only aggravating her shame.

At length Lord Cu'lugh's hand stayed, but he stroked her chastened, tender flesh so that it seared against his firm fingers.

"Do you think you can just do as you please?" he said in a voice shaking with anger. "That I am not a man to demand obedience? Do you think me so irresolute that I would accept such flagrant disrespect?"

"No, my Master!"

He was quiet a moment and she felt his anger subside a little.

"I have been too lenient, young lady, but no more." He spanked her again, with such intensity that at last a wail broke through her lips. But still the chastening blows continued. And when Lord Cu'lugh stopped this time he drew a fingertip over her swollen buttocks and her sex panged its own immodest plea.

"You will know what to expect now for disobedience, do you not?"

Not daring to speak, Odette nodded, and he thrust her legs apart as far as the chain would allow. She felt her fluids drench over his thigh and she whimpered, sure he would spank her for that, too. Instead, he parted her swollen mounds and touched the moisture gathered there. Her face scalded with horror.

"*Please, not here,*" she whispered.

As in answer he probed the exposed orifice with two fingers, thrusting them back and forth slowly. Her entire sex and thighs radiated with grinding need. She heard a ripple of amusement from the men nearby and, letting go of her Master's ankles, covered her face.

Lord Cu'lugh caught her wrists with one hand and held them against the small of her back so she was forced to look at the men with their lusty smiles as he tormented her sex. Drawing the clip from Odette's clitoris, Lord Cu'lugh spanked it with a thumb. It swelled with each smack, quivering frantically. Odette felt an orgasm fast approaching, and her face went scarlet to know it would be in plain view of the onlooking strangers.

But Lord Cu'lugh seemed to realize it, too, and drew his hand back.

"I own this body, Odette," he said in a low and sensual voice. "I alone determine where it goes, how it is dressed, and when, if ever, it knows satisfaction."

Odette started to nod submissively when another round of blistering spanks fell over her buttocks. She wept as her hips bounced, uncertain what was more frustrating, the spectacle of her punishment or the nullified orgasm.

When it was done he lifted her up and placed her on her knees to the floor at his feet. He pointed to a the wall nearest the table and said, "Crawl over there and rise to your knees. Do not turn your face from the wall until I say otherwise."

Odette crawled at once, past the men who had watched every moment of her punishment. With her face bowed before the stones she tried to take comfort that no one could see her face or know with confidence the frustrated desire that simmered but would not relent. But by the growing din of voices she knew more and more people were coming in, and the tell-tale deep blush of her chastening could not be hidden from any of them unless she was foolish enough to risk her Master's displeasure again.

She heard Lord Cu'lugh order his dinner from one of the serving girls. He did not call her back, not even when the food arrived; and all the while he ate she remained in the chafing position. But after a time he rose from the table and captured the ends of her hair in his hand.

"Head upstairs," he said and though she tried to walk neither too fast or too slow he spanked her the entire way back to the room.

The fragrance of the rose petals filled the air as they entered, and the walls glittered in the candlelight. Lord Cu'lugh released her hair and bolted the door.

"On the bed," he said in an uncertain deep tone. Odette obeyed, her buttocks smarting harshly as she sat on the mattress. She could not look at him, but she heard him undress and step to the bedside.

"Look at me, Odette."

The sight of his robust limbs sharpened her aching desire. His manhood was already stiffening, though the anger still showed in his hungry eyes. She shuddered as they swept over her with a deliberate slowness that brought back to her mind his words affirming his claim over her body.

"I want you to be without doubt about my feelings for you," he said finally and sat down. With his key he unlocked her belt and slid the garters down her legs. Lifting her chin he kissed her mouth, filling her with his stern sweetness, and pressed her down on the petal-strewn mattress. He settled back on his haunches and his penetrating gaze laid her open as his hands unfolded her knees and massaged her inner thighs. Slowly, he found her clitoris and rubbed it gently, lightly with his fingertips. It beat needfully and Odette's pelvis rose to him.

"No, lie still," he said and stroked the flesh of her thighs and kissed her knees. "I have many things to say to you, Odette. Some details can wait until you have been adequately punished. For now, it is enough to say that I have never felt so possessive of a woman before…and that is because I desire no woman but you. I do not want to return you to Mistress Helrose. I cannot bear the thought of another man having you. I want you with me, always—but only if you return this passion."

Odette's eyes widened and her mind reeled. She thought she must have misunderstood him and waited, her brows knit and her arms folded protectively over her stomach, for her understanding to open.

He caressed her legs tenderly, his fingers lingering over her calf muscles. When he looked in her face again Odette could see the soberness behind his thoughts.

"I have spoken with Mistress Helrose of this," he continued. "She agrees, on condition it is what you want. You see, I cannot see my future without you, my flower, my beloved. I do not apologize for punishing you—no, not that—and it would not be so severe did I not love you so. It may be I have insulted you with my presumptuousness, and if this is so, tell me now and I shall return you to your Mis—"

"No!" Odette raised her head and did not care that she'd spoken without consent. All that mattered was the memory of his words—*did I not love you so.*

"Master, I love you," she said breathlessly. "I love you, dearest Master—I have loved you for all time though I do not know how I know! I feared I was a selfish fool to adore you as I do, and chided myself for wanting to cling to you."

Tears gushed over her cheeks, but she could see his eyes, the indescribable smile that formed on his lips. He cupped his hands to her face and kissed her mouth, deeply, lovingly. His voice caressed her soul.

"Then you will marry me, Odette—be my bride, my companion, my slave, belonging and wanting to belong to me and no one else?"

She gasped and kissed his brow, his strong hands. "Yes, oh, yes, as I have wanted and do want and shall for all time!"

He drew her into his arms and pressed his mouth against her ear. "You know your punishment isn't over, don't you?"

She nodded, and her breast beat with a fierce toll. He lavished kisses over her face and throat, whispering in his silken tone, "Turn, onto your knees and hands."

Odette's lips grieved to obey even as her sex pulsed madly, and as she turned he gently pressed her head to her hands on the bed and separated her thighs. His fingers delved into her vagina, inflaming the entire orifice, charging her clitoris. He grasped her hips, the crown of his rigid phallus pressed against her fount. Odette gasped wantonly as he plunged in. So consummately he filled her, his thighs slapping against hers as he thrust in and out, slowly igniting her hungry core with each torturous stroke.

She moaned loudly and turned her face toward him and made an imploring whimper.

"No one told you to look back," he said and spanked her upturned buttocks. Chagrined, she laid her chin over her folded arms and looked straight ahead. She focused on his pleasure, commanding her needy orifice to grasp his pounding organ like a fitted sheath.

Gradually, his hips drove faster, harder until she thought her womb would surely shatter from the heavenly cruel sensation. Just as she was about to orgasm he clutched her hips adamantly, and with one last titanic thrust his life fluid burst through her.

His soft moan was the purring of a lion against her ear. Drawing his spent shaft from her he lifted her arms and drew her to her knees so that her back pressed against his damp chest. So brutal was Odette's need her hips rocked against his pelvis, and careless of punishment she whimpered again for relief.

"No," he said and kissed her throat, sending a shiver through her.

Even as Odette's body screamed for satisfaction, an unexpected rapture suddenly swept through her. It crowned her passion and refined its purpose.

"I love you, Odette," Lord Cu'lugh whispered. He turned her to him and his face seemed suddenly so vulnerable in its very stern bearing. "I love you."

"I love you, my Master," she said and understood now that as he had given his heart to her, in turn her body and spirit had relinquished themselves utterly to his will.

The affirmation of all I wanted but dreaded to believe possible!

The sense of selfishness she'd felt before subsided into the oblivion where it belonged, and never again would she be misled by guilt or self-doubt. She wanted to please him and make him happy, to be guided and possessed under his resolute command always.

And as his fevered mouth fed on her lips the essence of their reciprocal bondage whipped the flames of the candles and tousled the rose petals into the night breeze.

Chapter Twenty-Nine

Cu'lugh was tired, but in his joy he could not sleep. He leaned up on an elbow and looked at the cage by the wall. Odette lay curled up on one side, asleep in her prison, her golden tresses strewn beneath her arms and lovely back.

She loves me.

Cu'lugh's chest pounded, and he had to fight the urge to release her, to take her once more. After he'd brought up a bowl of the kitchen's last porridge for her, they had made love again. He almost relented on the decision to make her spend the night in the cage both for his own satisfaction of having her close to him at night and the unhappy tears that came to her eyes as he told her. Yet, he knew she unconsciously expected a firm hand, and her respect would wane if he proved weak.

Before locking her away he had removed her boots and gloves, all the dainty accessories, so she might sleep a little easier. In the morning he planned to find a fitting conclusion to her punishment. He could not deny he looked forward to it, that he enjoyed punishing her even when he had been so angry at her. He craved her obedience—at least her inclination to obey—but punishing her aroused him, especially watching her suffering little buttocks move under his hand and the tremble of her lips as she fought to control her passion.

That he had fallen in love with a woman with such vitality and host of graces still amazed him. Before Odette came into his life he had sought no more in a woman than the material or carnal things they could offer. Odette fascinated him, comforted him, and she possessed a sense of self-worth and acceptance of herself that he'd rarely found in others, whether female or male.

He would disclose to her on the coming day all that he'd kept hidden, and there was fear in him now of losing her for that disclosure. She would be unavoidably wounded—that he regretted deeply and was prepared to face. But if he was certain of anything in Odette it was that her capacity to understand and forgive equaled her sensuality.

Cu'lugh pressed a cushion over his erect cock, willing his lust to lull, and wondered if he would ever know such anger with his tender Odette as he had earlier. She had disobeyed, and she would break rules in the future, yes; but it was not just her behavior that had ignited his fury. Part of his reaction had stemmed from the identity of the man to whom she had spoken, that steward and brother of Helrose. As soon as Cu'lugh met the man's eyes he had recognized at once the nature of the passion that shone so brightly in the other's somber face. He had seen it in the faces of other frustrated men who could not abide a woman's love for another. Those other men had proved dangerous to the objects of their desire. Cu'lugh was doubtless this one was just as volatile.

As soon as he could arrange it Odette would be his wife. Surely once they were wedded this Lord Eryan would not dare challenge the strict codes of the Athlan laws.

Cu'lugh sighed and turned over on his back. At last sleep came, but it was light and molested by a recurring dream of a dark, ravenous scavenger bird that haunted Odette's every step.

In the morning, after a small meal, Cu'lugh took Odette to the public grounds so she could bathe in the brook. When she was clean and dressed again, he plaited her hair in two adorable braids and led her back to the portico at the inn. There he ordered her to wait as he fetched the youth who oversaw the inn's serving girls.

Cu'lugh explained that his slave was in dire need of strong chastisement, and the boy agreed with him that she would likely benefit from a lengthy kneel at one of the punishment benches. Another girl was already fettered to one of the benches, and by the redness of her buttocks it was evident the boy was diligent in using the paddle he carried. He suggested to Cu'lugh that it would intensify Odette's frustration to have her facing the other girl. As Cu'lugh selected a pair of manacles for Odette on the opposite bench he noticed her wringing her hands nervously.

"Here," he said at length, patting the cushion between the middle pair of fetters. The boy caught Odette's hand and pulled her toward the bench, telling her to kneel on the tiles. She complied, and the boy set her chin carefully over the cushion and locked the fetters about her wrists so that her hands lay against her cheeks. With each turn of the key she made a fretful sound. She was sufficiently bound, with her clamped nipples swaying behind the bench and her buttocks propped high, her face helpless to hide its scarlet blush.

But Cu'lugh thought it was not enough and asked the boy had he anything with which to guarantee she could not complain. The boy promptly fetched one of the leather bits he said were kept for the most insolent of the serving girls.

The boy bade Odette open her mouth. She frowned at this, searching Cu'lugh's face incredulously, and only after the boy ordered her again did she comply. With the pap inserted into her mouth the boy buckled the strap at the back of her head.

"I think that will suit the need, sir."

"Yes, perfect." Cu'lugh said and saw how Odette's eyes had widened and her hands twisted against the fetters. She was the sublime image of the punished slave now, and for several minutes he stood with his arms crossed and gazed at her, savoring her helplessness and the pride he felt as other men passed through and contemplated his lovely possession.

At last he stepped behind the bench and stroked the length of her back with his fingertip. She trembled as he did this so that the little bells at her nipples shook.

"I need to go into town for a time," he said to the boy. Cu'lugh looked down at Odette's face and saw that her cheeks were damp with tears. He felt a moment's weakness but he controlled it and ignored her weeping.

"She will be most safe, sir," the boy said and brandished before Odette's eyes the paddle he used to discipline his regular charges. The sight of it made her breathe rapidly, but Cu'lugh noted that in her growing fear the tears did not fall so easily.

He reached down and tweaked her nipples, just hard enough to bring a stifled cry to her lips. Satisfied at last, he left her to her discipline.

He first made a visit to the livery stable to pay the proprietor. His horse was in the yard outside when he came, looking rather plumper than Cu'lugh recalled as he watched him circle a grazing mare. For a time he and the proprietor watched the two of them.

"We brought her in from the pasture when he started getting edgy," the man explained. "If you plan to stay there's an exchange of promise for any horse allowed to roam." Seeing the uncomprehending look on Cu'lugh's face he continued, "We prefer to see the animals allowed to go as they wish, excepting the warrior's mounts and private pets of children and ladies. The king's men, of course, keep theirs in the royal stable. I am sanctioned to offer twice whatever you paid for him."

"Truly? Does that not create an overpopulation?"

The man grinned. "No, sir. Nothing in Athla procreates without considered design beforehand."

Cu'lugh raised a disbelieving eyebrow but he answered, "I shall think on it." Before leaving he asked that the horse be ridden daily.

"It will be done," the man promised. "He's a fine animal."

Next Cu'lugh visited some of the shops at that end of the city. In one cozy establishment he found some lotion for Odette and honeyed soapwort for bathing. At another shop he came across a fine little purse of gold muslin for her to carry coins when he sent her on errands. In the same place he also bought a new razor for himself and a vest of beige silk. At a small open market he came across a man selling whetstones, of which he bought several. Lastly, he visited a baker's house where he picked up a loaf of rye bread and a pouch of freshly baked pastries for Odette.

The sun was burning high in the sky when he walked back to the inn. Delightful reveries filled his mind: of taking Odette while she was locked over the bench, not just her succulent sex but her mouth. As he entered the portico three men sitting at a table raised their cups in greeting, the same men he recognized from the night before. The girl who had knelt at the bench opposite Odette was gone and to his surprise a young woman knelt at Odette's face. By her tight blouse that molded tightly over her bosom and snug breeches of green linen he knew she had to be a free woman. Her black hair fell in a loose braid down her back and a wide paddle was hooked to a loop on her leather belt.

She was smiling in a most peculiar way at Odette, and by the movement of her lips he knew she whispered something to his slave she didn't want overheard. Distressful little lines furrowed Odette's brow and her hands were clenched white-knuckled at her cheeks. As Cu'lugh approached quietly he noted the animated expressions that livened the newcomer's face as she spoke—hardly a self-contained priestess, this one. Nevertheless, the thought of offering her the privilege of spanking Odette for his own pleasure was quite tempting.

Odette noticed his advance and even with the bit in her mouth he could hear her whimpering plea for him to intercede.

The freewoman looked up as Cu'lugh neared and stood to meet him. "The boy here informed me this is your slave. I was impressed to see her gagged —so many Masters and Mistresses are too lenient these days."

Cu'lugh beamed and looked down at Odette proudly. But she was attempting to fight the restraints now, straining up on her toes to rise and fussing behind the bit. He was disappointed by her behavior, and it would not take much more to persuade him to make that tempting offer he had just considered.

"Settle yourself down, young lady," he said coolly.

Odette did settle back onto her knees, but her green eyes flashed at him, desperate with anger; and raising her chin she tossed her head impertinently over the cushion.

"If you'll excuse, me, I must tend to this young lady."

The girl laughed. "Ah, I hope that might wait a moment, sir—I've an offer to make to you."

Cu'lugh sighed, his bundles weighing on his arms. "I'm sorry, she is not for sale."

"Oh, I am looking more for a hireling for the afternoon," the girl explained, her laugh suddenly pinched and impatient. "My companion and I need our new household swept and mopped and the furniture cleaned. The king's men are keeping their own girls quite busy today plowing the royal fields, and as I passed I saw how capable this girl looks. I am willing to pay for her services."

Cu'lugh lifted an eyebrow. "Just for the day?"

"Yes, good sir. I can return her tonight."

Cu'lugh looked down again at Odette and he knew a moment's pity for the devastation in her face. It was all he could do to keep himself from releasing her that moment, taking her into his arms and forgiving this latest exhibition of arrogance. But, no, if she had not learned from the punishments so far then she needed more.

"Very well," he answered. "Give me your name and the location of your household. I will bring her there shortly."

The girl's sable eyes sparkled. "I am Brune and our household sits within the guilders' district. But you should not be so troubled for your generosity when I can take her and bring her back."

Cu'lugh remembered that King Larsarian had promised to send a messenger that evening, and he did not want to risk missing the man.

"It is but you and your companion? Who is this companion?"

"An old friend of mine who was a student of the holy mysteries."

"Mistresses?" And seeing the confirming lift of Brune's chin, "My Odette does need a thorough lesson in humility, I regret to admit. You may take her, Brune, and all I ask in return is your promise to discipline firmly if the need arises."

Odette suddenly squealed behind her gag, a baleful, indecent sound. Cu'lugh stepped to the table, ready to throw down his merchandise and spank her soundly right then and there. But Brune laid a calming hand on his arm.

"You are most generous, sir, and you speak wisely. Often when a master is fond of his slave the slave naturally tests him or, worse, believes that fondness grants them certain privileges. Leave her fittingly gagged and call the boy to release her into my custody for a time. I even have a leash here—" Brune patted the object at her left hip. "An afternoon under the strict hand of another, and she will understand her privileges rely only on the good behavior she yields to her master. I dare say, it will be long before she again demonstrates such disrespect."

"I think you are right," he agreed and set the merchandise on a table to go and fetch the key from the young overseer. As he came back and unlocked the fetters Odette's hands flew to the back of her head. At once Cu'lugh pulled her arms down and bound her wrists to the small of her back. She danced on the tiles, murmuring still behind the gag, trying her best to get away. Taking the cord that the merchant had used to wrap the soapwort, he tied her hands securely behind her and spanked her harshly. And yet she wriggled and stomped her feet, throwing her head back and forth in the attempt to spit the gag from her mouth.

Trembling with anger Cu'lugh asked Brune for her leash.

As he reached for her collar Odette sank to her knees and knelt at his feet. Her whimpers were unconstrained, desolate, now; and she bowed her forehead over his boots.

"Oh, no, no, no," Cu'lugh said, touched by her contrition even in his anger; and pulling her up by her arms spanked her until her buttocks were the color of reddest rose and she danced for pain, not insolence. When he was breathless he stopped, and the tears streaming down her face again made him want to comfort her. But it was too late; he'd given his word to the girl.

"You will go with her," he told Odette and dried the tears away with his sleeve. Her eyes held onto his, desperate and red-rimmed; but he kissed her brow and turned her toward Brune.

"You will go, my love," he whispered, loving the touch of her small ear against his cheek. "And you will behave if you do not wish to be knelt over this bench when you return, to stay here until tomorrow morning."

Brune had already slid her paddle from the loop.

"In the guilder's district? Which house?"

Brune sighed and pursed her lips. "This one has truly vexed your warrior's heart, sir—shall we expect a visit?"

"No." Cu'lugh sounded defensive even to his own ears. But she'd guessed correctly—he had planned on coming to make sure Odette was well. His pride, however, would not allow him to make a spectacle of his love for her.

"Well, 'tis second past the hall of the Silver Masters. A small house of white ash logs."

He nodded and snapped the leash to the eyelet of Odette's collar. The next moment Odette stomped her feet in pure protest. Cu'lugh started to grab her, punish her himself; but Brune yanked her in the direction of the street so roughly that his eyes widened as much as Odette's.

"I shall see my promise kept to you, sir," Brune told him and bade Odette to walk before her on the leash. When Odette hesitated, the girl whipped the paddle against her thigh. Odette jumped and glanced back at Cu'lugh sadly. Only after the second strike of the paddle did she begin to trot her chained legs toward the entranceway.

The overseer emerged from the inn as Cu'lugh watched the two women head down the walkway. He cleared his throat gently and said, "Come in and have some tea, sir, it is my own special brew."

Cu'lugh felt a niggling little urge to run after Brune, to reclaim Odette and bring her into the shelter of the inn. But with considerable effort of will he discounted it as but his passion for Odette and followed the boy inside.

Chapter Thirty

he walk to the center of the city had never seemed so long to Odette. As she endured the merciless strokes of Brune's paddle she searched the faces of those they passed, desperate to find an understanding eye. Surely, she believed, someone had to understand what was happening, any one of the people who knew her by sight—or at least Lord Cu'lugh. This was kidnapping, pure and simple; she did not know the girl but she understood at once her wicked taunts back at the inn. This Brune knew *her* name, the name of her Master as well. And she had vowed in her mad, hateful whisper that Odette was about to be taken away forever from her *indulgent Outer Realmer.*

Odette's imploring search went unheeded. Then, when a careless merchant blundered betwixt the two girls Odette felt Brune's hold on the leash give way. She stumbled across the street, seeing at the last moment a mule cart moving toward her. Only then did anyone else notice her—one of the street sentries. He leaped across the stones and pulled her back before the mule collided with her. As he delivered her to the walkway Brune came running up. She clutched Odette's arms, shaking her violently; and her hysteria at the near-accident put a tremble in her admonishing voice.

Before he turned away, the sentry advised Brune to better discipline her slave.

Odette had no doubt the deceiving girl would do just that and worse. Soon enough she realized the extent of Brune's lies, for though they did enter the street where stood the temples and guild houses, they turned down an alley and walked to the side of a dark cottage she thought she recognized. It was certainly not the house of white ash Brune had described to Lord Cu'lugh. Opening the door, Brune shoved Odette inside so roughly she fell to the wooden floor.

A startled murmur rose from the front of the house. Odette twisted off her bruised hip as the door slammed shut. Brune turned and wrenched one of Odette's braids with a shaking fist.

"You could have gotten yourself killed," she seethed and gave Odette's thigh a hearty kick. Behind her gag Odette cursed her, and as she tried to rise to her feet Brune yanked her back by the braid and raised her fist.

A calm voice stayed Brune's delivery. "Leave her be."

Brune's face darkened, but she let go of Odette's hair; and the man who had spoken stooped and helped Odette to her feet. It was then she recognized the bearded giant owner of the house—Lord Eryan's brother, Harold.

"The stupid beast nearly got herself killed," Brune railed. "Where is Yolande?"

Harold motioned toward a curtained door beyond the tables. Brune made an ugly grunt and took the leash again and yanked Odette about, shoving her through the curtain and into a narrow hall. Wooden bins crowded this space, all crammed with what looked like worn parts from musical instruments. It was the door at the end of the hall Brune led her to and here the dark girl knocked with a modicum of restraint.

The face that greeted them brought no surprise to Odette—Yolande, with her hard eyes and smug pout, standing there more proudly than ever in a matronly blue peasant's smock and starched white blouse. Brune pushed past into the small bedroom with deep-paned windows and plastered walls washed a bright, clean cream. In a drawing room beyond someone sat on a bench before a small wall hearth. As he turned his face turned them Odette's strength washed from her, and she would have fallen to the floor were it not for Yolande's hands at her waist.

"Tired, is she? Poor wench," Yolande cooed sardonically and, taking the leash, led Odette to Lord Eryan. His eyes pierced her like a dagger forged in ice.

He did not seem the same obsessed being he had just the night before. The savage emotion had disappeared, as had the aura of desperation. He regarded Brune.

"You seem to have met with success," he said. "Was there any trouble from the Outer Realmer?"

"No, he is the fool you said. But this wench nearly got herself killed trying to escape."

Eryan turned his eyes again to Odette, exacting and cool.

"Untie her hands, free her mouth."

Odette moved her jaw gingerly when Brune had released her, as her mouth retained a ghostly impression of the gag. She did not move otherwise but waited for him to say whatever reproachful thing he'd brought her to hear.

"Kneel before me, Odette."

She inhaled deeply, knowing protest was futile, and obeyed. He took the end of one of her braids and rolled the tuft of golden hair between his fingers.

"I cannot say I disapprove of your Outer Realmer's taste in apparel for his property. What say you, Odette?"

She shook her head, honestly perplexed for an answer.

"What kind of man do you rate this Master of yours? A better man than I?"

Odette fumbled for a reply for the unfair question. "I would not know how to answer that, Lord Eryan."

She expected anger; instead the frost thawed a little from his voice, "Of course not—he is your first. I suppose you're quite smitten with him?"

Odette blushed painfully. She hated deception, but she suspected strongly that to divulge her true feelings would only incite Eryan's wrath.

"I-I am indebted to Lord Cu'lugh."

"Indebted? And has he shared with you *his* feelings?"

Odette heard one of the other girls yawn.

"Answer me, Odette."

"He tells me my company is enjoyable."

Lord Eryan leaned forward and tented his fingers over his knees. His smile brought crinkles to the corners of his eyes that at any other time Odette would have found flattering to his features.

"What did you tell this knight that day you met him in the domicile of Holbarki? Did you promise to satisfy his every need? To yield to him all those precious lessons learned in my sister's household?"

Odette was appalled by the insinuation. "Certainly not, Lord Cu'lugh. It is not for me to decide to whom I am to go."

"No? And you would not even pretend otherwise? Say to vex the heart of another man, whether as a test of his ardor or just from blatant wickedness?"

Odette's indignation hardened her voice. "No."

The tenderness vanished from his face and he hauled down on the braid, forcing her brow to the floor at his feet and pressing the heel of his palm to the nape of her neck. But his voice was smooth as polished marble as he said, "You are young and inexperienced, Odette, and so I understand your lack of appreciation for the consequences of the pranks you play. But I shan't allow you to destroy yourself—or let that barbarian destroy the potential I have always seen within you."

Odette trembled, more from anger than alarm, and before she could stop herself she shouted defiantly "*No.*"

Behind her, Brune and Yolande snickered, and though Odette could not see Eryan's face she knew by their abrupt silence his penetrating gaze had lit upon them. For several moments he kept Odette bowed in the vulnerable position. She was frightened now and wondered what Lord Cu'lugh would do when at last he realized he'd been duped.

"Yolande, I want you to tend to this naughty young lady," Eryan said at last, his voice thick but even; and raising his hand from Odette's neck, he turned the leash over to Yolande. "Do as you will—as long as it is with the efficiency my sister lacks."

Yolande pulled the leash so Odette was forced up on her hands. She took Brune's paddle and lifted it high, smashed the wooden face across Odette's buttocks with a resounding crack.

"Come," she ordered, and Odette crawled at her heels over the floor into the bedroom.

Yolande sat down on the bedside so that she faced the drawing room. Odette felt Lord Eryan's heavy regard as she dropped the looped end the leash over the post of the footboard.

"Remain on hands and knees, and lower your eyes humbly!"

Odette's obeyed at once, and she saw the hem of Yolande's dress rise, revealing the naked pair of creamy legs and thighs Odette had seen many times before. Brune's ungainly yet light footfalls came up close behind her, and Odette trembled to think what the evil girl might try. But she dared not glance back, for the most mortifying thing she could think of was to suffer another stroke of the paddle at Yolande's hand.

"Odette—love hostage of the exotic Outer Realmer! I never thought truly I'd be looking upon you from this perspective!" Yolande tittered and lifted Odette's face so that she was staring between Yolande's parted thighs. The girl's nether lips were plump and moist under the heavy brunette curls, and her large clitoris looked like a glistening stone above the vertical slit.

"Look at me!"

Odette raised her eyes at once and saw Yolande massaging her breasts through the front of her gown. The nipples had become erect and the aureolas were saucers peeping over the low-cut bodice. Yolande smiled lazily, her eyes heavy-lidded; and she leaned back on one hand and spread her long nether lips apart, strumming the large clitoris between her first two fingers. As she continued to masturbate it gorged to the size of a sparrow's egg. Her hand descended farther and she slid a finger into her vagina and pumped the orifice slowly. The musky fragrance of her mounting passion perfumed the air, sweet and thick as costliest incense.

"You will pleasure me," Yolande said, "and you shall perform well, for if you attempt to do anything but that, Odette, it will be a choice sorely regretted."

Odette swallowed, numb with shock, and bowed her head. Gingerly, she placed her hands on the creamy skin beside Yolande's pubic mound. They were hot, but so were the hands that unexpectedly grabbed Odette's buttocks and pried her thighs apart. Odette gasped, terrified at whatever Brune planned, but dared not look back. Instead, she tried to concentrate on the command she'd been given and lowered her mouth to Yolande's sex and lapped her tongue over the inner folds of the nether lips. The heady incense filled Odette's mouth, and as she gently suckled the lips and licked the bulging organ Brune laid a hand over her sex. With her fingertips Brune pressed Odette's clitoris and then slid a finger into her vagina. Several times she probed it, then, withdrawing, she parted Odette's buttocks and inserted a finger into her anus. Odette chilled, paralyzed, until she saw the impatient look on Yolande's face. With all her effort she tried to ignore Brune's intrusive touch. With her tongue she dove into Yolande's fount, filling it as deeply as she could, canvassing the pulsing clitoris with every rise of her face before plunging back into the cavity again.

Yolande moaned and fell back on the bed. With Brune still pumping her anus Odette rose and draped herself over Yolande's thighs, kissing the nether mouth and drawing it open carefully with her teeth. Her tongue bored through the pink slit as her fingers massaged the clitoris. Yolande writhed on the bed, clutching the coverlet above her head. Odette felt her own sex rock with desire as she inserted two fingers into Yolande's. Back and forth she pumped the orifice until suddenly Yolande's hips hurtled forward and a cry of exultation broke through her pouting lips.

Odette watched Yolande's clitoris twitch and her thighs and stomach flush. Brune's manipulations grew ever stronger. Odette's sex hungered after attention and her hips plunged shamelessly. Below her Yolande's eyes fluttered open and she reached up and grasped Odette's breasts. She groped them roughly and pinched the clamps into her nipples. At last she sat up on her knees and thrust her hand between Odette's wet thighs.

Odette moaned and reared her sex forward now. Yolande drove two fingers into her eager nether mouth, and Odette felt her muscles clamp them eagerly as Yolande assaulted, worked the opening. With a cry of humiliation and abandon Odette orgasmed. Her orifice quaked with a relief that tided into her stuffed rectum and spread through her midriff.

At last Brune backed away and Odette fell gratefully into Yolande's embracing arms. Yolande kissed her quivering mouth and stroked her face. Odette felt close to weeping when Brune spun her about. The girl had stripped off her breeches and boots and stood with her feet spread widely apart. She did not even attempt to hide the contempt in her grin and, gathering Odette's braids up in her hands, pushed her to her knees again. Odette's face was pressed toward the heavy triangle of hair between Brune's thighs. Odette bit back the little resentful growl that rose to her throat. Her hands were trembling as she peeled the blonde curls aside and exposed the eager sex. She pleasured the hateful girl just as she had Yolande, with only Eryan's unreadable watching eyes for comfort.

When Brune climaxed Odette's braids fell from her weakened grasp. At once Odette turned back to Yolande and bowed her head over the other's knees and kissed her shoes, hoping to find the comfort of shortly before.

Yolande smiled and stroked the back of her neck. "You did well, very well. I understand why your Master may be covetous."

Odette heard an unpleasant sound from the drawing room. Footfalls fell heavily over the floor, a shadow over the bed. Turning her eyes she saw Eryan standing over the three of them. She knew by the look on his face he'd overheard Yolande's words.

He snapped his fingers loudly at his side. "Come here, Odette."

She raised her head and crawled to him, making certain to bow over his feet as she had Yolande's. Brune laughed spitefully and threw herself on the bed.

Eryan's stroked the nape of Odette's neck, sending a bolt of new fear through her stomach.

"Indeed, Yolande, her Master does covet her. But I think you have become too hasty with your compliments. She still has tests to meet."

"Lord Eryan," Yolande said slowly. "I don't understand...you are surely not trying to claim this girl for yourself?"

He snorted. "That ownership is temporary at best, bogus overall. A result of fraud and the flattery of my naive sister—even the High Priestess, I would gamble. I would have offered high for Odette's deflowering upon her proper Unveiling. The Outer Realmer stooped to deception to have her."

A heavy silence weighted the air.

"If that is true, why have you not brought this to the attention of the king," Yolande asked. "Especially as Odette is kinswoman of his through marriage. I should think he would act promptly at any misdeed."

"And have my sister punished, her estate taken? Surely, you do not judge me so unkind, Yolande."

Another long moment passed, and Yolande said pointedly, "No, not so unkind, Lord Eryan."

"I do not care for your tone, Yolande."

The bedsprings creaked as she rose to her feet. "I do not care for duplicity, sir. When you approached me so bravely in the yard this morning and asked for aid in bringing Odette here, I was under the impression that Helrose surely knew. Your passion for Odette was no secret in the household—I thought Helrose had decided to just pretend ignorance out of love for you. But Helrose offered no consent, did she?"

Eryan's voice cut the air like a shard of glass. "Had you consulted her yourself, Yolande, you would have known. Fortunate for me that greed and revenge overwhelm your sense of duty. And you will not tell Helrose now—and risk the authorities learning that you enlisted the assistance of your old friend, a released felon who has already attempted to murder another, and who by the conditions of her release must wander the streets and beg for alms, proclaiming her crime to all she approaches until such time as a man shows mercy and takes her as slave."

Odette shivered fearfully as Yolande replied, "She is my sister—am I to let her beg when I can feed her?"

"She killed a man, Yolande," Eryan said. "The king showed extraordinary mercy to grant her a second chance."

"I shall not defend her, Lord Eryan, but you surely you will not extort my love for my own sister."

"As I see it, Yolande, you both benefited…and I look forward to giving you, at least, a place in my own household."

"Household? That is madness, Lord Eryan, if you plan to take Odette! The king himself will seek you out."

"Only if he knows, dear one. And think of the possibilities—you, the Mistress over my servants. And Brune may come as well. I have a house in the western region, an inheritance. Secluded this estate is, yes, but that seclusion will hinder the interference of others. The Outer Realmer will not tell of Odette's disappearance even if he is fond of her. He knows the consequences too grave for himself. He will ride out of Athla and return to Midgard, forget her as a fleeting entertainment. Helrose will think he took Odette with him, and she alone will face the king's penalty."

Yolande spoke sharply. "You would do that to your sister? I thought you feared her estate taken?"

"I doubt not King Larsarian will see it as a sign that stronger hands need to reign at the school established by our father. Larsarian's High Archer has developed a strong passion for Helrose, so much so she has already yielded to him much say in the running of her household. Upon discovering the king's displeasure, the archer will no doubt offer to wed her right away. The king will be satisfied to just know his archer will deal a fitting punishment to his new bride. But even in that, Helrose shall have the life she has shown she yearns for since the man came into her life. She will lose nothing but her tainted pride. Think not, dear, I have not considered all the possibilities carefully…as you love Brune, I love my sister."

Odette was shocked and turned her ashen face a little from him and so caught the doubt that darkened Yolande's.

"But is this is still kidnapping," Yolande said, "to take your sister's possession—one of Freyja's sacred vessels—without the granting of her Mistress."

"Did not Helrose commit sacrilege by ignoring the customs of the holy rite of Unveiling? Who is my sister to slap the face of the Goddess? To assume such arrogance? Her conscience is frustrated by her personal quandaries, Yolande, and if it were known that she acted under duress she would be stripped of her position by the Vitki Council. No, what she shall face is a leniency. But I can set right this sacrilege, insure Odette is again a sacred maiden of Freyja, and at the same time clear the school of all vestiges of impropriety."

"You shall possess Odette—and that is what this is all about."

Eryan's voice was condescending. "You should be grateful I want her, for otherwise I might have too late grasped Helrose's capricious behavior. Do you not realize that it was only by my prompting she finally decided to give you your freedom, and at my suggestion offer you the position of steward?"

Yolande bit her bottom lip thoughtfully. "I did wonder." She sighed, glanced at Odette. "And you will take Brune and myself into your household?"

"I could not reveal all to you before, but now I have. You can depend on my word. You shall be given the position of Mistress in my household with your sister welcome to serve as steward or slave, as is your preference."

Brune snarled, "I shall never be a slave again!"

"You shan't," Yolande agreed, shaking her head to reinforce the assurance. "Very well, Lord Eryan, it is a bargain to which I agree. But I advise you to keep Odette hidden here until you take residence in your house in the western region. In the meantime, I must soon return to the manor."

"That is a sound thought. I shall send for you in a day or two." Eryan eyed Brune and said, "I would have you watch my slave when I must be out, to keep a vigilant eye on her lest she attempt to escape."

"Is that is a request?"

"Certainly," Eryan replied, and he lifted the leash from the post and reined Odette to her feet. She did not even know she was weeping until he wiped a tear from her cheek. "My very insolent young lady," he crooned, "I shall punish you myself this evening. But for now I have business to attend to, and so advise you to do as your guardian bids if you do not wish to exacerbate what awaits."

Odette's limbs were numb with horror.

"Do not do this," she pleaded, "I love Lord Cu'lugh and he loves me!"

Eryan's face dappled crimson and purple, and he grabbed her by her arms and shook her violently.

"What fantasy is this? Let me warn you, spoiled flower. I love you enough to make you forget that barbarian forever!"

He flung her down onto the bed beside Brune. As he went to the door she tried to stand up, intending to go after him, plead or demand, whatever it took to reason with him. But Brune's hands clamped on her wrists and pulled her down to the mattress.

"Lord Eryan!"

The door slammed as the name flew from Odette's throat. She shrieked angrily and twisted and jerked against Brune's restraining hands. When her hands were free she struggled with the shocked girl, pushing her down on the bed and slapping her face.

The mattress sank beside them and the next thing Odette felt was Yolande pulling her back from Brune and slipping the gag over her face. Brune was up immediately and clutched her legs about Odette's hips and bound her arms. Odette pushed her back with a shove to the breasts. But the girl growled and caught her hands. As Odette tried to wrest them away Yolande pressed the bit into her mouth, cinched the leather taut behind her head and buckled it tightly. Odette tossed her head and tried to spit the gag out, but as before it was futile

The sisters worked to flip her over onto her stomach. Each took one of Odette's arms and pulled her toward the head of the bed and with a thick silken cord Odette had not noticed before tied each of her hands to one of the heavy corner posts.

Brune sat up breathless beside her and lifted the paddle. With furious, uneven strokes she spanked Odette, giggling hatefully as Odette's buttocks flared and her hips moved frantically in the attempt to avoid the angry strokes.

Through her tears Odette looked up at Yolande standing by the bed. She attempted with all her willpower to reason with her, to somehow make her stop this outrage.

But Yolande looked lost to her own thoughts. She turned and walked into the drawing room while the sound of the paddling echoed off the deceptively bright walls.

Some time after her buttocks had finally started to cool, Odette fell asleep. She dreamed of Lord Cu'lugh, desperate, yearning dreams spoiled by frightful shadows and a looming image in the unspecified ethers. Then the shattering of glass jolted her awake. She felt relieved at least to be out of the suffocating darkness of her nightmare but despaired to find herself still gagged and bound to the bedposts. Brune lay beside her, fully dressed now and sound asleep under the covers. Odette closed her eyes and laid her cheek on the mattress.

Hands were suddenly on her wrists. She looked up, dismally expecting to see Yolande or Lord Eryan. But the face she saw was not one she knew—defined and menacingly tender. She screamed without thought, so shrilly over the gag that Brune awakened beside her.

"What is—" The girl's words were silenced by another set of hands that threw a hood over her head and cinched it so tightly Odette was sure Brune would suffocate. She screamed again and thrashed her legs as well as she might, but the swarthy, childlike figure ignored her protest, intent, it seemed, on damaging her with its loathing eyes alone.

He dragged her off the bed and lifted her toward another much like himself, who held up a long, open linen sack. Despite Odette's thrashing limbs they managed to draw it over her head and pull it down the length of her body. She felt the drawstrings cinched under her feet. The sack was loose enough she could breathe and she beat at the cloth with her hands and tried to rip it with her fingernails. She met no success and felt herself lifted up and thrown over a shoulder.

She could not forget Brune—as much as she hated the girl she did not want her harmed—but as the stranger who carried her turned she heard a feminine moan. Someone whispered and her captor heaved her to the hands of another. The cool night air penetrated the sack as she was tossed this way and that, moved she knew not where. Again she was thrown over a shoulder and carried for some distance. They lifted her over what she was certain was the back of a horse. The rider pressed on her back to keep her in place and she heard him sniff loudly and grumble words she could not comprehend. He must have been waiting for his companions—for a few minutes all was still but the movement of the sack about her as she tried to wrestle free from it. Then one of the strangers barked a command and the horse bolted beneath her. As the animal ran the air rushed through the fabric of the sack over Odette's face, threatening to steal her breath. The horse's hooves thundered over stone and earth and she closed her eyes, terrified to move lest she fall.

And as the captors charged on into the night she thought she heard Yolande scream her name.

Chapter Thirty-One

hat man will not keep his position long, thought Arduin as he thanked the mercenary who allowed him through the gate. The opinion he kept to himself; surely the man knew what he risked. Other mercenaries had seen their wealth confiscated or had faced banishment for less.

The women serfs had reported to this man that Arduin's mother, Blichilde, was near death. Arduin was acquainted with him, knew he'd already provoked Lady Vanda by sneaking in certain healing herbs and giving away his rations to the neediest of the female serfs. Everyone in town knew that were it not for his formidable dimensions and skill at weapons the softhearted giant would have been dismissed long before.

As they stepped onto the compound's yellowed grass, Arduin felt as confined as his folk surely did. Like the men's compound this was bounded with a high timber fence that segregated the inhabitants from the rest of the world. A dozen or so small hovels stood in a circle, but no smoke rose from any of the chimneys, for all the combustible material had been confiscated months ago. Arduin saw small squares of barren earth—the gardens the occupants were accountable for. The compound had been part of the sprawling fecund Saxon farmland, where Arduin's people had raised gourds and rye, sunflowers and edible herbs. Now, as with the rest of the fief, there was nothing but fetid soil and hunger.

The men and women bore all responsibility for the success or failure of the crops in their respective compounds. Failure, of course, brought rapid penalty under her Ladyship's laws.

He saw shocking remnants of the sunflowers his mother and the other women had used to decorate their homes long before—black stalks here and there, their grey and rotted heads bowing over the sterile earth. A distinctive foul odor assaulted his nostrils as he headed toward the hovels. He shivered to think of it— the spring air bereft of warmth and life. The clouds that never left the land anymore seemed to drape over the serfs' compounds with particular vengeance.

Because of his mother's Burgundian parentage, Arduin had been spared the fate of most of his childhood companions. While they were carted off to distant lands by the slave traders or into the equally hopeless villages administered by the followers of Boniface, Arduin was sent to the artisans' quarters in town and given a position in the house of the furniture maker, Emmanuel Galbos. The man was one of Lady Vanda's most favored artisans, a minor nobleman in his homeland.

But Galbos was a drunkard, too, apt to squander the silver and gifts he received instead of buying what lumber the woodcutters had managed to save from the diseased trees in the forest. Under Galbos's supervision Arduin had learned to play cards, to swear in Lombard and to make excuses to the mercenaries who were constantly banging on the door demanding payment for the items they had smuggled in for the man. Often Arduin went hungry between the times Lady Vanda's generosity intervened. There were always a few mercenaries who enjoyed Arduin's delicate looks enough to suggest another kind of exchange for food. Arduin hated these men but the pangs of hunger obliged consent, and they had introduced him quickly into the means they pursued in their unwillingness to protest her Ladyship's laws that forbade carnal relations between men and women. With his pale locks and great blue eyes Arduin was an adequate substitute for the company of women, and most of these craven men were at least more gentle in satisfying their desires than Galbos when he was in his cups.

Those times when Galbos got so delirious from drinking he locked Arduin out of the house there was always a bed to be found in the quarters of the mercenaries, even if they had to sneak him in behind the backs of the Vanda's priests. And sometimes her Ladyship even sent Arduin clothes that he might continue to look the proper apprentice.

His mother had to remain in the tiny hovel allotted to her. Arduin's father had died in the brief clash when Martel's men descended on the tribe. Arduin yet carried the memories of how his family and neighbors had looked. He cared not to remember the fateful morning when he'd been awakened by his mother's screaming from outside their house. He had run to the door and saw his father lying in her arms, cut down by a Frankish blade as he sought to protect the village from the unexpected invaders. As chieftain Rulf's oldest companion, Valhelm had tried to rally the Saxons; but the Franks were too many for the surprised people. Only later, when the rest of the tribe were ordered into the forest to collect firewood for Charles's warmth were the sentries found—poisoned, it was reasoned by the frozen and tortured features of the victims, though just how was never discovered.

Now, as Arduin walked to meet his mother for the first time in years, he wondered what fate would have dealt the tribe had Lord Thierry lived. It had been Thierry who had chosen Blichilde to serve as caretaker for his private garden, as she had been born in the same Frankish village as his own mother. He even gave her and Arduin a room in the Hall.

But with Thierry's passing Blichilde was sent to live with the other women serfs. Lady Vanda was sufficiently generous to make Arduin an apprentice—something she'd done for not a single other Saxon child. Blichilde had kissed him and told him he was most fortunate and sent him on with his escort with the promise that someday they would be together again.

Arduin had sent what food he could into the compound through the more tenderhearted guards. Once he'd even managed a blanket, one that hung on a forgotten peg in Galbos's house. And from the guards he had learned of the deaths of Blichilde's companions over the cruel winter. Many had been relations, others friends. He heard of how when his mother's garden failed to produce the Lady had her branded with the sign of the cross on her brow; and how during the harshest month, when the snow lay as high as a man's knee on the ground, the bones and skin of a goat had been found in Blichilde's hovel. For eating Vanda's livestock the overseer had flayed the skin from her hands. She had cut her long roan-colored hair and sent it to Lady Vanda in exchange for a bag of wheat for the women, but while Vanda had the hair stuffed into a cushion for her footstool the bag of wheat when opened was found to be tainted by black and oozing worms.

Arduin's chest pounded as he passed through a gap between two of the hovels and entered the small, circular common ground. Several elderly women sat on their haunches at the thresholds of their decrepit homes, stripping unhealthy-looking flax with their worn hands. They were clad every one in tattered garments and their feet and thin legs were bound in strips of raw flax. Arduin was shocked, especially when he realized the stalks they worked to strip would most likely be taken as levy, for news had reached the town that not a solitary sprout had issued this spring from the seeds and roots sown in the fields.

Between two of the hovels Arduin saw what might have been a woman of childbearing age knocking the rocks from the sod with a hoe—looking for edible mushrooms or roots, no doubt. She was bent of back and thin, and the front of the strips of flax across her belly and down her legs was soiled with blood. Her hair had been shorn recently, and the wiry new growth was of an unhealthy grey tint.

Arduin bit his lips. He felt wracked with disgust and guilt. At least he had shelter and a meal three or four times a week, clothing to keep him dry and warm against the cold rain.

"Arduin?"

The gravelly voice brought Arduin about on his heel. A figure towered over him, and for a moment he did not recognize the wasted face and sunken grey eyes. But the smile on the parched lips, as pained as it was, brought back memories of running through high-grown fields of velvety green, of laughter and the scent of honey filling the air.

"Irmina!"

He embraced her tenderly, carefully. He realized how far now his arms reached about her, almost encompassing her shoulders and back. How long ago had it been since this girl had watched him for his mother and father, chased him as he ran a naked, happy little boy through the sun-kissed fields? She had taught him how to sing to the wild bees and make them drowse on the flowers so he might pilfer their hives with his bare hands. Why, he had almost forgotten it had been she who taught him to sing the ancient songs of the gods and how to carve boughs into animals and figures. Tall, patient Irmina, whom his father had said was surely destined to wed one of the spirits of the fields, for no walls built by a man's hands could contain her wild spirit.

"You live," she whispered. "We had feared you dead."

They released one another, their fingertips touching; and with the insight of his approaching manhood Arduin understood why Irmina had been spared by the slave traders and missionaries alike—her eyes, her lovely eyes. Each orb contained not one, but two distinctive grey irises side-by-side. He had never noticed as a child, and none of their Saxon folk had cared. But this difference had obviously frightened the superstitious minds of those who had taken away the others. So now she labored and starved along with the sickly and old.

Her emaciated features and scaly complexion disturbed him. He pressed her palm to his lips and kissed it, ignoring the diseased smell that emanated from her skin.

"Oh, our sweet Arduin, our Brune…" she said and wiped a tear from the corner of her eye. "Your mother needs you."

He followed her through one of the curtained entranceways into a dark and tiny room, illuminated only by the smoke hole in the ceiling. But there were no coals in the small brazier that sat beneath it, only cold ashes. There were no furnishings, no tools and certainly no trophies or idols hung from the tar-paneled walls. Across the bare floor lay a simple rug of hooked yellowed leaves and grass, and atop this reclined a figure draped in the same flax strips as the women outside, even its scalp and hands.

"Blichilde, your son is come," said Irmina.

The chest of the figure heaved slightly, the eyes opened with effort. They were yellowed and gooey with sickness and hardship, yet he knew them at once; and he sank to his knees at his mother's side and encircled his arms about her tiny waist.

"Ah, Mother," he said, unable to stop the tears.

He heard Irmina pull the curtain back and step outside. His mother's lips were feverish on his brow, and the sickly smell was even stronger on her than Irmina. But he cared not, only that she was alive and recognized him.

"My babe," she said, and he was surprised by the strength in her voice. She pulled him into her arms and rocked him. Her heart beat solidly against his face, just as it had when he was but a tiny thing.

"I shall get you out, Mother, we shall escape!"

And for a time neither said anything else, until at last Blichilde wiped the tears from his face with her bandaged hands.

"You are well and stronger than I'd expected," she said.

Arduin sat up and kissed her face. So haggard and lined it was, nothing like the beauty that had once been hers. That beauty, he rued, should have been allowed to meet old age gracefully instead of being forced into it brutally.

He nodded eagerly. "Yes. I can barter, Mother, to get you out, I know I can."

Arduin could not fathom what it would take to fulfill that promise, except by those things he'd done before to glean the generosity of those who had ruined his innocence. Whatever it took he would do it, somehow.

"Arduin, sweetest Arduin." She sighed and touched his chin with the bandaged fingers. "I have not summoned you for that."

"Are you telling me you are…dying? No! I will not believe—not if I can remove you from here. I will take you to the caverns over the mountains, those the mercenaries speak of, where there are lakes of fish and lush grottos. They avoid them for the spirits they believe haunt there, but we are not such fools as they. We shall find shelter, you and I, and—"

"Arduin." She sealed his lips with a finger and kissed the flesh between his eyebrows. "I do not know when I shall die. It would be heartless, selfish, to have risked so much to get you here for just that." Blichilde kissed the protest from his mouth. "No, you must listen to me. The time is come for you to escape—time for you to take your inheritance and let it guide you to freedom."

Arduin stared, bewildered. "I do not understand, Mother. And I shall not leave you here to…to linger like this, to meet the pyres before your time!"

Blichilde shifted against the wall so that her back rested straight, and as she inhaled Arduin heard a thick congestion flood through her lungs. "The pyres burn no more for us, Arduin," she said. "There is only the barren sod and the monotonous rites to sanctify our pagan souls before the eyes of a heartless god. But, yes, you shall leave, if not for yourself then for me and, more importantly, to attempt the quest of hope our people dare still dream of."

Her face lit then with a peculiar light that Arduin found discomforting.

"You are our hope," she said, "for a measure of right to be brought here, though it must come from the most unlikely source. If the evil that has corrupted the soil and enslaved our people is to be eliminated, it must be done soon. So I offer to you earlier than I'd planned that which has the power to take you from here. With it you may relieve this land, or at least seek aid to battle the perpetuators of evil."

"What do you speak of," he whispered. He glanced to the doorway and saw Irmina's silhouette on the other side of the curtain, as if she stood lookout. "Do you mean Lady Vanda's mercenaries and levies?" His eyes burned to think of the woman, surrounded in luxury in the Hall of the father she'd forgotten while his mother sat here, a withered and dying thrall. "Would you have me kill her?"

"Kill…? No, she is protected by those holy men—those celibate, breathless half-men."

"Her counselors—the priests?"

"You have seen them, have you not? Encountered and spoken with them?"

Arduin nodded and felt his stomach knot. The encounters had been unpleasant in a way impossible to describe. He was averse to meeting them on the street, though never had they once harmed him physically nor even forced him to kiss some relic and pledge away his soul as had been done to the Saxon men spared by Martel's army.

Once, when he'd come to her Ladyship's Hall on an errand for Galbos, one of the priests had drawn him aside in conversation. The man had addressed him in native Saxon, and his tone had been patient, his words not singed with raging incriminations. But his almost colorless eyes had seemed to pierce through the secrets of Arduin's unspoken misery, and he'd commented on the shameful practices that had kept Arduin from starvation. The priest's reproach seemed to have little to do with the act itself but rather focused on the pleasure the mercenaries had known in it.

"Carnal union," the priest had said, *"even when bereft of the taint of the*

wicked goddesses, is corrupt for the pleasure it provides. Pleasure is a false doctrine, boy, and will only lead to spiritual weakness. Suffer hunger, accept the pain of this corrupted world, and let your soul feed on the essence of the Chaste Lord Who brings soon a world made strong by cleansing away of desires."

Arduin had made excuse to slip away, but before he could the priest invited him to visit the Temple of his brethren. Although the man had done nothing more than speak to him, Arduin was overcome with nausea more intense than even that he'd experienced the first time he'd pleasured another man. He had to run outside to retch, and for days afterward sour bile coated his tongue. He avoided the priests after that.

"They took all our valuables," he heard his mother say. "All that their heartless eyes fell upon they destroyed—except for that which by the grace of the Gods I managed to hide."

Arduin followed her gaze to the ceiling. He saw at first only layered smoke and speckles of old grease, but as he squinted he could make out the borders of tar paneling underneath, peeling and flaking under the cake of grime.

"There," she said, pointing. "Peel it away and you shall find it."

Arduin rose to his feet; but still seeing nothing he feared his mother was suffering from a fleeting moment of hunger-driven madness. Then, as he moved around under the tar he did notice something—marks of deep red, so tiny no one unacquainted with Saxon runes would have noticed. He traced his fingertips over them until he saw her nod.

"That one...peel it back."

The rune of Thor's hammer. Arduin scraped the corner beside it and the tar began to strip away. A large hunk of wood fell, but he dodged it and it struck the floor. He continued to work the tar until at last it opened and something dark fell over his head and slid down his shoulder onto the floor, too.

"Is this it?" He knelt and touched the coarse fur. A bear's pelt, with the scalp intact; and he turned it over with his hands and saw the pelt had been carefully prepared so that even the soft tissue that surrounded the eye sockets was as well preserved as the snout, teeth and claws.

"Bring it here," she whispered and Arduin did so, sitting down with her again, smoothing his palm over the fur.

"What—what is this?"

"The cloak of a Berserker priest," she said, and turned the scalp over and pointed out the runes painted so finely on the tanned flesh. "In battle it provides dauntless strength, imbues the wearer with the qualities of the animal whose life was sacrificed for its use. And to fight the crusaders of Loki, it instills the courage needed to carry out the secretive rites of Odin...for it is known that those who attempt to fight these creatures without proper rite will have their souls consumed, their minds replaced by the chaos from which their god was birthed."

"My father's," Arduin said, and suddenly the pelt felt very sacred in his hands, and his hands unworthy to touch it. "I-I am ignorant of the rites, Mother. Why would you entrust me with this?"

"You do not need to know the rites for this to serve as it must. The priests will recognize it immediately and will be too leery to approach you. And in it you may take the life needed to know the route to Martel's abode."

"Kill…" he said, aware his throat was as dry as the ancient tar. "Route to Martel's abode? Are you mad, Mother?"

She smiled sweetly and swept back the flaxen lock that had fallen over his left eye.

"You have a rich heritage, my son. A Berserker's son with a Merovingian grandsire. The heritage of the one will give you the power to leave this land…and the knowledge of the other guarantee a certain safety when you speak with Martel. He fears the consequences of killing a descendant of Merovech with his own hands."

Arduin was silent a moment. "Mother, I understand none of this. You are a Merovingian—I think I remember Father speaking of it—but what has any of this to do with me? Or our enemy, Martel? All this talk of killing…"

"My Brune, you will listen to me now." Blichilde laid the fur to the side of the rug and embraced him close so that his face lay over her breast. Softly, she spoke. "You shall don the cloak and kill one of the Frank mercenaries. From him shall you glean the way to their homeland, and from there the route to Martel's keep. For you must speak to him, demand he come here—"

"Demand?"

"Ssh, listen. Our halest men are dead or taken far away. Not even the priests of Boniface know what goes on here under Vanda's rule, Arduin. She thrives and gives her priests what they will so she might thrive even stronger. And these priests are not ordinary men, Arduin, I think you have guessed that yourself. They use her as surely as she uses them, but of the two Vanda is the most dangerous. To get into Frankland you must get past the priests. And only by donning the cloak can you hope to do this."

"And how is this, Mother?"

"They are the feeders on flesh, my son, the Blodsaukers. Those whom the Berserkers fought with their magic, for they alone knew the secrets of life and death as Odin allowed. Neither dead nor alive, Blodsaukers seek always the blood of the living and the power in that blood for their obscene god. Only the Berserker knows how to destroy them without tempting the chaos of their god to infect the mortal, living mind.

"But for all their power the Blodsaukers have other enemies—the other children of Loki, and the priests of his other manufactured religions. Ignorant and zealous in their respective beliefs, these fail to recognize their god works in other sects. The mighty Church is one of these intolerants, and its members would seek to drive the Blodsaukers away if they knew how they had infiltrated this, a Christian fief. Martel is the Church's new champion. Therefore, to defeat them he must come—and defeat them he must before it is too late."

Arduin frowned. "But you said the Blodsaukers cannot be defeated but by the Berserkers."

"Yes, but it is their host who binds them here, Arduin. For Martel to discover Vanda's secret would mean her end. And believe me when I say the Blodsaukers have no use for politics, no use for battle either. They know Martel holds final reign here. With Vanda's power taken away they will disband and leave here."

"And Martel? Never would he give us back our land, Mother."

"No," Blichilde sighed. "But better to have our land and our health than what the Blodsaukers plan."

Arduin sat up and looked at her. "And what is that?"

"I should not go on," she answered. "It is not to say, but think you not it strange our chieftain's youngest was spared to live in Burgundy?"

"Odette?" Arduin remembered her a little, a tiny golden-haired girl, not much older than himself. She had played with all the other children before the Franks came, just as her mother had run naked with the other women in the fields. He had not seen Odette since that fated day, the same day the chieftain and her mother died, for she had been closeted away in the Hall afterward until Lady Vanda sent her away.

"When you put on the cloak I think it shall all be revealed to you. But a sacrifice must you take to know the way to Martel—and that is conveniently close.

"Once in his dominion, however, you must take the cloak off. Keep it on your person, wear it as a cape, as long as your head is bared. When you speak to Martel remind him of your heritage from my bloodline or else he will kill you, thinking you mad to speak such things as you must of his brother's widow."

He looked at her, frightened. "How do I remove it? Will I not, once vested in it, possess the mind of the bear?"

"Not wholly, Arduin. Your souls shall intertwine. All you need do is rake the rune of your name in the ground and then it shall fall away and you shall be yourself again."

"And my head bared? But wh—"

"It will be an advantage, this sign of your Merovingian descent."

Arduin was not sure if she was sane at all, though he was glad to see the proud flicker of spirit that imbued a healthy shade to her cheeks.

"Her Ladyship and I share distant kinsmen, Arduin. Martel shan't dare to harm you himself, not with these." Blichilde clasped Arduin's face and bowed his head over and, taking his hand, combed his fingers through the roots of his hair.

"Remember?" She pushed his fingertips across his scalp. At first he felt nothing but the smooth, warm dome of his skull—and then, at the very crown, a small outline of bone.

"Do not dig in," she warned, then murmured, "When they took you away, I feared you would forget all I'd warned you and probe these, carelessly, as all children pick at scabs." And she helped him find two other indentations, one to either side of the back of his skull.

"What are these," he gasped, trembling now, relieved when she pulled his hands away.

"The mark of our men," she said, "the descendants of Merovech. In your veins flows the blood of the sorcerer kings to which the Church of Rome owes its power, and to which it avowed its everlasting support. Martel has coerced his supporters to arrest and imprison the young princes left in our land, destroying them by starvation in the abbeys of his Popish allies. He needs them eliminated, and yet he will never lay a hand upon them himself, for he fears the curse of his dead victims.

"So you will ask audience of him, to bring him news of his brothers in this land. These marks shall prove your maternal inheritance, and by them he will not question your words, for it is known the sorcerer kings cannot lie. You shall inform him what has befallen Thierry and that Cu'lugh has disappeared. You shall tell him how Vanda acts under the advice of priests unrecognized by his Church.

"But just as soon as you have had your audience, you must find excuse to leave his presence. Adorn yourself again with the pelt and flee…or else, my son, he will have you eliminated as surely as our other kinsmen, made to languish in an abbey where the ignorant priests hold no respect for the sovereignty of our ancestors."

Arduin closed his eyes and rubbed his tired brow. These things his mother revealed were almost too much to bear. He hoped, perhaps, when he opened his eyes she would say it was but a jest; and, oh, yes, the time had come for them both to leave. And he would find a way, yes, whatever the cost to his person. They would take sweet Irmina as well and live out their days where neither man nor beast knew of Vanda or the Blodsaukers or the Franks.

But when he looked at her again the power of the testimony was too radiant even with the pain in her eyes.

"Ah, Mother," he sighed, "it is no dream."

"I dream still, Arduin—of you taking a wife who will give you boundless love and pleasure. Of your children, many, many lovely children who will run, laughing, through the wild fields, who will tame the bees with the songs passed down from the generations. I do not wish to go to the Hall of Heroes—naked and youthful again to meet my beloved husband—without knowing I have done all I can do to leave behind a hope that my dreams will be fulfilled."

Arduin felt anger swell in his breast to think of her young, not so long ago, vital and pretty, when her personal dreams were colored with prospect. Events masterminded by others had stripped her of all right to be selfish, and that wrenched him most of all. He could not even take her away. She could not in good conscience leave or even think to leave yet. Ah, she had been a good mother, and so unjust was this trial of the heart forced upon them. Even if Blichilde were wrong about all these things she spoke, why, she would never truly know it and thus would regret all the rest of the days of her life to think her son had not done all in his power to free all the Saxons from Vanda's yoke.

"I shall do your bidding," he said and felt his parched tongue crack. "But when I come back you must leave with me, and Irmina, too."

She murmured assent, but her weary smile betrayed the belief she'd not see him again.

"The sun will be down shortly," she whispered, "and then you must take the pelt to the farther fields and there put it on. You will remember all I have said?

About the blood of the Frankish mercenaries to give you direction? And when to disrobe and again mantle yourself after seeing Martel?"

"Yes."

"Approach not the Blodsaukers, if you can," she said. "The sight of you will keep them at bay. To try yourself against so many would make a grave delay and bring the attention of Vanda's mercenaries, who could kill you."

Arduin kissed her hand and lay down on the floor beside her for a time with his head in her fragile lap. And as the dwindling light of day passed away she sang him a lullaby, one of the tunes she had sung when he was small. She stroked the dirt from his pale tresses and kissed his throat to make him giggle as so long before.

When at last a splinter of the new evening moon shone through the smoke portal he said, "I should go, before Galbos awakens and sends for me to steal some mead."

She bowed his head again between her hands, kissing the crown, and said something he did not understand. She looked so like a poppet to him, abandoned and broken on the flaxen bedding. He had to fight the urge to simply lift her up and carry her away.

As he withdrew from the place Irmina stepped aside, and he saw her eyes were filled with tears.

"Good evening, sweet Brune," she whispered and leapt away into the shadows between the dark circle of hovels.

He left them behind and started toward the field, glancing up only once or twice at the bordering fence. His feet crunched across the dead grass, and masculine echoes swept down from the other compound. The earth of the field was dry, and here and there gave under his weight so that the strips of leather and flax that covered his feet soaked up a foul-smelling sludge lying beneath the surface.

The fence at the rear portion of the field was constructed of a tall thicket of saplings strangled of their life by weighty needled vines. His flesh was cut in a dozen places as he entered this thicket, but here he knew no mortal would look for him.

Arduin raised his eyes to the moon, squinting against the glare of the bloody haze that sought to conceal it from view. From somewhere far behind heavy, urgent voices rose. His heart quickened; and he pulled the heavy cloak over his shoulders, fitting his arms down the drape of fur that had been the bear's arms. Loose upon him the pelt fit, for his body was still that of a child's due to years of malnourishment. For a moment he thought the shank fur tightened about his legs. He shivered and tried to shake off the feeling. He lifted the great skull from his shoulders, fitting the mask of face and snout over his head.

For a short time he felt only the heat of the pelt. The scent of the tanned flesh tickled his nostrils. But as he waited the discomfort did not pass. His flesh itched, then began to burn and his bones felt weighted under an unendurable pressure.

"Oh, Mother," he whispered, but his own voice sounded strange to his ears. He was sweating, but when he looked at his arms the folds of fur were moving about his limbs. With a gasp he tried to raise the skull from his head...and knew he looked now not through the pelt's eyelets but with a new vision. An overpowering stench stifled his senses; the plants he knew without process of words now, their fibers poisoned of vitality by the same foul presence that lingered, waited, watched in the ethers.

Arduin's heart filled with terror, anger, wrath; and he tore at the molesting weeds and brambles with his claws as he tramped the wounded soil. A great articulation of outrage roared through his throat. He heard, whispered through the haze, hissing, badgering threats from creatures not of the earth or the air or even the reflections of the heavens, conscious, never-dreaming elements that screeched in voices inaudible to humans, messengers, watchers and informants from a realm alien to Urtha's domain. They were agitated by Arduin's presence and buzzed in their unseen course into his face and beside his ears, vying to infect him with the desire to leave.

He would oblige them, as soon as he'd done what memory spurred him to finish.

He tore through the grove on all fours until he reached the sterile garden area. Standing on his hind feet he swiped the air with his foreclaws, testing his balance, and heard the heavy heels slogging toward him. The outline of a single man unfolded in the hazy darkness, and though he knew the man had still not spied him, the voice of another boomed from the circle of hovels.

The man stopped and raised his hand to his eyes, as if trying to discern what form blocked the twisted grove. He reeked of mead and unwashed skin and of manly virtues corrupted.

"Boy, 'tis time to go back home."

Whether it was the smells of the man or the way he spoke or something else, Arduin assented to the impetus his presence provoked. He reared on his hind legs and tore over the sod so quickly the man knew not what was upon him, had not even time to draw a blade. Arduin seized his head with his claws and lifted him up off the ground. The man screamed and went for the gleaming pommel at his hip, but Arduin opened his mouth and sank his teeth into the horrified face. The man's arms flailed and the next scream broke in Arduin's great throat. With his claws he squeezed the skull, compacted it almost instantly, so that the limbs spasmed wildly and the man's bowels loosed of their contents. Bone and brain matter spewed into Arduin's mouth; but more important was the man's last thought that swam in the blood.

Arduin threw the still-convulsing body to the ground and dropped to his four paws again. The blood he savored in his mouth, letting it ooze slowly down his throat. Scenes invaded his vision and emotions pumped through his bestialized consciousness; and closing his eyes he purposely calmed the current that would have otherwise swept away his own memories. From nearby he heard feet running over the sod. He put the Frank's memories away to study later, in a place that as an ignorant boy he had not even guessed was a part of his consciousness.

With the taken knowledge safely guarded Arduin looked to the west. He saw a breadth of fence not so well-guarded as that nearer the compound. He sniffed the air, caught the smell of Blodsaukers lurking beyond the fence. Several of them, on the lookout for trespassers and praying to their angry god over the disquiet of their famished bellies. His mother had said to avoid them if possible, but the men with weapons were drawing near so he lumbered to it.

As Arduin's claws hauled him up the timber he heard the possessed earth he'd left behind; it drank of the spilt blood as its right. The invisible creatures veered from the spaces, for they knew the Berserker escaped, and made haste for the invisible passageway that led to their brother's prison.

Chapter Thirty-Two

he captain of the street patrols was so distraught he did not even attempt to restrain his voice as he questioned the priest.

"This bear passed right before you—and you did nothing! Lugrene is dead, and you raised no weapon nor called for aid!"

Ungar's response was almost bored-sounding, and Hrowthe knew the reason for what he said next.

"It was a bear, only a bear."

"Only a bear! It killed my friend, priest!"

Ungar was not one for answering to men, and ignoring Piers, he tented his fingers over the soot-black robe he wore. Hrowthe had often thought that of all his brothers Ungar stood out as the most distinguished. His initiation had imparted a glossy blue sheen to his skin and an insect-like quality to his long, oval eyes. The rows of kinky curls across his skull before the initiation had taken a grey cast and become almost illuminated in the transformation, so that they stood out. This unnatural countenance, along with his impatience for mortals altogether had made him especially suspect amongst the mercenaries. And now their appointed captain stared agape at the priest, as if he'd discovered the rumors were true.

"Brother Ungar came and informed us, sir," Hrowthe said. "What more could an unarmed priest do?"

The man shook his still-drawn sword, as if at any moment the beast would reappear in the midst of this circle of mercenaries and clerics.

"I have never understood why she assigns priests as sentries," the man snarled. "We would not have allowed the beast to slip away."

Hrowthe understood the captain's outrage, the senselessness of his man's death, the questions. Yet he also wondered if or when the mercenary would realize that this death was the most natural the fief had known in a long while.

"I am sorry for the loss of your friend," he said mildly, "but Ungar said the bear was heading toward the wast. Surely it will not return." He turned to Ungar. "Have this man's body taken to the Temple and prepared for a funeral worthy of his heroism."

Ungar bowed and turned away; and the captain demanded, "I want Lady Vanda informed at once. If she is determined to take the station of a man, she should be roused the same as would be the vassal lord."

Hrowthe ignored the order. As much as he knew this sentiment from her warriors was exactly what Vanda wanted, he also knew her temper when awakened; and for the moment he had other things more important to attend to.

"You said you were searching for a boy when he was attacked? Why here, in the women's compound?"

The man's hesitant frown was telling. "We thought he might have heard word his mother is dying. You know the coarse sentimentality of these Saxons."

"Have you spoken with the mother?"

"Yes. She does not know where he is."

Hrowthe smiled coolly. "And did she say he had been here?"

"No. But then, she is very ill. I would not trust her recollection."

"And the other women?"

The mercenary shrugged. "They do not know if they would recognize him—its Galbos's houseboy, Father. Taken away years ago."

"The Saxon males have not seen him?"

"No."

"Galbos?"

"Dead drunk, I am told."

Hrowthe sighed. "Then it is possible the boy met the same fate as your man here, especially if the bear was wounded when he met the boy. It would also explain the fever of its bloodlust when it encountered Lugrene."

Past the captain's shoulder stood a throng of other mercenaries, muttering amongst themselves.

"Go and double your posts," Hrowthe advised, "and say nothing to the serfs, not even the mother of the boy. Not until I have had time to speak of this with Lady Vanda."

The captain was staring at the brutalized body near his feet, and his complexion was like chalk. "This was no ordinary bear that did this, Father. No, this was a monster."

"A bear it was, I assure you," Hrowthe said and drew near the man and laid a hand on the arm holding the sword. "'Tis easy to classify as monsters that which we do not understand. But it is not constructive."

The man's face was blank as he turned to go, and Hrowthe watched as he urged his companions to leave the dreadful field. When they were gone the priest listened to the silence of the compound beyond, and it struck him as strange the women were not about. They had seen the mercenaries run in, surely heard their cries of shock. If the boy who had been one of their own, had died as he suspected strongly, why was there no sign of worry in the compound?

I have not determined anything for certain—this is but irrationality speaking.

He squatted beside the gruesome remains, ignoring the tempting smell of gore and tissue spilt everywhere. The blood was fresh enough, he saw, to retain the memories of the man in his last moments of life. Hrowthe's stomach spasmed violently, but he ignored the craving to feed as he had for so long and dabbed a finger into a smear of dark blood on the man's shirt, taking only a sparing drop. Enough only to yield the answer he sought.

He licked the sticky fluid and his mouth contracted wildly as the ooze seeped over his hardened tongue. Within moments his tongue began to twitch; his veins swelled and convulsed expectantly. His skull seemed to burst with his quickening brain, and a flash of fire crossed his spine. So long had it been since he had tasted the essence of existence, so habituated had he become to his starvation, that now the world condensed before his very eyes and his enfeebled organs animated. The dimension of the living infected the vision he'd come to accept as natural; the black-and-grey silhouettes of his dead perception gave way to the colors of life. For the first time in countless years he saw the world as did living men—the glint of starlight that swept across the distant forested mountains, the sickly hue of the earth underneath his feet. He perceived the red haze that veiled the land and kept out the healthy influence of the heavenly bodies.

As the transformation continued, Hrowthe's undead senses prevailed over the emotional human perceptions, so that all the beautiful imagery turned into the indefinable haze of washed colors and the steadfast contours of the spirit. He retained only that mortal thing he'd intended to pilfer—the memories and the hearing of the dead man as it had been in those moments just before the Berserker came upon him.

The air had buzzed with testy mutterings alien, unfathomable, to the man. But Hrowthe, who had studied the arcane testimonies of societies long dead and who felt the shadow of their essence even now, knew what they were. The knowledge rocked his equilibrium harder than the invasive thoughts of that Darkling, Loic. Their essence, their purpose saturated the air, lurking in the ethers, invisible to even the eyes of his brothers.

They held no distinctive personalities, no disruptive individualizing qualities that would disturb their perfect state of chaos. That chaos lurked in the ethers now, summoned by the prospect which his Lord, their kin, offered. It/they hated humanity, with all its dreams of pleasures that tranquilized the soul, as much as Hrowthe hated the sin of man that necessitated the creation of ideologies to lead him from sin. It/they cared not how dominion was accomplished, only that it was and that it was cruel and devoid of sympathy.

But, most disturbing, this presence had fled straight to Hrowthe's Lord in His isolated prison. It/they were of His race and wanted the fulfillment of all He'd set into motion, forgiving of His fall into temptation but not oblivious to it. It/they cared not that once all that was so ugly and disdainful to them had seduced Him to know hope, desire. Loki's failure had corrected His purpose, propelled Him to make a vindictive move; and that move would benefit their unseen and feared host. His race would be free from its limited access to humanity, liberated from the necessity for outlawed, obscure rituals carried out only by a rare few and loyal humans. The fears, greed, intolerance and violence begat of Loki's tasking religions accommodated their endless appetite. Soon would they all banquet together upon a feast of cruelty the likes of which the world had never known. Hrowthe's Lord, His race, His kin—ah, they had existed from a time before times and expected, without doubt, to continue even after the death of the universe.

Hrowthe sank to his knees, as bereft of hope as when he'd been a living man, dispossessed now of the future he'd labored in the shadows to fulfill. He had only wanted to see humanity divorced from suffering and death, from despair and futility. For that he had loved Loki, had played the blind follower to His hypocrisies.

Hrowthe had not always hated life. When he was still a living boy—before that time when his parents died, before he was found by a Blodsauker and taken into the court of Loki—even the hardships of daily existence were accompanied by simple pleasures: friends and family, the hunt and friendly games, the warmth of the blazing hearth fire while the frigid winter gripped the world outside his tiny home village. He'd had a pet raven then, and he'd taught it to speak. A tiny sister, too, who had delighted in his riddles, had screamed to follow him when he went out on the hunt. His father, though averse to affection, had taught him many things; and Hrowthe had loved him. And his mother, quick to take offense, but always laughing. It had been her belly, swollen with growing child, which his lips had kissed before setting out that last day.

He'd returned from his spring outing, having taken a hare and a grouse for dinner, returned home to find the village buried under an avalanche of snow. For two days he tried to disinter his people and wept and wished to die when at last his frozen fingers and hands and feet had lost all feeling. He wept like a babe in arms and prayed to the gods to take him. It was not until the Blodsauker priest came across him that he knew the desire for revenge—not against the forces of nature but against the lies of life, the false promises of pleasure and happiness. And had he grieved instead of resented, perhaps he could not have been seduced.

The Brethren explained it was the essence of passive femininity that had ruined the prospects of civilization. The faces of that foul spirit had corrupted womankind and mankind equally. It made sense to Hrowthe; it had to, as life certainly did not. So, he willingly gave away his mortality and the inheritance of the afterlife to join their ranks.

Their gory deeds were for the salvation of mankind, they claimed, and in the end they would sacrifice all they'd taken from the men and women they killed to garner the ultimate sacrifice. The goddess would know their reckoning, her deceptions wiped utterly, permanently from the world of man. Once Loki had quelled the worthless pagan spirits called gods the malevolent spirit that was Freyja would have no sanctuary and, with the enlightenment of mankind, no summons to stay. She would have no choice but to drift away from Midgard into the desolation of the heavens. Life would return as it was intended for mankind, with no difference of gender, no sexuality, therefore no bonds. Women would be as independent and self-sustaining as men and men exorcised of the passions instilled by the eons of the perversions the Goddess had incited. A world without fragility or ignorance, without the despair that false dreams and desires whelped. With men and women liberated from their deceits there would be no need for governments or differences of religion, for all would worship peacefully under Loki's gentle example.

Lies. The word stamped itself in Hrowthe's mind, searing his assurance. His breast panged with human regret. He closed his eyes, praying for the return of his Blodsauker perceptions. Long minutes passed; and gradually his senses eased, his sound judgment flowed anew.

The secrets he'd sought to unveil he allowed to slumber in his veins. Frivolous information it was, but for that single confirmation; and the rest he hoarded away until the time when all the information the undead kept would be shed upon the roots of the World Tree.

Reality draped over him in its familiar dark shades as he started toward the gates beyond the compound. Suddenly, he heard His Lord speak his name. Hrowthe slumped within the shadows, making himself one with them, his long fingers camouflaged within their ink. For how long he hid there he was not sure— all he knew without doubt was the manner of Loki's need. Somehow, the comfort had disappeared from the rich, chaste voice; and Hrowthe did not know if ever he could answer it again.

He wept tearlessly, remembering the cause that had drawn him to be a Blodsauker. He told himself it mattered nothing, the revenge he'd sought; in the end he loved humanity more than he hated life. And it mattered not Who had bestowed upon him the powers of the creature he'd become, or even His intent. He, Hrowthe, would help fulfill mankind's liberty from the delusion of the fleshly world.

As he hid in the shadows he saw some of his brethren drift into the field and carry the body out of the compound. They comprised a wraithy procession, their eyes haunted by zeal. A quickening of the man's perception reopened his vision— only a moment, but long enough he saw his brothers as the living would, corpses that animated their veins with the blood of sound men, women and children. Grey, hard faces smeared with the gore of these victims, vulnerable to the life-giving sun and chased into the cavities of the resentful earth by the reflection of the sun's mate and companion, the moon.

His quickening passed with a retch. Hrowthe wiped the spent fluid from his lips and smeared it on the grass.

No, we are more than that. We are the children of a hope few mortals appreciate or can fathom, bringers of Chastity to this world seduced from wisdom.

His brethren called him *Father,* for he was older than most who had survived the magic of the Berserkers. Hrowthe had come to love them truly, and mortals even more. He had embraced the religion of his fraternity and the promises of Loki. When the brethren grew frail he embraced them, and they sought out his knowledge for solace whenever troubled by that lingering human frailty called guilt. He assured them of their place in God's design, the beauty of their purpose, the worth of their coming sacrifice.

But he could not embrace them now. The visions had worked too heavily and Loki's summons only reinforced those dreadful doubts. He stole past their midst unseen and made his way back to the Temple. He would leave them in the forest, to devour the corpse if they were so inclined.

Dawn's light pursued on stealthy golden heels as Hrowthe entered the Temple. The sun's relentless, clarifying rays plastered the Temple and sealed him inside. Alone, he buried himself in the protective dirt, and it was nearly noon before Loki's demand to feed on his veins fell silent.

Chapter Thirty-Three

he boy had not once flinched or made any suspicious gesture that indicated his claims were anything but true. As he fell to his knees before Martel and bowed his fair head the Mayor of the Palace was speechless, for the visions of all he'd labored for his adult life crumbled as so many parched autumn leaves beneath uncaring feet. With sweat-moistened fingers he parted the blonde locks of the malnourished young man and examined the small skull. He felt the familiar, undeniable indentations and he thought he heard the voice of the last Merovingian prince he'd imprisoned laugh from the mists of purgatory.

He glanced at the guards standing by, and one of them drew his dagger. But Martel had to act with care. The death of a Merovingian held the potential for revenge from the populace, especially when his plate was fuller than ever with the issues in Spain and the ever-aggravating German hostilities. Gregory had already expressed dismay he had allowed Boniface to slip back into Frisia. There the crusaders had headed, in all likelihood, to carry out Boniface's schemes that amounted to assured, if self-sought, martyrdom. The old Frankish nobles argued for a larger portion of Martel's government and would not hesitate to take advantage of his coming absence to pry into the affairs of his household, bribing whom they could for anything with which to contest his position. And this Saxon-born boy could certainly be used as an argument.

Martel drew his hands away, rubbing them briskly behind his back to dry the cold perspiration.

"Rise," he said. The boy stood and faced Martel's scrutiny. Again the Mayor searched for subtle tics or a shift of the eyes, anything plausible. He found nothing dubious about the dirty manchild, nothing that would spare him from having to turn his attentions away from important things to delve into these charges concerning both Cu'lugh and Thierry. Rather, that damnable unworldly look so typical of the Merovingian males was clearly evident.

Martel eyed the readied guard meaningfully so that the man put away his weapon.

"You have proven your reliability," he said to the boy blandly. "Your mother— a serf now in her husband's land? She believes some rumor that Lord Thierry died by his wife's order and Lord Cu'lugh has disappeared on some cunning plan the lady has devised?"

"Sir, they are both gone, your brothers."

Martel smiled thinly. "My brother Cu'lugh is a mercenary at heart, boy, a vagrant, hapless knight. And Thierry, I have been told, died of the sweating illness which struck in the winter."

The boy's eyes seemed to grow larger, distant like a soothsayer's. "Lord Thierry's screams issued from the roots of the tree, sire."

"And you are certain it was your vassal lord?"

The boy's voice resonated with the deep timbre of a man's. "He was taken by the Lady's mercenaries and at her order walled up alive in the roots of a great stump."

Martel licked his lips and padded across the cold grey stones, gazing for a moment at the banners hanging on the granite walls. His skin crawled as he eyed one he'd obviously forgotten to have taken down, one of the oldest, bearing the image of a bear standing on its hind feet over a low bough upon which hung a beehive.

"Arduin—that is your name?"

"Yes." The boy fidgeted a little on his poorly wrapped feet, and Martel noticed the bone that brooched the fur cape about his shoulders...and the Mayor reached discreetly for the wall in order to steady himself and not draw the guards' notice.

His voice sounded calm enough to his own ears. "Arduin, for what reason would my sister-in-law kill her husband? Or cause mischief for my brother Cu'lugh?"

Martel heard a muted laugh from the guards, but the sweet boy did not pale or blush or seem timid. "For to have the fiefdom to herself, sire."

"But she is a woman, Arduin. A Christian woman, despite the distant connection to your ancestors and even the pagan lineage from her Burgundian descent." Martel felt the dizziness ease a little.

"I think Lady Vanda little considers blood claims, but perhaps for the Burgundian ties, of which she is most proud."

"Ah, the imperial, murderous Burgundians—so many legendary houses, so little proof to their claims of godly ancestry. So what if she is proud? She is a Christian and that is proper and commendable. No more chaste a woman have I ever met. What proof have you of any of your claims?"

The boy glanced at the floor, not with the look of one unsure but as if hesitant to reveal more than he'd intended.

"Well?"

Arduin raised his eyes. "She banished her sister, the daughter of the old chieftain and his wife."

Martel laughed. "That is all? Why, she was more merciful than I would have been, descendant of the Bee-Kings." He relished the unease in the boy's face and drew near, feeling more generous than he'd imagined. "Lady Vanda was, then, quite benevolent, do you not think? To spare the pagan issue of her forsworn father?"

Arduin's eyes did not move, and his voice was steady. "She is a swanmaiden's daughter, sir."

"Oh, I have heard the rumors of Rulf's whore. I would advise you ignore such fantasies. With such rich imagination, no wonder your people were quelled so easily."

"Our people did not fall save by the aid of Vanda, for her hatred of her own people and, more so, her father."

Martel stiffened. "That is unchivalrous, young sir, even for a pagan."

"Vanda sent her sister away and has kept control of the government you left in the hands of your brother. If not for Lord Thierry's concern for the sister he would not have slipped away to take her elsewhere. She had his men banished or killed when he left and him murdered when he returned. I do believe, sire, with all my intuition, you are well acquainted with the depth of Lady Vanda's temerity. Have you not wondered once how she managed to have the Saxon border sentries poisoned before you invaded the land?"

Martel's heart leaped, and one or two of the guards made a shocked sound. Again the Mayor's head spun. Even with his Merovingian blood, this was but a serf, a thrall—how did he guess a man's suspicions?

But whatever dark powers the boy employed Martel could not care less for affirmation. Vanda had guaranteed him safe passage into the land, and she had given her pledge to insure the Saxons kept their Christian vows under Thierry's puppet authority. Since Thierry's death she had wielded her power openly and never failed to meet her levies or at least do her part in keeping his coffers filled. As long as she kept her vow to the Church he cared not even if she were guilty of patricide, for what worth a Christian who loved pagans? Cu'lugh had written him already reporting that Thierry had died, yes, but of natural causes; and that his grieving widow remained constant to all her alliances.

"You have no proof of harm to Lord Cu'lugh," Martel said, "but his own absence, the purpose of which was made known?"

The boy breathed heavily.

"He was not approved by her Ladyship's counselors. They are not Christians proper."

Martel chortled. "What is this mad revelation? I know the hearts of those I charged with the duty."

"The counselors you provided have all left."

"Ah, but that I know already. They left to follow Boniface. You refer to the mercenaries? Certainly, she has wit to choose her own."

Arduin shook his head steadfastly. "No, sire, I mean the Christian priests and monks. Some of them chose to stay…and died by her order or, at least, that of those who serve her now."

Martel frowned. "Do you know this for a fact?"

"I have seen them buried, sir; the man to whom I am apprenticed carved their caskets himself."

Martel blinked, unwilling to accept what he heard as true. "You would have me believe she has recruited Merovingian priests?"

"No, they are not that. Even I who know little of my mother's people know they are not that."

"I suppose you would." Martel turned and gazed at the walls with a deliberate air of boredom. "Boniface's brothers, the monks he left behind, and those I left, as well—were your fears grounded I would have received report from them."

"They cannot report to you, sire, not from the grave."

The floor seemed to heave under Martel's feet. He closed his eyes a moment and the sensation passed; and when again his eyes opened he clutched the boy by his narrow shoulders. Lifting him off his feet, Martel shook him until his pale locks quivered like beaten wheat.

"While I stand listening to this the forces of the infidel gather in Spain! I do not have time to waste on delusions, boy. But if any of this proves anything but the truth, your mother shall die at my own hands and you shall live out the rest of your days chained to the rock foundations of this castle."

Arduin gulped for steady breath, and the innocence of his blue eyes was more accusing than any malevolent machination dreamt up by a petty rival.

"As have all my young kinsmen here in your stolen territories, Lord Mayor?"

Martel's voice was guttural. "They are inbred idiots, all! Corrupted by their paganism and worthless to anyone!"

A fragile, sad smile touched Arduin's lips and his eyes hazed with understanding beyond his mundane knowledge. "Lady Vanda claims the same of the Saxons…and so proclaimed it of your brother, Lord Thierry, before he was taken away!"

Martel felt the blood rock against his temples. With a roar he lifted the boy and dashed him headlong into the wall. The fair head struck with an ugly thud. Before he'd fallen to the floor the boy's thin limbs began to thrash, the muscles of his face to contort; and his blue eyes jerked in their sockets.

One of the guards knelt beside the convulsing body and pinned the small arms gingerly.

"The Bee-king's heir is in a fit, sire!"

Martel stepped to the boy and saw the muscles of Arduin's face were rigid and his complexion turning from crimson to blue. A droplet of spittle ran from the corner of his mouth and fell toward the floor.

The moment the spittle puddled on the stones the foundations of the castle rocked. Yells echoed down the corridors and several of the banners fell from the walls. Martel cursed the boy under his breath and prayed something would simply whisk the ill omen away and from memory.

"You should have left it to a priest," said one of the guards fearfully. "If he dies, your descendants are doomed to be a curse on the face of this land."

Martel fell to his own knees and touched the boy's face. The muscles strained against one another so they were harder than the granite he'd struck. The Mayor bade the guards help him restrain the boy's limbs.

And still the small body contorted, the muscles shuddering as if propelled by some unseen force. The thin body suddenly bowed upward with a vehement intensity and Martel heard the spine break.

"Ah, Jesus," he muttered. The boy's chest now neither rose nor fell, and his flesh was changing from blue to a mottled shade of grey. Martel looked to one of the men, his voice so weak he could hardly hear himself, "Bring a priest at once!"

The man's mouth moved as if he were dazed, but he went; and before the door shut on its hinges Martel felt Arduin's taut muscles go limp. Frantically, he touched the chest, here, there, his ribs, too; but the boy did not breathe. He slapped the ashen face, looked into the unfocused blue depths of his eyes, struck with more strength—but no movement resulted.

"He is dead, Lord Mayor," he heard one of the men say.

For some time Martel could not move, only stare into the innocent face. The weaving in his head had stopped—in fact, he'd never known such clarity of vision and sound. Everything shone with colors painfully rich, details hauntingly dynamic.

"He is not from here," he said with feigned confidence when at last he could rise to his feet. "A Saxon he was—what blood of Merovech flowed in his veins was thin and diluted at best. His blood has no power to curse."

The guards were pale and did not comment, and Martel saw how their knees bent toward the floor as they looked on the slender corpse. There at his feet lay the dainty heir of his enemies, all right to title and claims crushed with the single blow to the trepanned skull! Were he king in name as well as by might he could have legitimately protested.

"Fools, did you not hear?"

Their superstition would not allow them to look at him. If only his own men possessed the shallow boldness of the priests who warded his prisons. He had spent most of his life ridding the land of the Merovingian princes, and yet the supernatural myths that surrounded the bloodline could weaken the bravest men.

Martel kicked the body angrily, was shocked to see them drape themselves over it as if now they would protect the boy. Yet, as he saw a tear flow over one stalwart cheek, he knew what they saw…for he had witnessed the healing touch of the other brats of the lineage. He remembered how those pairs and pairs of suffering eyes had stared at him through their prison bars—penetrating his thoughts, feeding on his knowledge, his ambitions, had registered to the memory of their souls the name of every village and tribe he'd conquered, the name of every woman he'd widowed, every pagan babe he'd let the crusaders drown…

The legends of their curse stagnated his rule, tempered his warrior's hand; and yet he knew they did not curse without justification.

But those enemies, which I imprisoned by sanction of the holy Church, were every one born here, on the soil of their ancestors. Even by work of the devil, what power has the soul of this Saxon boy over me or mine?

"He was not born here," he repeated, grasping onto the confidence he derived of the declaration. "He was born on Saxon land, sired by a Saxon, his heart and consciousness wed to that land. The power of his ancestors was made impotent by that fact."

"Perhaps," replied one of the men, his voice strange as he sat up and pulled the edge of the boy's cape into his hands. He turned the fur over several times, and then, turning the boy over onto one side, lifted the hood. And at once Martel saw what the guard had—no ordinary cowl but a head covering tanned entirely of the beast's face. The guard untied the cape from the boy's throat and regarded the cowl, the figures in red marked on the pelt that had once encased the bear's skull.

"But this of his father's blood he carried to the end."

Martel jerked the thing from his hands and stared at the tiny, blood-printed runes, the mark of the ancient order of the Berserkers.

"Ah, God," he sighed. His strength drained completely away now, and he thought again of all the responsibilities that awaited him, the favor of the Pope that was within his grasp if only he took the initiative. Power and wealth were his, but for appeasing Gregory; and he had worked politics and the religion that engineered it so that when he died the proper title of king would fall on the head of his favorite son. God almighty, frightful and jealous, demanded Martel focus on all these pressing earthly matters.

Now delay was forced into his hands. To ignore the allegations concerning his brothers invited more schemes than any man could control from a distance. Before he set out for Spain he had no choice but to do just as this brat had urged…and if he could meet that obligation perhaps this curse, if for a moment real, could be nullified; and he would retain without doubt all he'd worked to wrest thus far from the true kings.

The bear's cape was burned, consumed to ashes before nightfall, as the funeral rites had to be completed before Martel dared venture into the Saxon vassalage. He turned the body over to the oldest of those handmaidens who had served Anga, his father's beloved, when she still held sway at court. He gave them free hand to prepare the body in the old ways, and so they dressed the boy in a robe of costly silk and boots of virgin ewe leather. Children's toys made for him, and a small dog poppet stuffed with lavender that was pinned to his robe. A signet ring of gold was made for him, fashioned with the symbol of the bee and set upon the boy's thumb. His lips and eyes were sealed with thread of fleur-de-lis; his flesh tattooed all over with symbols of the very lily. At last he was laid in a coffin of unpolished cedar that was then carried on the shoulders of twelve virgin boys. A band of thirty-three maidens danced alongside the pallbearers, singing songs with origins so lost to time only the most rustic dwellers watching the procession recognized the melody.

Into the heart of the deepest forest they bore him, to a sepulcher gilded and coated with moss beside a splaying fountain. There, chanting the old dirges, they buried the young prince, far from shadow of abbey or monastery.

Chapter Thirty-Four

Cu'lugh watched without intervention as Queen Honi struck Yolande's face. He had been tempted to do the same when she found him at the inn and informed him who she was and that Odette had been seized. Only his concern for Odette and how to get her back had tempered his fury.

The girl revealed the whole sordid story—that she worked for the steward, Eryan, and that it was to her accomplice he, Cu'lugh, had given Odette. He had the overseer bring the closest sentry, and to him Yolande repeated her story. The man agreed to let Cu'lugh keep her in his custody as he went for help to question the harp maker, and Cu'lugh at once dragged her to Larsarian's castle. She did not protest as he wrenched her by the arm through the streets, except to plead over and over that her sister was not to blame.

The court guards escorted them to a waiting chamber as the king and queen were roused, and shortly Helrose arrived with the High Archer, Edred. The Mistress's anger was subdued compared to the distress of Queen Honi.

The billowy gossamer pantaloons the queen wore were but a shimmer of iridescent mist as she paced the white-and-gold-tiled floor and demanded again and again to know the reasons for Odette's abduction. Yolande sat on a stool, wringing her hands and twisting the hem of her dress, cringing as the queen raved and wept and admonished Cu'lugh and, as well, Mistress Helrose, who stood quivering under a window. The High Archer's arm was about Helrose's shoulders and every now and then his dark, accusatory eyes met Cu'lugh's. Even as his wife was near hysteria, King Larsarian was calm as he questioned Yolande and reassured Honi that no one was to blame but the sisters and, most of all, the treacherous Eryan.

While the king's men and the street sentries searched for Eryan, his brother was questioned in another room. The sister, the one Cu'lugh would never forgive himself for trusting, was being treated by one of the royal healers.

Although she was more voluptuous and paler of hair, Cu'lugh could see a familial resemblance between Honi and his Odette. Her blue eyes glistened with heavy tears that continued to stream down her already wet and wretched face.

"You are both abductors, you and that sister," she repeated to Yolande. Her eyes moved balefully toward Mistress Helrose. "How could you have been such a fool, Helrose—to trust one you knew already as devious? To betray the confidence I held in you?"

The Mistress's face was lined with remorse but she answered not.

"It is not her fault, Your Highness," Cu'lugh said, the urgency to go out and seek Odette edging his tone, "but mine. It was I who handed Odette over to the sister."

The High Archer retorted, "I agree."

King Larsarian spoke in his calming voice. "No. Lord Cu'lugh has done nothing more than any man is privileged to do under our laws. I am responsible for releasing Brune, for showing mercy that was foolish."

Queen Honi suddenly crumpled to the floor. They all clamored about her as Larsarian lifted her up. She clung to him, weeping bitterly; and Cu'lugh could hear her beg him softly to find Lord Eryan, to have him imprisoned, to have him castrated...

"Hush," Larsarian commanded quietly, and she bowed her head, though her anger sculpted her brow. "I want you to go lie down in your bed, my love. I will see he is apprehended." And with a glance at Cu'lugh and the archer, he led her from the room.

When they were gone Helrose strode toward Yolande. The girl braced just as Helrose raised her hand and slapped her across the face, leaving her left cheek as red as the queen had the right.

"They had better find him, Yolande, or your life is as worthless as your loyalties!"

Yolande's composure dissolved completely, and she slumped over the bench and sobbed in her hands.

"I am sorry, my Mistress. I did not mean Odette harm!"

Helrose grasped her by the roots of her hair and jerked her head back on her neck, bending down so that her lips grazed the girl's. "Never, never, say those words to me again, Yolande. I am not your Mistress, and you are not my concern any longer!"

The High Archer laid a hand on Helrose's shoulder. "Steady yourself, Helrose—"

She hissed at him vehemently. "You dare! I have been betrayed by those I love—why are you not out hunting for Odette yourself?"

Cu'lugh inhaled sharply and paced as the king had.

"I have sent all my companions to the cottage of your parents in search of her and of Eryan. I thought you'd want me here. But I shall go now myself, if that is what you wish."

Helrose shook her head thoughtfully and released her hold on Yolande. She looked at Cu'lugh.

"I do not blame this man, Edred, and neither shall you. When Odette is found, I want the two of you to deliver justice to my brother."

Cu'lugh and Edred eyed one another uneasily, but the High Archer promised "Yes, Helrose, as you wish."

Yolande was still sobbing, and Helrose folded her arms impatiently as she regarded her. "Oh, do not be frightened of the future, traitor. It comes surely, with the wrath of the queen and king to insure no mercy shall be extended to you or your contemptible sister."

The door opened behind them, and King Larsarian returned with three of his warriors.

"Your sister is mending from the attack," Larsarian informed Yolande and offered her a handkerchief to wipe her eyes. "You shall be taken to the Waiting House, the both of you, to hear my forthcoming verdict."

Yolande blew her nose and nodded, and she was trembling as she stood. Cu'lugh had no sympathy for her as the guards tore her garments off and ordered her to remove her shoes. She was as naked and vulnerable as any wife or slave now; but though her head hung listlessly as the guards flanked her and took hold of her arms, the contrition on her face did not glow with the sweet humility of a proper woman but only the pale understanding of the seriousness of her crime.

When they had gone Cu'lugh felt the weight of full mourning in his restless limbs.

"Edred," the king said, "I wish you to take Mistress Helrose home. Although I do not expect further problems, I think it wise if you remain there for the time."

"I shall not go, sire," Helrose insisted. "I will help in the hunt!"

"Helrose, I shall call upon you presently, but for now you need your rest. I wish to have conference with Lord Cu'lugh and shall have the details brought to Edred, who can relay them to you."

"But I am Odette's vitki—I am priestess of Freyja, and I demand to stay here and keep fully informed of all your plans."

Larsarian exhaled. "You overstep your authority, Mistress Helrose. I answer to the High Priestess, not you."

Cu'lugh saw Helrose's face bloom with color, and though her eyes burned angrily he sensed the desperation within.

"My liege, perhaps it is best to let her stay."

The king looked at him several moments. "Very well. At least let me have you shown to a room where you may rest for a time, Mistress."

"No. I shall remain here, just the same as they," she stated and sat down on a bench and crossed her arms. "When this is over, when my flower is returned, then I shall relinquish my position, as already I had planned. But for now, I will meet the responsibility of the position I have held, for it is not, I suspect, what my brother counts upon."

"Eryan," Larsarian muttered, his mouth hardening. "A great disciplinarian, except over his own affections. Such a waste."

"And Honi tried to warn us," Helrose concurred, "if we had but listened."

Cu'lugh cleared his throat and felt his hands draw into fists at his hips. He was not used to this sense of powerlessness, nor this waiting that seemed without purpose. He asked leave of Larsarian and stalked out into the hallway. The walls were narrow here, with intricate carvings across the whitewashed walls. The floor was carpeted with an exotic print. There was a sliver of a window at the end, paned with blocks of thick, milky glass making it impossible to see anything but the manifold hazy sweeps of sunlight pouring over the horizon somewhere outside. For some time he stood there, tired, restless, more fearful than he liked to admit.

"How could this happen," he asked himself, and the next moment he heard someone coming down the hall. He turned to see the deep blue fringe of Larsarian's robe sweeping over the carpet.

"Not a good view," the king said in a distracted voice. He drew a fingertip across the surface of one of the upper panes and a silvery note sprang from his caress, the song of pure crystal.

Cu'lugh stared into the milky streaks and felt Larsarian draw a weary breath.

"She is no longer in Athla, Cu'lugh," he said, and Cu'lugh's chest pounded. "We can search a lifetime and will never find her here."

"That steward—Eryan—"

"No, I do not believe so. During the night, before you came, the queen awoke from a terrible nightmare. When I asked what she dreamt, she said she had seen a pool within caverns beneath a hidden waterfall upon the mountains. There was a hungry shadow, she said, who took with it a piece of the altar from Freyja's Temple and it seemed to her mind the legendary thing called the keyfrost. I summoned my huntsmen and had them search the mountain area she saw in the dream, and their hounds picked up a scent. But the pool had dried up when they reached it, and as one of them touched the muck left behind he fell ill. That is a rare thing in Athla, Cu'lugh. Moreover, a priestess arrived a while ago from the Temple to report the High Priestess cannot be awakened. She has never slept before, Cu'lugh."

Cu'lugh's blood pumped quicker but he was cautious still. "I do not put much faith in superstitions."

"You should know by now what is real and what is not in Athla, my friend," Larsarian criticized mildly. "And you know as well as I that she is gone."

"What will we do?"

Larsarian thought a moment. "I have brought the merchant Holbarki here to explain all he may know, as he has quite the reputation for doing business with the Darkling elves."

Cu'lugh's eyes sprang open. "You think she is in that terrible realm?"

"Not likely. They detest our women. But they may have other use for her. It is not unimaginable that if they encountered her they detected her bloodline with their innate capabilities."

Cu'lugh's palms were damp with his frustration. "I will fetch her, no matter where it is they've taken her."

"I know. But hear me out, Cu'lugh. This is no small warning to find our High Priestess asleep. I fear there is great danger in Midgard—for you, for your brethren. If this is so I must summon a conclave of the vitkis to perform the Rite of Resistance, so that every passageway is barred utterly to the Midgardians. We cannot allow evil to penetrate our boundaries."

"How could it penetrate? We cannot even enter but by permission of whatever invisible force supervises."

"Mortal men and women, yes, Cu'lugh, but the wards that screen the souls of human beings do not apply to other creatures. So have the Darklings come and gone, under limitation, by the grace of their initial maternity. The Blodsaukers, of course, would never enter, nor the Trolls. But there is one creature that for its own ill mind-set toward us so far has chosen not to enter. If, however, this being gains entrance it might have the power to invade unless we take the proper precautions. Precautions that have been known to cost the lives of the priestesses who invoke it and which wanes after a time."

"And what is this creature?"

Larsarian shook his head. "I do not know, only that it is the timeless and perpetual enemy of the gods, of mortality, of all the worlds it broaches. We have detected its proximity only once or twice in all our history, and we know not what it is or from where it comes. It is said that even Freyja, after She encountered one of its number, could not endure its design, that the very essence of its familial purpose filled Her sacred heart with utter loathing."

Cu'lugh rubbed his brows with the back of his hand. "So the High Priestess sleeps. And you feel that this has something to do with Odette?"

"Remember what I told you about her mother? Of the mantle?"

"Yes, but—"

"Silfr was a daughter of the Goddess Herself, conceived with Freyja's mortal consort. The blood in Odette's veins, as human as it might be, still is imbued with some of the divinity of her Granddam. And an entity from amongst this nameless hoard cursed Freyja, cursed all Her temporal world. I suspect it still harbors resentment for Freyja's spurning when it sought to seduce Her."

"Seduce the Goddess?"

"Love recognizes few laws, my friend. And love spurned transforms easily into hatred. So this entity cursed Freyja and vowed to destroy all She loves—the gods of mankind, the shores and mountains and seas of precious Midgard, the hope that breeds ever perpetually in the hearts of mankind. If it has Odette, it will seek to destroy her, as its schemes are boundless in the effort to destroy what the Goddess loves."

"Oh, that is impossible. Odette is but one girl. Such villainy as you describe could take scant reward in the abduction of one girl."

"She is the granddaughter of Freyja, Cu'lugh, and she is not the first swanmaiden to be pursued by this entity. The others, knowing their pursuers, fled back to Freyja's abode or took haven here until their trail was obliterated. Odette, who knows nothing of her mother's heritage, cannot do that. Nor could she in any case, without a mantle."

"Does this entity have a name?"

"It goes by many, so I have learned. It has donned many lesser guises in order to trick the Midgardians into worshipping it over the centuries. Few tribes of man still recall the real strength of the entity or know that it changed forever the grace of Midgard. They do not recognize its original countenance, its true nature. Amongst those who remember are the Saxons, and they call this deceiver of mankind and designer of havoc by the name of Loki. I doubt its race has need for names, as its members are but branches of a single consciousness. In the case of this one, it severed its kinship when it became infatuated with Freyja. But when it damned itself by its resentment against Her it called out to its kindred. They seek a way to take this member back into their fold and, as well, ruin the beauty of Midgard, which was the entity's original task when it first broached this world."

Cu'lugh contemplated these things. He still had difficulty in believing the tale. But if Odette were truly in Midgard he must leave without delay.

"You need the vitkis to act at once," he said and saw Larsarian's head move in confirmation. "I will set out immediately to find Odette. Have you any idea at all where it may be the abductors—?" The next word fell hollow on his tongue and the back of his neck prickled with heat. "I know where they are taking her," he whispered. He shook with anger at his own stupidity. The answer was so simple only a fool would have not have seen it.

"Where?"

"The same damnable place I came from!"

"Where, Cu'lugh?"

He stared at the hopeful king; but, no, there was no hope he could offer, for no entity or elf or other monster nurtured thirst for violence or revenge, he realized finally, as that which lay in the heart of Odette's own sister.

"Have the priestesses perform their rites, do what you must, I understand. But I must leave now."

Larsarian's face tightened. "If you think you can get her back, I shall send a host of my best men to accompany you."

Cu'lugh considered it. "Your men are surely well trained, sire, but they have no experience with the treacherous force I go to face. And they would be on foreign soil, which I suspect would make for a thorough disadvantage."

Suddenly, Larsarian grinned. "You are more perceptive than you realize, Cu'lugh. Yes, their dexterity might be damaged, their senses affected somewhat by the unfamiliar ethers. But they are warriors and pledged to defend our women, and Odette is one of us."

Cu'lugh assessed the situation waiting in Vanda's land. She had a considerable army at hand, and yet he could not help but feel that it was not the mercenaries he should beware so much as what he had felt once in that dead forest. And if he were right, perhaps the Athlans with their own keen perceptions might stand a better chance to recognize it where he had not, until it was almost too late.

"Give me half a dozen," he said, straightening. "They must be acquainted with stealth and hand-to-hand combat…and I'll need at least two good archers."

Larsarian's face brightened. "You shall have them."

Two warriors, their uniforms and boots stained with mud, approached from the far end of the hall. They bowed before King Larsarian. One of them spoke rapidly.

"Lord Eryan has been found, sire, trying to ride to the cottage Mistress Helrose described. We have him in the hold."

"What does he say of the girl?"

They shook their heads grimly. "He claims not to know where she is, that he is as shocked by her abduction as any."

Larsarian's mouth broadened into a contented, almost dangerous smile.

"Ready and bring him to the public arena for scourging. I shall be there promptly, but for now deliver to him this message—if he lies about his knowledge of the girl's whereabouts, he shall suffer worse than death or banishment for it."

The two bowed again and went at once. Cu'lugh was eager to confront Eryan, to wrest him from his captors and strangle him with his own hands.

"Come, let us attend, Cu'lugh."

Cu'lugh blinked, unbelieving. "I leave that in your hands, sire. I must be on my way. Just direct me where I might find the men I need—"

"They await you at the public arena, my friend."

Chapter Thirty-Five

u'lugh looked at Helrose who sat still as a stone on the bench brought up on the dais for the queen. He did not mean to stare, but he was struck by her profile, so greatly of an idol of a mournful goddess did it remind him. She had not spoken a word since Larsarian informed her they were going out to watch her brother's scourging.

A crowd of male citizens was already gathering to investigate the commotion on this portion of the royal lawn designated for the public chastisement of male offenders. Their faces were sober as they contemplated the timber post standing the grounds and watched as one of the king's men hammered a newly forged iron ring high up on the wood. Guards armed with wooden staves stepped forward to block any nearer approach, and a few of the citizens asked the name of the one who was scheduled to meet this terrible justice. The guards kept their silence, and soon enough another guard emerged from the door leading Lord Eryan by a rope tethered about his wrists. There was little of the fear Cu'lugh had hoped to see in the steward's face, but at least the brazen pride he had stared down before had vanished utterly.

A herald walked out to the arena and announced "Upon charge of betraying our laws, specifically for thievery of another man's property and for the heinous neglect leading to the abduction of a woman by a foreign agent, Eryan, of the household of Yan and Aani, stands ready to deliver his testimony before the descendants and direct seed of our divine Matriarch."

A few disquieted shouts hailed from the citizenry, but none attempted interference as the guard took Eryan to the post and raised his arms over his head. The man laced the rope through the ring and knotted it securely. Removing the gag from Eryan's mouth he then turned and stood dutifully facing the dais.

King Larsarian stepped down to the lawn and went to stand beside Eryan. Their exchange was inaudible, but on the trek to the arena Larsarian had explained to Cu'lugh that, before rendering his final decision, he was bound to ask the prisoner to confirm or deny his guilt. If Eryan denied the charges he would have to wait on the post until the High Priestess arrived to give her judgment, which prevailed over all others. On this occasion, as circumstances necessitated, a proxy would be summoned, one selected by vote of the Temple priestesses. If, however, Eryan affirmed the charges he would meet immediate punishment, which Larsarian said would be kinder than what awaited a man found guilty under the divine oracle.

After several minutes the conversation seemed ended. Larsarian raised his left hand and, shielding his eyes with the first two fingers of his hand, turned his back on the steward. Loud jeers erupted from the crowd, and Cu'lugh saw the anger smolder in the faces of the guards. Larsarian returned to the dais to stand beside Queen Honi, and he held her hand as the towering guard advanced to the post and displayed to the crowd a hood of thick leather. It had been designed in the shape of a toad's face without eyeholes—a device to protect the prisoner's face as much as to denote disgrace. As the guard pulled it down over the steward's head the sound of the crowd grew uglier. Here and there men cried that Larsarian had showed mercy; others shouted their dismay directly to Eryan, calling him barbarian and traitor. Cu'lugh saw a few simply wring their hands and speak his name as if too shocked to believe the steward capable of the crime.

The guard took a dagger and shredded Eryan's shirt from his back and arms. A young boy ran up carrying a long pillow of black velvet upon which was laid a whip with five cords, the ends of which were set with small, iron spiked balls. Taking the handle, the guard positioned himself several paces behind the prisoner and snapped the cords two or three times in the air. The crowd went silent, and Helrose shuddered, pressing her lips together so tightly they glowed white under the sun.

The first lash descended, tearing Eryan's pale flesh in several places and bringing a muffled cry beneath the mask. Merciless was the guard's hand as he again and again bore the whip down. Eryan's body jerked with each blow and rip of the spikes, and soon his blood coursed over his waist and down his legs to pool in the lush grass below. Nothing like the loving discipline given to correct slaves and wives was this punishment, but one befitting a man. Eryan's screams filtered through the leather, wretched, bestial cries. Thirteen strokes in all the guard dealt, not one less or more.

And when it was finished and the guard turned and bowed to Larsarian the queen jumped to her feet.

"It is not enough! In the name of decency I demand more!"

Helrose looked ill, and she gave no protest as Edred bent her face over his shoulder and kissed her brow.

But the king was thoughtful. He nodded to the guard and the other obliged the queen with an additional nine strokes.

When the rope was at length untied Lord Eryan slumped to the ground. The guard and two of his compeers carried the steward off the lawn and back through the door of the hold. The king called his companions to attend him in the hall and asked Cu'lugh to come as well. Edred had to leave Helrose now, but the queen came and embraced her and Cu'lugh heard their muffled shared grief as he stepped from the dais.

Eryan lay on his stomach on a rough wooden trestle while the royal healer washed his wounds with honey and oil. An assembly of the king's men stood about watching, making room when Larsarian entered.

"So, you know not where Odette was taken," Larsarian demanded of Eryan.

The steward raised his head weakly, but he managed to bow it and press his lips to the edge of the trestle as if attempting to show the king his obeisance.

"No, sire," he said, speaking through teeth gritted against his pain. "But...they have told me that...Yolande claims the abductors appeared...to be Darklings. I...should not be surprised if the merchant...Holbarki has a hand in this. He...desired to purchase Odette. We all are...aware of his past dealings with...the dark elves."

Larsarian looked questioningly to one of the guards.

"They have questioned the merchant, sire," the man said, "but he claims to know nothing. He was sound asleep in his bed when we got there. We investigated the property and found her not."

"If he is involved, he shall suffer later," Larsarian said. He looked at Eryan again. "At the moment it is inconsequential, as we know where they exited the realm."

Eryan's eyes widened, and Cu'lugh saw a flicker of hope in them.

"Then you have sent...searchers?"

"Not as yet. This is why I have spared you from banishment, Eryan. You shall accompany the search party to hunt for Odette and bring her home."

Cu'lugh felt the air knocked from his lungs. "Sire, this was never discussed!"

"Thank you, sire," Eryan said, biting off a moan. "You shall not...be disappointed."

Larsarian grunted directions to the healer to have Eryan bandaged and prepared to come to the royal stable. Cu'lugh argued against the king's command, shocked by this decision from a man who had won his deepest respect; and when Larsarian tried to pull him away from the trestle he shook his head.

"I will not agree to this," he said heatedly and saw the concurring looks his words elicited in the other warriors about.

Larsarian was adamant. "Go fetch your horse and your gear, Lord Cu'lugh, and wait for me at the royal stables."

"I will go, yes," Cu'lugh replied, "but forget your escort—I go alone!"

"No, you shall not. I will have the sentries bar your exit if you dare this foolhardiness!"

Cu'lugh trembled with an anger he did not know how to release. At last he made a rigid bow to Larsarian and shoved his way through the men to the doors.

News of Odette's abduction had already reached the inn. The young overseer bore a regretful face as he opened the door and asked what had been discovered. Cu'lugh told him what he could, and the boy assigned one of the serving girls to help him prepare. But as she started up the stairs the proprietor called her down again, and his eyes were dark and accusatory as he watched Cu'lugh.

As Cu'lugh geared in his scale mail the walls of the room seemed to cringe from his presence. So cold and empty the bed looked without Odette lying on it, the cage a meaningless structure of metal. But deliberately he put the thought from mind and left with haste to fetch his mount.

The royal stable was a huge building with dozens of well-kept stalls and tables decked with the finest riding equipment. The gaily garbed young attendants who worked there took the reins of his mount and led the animal to one of the stalls, inspecting and adjusting the saddle and bridle as Cu'lugh waited for the king.

He still did not know exactly how to best return to Vanda's land. When he set out for Athla he had sensed her sentries' eyes like a drill boring into the back of his skull. Not one man had he glimpsed hiding in the barren fields or the lifeless groves, but they were there—they had to be for the mercenaries to have warning of the trespassers who provided the goods that Vanda coveted. Recruited for the most part from the dregs of their own respective societies, Vanda's men would make no allowances for title or gender, right or wrong. If their patroness wanted to make her sister prisoner they would defend that desire to their last dying breath as long as she was paying them.

So, it was the sentries he had to concentrate on first. But how did one maneuver around a force that, for all practical purposes, was invisible?

King Larsarian arrived shortly with the High Archer and a valet toting his bow, quiver and riding bags. Over his padded armor Edred bore another large quiver and on his feet high boots leafed with vertical strips of gleaming iron. A younger man of similar dress and flaming red hair cinched back in a braid hastened in just afterward, carrying more quivers of arrows and a bow. Helrose followed the men; and she had changed, too, into a vest and riding pants and thick leather boots. A bronze breastplate was slung over her shoulders and bronze gauntlets covered her arms. A long sickle knife swung in a sheath at her left thigh. Cu'lugh watched as she donned the breastplate, surprised that she was actually coming along, and wondered if her presence would be more of a help or a hindrance.

Other men tramped in, experienced men, he knew by their bearing. King Larsarian drew Cu'lugh aside.

"Helrose will be accompanying your party," Larsarian said.

"Yes, I see that. Is it wise?"

"I ordered the spirit of welcoming closed about our borders so none might enter, not human or otherwise. As a vitki, Helrose has the power to open a portal at close range and to close it at will. Besides, I fear until this is over, and with Edred gone, she will be of no use to her girls."

Cu'lugh was still bitter. "But her brother? He is responsible for this!"

"I know, Cu'lugh, but he is our best tracker. We are a sensitive race, but even amongst us his senses are quite refined. It is hard for you, yes, but I know this man well. As much as you now I am familiar with his passions. But I also know his morals and know his remorse is true for what has happened. I give you my own word that Eryan will do his utmost to track these abductors and to aid your party in any way necessary."

Cu'lugh was touched but unconvinced Larsarian was not, perhaps, being naive. "It is his passion that disturbs me. How can he be trusted not to abduct Odette himself if, indeed, we find her?"

Larsarian's eyebrow quirked good-humoredly. "Preventing that is your duty, Cu'lugh."

Cu'lugh reddened. "True, sire. And what of when Odette is safe again?" Cu'lugh ignored the disturbing doubt the words brought to his heart. She had to be alive;

she would be rescued. "What will befall him, if he is not to be banished? What of the next young lady toward whom he directs this irresponsible passion?"

"He has little choice but to enlist his services to the army. The citizens will not tolerate his presence out in the streets."

Cu'lugh saw a figure enter through the stable doors—Lord Eryan, garbed fresh in black padded armor. His hair had been washed of the blood that had splattered there from the bathing of his wounds; and he carried a small traveling bag and a rapier sheathed at one hip, a dagger at his ankle. By the way his mouth tightened with each step Cu'lugh knew he was in pain from the bandaged, hidden wounds.

Trifling justice, Cu'lugh thought fiercely.

Larsarian introduced Cu'lugh to the others who would be accompanying him. Prage, the red-haired youth he'd noticed before, was long-armed and sinewy—an archer, as Cu'lugh had surmised. He smiled modestly when Cu'lugh complimented the short bow he carried. Constructed of a glossy white bone and strung with black sinew, it was a beautiful weapon.

"The bone is of the beast that attacked the sacred flock some years ago. My father gave me first choice of its carcass."

Cu'lugh touched the smooth recurve. "Dragon? I heard their bones are slimy and evaporate to smoke when touched by air."

"Not this one," Prage answered, and Cu'lugh almost smiled at the modest look on the boy's face.

Amnoc and Yori were personal guards of Larsarian's. Huge men both, they had primed for battle in full studded leather armor, breastplates, helmets and spiked shields. Amnoc carried a great double ax, Yori a magnificent double-edged sword. The two were as formidable-looking opponents as Cu'lugh had ever encountered, and he was surprised when Larsarian confirmed they were not Midgardians but Athlan born. Another swordsman, Sylreth, wore simple black padded gear with studs. Larsarian told Cu'lugh that this nobleman was the palace champion, and the man had the scars to prove his experience. With his black hair and flashing eyes and pale face Sylreth had a similar look to Lord Eryan, but his easy demeanor contrasted sharply with the somber steward.

When the horses were at last prepared, King Larsarian told the party that once Helrose had opened the passageway that would lead them on the trail of the Darkling force they were to rely on Cu'lugh's advice if it were, indeed, Midgard where the pursuit took them.

"Yori and Amnoc, acquainted though you are with Midgard, be not so careless as to forget that land is alien to us. What might seem familiar sights and sounds could easily prove quite unfriendly."

The king made a gesture with his right hand, a blessing of some sort Cu'lugh was sure, and went to stand by Helrose's dappled mare. He handed her a stone—a simple river rock, it appeared—and this she pressed to the center of her forehead. For several moments she held it there with her eyes closed, and when she opened them again stuffed the stone into a tiny pouch tied at her waist. She glanced at the men, met Cu'lugh's nod and clicked her mount forward. As the men rode out after her Cu'lugh saw that children lined the streets. They were shouting words exotic to his ears and pelted the passing party with what appeared to be green sponges. One clung to the mane of Cu'lugh's steed, and he saw that it was a tiny toad. He picked the creature up and was about to toss it back to one of the children when he noticed Helrose lift one that had landed on her shoulder. She popped it into her mouth just as one would a baked sweetmeat. Cu'lugh shuddered but followed her example.

Then, as they headed out of the city by a track leading westward Cu'lugh felt a bolt of heat spread through his stomach. It passed quickly, imparting a wave of confidence and vitality through his system and an almost feverish rutting lust. But this lust clarified his thoughts so he knew only one consideration, that of finding and rescuing his Odette. Even the simmering desire to reckon revenge against Eryan dwindled into a matter to be indulged at another time.

They reached a field, and Helrose spurred her mare into a full run. The men followed until she signaled, slowing at the entrance of a path between two ferny hedges. The path grew dark for the strange, fecund trees here, so dark only a tinge of light penetrated. But it ended abruptly enough, and Cu'lugh saw Helrose had stopped at a stone wall covered with thick brambles abloom with great waxy white roses. The fragrance of the roses was so heavy Cu'lugh felt a little lightheaded. He watched as the Mistress dismounted and took her sickle knife in hand. She inclined her head to the brambles and cut some of them away, enough to reveal the seams of a door hidden in the stones. She knelt, then, and re-rooted the severed brambles into the black earth.

"'Tis wonder the touch of the Darklings as they passed did not wilt the flowers," commented Edred.

"Odette was with them," Helrose answered by way of explanation. She reached for the blackened iron handle of the door and pushed it down.

Chapter Thirty-Six

Cu'lugh did not know what to expect as the Mistress pulled the door open. What met his eyes made him reel in his saddle.

Never had he imagined the color or shape of utter nothingness, although that was exactly what his brain confirmed he saw. Shadeless, colorless, formless, without subtle dimension or texture, the alien oblivion was beyond any hue the mind could conceive. No sound issued through it, no movement ensued within its depths.

His mount pranced with a fretful whinny. He spoke to it reassuringly until it calmed a bit; but it still strained to pull its face away, as if the void would swallow them all.

He whispered, "What is it?"

Helrose returned to her saddle. "A passageway through the bowels of that dismal place your people call the Wastelands."

Eryan frowned. "What is this Wasteland, sister?"

"The Helsroad—the fearsome paths between the worlds which for their disquieting ambiance appeal to the Darklings. It is not an easy way for mortals to travel, as they abhor enlightenment as much as they pursue it. But, as they have bred for so long, their collective awareness is very strong, and its blind desire demanded of the World-Tree a path to match the purblind consciousness from which it was birthed. When the time comes mortality at last tires of its games and is ready to accept what is, these fearsome passages will be no longer needed. Then mankind may travel between the realms at a whim, just as we."

Cu'lugh felt the eyes of the other men skim over him.

"But are you not all as mortal as I am?"

"Yes and no, Lord Cu'lugh," said Helrose, "We have no need for this as you do. Our bodies know no reason for corruption, and by that I mean aging and death." She flipped him a confidant grin. "However, we can *pretend* now to be ignorant and in love with suffering to help you pass in haste. It is a game of the perceptions, and we can play it when need requires."

This brought a round of laughter from the others. Cu'lugh reddened, impatient to move on.

"Then play, Mistress."

Helrose exhaled and drew out the stone again and put it to her forehead. This time, though, her eyes became unfocused and the muscles of her face grew slack.

"Yes, they have gone to Midgard," she whispered.

Edred took the stone from her and brushed her cheek with the back of his hand until she recovered. She told Yori and Amnoc to gather what they needed to create a light to see through the passageway. The two dismounted and collected heavy limbs and material for wadding, some of which they put away in their packs, keeping two of these torches at hand. With flint and steel they lit the ends and handed one to Helrose and the other to Cu'lugh.

Helrose reined her mare forward through the doorway. As the last to proceed, Cu'lugh coaxed his steed through and in the shuddering emptiness turned to close the doorway. Indeed, the place now reminded him of the Wasteland at nightfall, with its suffocating shadows and sterile ground. He rode toward the flickering silhouettes waiting ahead.

Helrose's voice broke through the baneful silence. "Are we ready?"

At the men's affirmative she whispered something into the mare's ear. Like an eagle it bounded through the merciless landscape and the men gave chase.

* * *

The skies were clearer than they had been for months, and the light that bathed Vanda's face felt like genuine warmth pouring through the window. Outside, some of her men had stripped off their jerkins as they patrolled the Hall grounds. She was not likely to be disturbed by their muttering today, however, for she had began to pen ultimatums, the future orders to the lesser Frankish chieftains. They would have to willingly give their loyalty to her once the entire world had transformed before their narrow vision, unless they wished to see themselves and their children turned out of their ancient homesteads.

As your former liege, Charles Martel, by reason of his refusal to obey the Lord cometh...

She had no illusions as to his reaction when the earth trembled and the sky grew dark and the Eternal Father of established religion reclaimed the world. More moral than any man she'd known, Charles was proud, grasping and would do whatever it took to secure the hereditary rights of his legitimate children. Martel would not willingly yield to even God's will.

The chieftains would surrender all titles and positions, submit their power to those Vanda named overseer under her rule—women who had served her mother and now resided in communities dedicated to certain orders of the Church in order to protect their chastity. And though they were all ancient, in the ultimatum Vanda allowed them to choose their successors—with the stipulation that successor was female and celibate.

She sensed the time was running out to get the ultimatum prepared and forwarded, and took some comfort in imagining the blow these men's pride would suffer when their forces fell to the army of a woman.

When Piers informed her about the rogue bear she was incensed they had waited to tell her, as if by virtue of her gender she was to be spared such news. But it was the demeanor of Hrowthe, who had not showed up until the next evening, that most irritated her. He seemed hardly concerned about the insult, interested more in some issue concerning the distant kinswoman who had whelped the boy they suspected had also been attacked. She cursed the priest for his irresponsibility, ranted and dismissed him. He had not even apologized, merely misted out of sight as she spoke.

Where he had slinked off to she neither knew nor, for the moment, cared. So great was the affront that she smeared the juices of a certain bulb across her windowsills and over the threshold of the door, leaving that scent that so wounded the Blodsauker's sensitivities. She had not seen him for a few days; and though she'd given up expecting his regret, she was mystified he had not played upon her serving women as he'd done many times before, convincing them to speak on his behalf and then, when she relented, behaving as if nothing had gone amiss between them since their last conversation. She had pointed out to him often enough he could not have too much pride to stoop so to beg the servants, to which he always replied he should be grateful, as pride was a sin.

Piqued as she was this time, she missed his company as never before. He had a knack for calming her when her emotions built. And she sensed the pleasure she knew at the moment was fast veering over the boundary into anger toward the buffoons she addressed. Her anger was what provided weight to every decision that had secured what power she held. Yet, the wrath could be uncomfortable without a sounding board. She knew not how to control it any more than she knew how to castrate all of civilization with a mere thought. Only Hrowthe could assuage her fury; and it was close, she knew, despite the pale sunshine and the new silk gown she wore and the poignant smell of the expensive indigo ink on her desk.

She tapped the windowpane restlessly and started to turn again to the desk when she glimpsed down the street far beyond the men a group of riders passing through on mist-dun horses. The animals moved with a grace defiant of their size, making it look as if their hooves were one with the dirt foaming before them. Vanda blinked and looked again, and saw now only the natural shadows of the beasts. And yet their small riders were not her men or any she knew by sight. She sighed and looked dourly at the parchment waiting for her.

Soon old Rachel came rapping at the door of the apartments with the tidings Lord Loic had returned with a parcel to deliver to the priests in the Temple. Rachel's disapproving frown gave her ancient brow the look of a patch of crisscrossed wicker. "He has sent word that he and his companions shall be taking room in your stable, my Lady. Should I have your personal guards informed to have these riders watched?"

Vanda laughed and clapped her hands together. "Certainly not. Lord Loic and his companions are more trustworthy than most of my men, dear. Take them bedding and wine and whatever else they may require for comfort."

Alone again, Vanda drew the bar of her door. The ultimatums were forgotten now as she walked to the back of the room. A tapestry of a black unicorn hung on the wall, and she lifted it carefully from the pegs that held it. The sender of the gift was a minor nobleman from Brittany who had proposed marriage. Though she had forgotten his name and even his house, the tapestry she had fallen in love with. She spread it over her bed and came back to the low door it had concealed. Unclasping a chain from her neck she fingered through the line of keys suspended from it until she found the one she needed. Inserting it into the keyhole she unlocked the door. The hinges moved with a lonesome creak.

The lamp from her night table she retrieved and held to enter. The light pitched cozy patterns across the walls of the tiny room and illuminated the velvet surface of a drape hanging over the narrow slit window. The mustiness of the room tickled her nose, but she ignored it and surveyed the dusty furnishings: a padded bench, a small table, a high-backed armchair. She saw the rosewood cradle her father had built for his whore's child, still filled with stacks of old wool blankets and heaps of tiny stockings. There were infant's caps as well, of pure white flannel embroidered with a rich blue thread and sewn at one corner each with the runes of Nana, goddess of babes-in-arms.

Vanda set the lamp on the armrest of the chair and knelt on the floor beside the bench. Warily, she thrust her hands beneath the seat. Her fingers grazed the flat outline of a narrow brass trunk she'd hidden there years before. Skimming the side of it until she touched the iron handle, she pulled on this until the trunk slid forward. A fat spider ran across the tarnished lid; she swiped it off and watched as it scurried into the safety of the cradle's shadow.

A chain girdled the trunk, padlocked by a tiny ball made of pieces of deer antler over-and-underlaid in such a way as to form a puzzle. It was a gift from a trespassing gypsy in return for her sparing the lives of himself and his family, and Vanda had not shared the secret of unlocking it with any, not even Hrowthe.

She rotated the ball gingerly with her fingers, removing the pieces in the intricate sequence the gypsy had shown her. Her heartbeat accelerated as one by one the sections separated into her sweat-dewed fingertips. At length the clip sprang back from the core of the ball and a last gauzy strip of antler released from the chain.

Setting the pieces of puzzle aside she lifted the lid of the trunk. A waft of earthy fragrance assaulted her nostrils and eyes. She shook her head and blinked until her eyes smarted no more.

Like whirls of cream were the layers of soft, stainless feathers within the chest. She was seized with an impulsive desire to stroke the lovely things, but put the feeling aside and wiped on her gown the perspiration from her shaking hands. A sharp needle she took from a small pocket of her robe, and with a sharp intake of air she pricked her thumb.

Two drops of her blood fell on the feathers; the other five she was obliged to squeeze out. She muttered the ancient binding—once, twice and three times. As she let go her breath the feathers fluttered inside the trunk as if stroked by a breeze passing through the room.

Vanda smiled to herself. *So, so simple.*

Immune now from the protective wards her father had placed on the thing before wedding Silfr, she drew the garment out of the trunk. She held it up by the taut cowl against the light from the outside room. No seams, no stitches, no lining could she see anywhere on the mantle. More than a mantle, truly—whoever had tailored it had made it into a tight-fitting gown. So unworldly beautiful and perfect was it she had no doubt the barbarian Saxons were right in their assertion that these swanmaiden's gowns were created by the light elves themselves.

The thing was Odette's only link to her heritage. Over the years Vanda had dreamed of taking it out and using the hereditary proscription of the thing before all was set in motion to summon Odette to her, force her to kiss the hem of her robes, to place a knife in her lily-white hands and make her cut her own heart from her breast. But due to Thierry's interference, Odette had been removed to the haven of the Athlan realm, with its demonic incantations that shielded against a summons from across the borders.

Vanda had another fancy from time to time—of donning the gown herself. To know flight as did the daughters of Freyja—ah, that would be sublime irony to insult the goddess of whoredom! But the warnings against such a deed had been many, and in the end she always discarded the idea. Besides, that insult would be only to Freyja, and what Vanda truly wanted was an insult so complete and overriding that even in death Silfr would reel from its barbed design.

Soon enough would the pagan gods be destroyed forever and Loki turn His face to the spirits of Vanir, the evil spirits that had plagued the universe from its conception. The time was fast approaching when the world would be washed of every form and vestige of sensuality by the hordes of the godly who worked for Loki under His varying faces and tenets. With the world chaste once more, Loki would issue His long-anticipated demand that Freyja and Her brethren leave the Midgard ethers forever. And then the decadent goddess would be permanently expelled from the collective consciousness of the abstemious mortals left.

The one fancy Vanda had never forsaken was the single request she would make of Loki when He dashed off the chains of his prison: to allow her to deliver the eviction notice to the Vanir Lady…wearing this gown of Her own child.

It was an ambitious dream, and even if Loki wanted to keep the entertainment to Himself at least for now the mantle belonged to her. With it she would make Odette forswear herself of her own demon gods, her mother, her father. A priceless moment Vanda had waited for all her adult days.

She laughed softly and pressed the gown to her breast, indulging herself with a few moments of the gown's intoxicating, deceiving fragrance.

* * *

Odette awakened to the feel of a wet, damp sponge bathing her flesh. She was lying down and her wrists were bound above her head. For a moment or two she thought she'd just roused from a particularly sensual and disturbing dream and would open her eyes to find herself bound for punishment somewhere in Mistress Helrose's house.

It was a noxiously unpleasant smell that at last prompted her to open her heavy eyes. The room was strange to her and ill lit; she thought she saw a torch or two hanging from the walls but they were too far away to make out. She felt nauseous, giddy, but on turning her head she forgot everything else but the frightening sight that met her gaze.

The gaunt, bloodless creature that stood at her side did not notice how she gasped, not until she screamed. He looked up from his task and regarded her through passionless, phlegm-tinted eyes. His complexion was as devoid of color as his features were of expression. The hand that had stilled upon her was so lifeless she could feel the frigidity of his hard skin soak through the sponge and creep into her bones.

She screamed again and pulled on the fetters; and finding them tauter than anything she'd been imprisoned by in Athla, she pulled her legs up at the knees and kicked frantically. He stared at her and stepped back a pace, watching emotionlessly as she managed to topple the basin of water that had been set upon the table near her legs.

"Let me go," she panted, looking desperately at the unfamiliar walls. "Or I swear I should not wish to be you when my Mistress and Master discover your treachery!"

He looked rather harmless in the shapeless grey robe that was too large for his proportions. As he made no move to touch her again she at last stopped kicking and searched his face for a hint of understanding.

"I am not speaking rashly," she advised him. "My Master is a formidable soldier. Let me go now and I promise not to reveal your name, good sir!"

She heard a rustle from beyond the fetters, followed by a whisk of footfalls over the dirt floor. Odette twisted her head this way and that, but she saw no one, not until the strange young man bowed his head and backed farther from the table. Like a hare darting from the shade a figure appeared suddenly at her head. She gasped and tasted the unmistakable flavor of death in the air.

"Welcome home, Odette."

She shivered under the gaze of the new stranger. And then, without warning, she felt a prick of familiarity. As suddenly as he'd appeared she now recognized the hierophant features, the smooth, timbreless voice.

"Father Hrowthe…"

He stepped closer so she could see him easily and lifted a lock of her hair, which he regarded with an expression of sadness.

"Welcome home," he repeated, now touching her chin. He turned her head gently from one side to the other and examined her face and eyes. "They tell me that after you fainted they gave you an elixir to keep you asleep. Do you feel ill?"

"Not now."

He released her chin and grazed her cheek with his fingers. "Good. But I must apologize—the Darklings are not apt to implement foresight."

Odette was beginning to shiver so with the cold and the dampness that her teeth chattered.

"You are cold," he said and, turning to the other, "kindle a fire."

The other did not blink; but now his features made a little movement, so that she could see he was disturbed, though she wasn't sure why. And it mattered not, she knew, and looked to the priest.

"I am here again," she said softly, her heart sinking. "In my sister's home?"

"You are in your homeland," he answered, "but this is our Temple."

"Home," she repeated, and wanted to sink back into sleep, find the way back to Athla. "No," she said, "this is not home."

He did not respond, and the way he looked at her naked limbs and torso made her uncomfortable for its unspoken disapproval.

"Why do you have me fettered?"

He met her eyes again with evident relief. "For the same reason this is not home in your heart."

She wondered at his words as he turned and produced a blanket. He spread it over her and pressed it snugly about her throat.

"Where is my sister?"

"She will be here presently. For now, abide my brother's ministrations. Truly, they will not harm you."

Odette's thoughts were wracked by all she'd heard. "Where are those Darklings? Are they the ones who seized me?"

Hrowthe smoothed the hair at the crown of her head. "It was necessary. But they are without, and have no desire to be present. It shall only be my brothers and I—and Lady Vanda, when she comes—and then you will rest."

She frowned, her skin prickling now with apprehension rather than cold.

"Lord Thierry took me to Athla—I wish to speak to him."

Hrowthe's eyebrows pinched a little. "That is impossible, Odette. The Lord is dead."

Odette shook her head in dismay. "No! Please, Father Hrowthe, fetch him here now!"

"I am most sorry, Odette. But her ladyship's husband died some months ago."

She felt tears brimming at the corners of her eyes. "It cannot be. Thierry was a very, very good man!"

"Good," mused Hrowthe and bent and kissed her brow with marble lips. "As you will to see it, child. Now, consign yourself to the care of my brothers, and rest as you can."

He stepped away, ignoring her repeated pleas to be unfettered. In the dark shadows of the room she heard the crackle of freshly kindled wood and Hrowthe telling the other something that made her wince.

"Cleanse her bowels and then glut her on honey till she's quite stuffed. It will enhance her sensations without dulling the awareness."

The other murmured in reply, and she heard the ruffle of Hrowthe's unseen feet exit from the room. She was terrified and began to weep in shallow, frantic gasps.

* * *

It was a twist in the blind passageways that Cu'lugh, even with a dozen torches, would never have discerned. But Helrose had no doubts of it and led the party through the narrow way. At once Cu'lugh felt a crushing weight on his entire body and the silent air sucked at his nostrils as if it wanted to steal his breath. His steed continued on swiftly, and had it been reasonable he would have thought the horses were not running but flying.

A glint of light pierced the horizon at last. Helrose allowed the party to slow now and coaxed the horses with a little melody; they whinnied in chorus and followed her through a voluminous cloak of pitching colors. Cu'lugh's eyes stung and he closed them; and when at length he felt the animal slow again he looked and saw that the whole party was emerging from a grotto toward the grassy bank of a shallow stream.

A waterfall plummeted down the wall of the grotto a ways, and through the woodland on the opposite bank Cu'lugh could make out the familiar points of the mountains that surrounded Vanda's lands. The trees on them were barren of foliage, as if still embraced by winter. A heavy haze bore down upon the peaks, and the rays of the sun scattered over this as if deflected from the valley by the ominous clouds.

The party dismounted once they were on the other side of the stream; and as the others stretched and made ready a temporary camp Prage set out to bring down some meat. The hares he returned with were lean, but the roasted meat comforted the hollow spot in Cu'lugh's stomach he'd ignored for hours.

Yori and Amnoc claimed the first watch while the others rested, agreeing to turn over their duty to Cu'lugh and Edred in an hour. Cu'lugh trod up the bank a distance to find a place to relieve himself and observed Helrose and Eryan speaking together deep in the bushes beyond. Helrose's hushed voice trembled with rage as she railed at her brother for his part in Odette's abduction.

"It was not enough to put her in jeopardy, but yourself as well! What if the king had not been so generous, you fool? Care you not for those who love you?"

She slapped his face and ran away, flying past Cu'lugh without meeting his eyes. As he looked at the steward he wondered if the pain in the man's face was honest or contrived.

Cu'lugh turned away and attended to the need that had brought him then went back to the camp. He fell asleep almost instantly, so deeply that at first he thought Yori's voice but the beginning of a dream.

"Lord Cu'lugh, we need you to rise at once!"

Only after sitting up did Cu'lugh see that darkness had already settled in. He groaned with some irritation and rose to his feet.

"Why did you let me sleep so long? It is night al—"

"We have been searching for Lord Eryan. He left while the rest of you slept."

Cu'lugh rubbed the ghost of weariness from his face and reached for his scabbard. "Why did you let him venture out there alone?"

The warrior looked at him stonily. "He said he sensed an unnatural tide on the wind, from that direction." Cu'lugh followed Yori's gaze to the woodland on the horizon. "He went to see, and when he had not returned after a time I went in search of him."

Cu'lugh looked about and saw Edred speaking with Helrose, who was just awakening. Even with only the starlight for illumination he saw the crimson in her face and her nails digging the earth.

Edred sighed and regarded Cu'lugh. "Is it possible he was taken?"

Cu'lugh shook his head. "By whom? You heard no one, Yori?"

"Not a soul."

All were silent for a time, and at last Cu'lugh called them all to gather before the fire. He told them the directions to Vanda's lands, the positions he knew were occupied by outposts, the passages and forest where he had sensed the waiting evil so strongly as he lay freezing. He explained the numbers and formations of the guards at her gates and the places least fortified by human sentinels. He described the layout of the streets, the districts where lay the artisan quarters, the compounds for the serfs, the heavily guarded Hall.

"Surprisingly, there are fewer guards at night than during the daytime," he said. "The quickest way to enter the city is from a spot I know of at the southern expanse of the boundary fence. But to get there we must avoid Vanda's sentries. From here we should first skirt the forest rather than cut through it, for it is likely dense with sentries or, if my suspicions are correct, swarming with the more fanatic of her priests."

Sylreth lifted an eyebrow. "Priests? What obstruction should priests offer to the rescue of a maiden?"

Cu'lugh chortled sourly. "These priests have no respect for Athlan customs, Sylreth—to them all women are fiends but those who abhor sensual love. And they will defend Vanda's lands and, more so, her will with a zeal like to the missionary priests' passion for desecration."

Helrose threw a stick into the fire. "This forest leads straight to the city?"

"Yes." Cu'lugh was shocked when she rose.

"Then I must go and subdue whatever ill results their prayers might yield."

Edred made a protesting sound, but at her adamant glance he sighed and let go whatever he'd intended to say. He turned to Cu'lugh.

"You calculate at most ten men per hundred foot of wall?"

"Yes."

The High Archer nodded and jostled the bottom of his quiver thoughtfully.

"Perhaps Lord Eryan is hidden in the forest," suggested Yori. "Should we wait for him?"

"Whatever he has gotten himself into, we cannot wait," Cu'lugh said. "Vanda's force will be stronger by morning light." He looked at Helrose. "We will need you to do whatever it is you vitkis do to ward off the Darklings if we encounter them, Mistress."

"I know they have already sensed us," she said, "and the greater of their number have already headed back on their original route toward the Athlan borders."

Her misted eyes grew unfocused, and again she raked the earth, raising a palmful of it and inhaling it as if it were a bouquet of sweetest flowers.

Her voice was detached. "Thirteen Athlan vitkis have offered their own blood during our journey in the effort to close forever the entrances to the Darkling host. The king has sacrificed his own life. Mother Urtha trembles in her fecund abode, for She feels the advance of the unhealthy ones and is helpless to obstruct it. For the faithful and courageous are now too few and frail on this realm She birthed."

Cu'lugh wondered silently how many human days had passed during their journey through the Wasteland, for it seemed little time had passed since they'd said farewell to the king and stood before those heavenly roses. A mournful hush fell over the Athlans; and he wanted to say that Helrose had to be mistaken and that the king lived, but common sense confirmed her vision was true.

The air grew dense with unshed dew as his tearful eyes swept over the grassland. Something moving low across the ground abruptly drew his attention. Squinting, he saw it was a thick, yellowish haze rolling from the outer brambles of the forest beyond, bowing meadow flower and grass in its wake, bearing a malignant stench he'd encountered only once before.

Chapter Thirty-Seven

The chanting of Father Hrowthe's brethren, as mournful as it was, lulled Odette's anger and numbed her spirit even as the honey they pumped into her rectum incited her physical passions. How she hated these demons of the detached touch. She could feel their pity, as if her nakedness was something unholy, the passion they had deliberately incited some distasteful necessity.

They had unfettered her before cleansing her bowels, and she had struggled to slip out of their grasp and somehow reach the door. Between the seven of them they had restrained and moved, rolled and anchored her as they needed to perform their sterile rite. When they were done they sat her up and put a bowl of water to her lips. She was thirsty, but not thirsty enough to trust them; and so they pulled her hair back and pinched her nose. When she could no longer ignore the need for air her mouth opened and they spilled the liquid down her throat. This done, they rolled her onto her side again and held her down and inserted a larger pipe this time to fill her with the honey. The thick nectar entering had been more uncomfortable than the warm water, and she broke out in a cold sweat. She had wept nervously and prayed with all her strength the Goddess would let the bones of their wrists break so she could escape.

Now they laid her back on the table and began to chant again. Odette's sex was growing damp with desire. She hated it, not out of any humiliation but that these sexless men should see her hips move and hear the low moan she tried to suppress.

One of them pried her legs open with his frigid hand and stroked her sodden nether lips. His touch was mechanical, and his eyes hovered over her head as his fingers massaged her flesh and manipulated her clitoris. The hands of another clamped over her breasts, massaging them softly, then roughly, squeezing the nipples until they felt close to bursting. Yet another offered a bowl filled with oil and the one holding her legs apart dipped the end of a finger into it. At once the priests' chant changed to a low, unsettling monotone that raked coldly the length of Odette's spine. Her buttocks were parted gently and the priest slipped his finger deeply into her anus. Having thus anointed her, he stepped back from the table and one of his brothers lifted her and carried her through a door two others held open. She was taken into another room with a great towering ceiling and a spiral staircase circling the walls up to it. A great misty orb was set at the apex. Directly beneath this strange gem stood a dais, and upon the dais a great harp.

Odette squeezed her eyes shut hard as the priest who carried her stepped up onto the dais. But when she looked again the harp was still there.

A beautiful instrument, its colossal proportions exacerbated Odette's fear. The silver strings sparkled under the glint of the torches set about the walls, and she caught the unmistakable contours of a granite phallus rising from the forepillar. No, not just a phallus—a double-headed phallus. She was astonished, frightened; and as she strained in the priest's arms for a better look his companions clambered up beside him and reached for her.

She was lifted so quickly she feared falling and reached for the one who had carried her. But he only spread her legs and helped the others turn her so that her back was against the forepillar. They held her legs apart, slowly lowering her onto the phallus heads. Desperately, she fought the hands holding her arms, but they were like steel. She felt the head of the hind phallus enter her oiled anus, the anterior the font of her vagina. Her mouth fell open as they settled her down so both orifices were engorged with impersonal granite. The priests fettered her wrists above her head—with what she did not know, but that it felt like cords of silky-soft leather—and her feet in the same fashion. So fine were these cords they cut into her flesh, and she knew it would not be long before her hands and feet were numb.

With her now securely impaled on the harp's phalluses the priests jumped down from the dais. Terrified, Odette struggled against the cords, and when her wide eyes looked up at them she nearly fainted.

It was not cord of silk or any other fabric that bound her, but two slender, living creatures poking out from two small crevices, and they were entwined one about the other. Their sharp little snouts darted here and there as they flicked their forked tongues in the air. One of them turned its eyes toward her and its jaws flared open angrily.

"*No, oh, Goddess, no!*"

Odette cringed against the forepillar and looked to her feet. A second pair of the same serpents coiled about her ankles, their bodies laced just as the other two, securing her in place upon the insensate phallus.

"It is ready," she heard one of the priests say. She implored them with her terrified eyes but saw only a milky elation glowing in the lifeless orbs above the sunken, dried apples of their cheeks.

Odette tossed her head and gnashed the air with her teeth.

"Noooo! Release me, please!" Whether they understood her or cared it did not matter; their elation intensified. Their jubilation was like that of the zealots of Boniface, their eyes burning with a dark light that radiated through the sickly phlegm. It seemed as if they gazed upon some mystery so sacred and elusive it defied sanity.

Something stirred deep within the orifices they'd defiled. A slight touch only but enough to tickle her and agitate the lust they'd manipulated. When it passed the serpents binding her moved and hissed. Her stomach fluxed with revulsion and she glared at the priests.

My sister is surrounded by these wicked monsters?

The thought made her sure Hrowthe had misled her. Vanda must have fallen victim to them, too!

"Oh, Goddess, no," she gasped and jerked against the snakes at her wrists. The tickling started again. It thrashed against her core, through her vagina and pressed into her anus, stoking her passion with a savagery unwholesome and acutely painful. Yet, despite this pain she felt a great need to work herself upon the phalluses. She resisted it and screamed at the priests again.

"Damn you all, you loathsome creatures! You are not human; you are not men! May Hela oil you all and impale you on spears of fire!"

They did not flinch or seem to care, but regarded her with that mingling of fanaticism, indifference and revulsion that lit her soul as surely as they'd kindled her sex.

The door between the rooms opened. Odette looked up to see Hrowthe step in, changed from the somber robe he'd worn earlier into a clean one of deep crimson velvet. A wide belt of lambskin sashed his waist, and on the front of it hung a small sheath from which protruded an ivory hilt carved into the shape of a serpent. A woman walked at his right, a woman in a high-collared and tight-fitting gown of black-and-gold brocade. Four hard-faced soldiers followed her, but they kept to the back near the door, barring the entrance. Odette saw their eyes drink in the sight of her lashed naked to the harp, their horror secondary to their coarse, instinctive lust.

It was the woman, however, to whom Odette's focus was drawn. Her face registered no unnatural zeal as did the priests', no bestial fascination as those of the soldiers. Hrowthe's brethren bowed to her as their leader escorted her to the dais; and Odette could not help but notice the beautiful thing draped over her right arm, some garment faced solidly with snow-white feathers.

The woman brushed the bejeweled fingers of her left hand idly through the pelt; and Odette looked into her face pleadingly, wondering if she, too, were some victim of the unholy priesthood. But as their eyes met, Odette felt a wave of staggering recognition.

"Vanda!"

Her sister looked young, as she never had in the shapeless, somber gowns she wore before the invasion of the Franks. She was regal now—beautiful, truly—and attired so exquisitely her familiar ruddy complexion took on a queenly mien. Odette had never known any who blushed so deeply as her half-sister; and she remembered how her mother would grieve, saying, *"'Tis a woeful thing for a girl to blush only for ripe and unseemly anger!"*

Vanda's mouth was quirked in the complacent caricature of a genuine smile. Odette remembered that smile, too, as she had seen it often when she would knock on Vanda's door and beg her sister to come out awhile. Vanda would pat her head and explain she was in prayer and had no time for senseless games or picking flowers.

And before shutting the door again Vanda would say, *"I suggest you do the same, dear sister, as life is precarious at best."*

How much tighter had those lips pursed when Charles Martel announced his wish that Vanda wed Thierry. How much more relaxed that day Vanda summoned

Odette to her and explained that Thierry was taking her away to Burgundy in order to stave off the discontent of their father's surviving supporters, those who might use a child of Rulf's pagan harlot as excuse to challenge Thierry's position.

But Thierry is dead, Odette thought grimly, *and she has brought me back and allowed these awful men to mock me...*

A curtain drew back somewhere deep in Odette's consciousness. She seemed to peer into a room, windowless and cramped, littered with tapestries of the most lurid, godless scenes. Images hooked and spun from thread upon thread of stringy, soured bile.

"Odette," Vanda said languidly, "you have decided to come home."

Odette's mind cleared of the disturbing image. "Please, sister, tell these men to release me!"

Hrowthe spoke contritely to his mistress. "I cannot gag her, my Lady, else it would—"

"Yes," Vanda said, "impede the task at hand." She stepped up on the dais and scrutinized the Harp, gliding her fingertips over the forepillar. "All is ready?"

The priest she'd addressed answered, "Yes, My Lady. We commence at Father Hrowthe's word."

Vanda came before Odette and her whole face contorted as Odette's hips flinched in protest against the swelling passion. She turned to Hrowthe. "My presence will not be an interference?"

"Certainly not," Hrowthe replied, "but have we need of *that*, my Lady?" He looked balefully at the pelted fabric Vanda carried. "Why not give it to one of your men to keep out in the hall?"

Vanda beamed at the garment folded over her arm. "I brought it as a gift for Odette—so she might receive illumination."

Hrowthe bowed his head. "As you wish, Vanda—you have waited long enough."

Vanda laughed deeply and, regarding Odette again, raised the garment so that the hem billowed to the floor. It was an exquisite gown entirely created of swan pelt, with a cowl of softest down.

"You see, sister, not even that knave Cu'lugh can spare you from purification."

"Lord Cu'lugh?"

"We are well acquainted, Cu'lugh and I. Did he not tell you that it was at my request he came to Athla—to fetch you back?"

Odette blinked, stunned.

"Matters necessitated more expeditious methods, however," Vanda went on, admiring the feathers. "He knows, I am confident, of your absence; and perhaps he will join us shortly, to witness that which he helped to achieve."

Odette was not convinced. "Why-why would he do that? He loves me, he has told me so."

Vanda's crimson cheeks took on a darker cast. "I have no doubt he told you what he thought best would persuade you to come by your own choice. Half-truths, deceit—God undoubtedly understands such methods from those who must enter

Sodom and Gomorrah to fight evil."

The words were wounding to hear, for Odette knew Vanda had to have known Cu'lugh to make these charges. No doubt there was some underlying grain of truth to base them on, but she was certain Vanda had perverted that truth just as her priests perverted the sanctity of sensuality. Master Cu'lugh had never lied to her, and whatever he may have neglected to acknowledge she did not doubt his vows of love and devotion. Too long had she dwelt in Midgard not to have learned to see evil when it neared...and too long in Athla not to recognize truth.

"Lord Cu'lugh's intent when he came to Athla may have been to take me away," she said, "but he loves me, Vanda. He wants me as his wife, to live with him in Athla. The boundaries of that realm would never have opened up for him were he party to this spectacle you put on. Whatever lies you used to deceive him into going, sister, they falter like the wind-blown candle against his chivalrous integrity."

Vanda clutched the gown to her breast and laughed wildly, but by the glowing white of her knuckles Odette knew it was only a façade of humor.

"They have taught you well to twist the truth as well as your foul body, haven't they? You are surely not so stupid as to believe a nobleman such as my husband's brother would actually consider wedding a whore? Why think you he accepted my hospitality? Pleaded for my kisses? Went to do my bidding? Just to wed a harlot?"

Odette was speechless a moment, for, indeed, she had not known her Master brother to Thierry. But it mattered not—she trusted him and her confidence did not falter. "And when he pleaded, Vanda, did you forget Thierry altogether...or was that accomplished with your husband's convenient passing?"

The blue seeped from Vanda's eyes, and her next guffaw hung on the air. She wrenched the cowl between the gem-clustered rings on her fingers.

"Still your heart flutters for Thierry, doesn't it! You bewitched him into coming to Burgundy, to deliver you to Athla, there to hone your depravity!"

Vanda lashed the gown by the cowl against the forepillar again and again until she was breathless. "No one can free you now, Odette! I have your mother's precious mantle—I possess your will as our father possessed the willing body of your demonic mother!"

Odette frowned and stared at the gown. "What is this? If you wish me harm, be done with it, Vanda, but cease the senseless prattle!"

"It is not prattle!" Vanda's eyes glowered as she held the garment before Odette's face, her fingernails burrowing into the feathers. "The swanmaiden's gown, Odette! I own you, and I command you now to tell me the truth of Thierry! He bedded you, did he not? And came back to harm me in your name!"

Odette shook her head. "He did not bed me, Vanda. And I know by his own words he returned here solely out of concern for your welfare."

"He came back to destroy me," Vanda spat, "so he might send for you and pompously marry you as our father wed Silfr. Speak the truth!"

"I do speak the truth." Odette looked past Vanda and saw Hrowthe standing amidst his brethren. His face alone amongst them was touched with the same pity she felt now for Vanda. "That is why you have allowed them this, sister? You believe

I seduced Thierry?"

Vanda laughed again, but the brittle sound had now lost its veneer. "As shallow as Thierry was, what could have tempted him away from *me* but for sorcery's nudge! You seduced from afar with your evil magic, determined to have what was mine, just as you always have!"

Odette stared at the garment against Vanda's breast. She did not know where her sister had come upon it, nor even if it was the thing Vanda claimed. But Vanda believed in its power even as she despised it.

"This gown you hold binds me to speak the truth? Then I declare this before you and your priests, Vanda—I never bedded with your husband. He loved you well, very well. And I have never sought to sunder or take anything given you by Charles's decree. I want nothing you possess or this land. My only wish is to return to Athla."

Vanda was panting with rage and disbelief.

"Hrowthe, compel her to speak the truth! Whatever it takes, force her!"

The priest stepped toward the dais. It seemed he struggled to hold on to his stoicism as he said, "She speaks true."

"Have you also fallen under the seduction of this vulgar brat?"

Hrowthe grimaced in a gesture reminiscent of a smile. "Vanda, you know I have touched enough human hearts to distinguish the truth from deception."

Livid resignation swept suddenly over Vanda, and the ice of her voice seared into Odette's soul. "So you have...and so I am left to believe she did not seduce my good husband. Very well. But still..." Her eyes pored over Odette. "I have known nothing but distress since your mother seduced my father—since the moment he carried that wretched creature into the home that he once shared with my mother, when he turned his Hall into a den of debauchery! And now his bastard wants nothing more than to whore herself in a lawless land, shaming and mocking me all the days to the end of my life. No, it shall not be, Odette, it shall not be."

Odette shook her head pityingly. "For this you have brought me back into your land, allow yourself to be shamed? Why, Vanda? Why can you not live your life and forget these insults that are real only in your eyes?"

Vanda did not answer save to drop the mantle to the floor. With the nail of her forefinger she traced Odette's bare stomach, scraping a light line across the flesh. She spoke most rationally to her counselor now. "How long will this rite take?"

"Only as long as necessary, My Lady."

Vanda nodded to one of the mercenaries, who turned and fetched a chair from the anteroom. As Vanda descended from the dais Hrowthe lifted the gown from the floor. Odette noticed his hands trembled as he laid it on a small table nearby. Then he stepped onto the dais and gestured to his brethren, who circled it. As they knelt on the floor Hrowthe raised his arms from his sides and closed his eyes. In a language unknown to Odette he spoke, and a murmur rose from his brothers. It grew louder and more articulate, until the sound of it was a deep and chilling chant.

Odette grew drowsy as the monotonous words echoed through the room.

Through heavy lids she saw Hrowthe step before her. He lifted her face with his fingertips; and his voice was singsong as he spoke now in the native Saxon, not to her but something unseen.

"We come before you, O Divine One, and offer to Thee this creature of sin in Thy holy name, an offering of our constant devotion, the epitome of sin most foul. Take this offering in the spirit it is given, the degradation of Evil for the uplifting of Decency, a symbol of our constancy to abstinence, of obedience to Thy will, of perfect denial of the senses that bind us all to earthly suffering. Allow the song of its mockery to resound through the depths of hell and the summits of heaven. For this is the reckoning in Thy name, Wondrous One, the symbol of the rejection of sin from Thy world and the refutation of the human love for sin. We ask Thee to remember this humble symbol of our devotion, to hold it in Thy heart as demonstration of our dedication to abide in purity until Thy deliverance from Thy most selfless sacrifice—that sacrifice delivered by the Evil Ones and endured for us, Thy ungrateful and unworthy children. This is our show of fealty to Thee, O blessed One of a Thousand Subtle Faces, Father of the righteous gods, Eternal One, Truth consummate and enduring!"

Hrowthe's invocation rattled through the spaces, and Odette felt his hands fall away. Her eyes had almost closed when she felt the phalluses move again. The pulsation did not only tease this time but undulated deeply within her stuffed orifices. Her sensations expanded, clarified, billowed along upon wave after relentless wave of manipulated passion. Her body responded irresistibly; her breasts swelled and her nipples hardened, her orifices contracted about the intrusive phalluses. Her hips were driven by the hidden stimulus, and she began to move up and down the smooth granite. Tears of anger seared her eyes, and as she blinked to let them fall she saw again the tiny serpents about her ankles. Their little heads darted back and forth in rhythm with the urgency within her.

Odette's heart surged with such violence she nearly fainted.

Inside me, there are more inside me!

Over the roar in her temples she heard Hrowthe speak. "It is done, my Lady."

He clasped her face between his cold, heartless hands and, bowing her chin forward, kissed her brow as if in blessing.

"Repudiate this deceiving sin, Odette. It is not too late yet for redemption."

Odette threw her head back and implored the heavens through the orb. *"Goddess, help me!"*

The priest sighed softly and rejoined the ranks of his brethren, kneeling and bowing his head in the same way. Vanda watched from her seat, her poise so cool it was like looking at a carved image of a woman but for the glow of her cobalt eyes.

The snakes inside Odette ceased their manipulations. She sighed and fell against the forepillar. Her hands and feet wrested against the snakes with what strength the priests had not already stolen. But it was useless—the serpents were as inelastic as bands of steel.

Her rest was short-lived before the tone of the priests' chant changed. Deeper still droned the monotonous invocation, and the serpents within resumed their torment. Her whole body shuddered as they danced and wriggled inside her. A tide of mounting pleasure seeped into her mind, pressing all wit from her thoughts. She felt carried away now on that tide of pernicious sensation, toward an end in a darkness alien and anxious.

Her body was hardly her own as she rode the phalluses. Closing her eyes to the dreadful audience she tried to swim the suffocating waves. Through the crest she glimpsed Cu'lugh; she tried to reach out to him, to clasp those steady hands she knew so well. But another surge billowed her up again and the murky waters drowned out the handsome image.

Through the flood a rich note struck the air. The silver strings trembled between the pegs and a deep vibration passed through the soundboard and the neck of the Harp. The music whipped Odette's desires from the clasp of her soul so that she felt like a figurehead lashed to the bow of a ship plunging through the heavy night sea. Her discharged soul sensed no good will in the waters but rather monsters lying in wait just beneath the surface, monsters that no man or woman was meant to set eyes on.

The serpents' tease stopped once more. Odette sought for Cu'lugh again and, thinking she saw him, jumped into his embrace. She sat atop his lap and covered his mouth with kisses. He entered her then, thrusting her hips forward with such force she knew her very womb would shatter if he continued. Leaping up, she tried to turn and run away, but his hands stuck fast about her wrists and he shoved her down again, penetrating now not just her sex but her anus as well.

Above Odette's moans and tears of grief the serpents perceived the coaxing summons of the priests, and with the next moan that splintered from her throat the Harp strings strummed. The rich resonance wafted to the ceiling and caressed the glassy orb. A veil of light rippled across its surface, through its core, to burst out again into the leaden haze that saturated the ethers. The skies quivered, but the roused haze scraped against them again and again until lightning jarred the night. A peal of thunder blared and pounded angrily upon the nether steps of the heavens.

Chapter Thirty-Eight

s steward in the house of a Freyjan priestess, Eryan had been expected to act with integrity and the will and determination to defend those who depended upon him. These things had he accomplished; it was the more subtle virtues he'd taken for granted, the attitudes that blessed every aspect of Athlan life. In these he'd failed miserably, putting his obsession for Odette before his regard for her happiness and education. He could never expect to find a position as steward again, and it would take bravery to bear the inevitable social consequences that waited for him on his return.

He had not considered his intentions when he broached the dead forest; he only wanted to find Odette and spare Helrose. But as the lifeless cold bit into his flesh and the unuttered warnings from an uncertain source pressed into his consciousness, he knew this action would test his bravery.

There was no snow to hush even the most careful footfall over the dead, crisped bramble that covered the ground, and so he relied on the talents that had once earned him a place in Larsarian's personal fellowship. From toe to heel he tread, envisioning his skull filled with an ether lighter than the air about him, taking a breath with each descent of his toes, exhaling only with the light crush of his heels. And when he looked he did not scan for texture or obstacle, but followed where his senses bade the safest turn and path lay.

It did not take long for him to know he wasn't alone. Watchers—sentries, he determined from their myopic thoughts, protectors of this land. He honed in on their emotions, what there were of them, and let his mind seep into the primal drive that gave rise to them. There the consciousnesses of the sentries unfolded, and behind some temporal allegiance that had sent them out to this forest lay an agenda callous and consuming. They all shared it, every one, the clinging of despair to comfort despair, the cravenly resignation to an order of birth and suffering and death that compelled them into a fantasy of martyrdom.

They were not human, but neither were they true beings in any form Eryan had ever had dealings with before. Their intelligences were laden with memories that were not unique in any one of them and hoarded wisdom they'd not learnt from their own experiences. All the more horrific, these beings despaired of the very emotions that had formed and were part of the memories, especially the sweeter ones, those things that had offered consolation to the lives of those from whom they had been pilfered. The memories and the wisdom these creatures craved, and yet not strictly for their personal gain.

Self-made abominations, Eryan assessed. He felt how they had already sucked the life from the flora and extinguished every mortal creature that had once taken shelter in the region. As he contemplated their nature he slowly realized what they were. He had heard tales of them, but never had he thought to encounter one. Tales almost unbelievable to him, of creatures who denied life and gave up their mortal essence to feed off the blood of the living in order to bring about eventual annihilation of all the world. It made him shiver even now to think anyone, even a mortal, could so abhor life and all its opportunities.

Eryan closed his eyes and willed himself invisible to them, making his heart beat so slowly they could not detect it were they even elementals. There were dozens of them in the forest, lying in wait like shadows against tree and rock, able to slink over the ground alongside the silhouettes of the thick, nettled vines trailing everywhere. Under the clouded twilight most would not have heard their soundless, inhuman movements; but as he passed by one and then the next he knew they detected something astir. Their unearthly eyes inspected, but only for human form; and their ears sought the pumping of mortal blood. They hissed and groveled and bit the air with their fangs, tasting for some hint to give them advantage. At length he eluded them and emerged from the murdered forest into a clearing that opened onto a great valley.

He sped across the dead grass here, toward the city cradled in the valley. He stopped one time and surveyed it with the same trained eyes. A rotted field lay off one quadrant of the city; at another was a burnt grove. Not half the size of Athla, the city was deafeningly quiet, and the few lights he scried came from torches that flanked the streets. In the center of the city was a long, graceful hall, the only building that showed no sign of neglect. Not a single candle illuminated any of the windows of the place, though he saw a faint line of smoke escaping from a chimney.

His vision delved deeper, and he made out the silhouettes of patrols on the streets. No one else did he see, but when his vision shifted a little he found a great tower that rose above all the other structures and buildings. The pinnacle was set with a magnificent orb. It reminded him of a cold scepter lording over all else.

Suddenly, lightning seared the skies and struck the orb. Splinters of green flashed over its surface. When these passed he saw the thing had been splintered by the heavenly flash. The building was intact, but he wondered if it could survive a second assault to its pinnacle. And there would be a next time, he was sure, judging by the baleful lights clashing just over the brooding clouds.

He had no time to worry over it, for the next moment something flew past him so closely it scraped his cheek. He was still invisible, but he sensed it stop in flight just ahead. It pivoted and moved toward him, a mist of shade and muck; and it scrounged the earth for his presence. The beings had been summoned to the city, something to do with their insatiable thirst to vindicate their despair. Eryan did not try to understand this now, but held his breath and dared not even blink his unseen eyes. When at last he felt the mist roll over his face he sped through it with great, bounding strides. Over the suffering grass he continued, not looking back, for it had encountered him once, and once was all it needed to recognize him.

It spied him at length just as he reached one of the watchtowers on the fence that enclosed the city. A guard there perceived something and grasped a small torch. The man's eyes scoured the field but he did not see Eryan.

Eryan circled the fence until he reached the front gates, where the planks were considerably shorter than the timbers of the fence. As he leaped and caught the top of the portal it rattled with his weight. One of the two mortal sentries turned at the sound and blamed the other for the disturbance as Eryan clamored over.

The rainless storm raged over the city, but he could no longer feel the beings from the forest. He wondered if it had been the entire host that had rushed for the city, for he did not savor the idea of Helrose's encountering them. Of course, she had the warriors and her own worthy skills to aid her, while Odette was helpless amongst these mortals and their undead allies.

He walked to the lawn beside the hall—or what had once been a lawn before every blade of grass withered and crumbled on its root. He inhaled deeply, analyzing every scent he picked up until at last, through all the dead and foul things that tainted the air, he picked up on a familiar, sweet bouquet. It led him through the streets, past the men and houses filled with darkness and trembling drunkards, until he stood before the doors of the baubled tower.

Voices jarred the walls of the building, and even the mercenaries who passed regarded it with unease. He watched as one of them ascended the steps and pounded on the door. The man talked briefly with another warrior, and when the curious one turned away Eryan saw his unease had cratered his brow with outright dread. As the door closed Eryan crept about the building to look for a place to enter unheard.

As he came around the eastern side he felt the beings again. They were very close, but the unnatural quaking of the building and the scent of Odette made it impossible to identify exactly where they were. He scaled the walls with his eyes and shut out the disquiet emanating from within, and as he turned the corner he saw them.

Kneeling all together in the parched sod was an army's-worth of these beings, chanting in rhythm with the sound from behind the walls. The ground shook so violently here he could see cracks open and gape beneath their knees. The sterile dirt sifted into the catacombs below as the creatures floated from place to place just enough to resettle and continue their chanting.

Eryan knew he stood little chance to escape their wrath if he stayed here, and so he moved slowly back round to the front of the building. As he turned the corner a scream cut through the chanting from inside.

Eryan's skin pelted with sweat—he knew to whom that very feminine scream belonged. He ran to the doors and knocked the guard aside so roughly the man nearly tumbled over, then after righting himself, the man gaped at the doors as they seemed to open by themselves.

The guard yelled for whomever it was to halt. Eryan saw the glint of a blade and drew his sword. Pivoting, he gashed the man's forearm just above the drawing hand. The guard shuddered, glancing about skittishly; and Eryan swung his weapon again. With the hilt he struck the guard's chest, knocking him back. A second blow to the shoulder and the man fell, and when he started to rise Eryan battered his helmet with his hilt until the brim was ground securely over the guard's face.

With a growl the man dug at the brim but not before Eryan leaped forward and brought a knee into his collarbone. The man sank to his back with another growl. Quickly, Eryan drew the dagger from the guard's belt and flung it into the street. He turned to the door again. Just as his free hand touched the wood something clapped his shoulders and thighs at once.

He lurched back so quickly he did not even feel the hand that grappled the sword from his grasp. Face-forward he was tossed. His chin crashed onto the steps, and his face felt as if it had been split. Blinding pain flared through his skull as he was turned over and kicked from every side. Boots battered into his ribs, his thighs, the back and sides of his head. Each desperate move he made to roll away was met by another kick to the head. Through a film of blood and wavering black dots he saw a nest of faces huddled over him. Savagely child-like oval faces and great black eyes all, their mouths leered with a perverse satisfaction.

From nearby the guard roared, "You beasts—you dare!"

The Darkling holding Eryan's sword turned from the others and pitched the weapon to the guard's feet. Eryan thought he recognized the dusky features, though he wasn't sure.

"Protect your Mistress," The Darkling sneered.

The guard blinked as if doubting his own eyes. Eryan knew the man had no idea what they were doing as they seemingly attacked the air and so just sat, stupefied, as they lifted something up and stalked off in a clustered mass.

As they carried Eryan down the street the leader jogged past those who held his shoulders. His grin was like a tight black thread across his lovely face as he trotted beside Eryan, buffeting his head now and then and squeezing the shattered jaw with his small hand. The pain was so intense Eryan felt close to fainting, but somehow he held on to consciousness and tried to suppress his angry protest against his vile captors as they conveyed him to the end of the street like a corpse. There they let his head drag against the hard ground, raking his skull over stones and stepping on his sweeping hair so that his neck felt close to snapping.

"You are not beyond our reckoning, Athlan," chortled the malevolent leader.

From the city they took him to the charred trunks of the grove he'd seen before. They raised him high and laid him on a wide trunk. Two stooped at either side of his head, other countless arms holding him down by his limbs. The leader knelt at the crown of his head and propped it forward so that his small fingers pressed into the broken bones of Eryan's jaw. His smile was a perverse caricature of a child's, his large eyes wide and lit with all the black, seething, irrational hatred of mankind that made even the Blodsaukers' agendas inconsequential by comparison.

He spat in Eryan's face—a vile spittle, though the sting of it Eryan hardly noticed.

"Athlans are never beyond our reckoning!"

His eyes were perfect pools of endless evil, and in their mirror-like depths Eryan watched each rise and plunge of the Darkling daggers as they cleaved away his flesh and organs. But his eyes turned to the clouds retreating far above, to the ray of brown that oozed through a tear in the heavens; and when he heard a woman's soft call nearby he feared it was Helrose discovered or Odette brought to watch his destruction.

He turned his face now from his killers and saw a figure emerge from the diseased earth. Her ebony skin glistened; she was the only lovely thing on the whole blasted landscape. The long webs of Her shining, kinky hair clothed Her ample form, and Her dewy brown eyes beckoned as She came forward. Taking his hand, She helped him rise and led him from the body lying ravaged on the trunk. Down a chasm aglow with encouraging light they descended, deep inside the womb of Her abused world, far from the descendants of Chaos. Only then did he notice She was weeping. He embraced her, covered Her trembling mouth with his own...and for a time forgot all else in the sweet, reciprocating desire he had waited for all his long, long life.

* * *

In his prison cavern on the Gulf of Black Grief, Loki struggled in the enchanted chains that had bound him for eons unknown. His brethren had penetrated the ethers of Midgard from the porous spaces that surrounded the little domain where the Harp had been at last constructed; and now they danced throughout the cavern passages, flits of black flames through the layered shadows.

Sigyn's husband ignored their encouragement—for what were they who had abandoned him when the Asagardian host had first imprisoned him? But Sigyn knew that these brothers and sisters of his possessed no concept of loyalty or shame; and though there was no worry they would demand to share in the bounty of human stock, there was the risk that once Loki was freed and had cleansed the world of all he resented he would regress into that chaotic state from whence he had been birthed.

Sigyn clung to one chilled wall, glad to be forgotten in the restive winds that blew up from the entryway down deep in the bowels of the cavern. She hated these chaotic beings; she had not even considered the rumors true, those things whispered so contemptuously by Loki's first wife. Pure evil these beings were, assured that their unholy cause was pious and perfect and all else evil that had to be eliminated.

She looked upon the two haggard figures kneeling beside her husband's prison bed. Bloodless fanatics, as evil in their stupid, selective blindness as the priests of the other religions her husband had sired. But these she loathed most—for their utter hypocrisy and the pride they veiled their eyes with to ignore that hypocrisy. They carried a secret, each and every one, but dared never share it amongst themselves. For that secret to be laid open would surely crush the Blodsaukers' righteousness.

She had often wondered if, individually, they truly believed they were the only one to feed their Lord? Sigyn had overheard their conversations with her husband time and again, knew how he avowed that the offering to him was but a small thing, a show of fealty, a trifling act that allowed him to see as the proud gods see…

Yes, Loki saw with their blood. He drained the stolen memories and caches of knowledge carried in that blood. She had no doubt he took much more enthusiasm in feeding than the morose and pious Blodsaukers did when they gorged on their victims. He convinced them they had made an offering—but she had heard his laughter after they departed, and she had endured the cruel echo drifting painfully slow through the long, empty passageways.

She had never pitied them, for they had willingly given up hope, hungrily embraced submission to misery. They yearned for the end of the existence of life so ripe with possibilities. The new world as Loki had devised they sought—a world without suffering or pain or regret, no interdependence, no obligations to others. A world cold, sterile, replete with all a coward dreamed of.

And yet, despite everything, Sigyn had attempted to warn them all of her husband's true nature. Not out of disloyalty, but to corrupt this foul game he had initiated. It had gone on too long. The humanity he had once donned in order to cover the evil of his heritage was shredding to mere threads by his endless intervention in human affairs—from politics to religion to tribal associations. Why, with the power of the twice-taken blood that imparted the gift of All-seeing, Loki had spied into the dreams of mere children and worked upon their forming consciousnesses, seeding suspicion and bigotry, cynicism and outrageous fears.

She knew these things; she had warned them all—and most fervently of all her beloved. But she was a god's child and so he dismissed her words. They all dismissed her, just as certain sects of Loki's contrived religions dismissed femininity as evil.

But no one shall name thee evil, Loki had assured Sigyn. Yet she could not hold faith in that as she looked out and saw so many intelligent nations embrace the lies his sects perpetuated. How could he control what his fanatics would assume when the day arrived that true chivalry was dead forever? To spite Freyja's rejection of that single bid for Her love Loki had vowed to see the day She was no more, and human women could expect no deference for their tender gender. For this end alone Loki had modeled his religions, puppeteered governments, influenced leaders.

Already his propaganda had been taken up and used as the cornerstones of infant nations and used as a banner to quell the older ones. In their fear of their gods' expectations men believed they were masters of their societies without need of the counsel of the feminine principle and that to lust for them and to protect them made them weak, vulnerable. The ancient balance was teetering, and Loki would not be content until the whole world was rattled beyond redemption, thrown into utter chaos.

Sigyn could not imagine a world stripped of femininity, but she knew that time was fast approaching. A world once beautiful, tranquil in its balance. But Freyja had spurned Loki's love, and it mattered not that She had allowed him to come to Her palace and introduced him to Her handmaidens. It was there Sigyn had first laid eyes on him. She had loved him almost at once, so faceted in his brooding darkness he was. She had not cared that her companions were repulsed by him; Freyja had addressed their quandaries by declaring this foreign male had possibilities.

Sigyn agreed. She starved for his touch night and day, and when at length he came upon her in the sacred gardens and carried her away there was no thought to protest. Sigyn was sure Freyja would wish her only happiness, as She wished it for all Her daughters and followers.

Sigyn was never to have confirmation, though, for soon enough Loki had played his last trick upon the patient gods. He was dealt justice for the death of innocent Baldur and brought here to this lonesome cavern. They had asked her to let them take her back to her Mistress, but she declined. She still perceived his possibilities and would not give up on him.

But her beloved's tricks and games had continued even as he lay bound to the stones, and now his ultimate triumph loomed. The daughters of Man suffered— and their men, too—from his perversions of truth. The Blodsaukers had labored long to bring about Ragnarok, believing the lies of their destiny Loki had given. Even those fools on their knees beside him still envisioned shedding their stolen blood on the roots of Yggdrasil.

For the love of humanity, can they not glimpse through the deceit? Each one knows how Loki betrays his own codes regarding their bloodtaking—why do they never speak up! How can they play into this spurious rite he has contrived knowing his hypocrisy and their own?

The wind screamed about her ankles now, blowing up the gossamer skirts of her gown, chilling her so relentlessly that her long reddish hair fell like strands of ice over her arms. And in the hoarfrost wind she heard a voice she had thought lost to her ears forever.

They are as the indolent civilization they helped to nurture, Sigyn, and see only that which they wish to see.

"Ah, Freyja," Sigyn whispered. "I have failed you and betrayed the Great Balance! My love is as foolish as the visions of these corrupted souls!"

Sigyn wept as she had not wept in ages, mindless before the ravages of the wind that threatened to slam her against the stones walls. Somber, hopeless music flooded up from Midgard, its resonance distressing the watchful god, Heimdallr. He mounted his graceful steed and rode now warily the edges and borders of the Bifrost Bridge. Was that a quaver upon Yggdrasil's roots He heard? His hand tapped the sheath of his horn, listening, waiting with anxious breath. Guardian of the stairwell to the heavens, he was patient always. He would not yet trumpet the call to battle, lest the sound shatter the veil between earth and the bridge.

The blast would alert the gods—all the good gods ever worshipped by the lips of mortal mankind. Once they were summoned the vibration of their trooping ethereal feet would shatter forever the chains that bound the evil one and unhinge the door that had barred so long Loki's kindred.

The god heard Urtha, trembling with despair under the coverlet of Her beloved realm. She cried out to Her brothers and sisters to muffle the quaking of the World Tree, to silence the Harp, to summon defenders from amongst mankind She had sheltered and sustained for generations.

Sigyn knew no men would come, no army of truly righteous hearts. The wind roared through the distant entrance and pinned her against the wall. It cycloned about Loki's punishment bed and sucked one of the Blodsaukers into its core; and as he was carried down the winding passageways the lights of chaos reveled about Loki, cheering in their baneful drone. The other Blodsauker hunkered over the floor, and his wail was as terrified as any true man's.

From another vault in the cavern Loki's son Fenrir howled, and Sigyn knew his jowls foamed in anticipation of his own deliverance. She sickened—for that mindless perversion of life she had never dared feed, not as she had Loki, whom she loved, not in all these ages since she had made her choice.

She looked at her husband, and for once took no pleasure in his naked limbs and rope-taut sinews. He tested the chains, his beautiful face beaming. She saw that several of the enchanted links were cracked, and the dwarf-wrought bolts that held them into the stones were loosened in their sockets. She raised her eyes to the ledge above Loki's head, to the adder that had been chained there by one of his enemies so its falling venom would forever drip upon his brow and exacerbate his suffering. Never before had it slept, but now it lay in a loose coil with its head as still as the stone that supported it.

A glint below the serpent caught her eye. The virulent liquid swished in the goblet banded to the stone between the animal and Loki. She had fastened the chalice there herself to protect her husband.

His deep blue eyes flashed at her, but not even the soft lust in them cheered her. Soon, he would be free…and she had no doubt of the nature of the emotions that would blind him to all else. No relief to be liberated, no rush to take her in his arms. Revenge and revenge again, entirely. Never through all the dark ages had he once faced himself. He had summoned the Blodsaukers using the magics still retained in the brain of the material form he'd assumed. His chaotic kindred had never truly left him, no, for they reveled in his ambitions and aided him in their own way. And when triumph was realized, he would not know contentment or gratitude but only the madness of absolute power.

Sigyn closed her eyes to his beckoning mouth, pretending not to have heard his summons. She could not approach him again, not after the years upon years of her pleading and reasoning ignored. He would have her stand by his side to watch evil triumph and quell the world. No, that she could not do.

If I were pure mortal perhaps I would have taken comfort in the Blodsauker's resignation of hope!

She felt faint with the weariness of it all and backed away from the reach of Loki's voice.

The darkness opened into a blaze of golden light, stabbing her eyes. She heard the silvery music from those gleaming white corridors where once she had played and skipped as a handmaiden of Freyja. Billows of sweet incense rolled before her eyes and the lilt of bells wafted through the window from the gardens outside the palace. Two great gilded doors opened before her, and she walked into the high-vaulted room she remembered—the Merriment Hall, where she and her companions had entertained the host of the honored fallen.

But the sound of the drums and cymbals and other instruments, the talk of the warriors and the sighs and giggles of the dancers were still. The only sound was that of weeping; and there upon Her throne sat Freyja, surrounded by Her begotten daughters the Valkyries—even those long wedded, Brunhilde and Golda and Silfr. Their husbands paced the Hall with their weapons drawn and their brows heavy and expectant.

Silfr knelt at the pale and perfect feet and buried her face in her Mother's lap. Few times had Sigyn heard such a mournful lament; and looking up, she saw tears flow from Freyja's iridescent eyes.

She commanded Her unmarried daughters to don their gleaming helmets and shining breast shields of bronze and silver, to go and mount their white chargers and be ready to ride before the fallen host and their respective gods.

"You must succor the holy cause, give them mettle for all that which they are about to defend."

Sigyn's heart sank; and yet, in the despair that embraced her, she felt the irony of it all. Another lie disproved, one of those that had fed Loki's endurance. *At the first note of the Harp,* he had claimed, *the Vanir Lady shall abandon all—gods and men and women, the very earth where Her worship flourished—and in Her cowardice retreat hastily to the haven of a new universe.*

Sigyn's eyes opened again, and she felt drunk with elation. Loki still eyed her, his own jubilation heightening the color of his exquisitely sculpted cheeks, and though she could not hear his words she answered his summons now.

The Blodsauker that remained had taken shelter behind Loki's bed. He watched Sigyn approach, suspiciously, jealously. But neither his evil regard nor the pricks of the dancing chaotic lights nor even the velocity of the maddened wind held sway over her. For she was Freyja's servant still, and it was all the lessons learned from Her that had imbued her handmaiden with the courage that had sustained her all these years. She would meet the end without the hatred that consumed the one she loved; and she would see to it death came soon, for Loki had chosen triumph over the fulfillment of his possibilities.

He was able to reach a hand beyond the stifling chains, and at his smile she folded her fingers over his.

"It comes," he whispered, "a few more plucks of the strings and triumph is mine! Then shall we eat at the table of the vanquished, my love, and thrive on the fruits of those who have served my truth!"

"Your truth, my lord?" she mused and brushed a strand of black hair flying about his brilliant blue eyes. "Yes, all your labors now come to fruition. Freyja and all the followers of lust and happiness and hope will soon meet destruction. All will be righted, yes—all punished for the insult She gave you."

He frowned and squeezed her hand, crushing the bones warningly. "As it should be, as is meet and fair. Reproach me not, Sigyn, for leading mankind as mankind sought to be led. The majority of them have already come to despise the old ways of chivalry and pleasure—I have only sought to achieve completely that which they wished. It was Providence that She beguiled and spurned me, for without that rejection how would I have sought to destroy the wickedness She begat in the world?"

"Lies within lies, deception to cover the truth, truth corrupted with fantasy as it is uttered!" Sigyn bent and kissed his brow even as his grip grew crueler. "And you would have me at your side to enjoy the fruits of victory?"

"You know so, my wife."

She laughed and saw no trace left of love or lust in his regard, as if he had tired of playing with the emotions of gods and men altogether.

"You are coming home, my love," she said, "and you shall forget I was ever your wife, just as your kindred forgets that disloyalty which tempted you into passions and human form. For it is the outcome that is important, is it not?"

"You mock me!" With but his hand, Loki had the strength of the gods he had emulated so long and pushed her aside so that she slammed into the stone wall. "You will perish then, Sigyn—as you wish it."

She pulled herself to feet and listened to the baying of Fenrir down the corridors.

"As I wish it."

She saw all rationality blink from Loki's eyes. The dark lights swarmed about him madly, and they began to swell and take shapes and form and texture. Sigyn heard their voices, vapid and ghastly, bowed in hatred like anchors of sunken ships. As they gathered solidity the Blodsauker drew away into the shadows beyond, clutching the walls as he backed away; and Sigyn saw in his lifeless and marveling eyes his horror at understanding at last the nature of his Lord.

Loki snorted and pressed her hand tighter. The bones popped, and she swooned from the pain. Outside, the black waves crashed against the cavern while the ice of Bifrost began to crack under the strain of an invasive melody.

Chapter Thirty-Nine

he forest was a maze of unseen trees and great nettled vines, and were it not for Helrose's innate sense of direction Cu'lugh knew they could have never made their way out until morning. The small company had brought three torches, but the flames seemed determined to die. The lightning that whipped the skies over the canopy provided only the stingiest of illumination.

Helrose led the way, with Edred just behind her. The Mistress gave no indication she was aware of the baneful shadow that seemed to infuse every breath Cu'lugh took. He concentrated on the trail she followed, ignoring the voice inside that questioned why no night birds warbled from the trees or why the storm they heard overhead did not shake the branches of the dead trunks.

The unnatural vines grew everywhere, vines that had not been here when he'd broached the forest before. As wide as a horse's back and high as a man's knee, the vines and sharp nettles were impervious to their blades. Helrose had a sense of where the newer growths issued; and over these, where the nettles were smaller, they were able to cross.

Even so, at one point Cu'lugh heard a sharp intake of air behind him. Turning, he saw Prage crouching with his hands over his right ankle. The boy had stumbled somehow, and one of the nettles had sliced through the leather of his boot. Blood spurted from the severed artery. Cu'lugh signaled the others with a grunt.

Helrose came and knelt beside the boy, and Cu'lugh saw his complexion seemed bruised and his eyes looked unfocused. The Mistress, too, noticed; she lifted Prage's face and peered into his eyes and with her fingers pulled back his lips and studied them.

"Do you feel ill?"

"Y-yes, Mistress."

"'Tis not surprising," said Helrose. "The sap of this vine is malignant. I want you to sit so I may bind the wound." He obeyed, and Edred removed the boot while Helrose chiseled a clump of dead moss from the ground with her sickle knife. This she pressed over the wound, binding it with the cord from the end of her braid.

"I have no ointment, but you did not get enough poison to die." She cinched the strip with an unexpected jerk that made the boy flinch.

Helrose stroked Prage's cheek while Edred helped him pull the boot back on. "We are fortunate," she said to them all, "that whatever evil infested and made this forest barren is now gone. Were it still about the mere scent of his blood would have drawn them like starved leeches."

The giant Amnoc helped Prage to his feet. "I do not remember seeing vines like these in Midgard before," he muttered.

"Nor were they here last time I passed through," agreed Cu'lugh. "And they are strange, unlike anything I have seen, though the forest was dead even then."

Helrose sighed. "It matters not. As I said, we are fortunate. I suggest we make it out of here before the return of whatever uses this as wards. Are you well enough to walk, Prage?"

The boy nodded and took up his quiver from the ground, though it was evident he was in pain.

"Help him, Amnoc," Helrose bade, and they followed her through the maze of rotting timber, taking greater care now to scrutinize the tangles of vines. Forever it seemed they meandered through the dead forest, and several times only Helrose's perceptions saved them from walking into a vine-draped stone wall or one of the numerous sinkholes that wounded the forest floor. Just as Cu'lugh feared his dwindling torch was about to snuff Helrose led them across a wide matting of pine-needled sod and stepped out at last from the forest confines. They looked out across a great arid waste that was once a fecund valley.

Cu'lugh felt uneasy as he contemplated the city. He had never set eyes upon it at night from such a distance, for under Vanda's hospitality he had kept to her Hall at night except to venture out for the occasional conversation and rare drink with her mercenaries. He had not grasped the full desolation of the fief, nor even how imposing the watchtowers looked looming over the squalid serf compounds. The streets were unnaturally dark, and the inhospitable fence encompassed the entire city.

From his vantage point Cu'lugh studied the watchtowers, the only locations well lit. Two guards he counted in the lofts of each of these posts. The streets were empty, though here and there he saw a twinkling of light through the shutters of artisans' abodes. The tall oaken front gates looked quiet but for the sentry or two there.

He scanned the breadth of the Hall until he spotted what he was certain were the windows of Vanda's apartments. For all her frugal expectations of her servants, she was accustomed to keeping her own rooms bright with candles and lamps before retiring, which usually wasn't until the wee hours of the morn. Only the most fragile of light escaped her windows now—a single candle, two at most.

Where would she be this night when the thunder booms like falling titans over the valley?

His squinting eyes pored over the city's roofs. Something moved through the streets, a hazy moving mist so low and thick it was like watching a dragon's dying breath. Only the property surrounding the Temple of the priests was clear. There, a sickly light spilled from the sparse windows and cracks between the planks. He stared, frowning—a low murmur carried across the valley. Dreary, monotonous, it was almost hypnotizing; and in a moment he forgot everything but the sense that his blood was freezing in his veins.

A flash of unearthly green light licked the sky just above the orbed pinnacle, breaking Cu'lugh's trance. He looked away just as thunder drummed, and at once his blood flowed normally again.

Sylreth whistled softly. "Did you see that, Mistress?"

Helrose came up beside them. Cu'lugh followed her wary eyes; and now he, too, saw what the enchanting drone had steered him from—a great fissure in the haze directly above the Temple. Light, radiant but as diseased as the lightning just before, poured through this fissure. Squinting again, Cu'lugh noted how the hues of it drenched the Temple—embracing it almost—so that the now splintered orb took on the look of weathered copper.

"What is it?" asked Yori, his long fingers stretching tensely over the hilt of his sword, "A dragon?"

Helrose shook her head slowly. "No dragon, Yori. Listen…you can hear the summons, and the music."

Cu'lugh caught his breath—yes, over the chanting and under the heavenly grumble was what sounded like the strum of harp strings. The resonance was low and climbing in pitch ever so slowly; and yet it built, and the stale air roiled with the weaving pitch. Even the ground under their feet vibrated.

Helrose sensed this, too; and kneeling, she ran her palm across the dead grass. "Mother Urtha quivers and the roots of Yggdrasil respond to Her fright."

"But why?" wondered Sylreth uneasily. "There is naught that has the power to dampen the blithe essence of that most fecund Goddess."

"Only the suffering of one of Her folk."

Cu'lugh's breast pounded urgently. "It is Odette you speak of? Urtha is a goddess, as is Freyja—and I am aware of Odette's heritage." He hesitated a moment, not wanting to think what he feared most, let alone speak it. "Have they killed my Odette?"

Helrose exhaled slowly, and he saw that her eyes were moist. "I do not know, Lord Cu'lugh, but I sense with all the training of my years that mortal and immortal alike now stand at the mercy of that which has sired and cultivated all blasphemy."

* * *

A bolt of lightning struck the orb again; and Hrowthe, opening his eyes, saw the crystal glow with a thousand warped hues of green. He stood from the ranks of the genuflecting Blodsaukers and saw that the serpents were performing their task most adequately—the girl's skin was suffused, bathed in perspiration, and her hips strained on the phalluses. For all her seeming humanity her vocal cords could not deny her heritage; and as she writhed and undulated her moans plucked the strings. All was going as smoothly as expected.

But Hrowthe, for all the rigid care with which he and the brotherhood had prepared and even as the girl approached rapture in this self-mocking, indecorous method they'd created, sensed something more had happened.

Vanda watched, silent with anticipation. Even her trusted guards, bestial men that they were, did not move to interfere. The focus of the priests was so intent that the chant they sang now seemed as powerful an entity as the very voice that strummed the Harp strings. The united sounds had transcended the rite to become a single potent entity of the Lord.

Possessed of wisdom and knowledge the eons had provided, Hrowthe now stood a world away from the ignorant youth who had once wept in ecstasy to utter the name of the pagan gods—and yet something challenged his self-assurance, disturbing his sense of equilibrium. It hinted that the ceremony had gone awry, or that he was close to a revelation he had overlooked.

Why do I quiver like an ignorant savage?

Another whip of lightning struck the dwarven crystal high above. The brethren did not stir from their induced trance, but Hrowthe peered up and saw that the orb had evaporated. Surely, an auspicious sign that God was pleased.

He stepped to the dais once more and peered up into the girl's face. Such torment, such indignity—she had never expected this mockery of the wickedness she served. He felt a pang of pity for her—after all, she was half-human in nature, totally human by virtue of her ignorance to her true identity. As deluded as any other man or woman born to this world, no more sinful than any other man or woman nurtured by false platitudes. No more wicked than other women corrupted by the laziness taught by the Freyjan principles. Were he not trained in the appropriate expression of emotions he could have been tempted to release her from the wicked bondage, to sink his teeth into her coursing veins and drain the life-force from her, relieve her of the delusions that gave her the ability to stir the strings as no chaste woman could.

But sympathy was useless without constructive application, and when that day came he and his brothers tore open their veins on the roots of Yggdrasil then no more would young girls lose their souls in servitude to falsehoods.

Hrowthe bowed his head and experienced an unexpected and complete serenity in the hollows of his bowels, the serenity he'd awaited all the days since his initiation, the one thing he'd never thought himself worthy of achieving—liberty from hunger.

O Eternal One, he prayed, *I have done well, then? Praise be Thy name for acknowledging my humble endeavors to fight against shameful hunger. I look forward to the continued endeavor to please Thee and live rightly and abstemiously so that my wise-blood shall be worthy when we are called to make the sacrifice of sacrifices. O holy God of a Thousand Faces, praise be Thy purpose!*

If tears could have formed in his gelatinous eyes they would have fallen, and he knew a moment's passion to embrace the girl, to kiss her brow and tell her it was all for good and soon finished. The serpents had just stilled within her again, and her wide green eyes flew open. She stared at him as one dreaming awake, and he wondered what ill forms she saw and if she blamed Vanda for stealing her away from the land of sin. Hrowthe smiled sadly and begged Loki silently to have mercy on her young soul.

And bless Lady Vanda all her days for her worthy self-liberation from the lies that have corrupted her sister!

His entire body shivered in harmony with the chant and the music, and never had he known such tranquillity…and as he raised his head a great force bore down on him. It threw him forward so that his face struck the Harp. He raised and looked about, feeling how his sharp upper canines had sliced into his bloodless tongue.

He blinked. Surely, it was an apparition he saw, no more. His mother, lovely and young as she'd still been at death. His father, garbed in his winter vestments and holding his shield and stave. His granddam, Bora. His childhood companions. And, standing with Hrowthe's young sister, a young boy he wasn't sure he knew, with a complexion like snow and roses and hair resplendent as the sun. The boy's arm was wrapped protectively about Hrowthe's sister; and as his sad eyes settled upon Odette, Hrowthe's feeling of knowing the boy deepened.

Apparition, leave me!

Hrowthe passed a hand before the little company, invoking the words that banished the dead as well as glamour. They remained solidly before him, and the figure that appeared as his father spoke in a voice only Hrowthe could hear.

"You deny our souls as you have denied your duty as a man. All these years you have set to force the world to yield its humanity because you cannot face your own."

Hrowthe refused to play into the apparition's game; and again he performed the gesture of banishment.

"See, my son, the reward of your cowardly work."

The apparition's face lifted, the head craned on its neck; and likewise the others, and their eyes stared heavenward.

Hrowthe gritted his teeth, was again performing the gesture when he saw Vanda's disapproving stare. The apparitions did not vanish, not even waver. Warily, he followed their gaze.

Through the hole the orb had occupied he could see a dark, gaping maw in the sky. From the center of it seeped a reddish ink that devoured the lightning that shot toward it. A sharp outline seemed to take shape there, like the craggy edges of a mountain. Framing this entire scene the stars pulled back from the indigo heavens and the foot of an arch tumbled through the maw. Aglow with colors of every conceivable shade, the arch fell down through the torn spire of the Temple.

Hrowthe did not want to look, but his eyes were bound to a specter advancing down the arch upon a great beige charger. The beast's hooves thundered over the rainbow, and the rider had to wield much coaxing to convince it to enter the Temple. It pawed the curve fitfully, its fearsome whinny muting the chords of the Harp. The rider's yellow hair showered over his brawny shoulders; and his eyes, one of blue and one of brown, scrutinized the scene within the sanctuary. Suddenly, he looked back toward the expanding maw and bared his teeth angrily. Hrowthe glanced, and saw the inky core was opening.

The horse's eyes soaked in the light of the sanctuary's torches; and as it fidgeted impatiently against its bridle, Hrowthe caught sight of the rider's belt and chilled to see swinging from it a great horn.

He shuddered and turned away. He could not put any faith in this vision;

Heimdallr was, as all the gods were, but a false spirit. Hrowthe looked to his brothers again and saw they still had not stirred from their chant, nor the guards from their positions. Vanda glared at the playing Harp, bored and angry now, while her entranced sister rode on under the serpents' relentless prompting.

Hrowthe gathered his will and gestured again, but the apparitions remained. Now it was the young boy who spoke.

"You have betrayed your humanity, Hrowthe, and you have betrayed yourself. Do you truly believe that you alone have fed Loki the blood he swore was to be used to awaken Yggdrasil?"

Hrowthe's calm seemed to slip away. "You are but enchantments, all! No power here save the will of God Eternal governs my will!"

"The Eternal is both male and female, Hrowthe, and as there is but one Goddess, so there is but one God. And His respective countenances are more multifold than even the collectively ugly, baneful faces of Loki's invented ones."

The boy's chin lifted imposingly, and he kissed the tender cheek of the vision at his arm—and as he raised his vivid eyes heavenward again Hrowthe at last recognized him. *Arduin!* The Blodsauker's mouth quivered, and he felt the old blood that clung to his arteries and veins roused. It was needed now, to provide him vitality to nourish the mortality that had reclaimed his body.

He dared not look at Heimdallr again, and he could not bear his folk to look upon his chastisement. He heard again the wail of the storm outside and, looking up, saw the ink had spread like a bleeding leviathan over the Temple. An assembly of the chaotic horde now clustered about the torn roof, their vile, hateful shapes and forms beyond the scope of human description. Hrowthe knew he could not look upon them long without going mad. His eyes shifted and what had looked like a mountain was growing solid. It pressed against the Bifrost Bridge, denting the arch and jostling the mount of the God.

Hrowthe heard himself whisper some shocked protest. Heimdallr's eyes flashed to the Harp and His fair head turned to one side as if He were listening for something...

* * *

The lightning bolt blasted down near the watchtower, just missing the base and striking the door of the women's compound. The two mercenaries who had guarded the door lay amongst the smoking cinders; and the women, summoned from their hovels by the noise, stared at the line of flames still burning down the charred frame of the door. The bodies were scorched beyond recognition.

The sentries from the tower and the guards from the men's' compound gathered quickly. They argued like hysterical children, their long-unspoken suspicions aroused by the portent. At length it was decided one of them would go fetch the captain of the street sentries. Those who remained were uneasy. Suddenly, another bolt pummeled down from the sky, striking the ground amidst the lot of them. One was vaporized instantly, and his companions regarded each other only a second before they fled down the winding street.

Blichilde stood in the doorway of her hovel, eyeing the dreadful maw that continued to yawn over the skies and the shadowy figures that hovered in the entranceway of the celestial cavern as they emerged from the maw's dark core. This was more than a natural whimsy of the elements, of that she was certain. And as much as she respected the elements, she had felt painfully ill since the rainless storm began.

More painful, however, was the sense she had failed.

Irmina came running out of the darkness, breathless and excited. Blichilde clasped the girl's trembling hands and rubbed them between her own.

"Was it a strike against a bush?"

"No, my lady—the gods have destroyed the doorway of this prison and vanquished the guards! The others are releasing the men, come with me and I shall lead you out!"

Blichilde was silent; she could not speak of her failure, the terrible, hopeless quest upon which she'd sent her only child.

"Where do you think we may go, Irmina? If by miracle the street sentries have, indeed, taken shelter the forest is yet infected with Vanda's priests!"

"Does it matter? We have a chance to reclaim our lives! To remain here is to spurn that chance; and—who knows?—perhaps, even in this land where the impotent god holds reign, there is still some task the gods have for us. Surely they would not wish us to just lie down and give up hope."

Blichilde smiled ruefully. It was true, she could not argue. "Have the others taken anything to wield as weapons?"

"Yes," Irmina nodded. "And I have in my shelter a hoe and a spade. Let us go now and fetch them, the others wait for us."

"They waited?" For all her doubts the sweet tidings took some of the ache from Blichilde's diseased and weary bones. The women would not one by one be facing the hands of inhumane men as each and every one of them had when Vanda ordered them escorted into the compound. If they had to confront the mercenaries they would so at the sides of the menfolk. And the mercenaries, she had no doubt, were pressed with more immediate concerns than to expect an uprising of sick and dying prisoners. She also had no doubt they could not succeed, not in their condition—but death met in the struggle for freedom was much more preferable than dying in the compound.

"Certainly, I will accompany you."

Irmina pressed Blichilde's hand to her face and led her away. In her own hovel she handed Blichilde the hoe as she took the heavier spade, and together they marched out to the place where the doors that had confined them were now but rubble. The small group of eager Saxon pagans huddled in silent waiting. The men, their farming tools held ready, surrounded the women and the group left the compounds behind and walked into the street. The wind was sweeping down violently from the broaching maw, and the street was lifeless but for a few mercenaries running for shelter. The artisans kept behind the shutters of their homes. Only a single person did they meet along the way, one of the Lombards. His besotted face was swollen and livid, and the wine spilled from the jug he swilled. He stared stupidly at the approaching cluster of Saxons, and the mercenaries could not hear him when his accusative voice rang out.

"You—what have you done with my boy?"

Blichilde regarded the wicked man sharply, knowing this the one Arduin had tried to keep secret. But just as the gods had revealed the nature of Vanda's priests, so had they revealed the nature of Galbos. This mockery of manliness had abused and starved Arduin into perversities against his nature. The beast deserved no reply.

"Kill him," she said.

Bald Wehsson, with his hatchet, and Galmor, carrying a cart shaft, broke from the group. Galbos spewed a mouthful of the wine at them.

"Filthy Saxons, get back before I summon the guards!"

But it was the last the Lombard was to speak before his skull caved beneath the fall of the tools.

Chapter Forty

he breath of Heimdallr fell on the nape of Hrowthe's neck, and the anger of it seeped through his warming flesh. It quickened the blood in his expanding veins and renewing organs, filling him with the sensation of warmth that most mortals took for granted.

The God seemed uncaring what the priest did. Instead, He hushed His impatient steed and with His eyes half-closed waited for the next pluck of the Harp's strings. His great fingers tapped across the ridges of the readied horn at His hip.

But the ghosts had faded out of this realm, back to whatever Hrowthe had avoided so long. He took a breath, a true breath, and smelled the blood and foul odor of himself and his kind that tainted the air. It permeated the Temple just as it had the environment outside, fouling the earth and sickening every living creature. He was very aware of the ritual knife hanging from a cord about his waist, a thing of brutality; and he blanched with shame.

The others had not roused yet from the trance of their chanting, were unaware of the movement at the door. But Hrowthe watched as it opened, and one of Vanda's guards spoke with another mercenary. He saw the frustration and fear in their faces. Vanda rose and joined them, and her eyes bulged and her pretty lips formed an angry circle. The tidings could not be advantageous.

But Hrowthe could not worry over that—he had to stop the sacrifice before the torturous Harp and its little nightmare workers brought Odette to orgasm and her cries opened the unseen barrier that kept Midgard safe from Loki's reach.

The serpents had stilled again, and the strum of the last chords played echoed on the air. Odette's eyes were closed as Hrowthe drew a chain from the folds of his robe, and her breathing sounded erratic. He looked at the amulet hanging from the chain—a single ruby, enchanted so as to direct and sharpen the power of his will over unearthly creatures such as these serpents. With it he would have to lull the serpents, make them withdraw their hold.

Vanda knew of the amulet, and he would have to act with discretion. As quietly as possible he sang the rune of parting over the stone, relying on his brethren's ecstasy to keep them from seeing.

A hand struck his arm, nails clawed through his sleeve into his flesh. Vanda, moving with a stealth to match that of the Blodsaukers, grabbed the chain from his hand.

"What is this? You promised this sacrifice would be completed only at her death! Even I can see she is not dead yet."

Hrowthe sucked the moisture that dappled the inside of his mouth. "I feel it is enough," he said, hoping she would be content with the familiar assured tone.

But Vanda's face was livid. "You shall leave her here, Hrowthe. The Darklings have promised more than God's favor."

Hrowthe half-smiled. "The Darklings? Ah, I feared you might have been seduced by their lies. But tell me, sweet child, why do you listen to them when your wellbeing has always been most important to me? I was mistaken before—this is enough, there is no need for this girl to die."

He took her hand and sought to wriggle the chain loose from her grasp. Vanda grunted, her face scarlet.

"I was more than happy to help you and your brethren gather all you needed for this sacrifice, this show of fealty to your God. But you promised her death, and I warrant you realize not what bounties await when she dies! Ah, I have been so foolish to account you with having such knowledge. The Darklings are right, my friend—you are arrogant fools all! God does not want your paltry show of fealty, Hrowthe. He wants the end of this world!"

Hrowthe's heart beat anxiously as he tried to think of a way to get the amulet from her.

"I know, Vanda," he answered. He could not afford this conversation, but he was grieved by her childish rage, the grasping he should have helped quell instead of nurturing in his indifference. "I understand now. We are nothing but His pawns. He promised us an abstemious world free of emotions, and for that we have worked. Perhaps that is what He works for, too, to rejoice in our stupidity. He is as false as I, who suckled Him so He might steal the thoughts of mortal men and pry into their affairs. I fed Him, I confess it before my brethren and you. He fed of that reserve of generational insights and memories, suckled that which He committed us to reserve for His holy cause. It is a lie, my dearest child, all of it. He needs the sacrifice of a Valkyrie's child to instigate the commencement of Ragnarok."

The anger seemed to ebb in Vanda's cheeks, and she regarded him tenderly. "You delivered to God what He truly seeks," she said. "Does it matter how He worked to enlist your help?"

Hrowthe felt pain in his eyes, as if someone were trying to tear open a healed wound; and by the astonishment on Vanda's face he knew tears had welled in them. She blinked rapidly and inhaled, as if trying to ignore what she saw, and laid a hand on his arm.

"Come away, now, Father. Let us see finished what must be."

"No. You understand, do you not? It is of consequence, a testimony, Vanda, that we Blodsaukers have been wrong all these long generations. To resent life so much we compelled ourselves to ruin it just to usher in a world without feeling, without pleasure, without love. At least in our wrongs we believed what we did was for the benefit of mankind. Loki has no such delusions. He hates the true divine Grace from which mankind fell, and He will do all in His power to see it is never embraced again."

"I cannot let you do this to us, Hrowthe—not to me or mankind or the world.

What comes must come."

Hrowthe tried to focus his thoughts, touch her motives; but the skill was difficult to wield. All the things he had so easily understood as one of the undead now slid frustratingly out of his grasp.

"I do not know what bargain you made with the Darklings, Vanda, but I urge you to understand that the end of everything is coming!"

He raised his hands to her shoulders and pushed her back with such suddenness she had no time to catch herself, raking the amulet from her grasp as she fell from the dais before the brethren. One of the priests now wakened, his frown deep and guarded. The guards had seen, as well, and rushed forward. One of them lifted Vanda as the others drew their weapons. She screamed with outrage at the man's touch.

"I do not need a man's help!" She glowered at Hrowthe and gouged the air with a quaking forefinger.

"Remove him!"

The men advanced on the dais, but the next moment the still-chanting brethren rose from their knees to creep up on the guards and pull them away. Vanda's hands clenched into trembling white fists against her ribs.

"You fools! Do you not hear? Hrowthe undertakes to stop the ritual!"

They released the dazed warriors and turned in unison. Their eyes grew glassy, and Vanda felt their minds probe her thoughts. They must have found her words were true, for they did not advance further. Vanda heard their unspoken conversation, although she could not understand the ancient language. They were concerned that the Harp's strings were stilled on their pegs.

"The sacrifice has gone on long enough," Hrowthe insisted staunchly. "It is time to take the swanmaiden down. I want you to escort Lady Vanda and her guards out."

Hrowthe turned again to the Harp and saw the reason the strings had stopped playing. The serpents seemed uncertain as to their order of behavior. Those at Odette's ankles had loosened their hold enough that her knees buckled, and the pair at her wrists was beginning to unknot themselves. He began the song of release again, forcing all his will into his voice as once he had forced it into the amulet. By the relaxation of her hips he knew that those within her were drawing back into the phalluses. A few more recitations of the command and they would relent altogether.

The guards glanced warily from one priest to another, hesitant but ready to take hold of them. But Vanda commanded them to hold their ground and faced the brethren angrily.

"We wish not to harm you," one of them assured her; but as his long pale hands reached for her, she suddenly roared and grasped his lifeless shoulders and spun him about with such force that the guards gasped.

"Look," she shrieked in his ear. "Hrowthe sets to undo all Loki has commanded you! Did God not tell you to see this sacrifice through?"

The Blodsauker listened to Hrowthe's chant and said in his listless voice, "Perhaps Father Hrowthe has fallen under an enchantment."

"Hesitate not," she urged. "For the love of dear God, fail not! Remove the poor wretch at once."

As Hrowthe reached toward the forepillar with the amulet in his hand their chant recharged, deeper and more determined than before. One moved forward with the alacrity of a swooping falcon to the edge of the dais. His arms wrapped about Hrowthe's ankles, and he jerked on them. Hrowthe teetered; the swanmaiden looked on with dread. With a second sound pull the Blodsauker brought Hrowthe down. The others folded in about the dais and together they hauled him to the floor. He hissed at them, argued, twisted and beat at the rigid hands that clutched his limbs.

They forced him to his feet, and Vanda saw in astonishment there was luster in his grey hair and sweat on his brow. As he twisted and bucked against their hold his flesh flushed with exertion.

"See the damage wrought by the enchantment of the swanmaiden!"

They looked as Vanda bade, and for the first time she saw naked human fear in her counselor's face. A paleness akin to it glowed in the hardened features of the others. It was time to take a firm hold over them before the ritual was a complete waste.

"Take the amulet and the dagger of ritual from him and give him over to my guards. They will bind him securely so the swanmaiden's influence can do no further damage."

Hrowthe set his feet against the floor as the guards wrenched the chained ruby from his grasp and confiscated the dagger from the folds of his robes, and turned this over to the priests. He commanded the brethren not to touch him or use the ritual dagger. But his efforts were futile, and the mercenaries dragged him toward the door.

His cry of warning was a feeble croak. "We have been lied to, brothers! What we do will bring Ragnarok!"

When the guards had removed him Vanda lifted the swan mantle from the table where it lay and turned to the Blodsaukers, who were bickering—or so it seemed—in their dead language.

"Brothers," she said, holding the mantle up before them, "this is the cause of your High Priest's possession. I would suggest we do not give in to the dissension the swanmaiden has attempted to engender but continue the ceremony. Is there one amongst you who knows the commands to bind the serpents?"

One with features that once must have been handsome and swarthy spoke up. "I do, lady."

Vanda inclined her head humbly. "Please take over, brother. I, too, have done my share to insure the completion of this honorable occasion."

The others murmured their assent, and the priest bowed his head and approached the dais. He recited the binding spell as the others began to chant again. Vanda watched as the little serpents were driven back to their stations, and Odette's eyes teared. How exquisite her misery was to Vanda, how properly fitting. In shameless, eager undulations the whore's daughter rode the phalluses, raising her hips as far as she could before plunging back to the smooth base. The guttural moans she made awakened the Harp once more; and its disturbing, primordial music filled the air again.

Three of the guards returned; and, satisfied, Vanda slipped into the anteroom. On the same bed where Odette had been prepared earlier now lay Hrowthe, his thin wrists fettered as hers had been, his mouth stuffed with a dirty rag. His eyes were closed, and it appeared his breathing was much labored. Vanda went to the remaining guard, who stood looking out the slightly opened entrance doors.

"Have there arrived further reports?"

"No, my Lady. I assume the street sentries have righted the situation."

"Very well," she said, her mind on other things, and went to the brazier at the back of the room. Fire still burned in the brass basin, low but blue with intense heat.

She lifted the mantle over the coals, admiring for just a moment the skilled handiwork, the pure, stainless feathers.

"Such a waste of craft and beauty for but a garment of sin," she mused aloud.

"A lucid example of beauty's falsehood."

Vanda looked to the back corridor, where Loic stood with his arms crossed over his breast. He was dressed in an overcoat and breeches of exquisite brown velvet and boots of the finest seal leather. With his windblown black hair and unearthly large eyes he was more beautiful than most women. But she had no desire for him. Her triumph over the carnal passions was as solid as her ambitions.

No male shall bar my course again.

He came toward her, savoring, it seemed, the feel of the trembling floor under his feet. As he eyed Hrowthe she saw now the blood curdled over the fabric of his pants and the boots. Even in his thick eyebrows it was matted.

"No, never again shall you bow to the wishes of a man, Vanda. Your counselor now at last understands the innate foolhardiness of his breed, that which made them the perfect tools to give Loki what He needed. I hope Hrowthe lives long enough to understand that their weaknesses are as unacceptable to the everlasting guardians of the universe as those of mankind. The world of corruption is about to be cleansed, Vanda, and your invaluable contribution shall not be overlooked. Those humans who accept the righteous way instead of death will have you as an impeccable example of righteous conduct."

"I do regret Hrowthe had to receive illumination so soon. I would have liked for it to have been him to thrust the dagger into the harlot's womb. But another has taken his place."

"You should return now," Loic said. "The melody rapidly reaches its climax."

Vanda nodded and held the mantle over the flames again and released it this time. As it fell upon the coals a thick smoke resplendent with the aroma of flowers billowed up. She coughed once and stepped back, watching until the garment was consumed entirely. A scream issued from the inner chamber—feral, forlorn, bringing to Vanda's mind an animal being butchered alive.

Odette feels the last connection to her mother burn from existence. The lovely thought made her anxious to return to the sanctuary.

"I will not have cravens disturbing the priests," she told the guard. "Lord Loic is free to remain, but let no one else enter."

The man inclined his head, and as she turned to rejoin the priests she saw Loic pace toward the corridor again. She understood his repugnance to watch the indecent writhing of Odette upon the Harp, but it was one spectacle she would not forego.

As she entered the inner chamber, the floor and walls were quaking harder than before; and as she took her seat again several pieces of wood fell from the winding stairs above to strike the floor about the Harp. The priests did not pause in their chant; and the new leader stood at the foot of the dais with his head lifted heavenward, his face aglow with zealous passion.

Chapter Forty-One

A band of stunted, thin figures staggered hurriedly across the valley. A single member of their number glanced back once, maybe twice, as if expecting notice from over the high fence of the city. There were injured amongst the company, supported or carried along by the others. But even when the lightning scorched the ground right before their course the band faltered but a few moments, then proceeded on.

Cu'lugh climbed from the chasm where he and the others were hidden when he saw the chain ladder that had fallen or been dropped from the watchtower. The tower seemed empty, and this swinging access enticed.

"Come on," he said and motioned for the Athlans to spread out. They surveyed the high fence warily, and he understood their reluctance.

"Those who left," Edred whispered. "They didn't look like guards. Have you any idea who they were?"

"I do not know, but were there priest sentries amongst them we would have been discovered already." Cu'lugh looked at Helrose, but there was not enough light to read her expression. "Odette was not with them?"

"No. She…she is beyond these walls."

"We can continue on to the cleft in the wall I know, if it hasn't been altered already," Cu'lugh said and gestured at the chain, "or we can climb this and get in."

"Isn't it a little convenient?" asked Prage, massaging his ankle. "It may be we have been detected somehow, and those who came down are out to find us. Who knows what is atop that tower."

Edred stepped forward and looked the tower over keenly. "There is a way to know." He drew an arrow from his quiver and readied it in his bow. "Go, press yourselves against the foot of the tower, their blind spot."

The others stole to the tower while Prage, with his bow set, watched for danger from the field. The High Archer backed a ways and aimed toward the lookout. The arrow shot out, stabbing the air silently, striking wood by the cushioned sound it made. Moments later Edred aimed a second arrow, this time shooting it a little to the left of the first. The thick, neat sound of its strike confirmed that again he'd struck wood. He looked the shelter over cautiously and set another arrow against string and bow.

With another round of thunder barreling overhead Cu'lugh could hear nothing. His heartbeat accelerated, and he sensed conflict drawing near. He wondered if these warriors from peaceful Athla had faced enough enemies that their bodies instinctively prepared for this, if their minds blocked out, as his now did, everything but the objective. He concentrated on his internal warrior's compass; and in his mind's eye he saw Odette—not as he feared to find her, but as he was determined to return her, kneeling before him with her golden hair cascading over her back, her upturned face bright and smiling.

She was the only thing in life that made him complete. For her his desires had matured, and never again would he lust for fleeting gains. Not all the adventures in the world or every last harem of beautiful women, or even the gold he knew hoarded away in Vanda's caches could fill him with the joy he'd found with Odette. She was the complement to his soul, and beyond his wrath against those who had stolen her away and beyond even his own guilt he knew she had found completion in him as well.

Edred beckoned them to him with a toss of his head.

"There is no movement, no sign of life up there."

Cu'lugh eyed the ladder. "Then I say we make use of this godsend quickly. Are all agreed?"

At the others' concurrence he sheathed his sword and took out his dagger. It was a small blade, but he could hold the handle between his teeth and still manage the links. Amnoc followed him; the others fell in behind the mighty warrior. Edred brought up the rear, scanning the ground and the shelter both for sign of movement.

As Cu'lugh pulled his right leg into the lookout he could see into the city beyond. When the others were safely inside he returned the dagger and went to the edge and surveyed the rooftops and the streets. The air was visibly denser below, and even from the lookout Cu'lugh detected a hint of the same stench they'd encountered in the forest. Little light beaconed from the dwelling places of the mercenaries and artisans, and the Hall stood dark and silent. The ill light still oozed from the priests' Temple, and suspended directly over its roof he saw a black haze.

"Fire," said Helrose, and Cu'lugh had to force his eyes to look where she pointed—the watchtower between the serfs' compounds. The doors were gone, and grey smoke billowed up from a fire smoldering on the ground.

"Almost died down," he said. He glanced to the street just below and squeezed his hilt automatically. A line of bodies lay there, just crumpled shapes in the darkness; but the armor and mail told what they had been in life.

"Utmost silence," he warned and, with his sword arm ready, led the others down from the tower.

They encountered no one on the descent, and as they stepped onto the street Cu'lugh heard a moan from among the bodies. He crept toward the sound and looked down in the face of a man, mutilated—crushed, actually—so his features were hardly distinguishable. His helmet had rolled away into the moldy grass.

"Help…"

Cu'lugh went on to the one who had called out. He recognized the man, one of those whose faults discredited the very word *mercenary*. His arms were broken, his throat slashed by a dull blade.

Cu'lugh knelt at the man's side, and he gripped Cu'lugh's forearm.

"Who has done this, Bleiz?"

The man's voice was a gurgle, "L-Lord Cu'lugh…it wasss…the Saxons…they have es-scaped."

Helrose knelt beside Cu'lugh and tugged the man's bloodstained shirt with her hands. "Where is your Ladyship's sister, the Lady Odette?"

With much effort the man moved his head to look at her. His pained eyes softened. "Withhh the dragon w-woman, poor g-girl. Ahh, but you are a f-fine sight. My likely f-fortune that I cannot ssstay…"

His lungs rattled and his head fell back on the dust, and when Helrose lifted it Cu'lugh saw the life had left the man.

Helrose released the body. "A horrid death!"

"Do not feel too sympathetic," Cu'lugh said, rising. "These men offered themselves into Vanda's service and remained freely, knowing the depth of her cruelty and greed."

"Dragon woman?" Helrose wondered.

Cu'lugh drew his hand from the dead man. "Vanda."

"I believe those who did this were Odette's people," she continued, "and that they have suffered much at the hands of this dragon woman."

"The serfs?" Cu'lugh felt the blood leave his face. There was no use in pretending he had been anything but indifferent to how Vanda had treated her own people. For all his high-handed arguing against her priests' over-piety and of the basic wrongs committed against pagan peoples, he'd done nothing to stand up for the Saxons. His concern had been to bed their sovereign and to glean what he could from her gratitude.

"Yes, a situation I should have tried to remedy."

He suppressed his guilt with some effort, knowing it would only interfere with the matter at hand. He looked down the streets and saw an alley he remembered wound in its tight course to the street where stood the Temple. He gathered the others aside and pointed with his sword.

"If it is, indeed, the Temple that Odette has been taken to, that is our route. It winds through the part of the city where is housed the grain and, once, the timber. The smokehouses are there, the old breweries. Thanks to Vanda's use of her cellars to store the supply of food that enters the city, it is the least-guarded of the avenues; and it exits on the street that faces the Temple. The mercenary guards make the occasional round; and for that, Edred, you should be our lead. Sylreth, at our back."

The path was crooked, the buildings close-standing; and without Helrose's senses to guide the way their pace was much slower than through the forest. The ground was tormented, furrowed and cluttered with bones of poorly disposed-of animals. But Edred was a stealthy walker, taking pains to test the ground with his feet as he led the others. Cu'lugh tried to calm the urgent knot in his chest, knowing it would be foolish to run on ahead in wild abandon.

It seemed they walked for a lifetime through the narrow way. Nothing stirred here but the squall of the occasional plummeting gale. No rats dodged between the buildings, not even near a butcher's door that had been left, curiously, ajar, as if the building had outlived its purpose. At length an ebbing of the darkness appeared up ahead.

"Hold back," Edred whispered and crept on alone. Cu'lugh could see his back silhouetted against the lantern-lights from the street. For a short time Edred surveyed the situation, counting, Cu'lugh knew, the number of armed men beyond.

At last he padded back with his assessment. "I saw the Temple down the other side of the street, across from a square. Eight men stand outside its door, probably a dozen more gathered out in the street. There seems to be a concern over some of their confederates."

"The ones brought down below the watchtower, yes," Cu'lugh replied. It could be some time before those out in the street went to check on their companions, for through experience he knew Vanda expected to be consulted about any predicament that arose in her kingdom, whether of consequence or trivial. Something told him that the mercenaries dared not approach her now.

As he weighed whether it was best to wait and see if these sentries spread out he looked at Helrose, and an idea formed in his mind. It was not one he was comfortable with, but it seemed the simplest and most likely to dupe Vanda's men.

"I will lead now," he whispered to the others, "and when we enter the square, your weapons must be down."

Amnoc grunted. "Is this not rash?"

"Hear me out. Helrose, you will be at my side, and you men follow my lead. Unless a weapon is drawn by one of Vanda's men, show no aggression, not till I give the signal."

Amnoc grunted again, but it was Edred who gripped Cu'lugh's arm.

"I am not comfortable having my Lady enter the square without front protection, Cu'lugh. You had best be certain of your strategy."

"I am certain this is the wisest course, Edred, as long as we control our offense. This is, of course, if Mistress Helrose is willing."

He could see her white teeth behind her sober smile. "I did not come for nothing, Lord Cu'lugh. Please, share your strategy."

* * *

A disruption had compelled the serpents away—that much Odette comprehended, though she had not felt their withdrawal. Her mind had separated from her body; she knew but did not feel the torment the priests regulated. She could not even say if their snakes had withdrawn entirely or just rested in order to prolong the build-up of pleasure before the final release. Only with much concentration could she open her eyes, and then she was not certain whether what she saw was real or some baneful vision brought on by the combination of magic and physical torture.

For a time she drifted between visions. The young boy who had spoken to her in the vision in Athla came to stand before her. The inconsolable sadness in his beautiful eyes made her want to weep.

She thought she saw Lord Eryan. He walked along an ice road through a deep chasm in the earth, his arm wrapped protectively over the shoulders of a comely young dark woman. As the two of them drew to the end of the road they stood before a wrought iron-barred portal. A frightful woman, the one who had watched over the infants in that long-ago vision, stood on the other side. A great key she held in one hand; and she bent now and with her bluish lips kissed the tousled fair head of the boy, who had joined her.

The dark young woman took hold of the bars, weeping to look upon the boy.

"'Tis too soon, dear Lord, too soon!"

The boy kissed her knuckles; and suddenly his countenance changed, swiftly, from that of a small boy to a bronze-skinned warrior, ferocious of face and lusty-jawed, naked but for a loincloth and sandals. A moment later he changed again, appearing now in a simple robe of undyed cloth, a lengthy beard upon his face and having great almond-shaped eyes. In the sweep of a moment he transformed again into a handsome youth with olive skin and long-flowing raven locks.

Again and again he rebirthed himself, each time taking a new countenance. Yet, Odette knew that with each respective form the emanating persona remained constant.

"But it is this banishment of all hope the mortal world has embraced," he said, appearing now as a tall, robed figure as black of skin as Eryan's companion. He kissed her knuckles a second time, his lips lingering a moment. "They would see me not as I have come to them, but as they wish to remember me."

His face lifted, again the flaxen-haired child's. "Seek they the nourishment of the stainless fruit when they have grafted the very vine. Soon the gate opens, and I shall appear, just as they have expected so long. But they cannot see me, for willingly have they allowed the ancient enemy to blind their eyes, accepting his guises in pretense of me, Thy divine lover. Their own proud will blinds them when I walk amongst them, whether as Baldur or the Bee-king, as Osiris or Krishna, Dionysus or Manitou or the foreseeing Quetzalcoatl. Yea, I even came and departed as the Nazarene carpenter, he whose words have been corrupted by the followers of the false disciples; and they deny me as always before. In my every avatar I shall battle the pretender, and I shall die under the blade of the willfully damned.

"Shower Thy mercy upon mankind, O beloved Faces of my Wife, for when the ancient enemy has eaten its fill and consumed the last spark of humanity from the dying shells of those who have stayed loyal to evil, their souls shall tarry in the mists of the world they help to destroy. They shall know then the depths of treachery consummate and long to turn themselves from the face of those who misled them, who come now to drive Thy essence from the world. For unless it be a secret of the Eternal not revealed to me, I must die again, without rebirth here in this world.

"From the comfort in Hela's court I must depart and say farewell to the solace She extends to all, even soldiers filled with cowardice. Here I have dined at the table of the damned, to teach them wisdom and brotherhood before entering a new womb. But many times now have you birthed me, and I find these souls unrelenting in their mortal stubbornness. Most all have chosen to ignore the lessons during the in-between, and as a whole they have rejected the joys natural to their own race. It is gone, the time for hope in their world. Mankind covers its own eyes and dares blind itself lest it see me for what I am.

"Thus I give you my final blessing. And when you arrive in that next universe to which you must soon retreat to find shelter embrace the Eternal One, my Father, and She, Your Essence, most passionately; and know I will again be delivered to Thee and by Thee. In the guise of goddess You sometimes forget—such is the fate when we are wearied by ungrateful children. But then again in that sweet time we shall pursue our pleasures and aspire to teach pleasure and love to that race we will beget. This is the inescapable truth the enemy can never destroy. As they forever seek to devour that which begat them, never can they know satisfaction. In contempt of the will they pretend not to possess they will themselves unto infinite misery, and for their proud contrariness to help themselves seek to make all others disciples to their misery.

"Your grief is my wound, Beloved One; your joy, my nourishment. So bind with the thread of sentiment these truths and carry them deep within Thy essence, as these truths shall provide You solace when to the next world You flee. They shall comfort you when comes Thy twin, Thy brother and Thy husband to sire me and all Thy lovely sisters once more."

The monstrous lady began to sob uncontrollably. "Cruel, sweet farewell, beloved One. But must you resign hope as if it were already decided?"

The boy grew into to a man again, lean and amber of eye; and he gathered her into his sinewy arms.

"Forgive my perceptions, Comforting queen, that I cannot hear the voice of Fate. But the Farewell music already cleaves the boundary between gods and men, and Heimdallr lifts Gjallarhorn to our lips!"

The ghastly one nodded, sobbing; and Odette saw her lift the heavy key to the lock. The other threw her head back and screamed. All faded from Odette's sight, but she heard a distant voice through the gathering numbness of her consciousness. Arms slipped over her shoulders and a cheek nuzzled her own, and the skin of it was ripe with the scent of water lilies and the musk of lovemaking.

"Odette, awaken!"

Another time Odette would have been alert at once to the sound of her mother's voice, but the numbness was edging over the threshold of Death's cold embrace.

"Daughter, time is drawing close to our Mother's end. But you can turn it back, for you have mantled yourself, won the grace of power by self-acceptance."

Odette saw a flickering light in the darkness. The light wavered, opened into the flower-caressed fields of Athla. The gilded turrets loomed gently over the streets where the pedestrians went about their daily business and pleasures. Lovers embraced on the open lawns and children ran happily in the streets. A novice priestess, her buttocks reddened and glowing in the sunlight, hung from the public thrashing bars, trying to hide her blushing face from the street sentry who stood admiring her.

"Look here, Odette—hear the sweet refrains of liberation and put away the words of the ill."

Torpid mists shrouded the beautiful Athla. A mirror bulged from the filthy air. Odette peered into it and saw herself, a little girl again, standing before her fosterling mother Irene, a privileged noblewoman with a wealthy estate garbed in her rough masculine garments, her grey hair cropped dramatically over her ears. She demanded Odette wear such garments, but Odette loathed the balloon-sleeved tunic and trousers of stiff linen, the pair of shabby leather shoes Irene had taken from the paltry estate of her dead gardener.

Odette heard herself utter the question she'd spoken then, when only newly arrived to her fosterlings' home and still innocent of the repercussions for questioning Irene.

"Might I not wear a gown, madam? Even the coarsest of servant's gowns would I prefer to the garments of men."

She watched Irene strike her across the face with her open hand, sharpened little nails scraping her cheek.

"I am the mistress of this land, Odette. Never have I tolerated the trespass of weakling and vain women, nor shall I now. If for one moment you think to seduce my serving men or good husband, I demand you leave this house and these lands and run to the woodlands beyond where may you rut with the unseemly beasts!"

Odette had been too frightened to argue, and she had worn the manly garb and done all the manly chores demanded of her. Still, Irene had never been satisfied and criticized her daily, relentlessly, month after dreary month, her vehemence countered only by Bierns's depraved overtures; so that it was not long before Odette feared she might, indeed, have lost her own soul to evil.

"But you knew better," Silfr said gently. The reflection disappeared, and the clouds began to dissipate. "And found your own vindication, your own true self in Athla. Would you now lose yourself again to the fantasy of the corrupt?"

In tight swirling layers the mist completely digested itself. And then she saw Lord Cu'lugh—his stout, masculine limbs naked in the moonlight sprawling over the bed they had shared in the inn room. He lay beside her as she slept, skimming his fingertips over her stomach, her nipples; and his eyes were agleam with unshed tears. She heard him whisper a prayer of thanksgiving to his Celtic gods, in gratitude for leading him to this, his love...

"Take the heritage which is yours by right of choice, Odette!"

Odette understood at last—and it was her own will that banished the shades of deception once and for all. She felt her throat first, so parched it cracked as she halted the next moan already rising to her lips. The crud that glued her lashes cracked as her eyes opened. The stimulation of the phalluses and the evil serpents she refused to think about, not even the skipping of her pounding heart. She was cold from the sweat that sheathed her flesh, and her muscles cramped. She struggled against it all, concentrating on the image of Cu'lugh and all those she loved in Athla and all those precious things taught, and directed her thoughts into a single coherent desire.

The pores of her skin widened and inflamed, like molten fire rising to touch the porous cavities of the earth's surface. Her organs seized and then spasmed, and the internal reconfiguration of her bones was so painful the pulsating lungs in her chest stopped.

As she battled for air the Harp responded to the last sound she'd made. A chorus of somber notes waved across the strings. Odette's blurring vision lifted just as the sound of the notes pealed upward, blasting the ceiling open. The high stairs were sucked loose from their bolts and inhaled by the inky ethers above. The timbers clinging to the blown ceiling curled back like broken fingers over the silver-plated roof. In the frightful black space that loomed just over the Temple a smell of ancient waste and restless bitterness wafted thickly from the prison cavern.

She feared her understanding had come too late, for even as she screamed from the shifting muscles and bone, the transforming flesh and organs, the serpents worked their evil magic and elicited another unintentional moan from her shifting throat, all too human…

* * *

The inhospitable weather was working on the temperament of all. Piers knew the men under his command outside the Temple were gripped with uncertainty and fear and that they resented that fear. When suddenly a band of men emerged from a nearby alley it took all his self-confidence to cow them into staying the aggression their unwanted trepidation inspired.

As captain of the street sentries, Piers was acquainted with Cu'lugh. They had shared a draught or two before Cu'lugh set off on the quest for Vanda's sister. His return at just this moment was certainly unexpected, even for one as headstrong as the Frank, and especially on such a night as this. And why had not the men at the front gate reported his entrance into the city? No matter—his companions offered no threat, and as for the woman under Cu'lugh's arm, her beauty was a most welcome sight.

"Lord Cu'lugh," he said as they advanced. "We were not expecting you."

Cu'lugh grimaced. "Not a hospitable night for any. This city is like the dead. I feared to bring her Ladyship's sister through the usual routes from the entrance gates."

Piers frowned. "The Ladyship's sister? But the dark elves have already returned her."

Lord Cu'lugh's face darkened, and he snatched the arm of the woman and pressed her toward Piers. Her eyes lowered and her arms folded nervously over her breast.

"I have faced the wilds of an uncivilized realm but to face the treachery of the Darklings? Ah, so they tell you it is the sister they brought? Take me to her Ladyship at once!"

"She has issued a warning that she is not to be disturbed. Besides…" Piers glanced at Cu'lugh's companions. "...we were informed you journeyed alone."

"These brave men have accompanied me from Athla to safeguard our precious burden."

"From Athla?" Piers had never believed it was truly to the legendary realm that Lord Thierry had taken the old chieftain's daughter; and now, seeing Cu'lugh's nod of affirmation, he was even more apprehensive.

"Lady Vanda cannot be disturbed," he repeated, "but I can have her informed you have returned."

Cu'lugh studied the Temple beyond. "Is that where she is? I must see her without delay if my Lady is to be spared from this Darkling ruse!"

Piers contemplated the situation. He did not know the Darklings well enough to attest to their schemes, but from his brief exchanges with them he knew they were not to be trusted. It might well explain the unearthly change of weather if the girl they'd brought was one of their own...and now she was in the Temple with the pious priests and her Ladyship.

What the priests were doing he had not been told, but he was not stupid—something had drawn this ill havoc. All the Darklings but their leader had disappeared, and the priests gathered behind the temple were too immersed in chanting to suspect an attack if it came. Piers had more integrity than he admitted. He would not idly put Lady Vanda in jeopardy...and all his experience told him a single Darkling posed more threat to human life and limb than these half-dozen Athlan warriors.

"I do not doubt your word, Cu'lugh, but by my duty we must have confirmation."

"Fair enough," Cu'lugh answered, "but understand my pledge to my Lady bids me act with conscience, too. I must insist you let me proceed to the Temple with this girl. It was Vanda's request that Odette be brought to her as soon as I returned."

Piers' next words were delayed by a corkscrew of lightning that shot down into the alley from which Cu'lugh and his party had emerged. It blasted the tin shingles off one of the lower sheds, and the ricochet of the metal glazed the passageway in blue-orange light. An errant course of wind then poured through the passage and into the square. It snuffed several of the torches and whipped the helmets from a few heads. Some of the gaping mercenaries exchanged superstitious looks, others moved from the square to the far side of the street.

Piers took a deep breath and said, "We will escort you to the Temple door, Lord Cu'lugh, and there send word to her Ladyship of your arrival."

He motioned to the six mercenaries who had not fled, and these trotted forward to encircle the band. Cu'lugh looked angry, and his arms encircled the woman's protectively. Piers understood his impatience, as well as the scowls from his companions. But there was naught else he could offer.

* * *

Vanda's attention had strayed from the tedious ceremony when the ceiling blew open. Quickly, she moved back, bracing her back against the wall, and watched amazed as the stair and all the loosened timber was sucked out into the black air.

Ah, take your last godly breath, Heimdallr, and sound the horn—the twilight of the gods is now!

The excited beat of her own heart drowned even the Harp's dismal dirge. But as she looked at it her own scream silenced everything.

Odette still hung upon the Harp, but the serpents at her ankles were flinging themselves angrily at flesh that was shrinking out of their reach. Odette's entire body was convulsing, her face was livid blue; and tightly rolled spears of blazing white light popped through the pores of her naked flesh. As each spear emerged it unfurled into a white plume.

Vanda forgot the tempest and stormed across the floor, pushing the kneeling, chant-drunk priests out of her way. The Blodsauker who had taken over the rites stared dumbfounded at the girl.

Vanda yanked on the hem of his robe. "What is this, priest! I was not told of this!"

The vampire peered down at her, and had he blood in his veins she knew it would have evaporated that moment.

"No, Lady! I do not understand what is happening!" He looked to the blown ceiling, and she saw that at last he'd been truly roused from the ecstasy of the rite as his fervor turned into disbelief.

Vanda saw that her sister's arms were rapidly misshaping as grotesquely as her legs. Her body shrank, compacted, shifted beneath the ever-blooming feathers. Her throat stretched to a visually painful length, her head now a nightmarish creation upon a swan's throat. Within moments Odette's arms—no, wings—would slip free of the binding snakes.

Vanda controlled the panic in her voice as she commanded, "The dagger, priest—the moment is upon us!"

The Blodsauker was paralyzed under the glistening black pools that were now Odette's eyes. The girl screamed, with such ferocity of pain and resentment even Vanda recoiled. But her mettle was second nature, and with it she forced the fear away and crawled onto the soundboard. The priest looked at her stupidly.

"Kill the whore or let me do it, now!"

"Lady, I cannot—I dare not—touch this creature!"

In his face was written the testimony of his repulsion and horror of what was now birthing on the Harp—a creature of life and eternal hope, all the things contrary to the Blodsauker nature. No wonder Hrowthe had not wanted the mantle in the sanctuary.

There was no time left to argue. Vanda grabbed the dagger from under the cord of his robe. The Blodsauker did not argue nor did he speak another word, but jumped down off the soundboard into the midst of his brethren.

"Awaken, brothers! Hrowthe is right, this is ill-omened!"

Vanda heard their chanting halt, but she had no time to fret and turned to

Odette. The black eyes bored into her own; and Vanda could feel the probing, accusing intelligence that sought to drown her purpose, rob her of her intentions.

Vanda raised the dagger and aimed it straight for the spasming white-pelted belly. She fought the attack of the swanmaiden's thoughts by seeing her father—the weakling warrior—crushing Silfr's sensual lips with his hungry mouth. She envisioned her mother standing behind them, crying out for revenge. She remembered the triumph she'd known as she stirred the elixir of monkshood and mandrake into the wine she offered to take to her father and the whore.

"An offering of devotion," she'd told Rulf sweetly. And so it was, in devotion to her mother's memory and to her own hatred for all Rulf and Silfr represented.

The swanmaiden's will snapped and reeled. Vanda laughed and thrust the blade into her sister's flesh. Blood showered over the plumes onto Vanda's glowing face. Odette cried out in a voice that was neither human nor animal.

* * *

The guard who had opened the Temple door seemed remorseful as he looked at the girl shoved toward the pike across the doorway.

"It cannot be, Lord Cu'lugh" he said, but Cu'lugh felt the uncertainty heavy in his voice. The man was more than apprehensive. "I have seen the Lady's sister inside the sanctuary."

Cu'lugh pressed Helrose behind him and pointed a finger over the man's shoulder. "There will be no sanctuary to protect if you do not let us in!"

Piers grumbled warily, "Are you not anxious, Lance? This is no manner of natural storm—the very roof of the Temple vanished as we came up the steps!"

There were sounds from within the anteroom, and the faces of the other guards peered over Lance's shoulders.

"There is truth in their words, sir," said one of them. "We should at least see to the Lady's safety."

"Damned the Lady's safety," growled another. "I am sickened by what I saw!"

Cu'lugh's face hardened, and his hand moved to his hilt. "Say what you have seen!"

Before another word could be spoken he heard the distinct twang of a bowstring from the shadows. An arrow struck the doorframe, and the guards turned. Lance's eyes narrowed toward the corridor at the back of the room.

"You dare!"

A voice, husky, familiar and lushly baneful, replied, "No one is to enter—you heard the Lady. I shan't suffer another fool within these walls."

Piers sneered and drew his sword.

"Let us through," he said to the guard holding the pike.

The man glanced at his leader; and Lance, his face worn, nodded curtly. Piers and two of his men entered the anteroom, and Cu'lugh listened as he said, "Darkling, your companions are not accounted for—and things are greatly amiss out here in the streets. I dare say you have less business here than any!"

Helrose eyed Cu'lugh steadily, but neither this nor her warning hand on his arm could assuage his fury any longer. He pushed her back toward the steps and advanced. Lance turned and had opened his mouth as if to object when the entire building—ground, walls, ceiling, all—quaked violently. A heavy beam crashed down in the middle of the room, crushing one of the guards to the floor. Two of his companions moved to his side. Cu'lugh saw into the recesses now, and the figure, dark and small and colored with resentment beyond telling, leered back at him from a corridor.

"Ill omen," Piers grumbled and cast a threatening look to the Darkling. "Loic, I think Lord Cu'lugh speaks wisely. This Temple sits beneath the eye of a heavenly schism. Let us fetch the Lady now before the place comes down!"

"No," replied Loic, and he pointed at Cu'lugh. "It is this sacrilege that you allow! That one has betrayed Lady Vanda. You know the priest's warning, Lance—destroy him if you would protect your Lady!"

Above the dust of cinders from the ceiling the reek of death and decay clung to every fiber of timber and minute mite of dirt on the floor. Cu'lugh could not believe these men would even consider the Darkling's lies. He noticed then a withered corpse fettered to the table, and he confirmed at last there was more evil involved here than merely that of the dark elves.

"And what is that at the threshold?" the Darkling continued. "What immortal creatures do you try to keep from my eyes?"

Cu'lugh saw a door in the wall to his right. "She is beyond that door, guardsman?"

The Darkling's face bloated with rage. "With these eyes I saw that one betray Lady Vanda! Your duty is to dispose of him!"

Cu'lugh heard the Athlans gather behind him. The bodyguards regarded the Athlans skeptically, but none on either side had yet spoken when another tremor brought more broken timber over their shoulders. Through the falling debris a dun shadow lunged from the doorway. One of the bodyguards coughed and made a threatening sound and Piers cried out some warning, but the next moment Edred leaped to his feet in the midst of the dust. His recurved bow swung forward before the man's words left his mouth, the string released and the arrow flew toward the corridor. There was no sound to confirm that the dark elf had been struck, only the clamor of the other sentries charging through the door.

They had hardly drawn their weapons when an arrow pelted into their midst, piercing the breast of one guard straight through his scale. Edred pressed Helrose behind him as the other Athlans raised their weapons and the bodyguards flew after the Darkling down the corridor. Cu'lugh unsheathed his sword and rushed at the shadow that clung to the walls they had passed. It flinched and dissipated. He had sliced nothing but air.

Mad shouts roared from the door. Cu'lugh turned in time to see a small horde of Darklings storm into the room, their elven blades raised and already bloodied. Yori, Amnoc and Sylreth engaged alongside the sentries as Prage stepped back and prepared to launch. Cu'lugh bolted to them and drove the end of his sword through the first Darkling eye he saw.

The creature hissed as the blade rammed through its brain. Oily black foam spurted from the eye socket and from the creature's mouth, but still it screamed; and Cu'lugh had to shove it off with his knee to draw the sword out. The Darkling sank to the floor, convulsing in hissing screams. One of Prage's arrows missiled into its throat. Even with his face drenched in the corrupted blood Cu'lugh saw its childlike features contort and dissipate.

Yori had just parried one of the elven blades and driven his sword through the gut of his attacker. Throwing a nod to Cu'lugh he shouted, "Go—find the girl!"

Prage shielded Cu'lugh's back as he went to the door and laid his hand to the bolt. At that moment he heard the whispery release of a shaft from the corridor. He jumped aside just quickly enough that the arrow sailed by his shoulder and stuck in the door. Prage spun about and discharged once before another shaft flew toward Cu'lugh. He crouched, regretting he had no shield but this lean boy. Another arrow hit the padded armor at Prage's shoulder, buffeting him backward as a second penetrated his collarbone. Cu'lugh glanced at him, saw the blood soaking into his shirt. There was no time to think; he crouched and rolled to the table and, straining to listen, heard the Darkling's angry murmur, the bare breeze of its feet as its aim followed him. Edred, seeing the fallen boy, ordered Helrose to crawl under the table and, still crouching, let loose a shaft toward the Darkling. The creature dodged it, spun and lifted his bow.

Helrose cringed on the floor, watching her archer as one frozen. Cu'lugh scrambled to her and grasping her hair, yanked her under the table. He heard a feline hiss from the corridor and glancing up saw Edred's last missile had hit the Darkling in the hip. Edred pursued it into the shadows.

Cu'lugh hopped up and engaged a spearwielding Darkling that bounded out of the fray. Its point sliced through his scale plates just over his hip. He brought his blade across the spear but it did not splinter. The Darkling drove further until he felt it rend bone. With a scream he brought the sword up, hewing the creature's jaw. It hissed, black foam spewing from the division in its face. Cu'lugh struck again, this time taking its left arm. It fell back into the huddle of fighters. Amnoc turned from the Darkling he'd just beheaded and brought his ax down, hacking off the creature's other arm at the shoulder joint. It sank to its knees, its ooze spuming into the air and over the floor.

Cu'lugh noted there were only two or three of the creatures left standing. As he ran to Prage he saw Piers fall under one of the elven swords, and his attacker leaped over the fallen guard and charged for the table. Helrose drew her sickle knife and threw it just as the Darkling's blade swung toward her. It penetrated the creature's scrotum, and the Dark Elf wavered on its feet, scowling, and rammed its blade through the wood. She screamed and clambered for the other end of the table as an arrow sliced the air and lanced through the Darkling's brow. As it screamed Cu'lugh leaped on its back and finished it off with a slice through the throat.

Again the Temple trembled, and dust and cinders fell over invaders and protectors alike. Prage was halfway to his feet when Cu'lugh returned, and he saw another Darkling die under Sylreth's blade. There was only one left now, and with a hateful hiss at the sentry with whom it sparred it spun and ran out the door. The sentry and one of his companions ran after it, leaving the Athlans alone with their captain.

Helrose crawled out from under the table and bent down to Piers. As she turned his head he coughed deeply, and the blood in his throat undammed and spilled over her hands. He smiled weakly into her face and mumbled something as the last breath rattled out of his spent lungs.

Edred ran back in from the corridor, his relief addled with discomfort.

"The guards are dead, all, and I never caught up with the Darkling."

Cu'lugh heard the sentries outside hoot vengefully. They must have taken the other dark elf. His eyes shifted to the door and another quake rattled the Temple, so hard they saw a split crawl down one of the corridor walls.

He glanced toward the table where the corpse remained.

"Edred, stay with Helrose," he ordered, and meeting the expectant faces of the others—" Let us see what they were sheltering behind this door."

* * *

With a final wounded cry the swan's slender neck keeled over its bloodied breast and the creature's wings slipped loose of its heartless bonds. It fell to the soundboard at Vanda's feet. She stared at it, laughing as she had not laughed since she was a small and carefree child. That last cry had prompted a discordant clash from the Harp strings, a sound almost deafening; and it ascended, thickening the air with such reverberation of ominous notes that what was left of the ceiling burst apart. The air of the sanctuary was sucked away so fast that Vanda's lungs felt close to collapsing. Faint, she leaned on the forepillar, and the vibration passing through it was so intense her teeth chattered. But it kept her conscious; and she watched with delight as the blackness reached into the sanctuary. The stones of the celestial cavern burst apart, blowing air back into the Temple.

A woman approached the sundered entranceway from the depths of the cavern. A giddy howl could be heard echoing from those depths, and a laugh as brittle as hoarfrost. Breathing easier again, Vanda stood straight and saw winking black flickers sputter forth from the shadowed gap. The woman sank to her haunches, and her face was wretched and tearstained. The flickers ignored her to drift down into the sanctuary like hundreds of butterflies fashioned of midnight. Behind them, in the heavens edging Loki's prison, the great bridge of flaming iridescent hues arched down toward earth. Its end seemed to plummet into the Temple, though Vanda had not noticed before. And now its guardian met Vanda's gaze from atop His wailing horse. Gjallarhorn was raised to His lips; and His eyes were baleful, reluctant, even as His fair cheeks ballooned in preparation. Vanda saw droplets of blood fall from His ears, blood of the Father of all the races, glistening as red as that of any of His mortal children.

At that moment Vanda's heart swooned in a rapture beyond any fleeting petty physical pleasure. She had triumphed where the Blodsaukers failed, where the Darklings dared not approach, where trifling men had feared.

She raised her arms, shaking in a joy sublime, and shouted fearlessly at the disapproving god.

"It is *I* who hath burst thy ears, O god of lusty and foolish men! By patience and liberation of carnal passions I stand witness as you herald your own destruction!"

The god's hand on the horse's rein tightened so His mighty knuckles glowed like the sun His worshippers flouted in their sin. His gleaming brow was heavy with a force that would have failed the heart of a weaker mortal. But more than any mortal were gods bound to destiny, and He had no choice but to obey the will of she who had summoned destiny.

The inky lights danced about Vanda and the Harp. The priests cowered against the walls. The Harp was silent, as if it waited to see the commencement of all it had labored to initiate.

One Blodsauker voiced the resigned horror of the brethren. "The sacrifice has been made and the roots of Yggdrasil shall stir."

A lamenting wail rose from their numbers, but the piteous sound did not stay Heimdallr's lips from Gjallarhorn.

Chapter Forty-Two

igyn's head rang with the echo of the Harp's crescendo, and it took all her effort to cling to the loosened stones and drag herself back into the cavern. Inside, she ran down the corridors toward her husband's chamber. The lights of Chaos skirted past her, so eager they were to descend to earth and enslave mankind they could not resist venturing on to listen as Heimdallr sounded the horn.

She passed Fenrir's chamber and heard the beast ripping his chains against the stones in which they were embedded. She dared not see him—this thing destined to devour Odin, this stepson she'd cared for long ago when it was still young without once expecting its gratitude or that of its father. She would take her own life upon Fenrir's escape, waken the adder and extend her wrist to its fangs. The pitiful serpent was a mere machined element, but Chaos was contriving and cruel.

A few of the evil lights remained hovering about Loki, and these began to take form and substance, ready to stand as warriors to meet the gods of mankind. They were an abstraction of a life form, or more likely, she suspected, the very opposite of life; and she knew she would go mad if she gazed upon them. She went to the stone bed, panting and weeping with anger and terror, and kissed the hand straining to cleave the weakening chains.

But when he looked at her the reason had vanished entirely from his eyes. Black and engulfing, they seemed to suck the soul from Sigyn; and she thought again of the poison, and grabbed the vessel as she had done a million times before. But now instead of emptying it down the chasm nearby she raised it to Loki's lips.

He snarled at her and batted the vessel with his brow. It fell from her hands all over his naked chest and Sigyn's hands and wrists. The scalding venom burned through her flesh so that she could not hold on to the vessel. Screaming, she tumbled back and watched as Loki's splattered skin smoked and peeled away. Beneath this ravaged semblance glowed the same kind of creature of chaos, hatred and darkness as those hovering above the bed.

"No," she wept, remembering the taste of his flesh, his mouth, the pounding of his heart beneath hers as she had comforted him in his misery. He had been the god her eyes had sought to behold, even as his impious actions had delivered him into banishment and punishment. Always had she perceived something there beneath his guile and deceit, something fine and good and brave as any god created by mankind's projections of the Eternal's virile aspect.

"Where has it fled," she gasped, sobbing, "that precious, precious virility you could have embodied?"

* * *

The door gave under Cu'lugh's push, slamming straight into the face of a guard. The man was speechless, white with horror; and his companions stood shaking their heads, babbling incoherently.

One of them was embracing a priest, weeping like a child. As the priest's sad eyes acknowledged Cu'lugh, he realized suddenly the body on the table in the anteroom was not a corpse, no, not strictly; none of these priests were, nor were they men.

The realization fled his concern as he saw the monstrous Harp. The strings gleamed dully under the countenance regarding them from above. It was the Heimdallr persona of God looking at them over the smooth brim of the horn at His lips! Amnoc gasped and Sylreth exclaimed something in Athlan.

Cu'lugh quickly assessed the situation. The guards were too frightened to move, the Blodsaukers were in shock. He saw Vanda standing on the soundboard, a bloodied dagger in her hand. Tethers of snakes dangled from the forepillar. And at Vanda's feet lay a swan of uncertain plumage.

His knees weakened and the sweat was cold on his spine. "*Odette!*" He charged toward the Harp, but one of the priests barred his way. The Blodsauker's hollow eyes shone with tears of blood and phlegm.

"'Tis too late, too late, too late."

Cu'lugh shoved the creature into the arms of his hissing brothers. Only their disbelief held them back. He heard one of the guards scream and run out the door.

Vanda looked down from the soundboard…and at that moment he knew he'd never seen a more beautiful face. The joy that radiated in her countenance paled even Odette's sweetest blush. But it was a rapturous beauty birthed of pettiness and evil sublime.

"You could have bowed before the feet of a brave and favored queen, Cu'lugh! But you preferred to rut between the legs of a whore—look and see the white breast to which you pressed your traitorous lips!"

Cu'lugh looked at the swan. The feathers, he realized now, were dark for the saturation of its own blood. Its elegant throat lay twisted over one crumpled wing. His blood went cold in his veins, and he wailed her name; but his voice was lost in the thunder released by Heimdallr's breath.

* * *

"Midgard trembles with the holy roots!"

Odette heard the words but she could not answer; her cognitive thoughts had been replaced by instinct and all she knew as her eyes opened was terrible pain and the weak coursing of blood through her veins. The beautiful woman standing before her was caught in her own rapture as the call of the horn blared. The black lights flitted in their dark joy, frightening the undead hanging back against the walls. Even the men—how they trembled; and somewhere by the reckoning of the gods she knew the slight alteration of the horn's blare slowed the heavenly army on the road to battle.

Through slipping consciousness she saw the familiar face she loved more than all—swarthy and shining, dark with horror. He leaped onto the soundboard and stroked the feathers over her eyes.

She wanted to stay with him; and she fought to keep her staggering heart from stopping, but her blood was draining so quickly!

And then at his shoulder a grey brilliance gathered, as if from the shadows of light that had been there before, all rosy and pulsing at its core. It spread over the soundboard, invisible to the others and unseen by the white god. Three faces pressed forth through its visceral folds, three heads upon a single pair of shoulders. And the center face, all maternal and wise and sane, looked up to Heimdallr; and He flinched as if feeling the soft gaze, and the horn's blare faltered.

"By her own impatience your sister changed the Harp's baneful melody," said the Norn. *"Now rise and confirm Heimdallr's suspicions that the crescendo was prompted not by manipulated rapture, but by blood and treachery."*

With effort Odette raised her numbing throat. As the face of Cu'lugh darkened before her she rolled over onto her bloodied belly and raised her wings. She saw the lips of the Norn form a circle and felt Her breath lift her body up. It was enough to give her knowledge, an infusion of all her mother had known and all the sisters of Freyja—the knowledge of flight. Odette hobbled a few paces down the soundboard, through the thick puddles of her own blood, and lifted the wings higher and brought them down in one aching swoop. She ascended, away from the horrible Harp, past the protesting flickers of evil. Toward Heimdallr she flew.

His eyes were closed, the yellow eyelashes damp with mournful tears as he expelled the rest of His breath into Gjallarhorn. There was no time to beg or plead. Odette wound about his head so that she hovered right above His fingers stretched across the horn. Then, gathering her wings she let herself plummet into the mouth of the deafening instrument.

The God's breath stayed. Odette's own breath failed; she hardly was even aware as He plucked her gently from the horn. Her head felt thick, weary; she craved to simply give in to the welcoming scenery before her eyes and walk through the hedges of violets and roses and other flowers, to run in the fields of Vanaheim waiting ahead.

But Cu'lugh was still there on the soundboard, whispered Heimdallr, and Vanda beside him, grappling for the sword that had fallen away in his shock and grief.

Suddenly, the colors of the hedge and the flowers deepened and took full hue; and a myriad of girls clad in flowers and giggles pressed through the greenery. They surrounded Odette, touching her face, the wound in her stomach. One of them grasped her head, and Odette gazed into her mother's beautiful and eternally youthful face.

Silfr said nothing, but pressed her mouth over her daughter's lips. A wave of sweetness entered Odette's throat and made its way swiftly into her lungs. She was filled with strength and the compelling desire to go with the others, to remain in Freyja's court, to wait for him she loved.

But her mother's lips drew away. *"Indeed shall you join us, Odette, as all loving women, but now is not your time!"*

Silfr pressed her away then, back through death's portal and into the realm of the living. Odette opened her eyes to see she stood in the palm of Heimdallr's hand. And following His gesturing eyes she looked down and saw Cu'lugh, amazed and careless to everything else, fall under the sweep of his own sword in Vanda's incensed hands. Vanda roared as he fell and, leaping to the floor, reached to the soundboard and dragged the sword off.

At once Odette unfurled her wings and plunged from the God's hand. She descended with all haste toward them.

* * *

One word stormed through Vanda's indignant mind: *traitor!* The tears spilling down Cu'lugh's face almost blinded her with rage. Laughing, she grasped the hilt securely and raised the sword again, determined to carve more on his belly this time than merely the scrape she'd dealt before. A crimson shadow glinted in the blade and as her face turned toward it she was struck in the shoulder with such force the weapon fell from her hands.

She screamed and retrieved it before the addled warrior could move. The swan squawked as it hovered about them, daring her to move. Every ounce of her triumph had been stolen away in a mocking instant. There could be no more waiting—Odette and all she loved had to die.

The swan swept past the blade and, pivoting in the air, collided with the back of Vanda's turning head. Vanda toppled onto her knees a humiliating moment, the next she was back on her feet. But as she raised the sword she saw that the blackness was slinking back through the torn rooftop. Heimdallr was nothing but a mist as He rode the Bifrost Bridge back to the heavens. And the delineation of Loki's prison cavern was fading from the portal.

The swan dove again; but Vanda crouched, avoiding the impact of its bill.

"Whore!"

Again and again the swan dove, trying to force Vanda away from Cu'lugh. Vanda lashed the air with steel and screamed.

"Face this, sister, face this!"

Out of the corner of an eye she saw a strange warrior approach. She even heard his threat…but her rage knew no limitations now. She pivoted, and with two clashes of blades disarmed him and stayed his insolent attack.

The swan ascended a ways and plunged back toward her, this time skirting the blade. Blood spurted from the stainless pelt, but the swan careened again. It evaded the flailing weapon and, making a sharp turn, fastened itself to Vanda's head. Vanda clawed at it with her free hand and tossed her head violently, but the damnable creature would not budge. It pecked at her eyes and her fingers on the sword hilt. At last, blinded by her own blood, Vanda felt the weapon slip from her grasp.

Only then did the swan relent and ascend again. Through her clouded eyes Vanda saw the other warrior run back. She drew the priest's dagger from her bodice and threw it at him. It punctured his throat; and he froze, gasping, and sank near Cu'lugh's head.

Vanda looked toward the soaring swan and, opening her arms, willed her rage and disappointment—and most of all her hatred—into every particle of her being. The agony of her fury dimmed even that of her shifting body. As the swan turned and plummeted again Vanda welcomed the little squawk of shock it made.

Vanda's black raven-wings fluttered gracefully; and she swept toward the doorway to gain speed, then circled quickly and hurled herself toward Odette. She flew straight into Odette's wounded breast. The swanmaiden teetered a moment before righting herself and flapping upward. Vanda followed directly and clamped her beak about Odette's leg. Odette tried to shake her but Vanda did not yield...until she realized Odette was flying straight toward the Harp with the aim of scraping Vanda off on the neck of the instrument. Vanda released her hold and flew one way while Odette went the opposite. The two turned in their respective courses and sailed toward one another.

Vanda was the faster; and as she careened toward her sister her dark, yellow-rimmed eyes glimpsed a horde moving into the sanctuary. Strangers, most of them, bloodied and combat-worn; and the Blodsaukers cringed and transformed themselves into cowering shadows and tried to hide against the walls. Odette swept by her, grazing her beak with a wing. Vanda turned and skimmed past two of her bodyguards, screeched at them to rise to their duty. But their bravery had vanished, and as she ascended again they slipped out of the chamber.

Only then did she see Odette plummeting straight toward her; but determined it was her sister's turn to bow, Vanda kept to her course. Just as they were about to collide Vanda altered her position just enough that her beak caught Odette's white throat. The swan was knocked from course; and as she fell Vanda plunged afterward, her beak ready to pierce Odette's eyes.

Unexpectedly, the swan reeled and gained momentum. She flew past Vanda again. Vanda followed, undaunted, vying now for the soft flesh above Odette's legs. Once and then again Vanda struck; the swan faltered, and Vanda dove for its face.

A thrash of wings struck Vanda blindside—she fell back, spiraling, unable to right herself until just before she would have crashed to the ground. She skirted the floor and had turned to fly up again when she saw the webbed feet spiraling down fast upon her.

She felt the swan's feet sink into her breast; and as she was buffeted down, Odette caught Vanda's ruffled neck in her bill. Odette had not the agility or reserve of strength to carry Vanda far, but with a heavy flap or two of her wings she flew over the dais. Vanda's wings beat furiously, so furiously she did not see the Harp until her side smashed into the top of the forepillar. A tide of pain washed over her with the breaking of her wing and she fell to the floor. Her uninjured wing flapped once, twice, and then she fainted.

* * *

The battle between the sisters had seemed a fantastic dream to Cu'lugh until Helrose's incantation brought him back into full consciousness. She knelt beside him with her eyes half-closed. Under her slowly moving fingertips the wound over his abdomen healed. The chamber resounded now not with a heavenly tumult but with inhuman, resisting cries. Pushing Helrose's hands away he sat up and saw the frantic Blodsaukers running in all directions under the attack of the swanmaiden— his swanmaiden.

Prage crouched nearby, holding a hand over his own newly healed wound. Seeing Cu'lugh rise he handed him the sword he'd lost. They watched with Helrose as Odette glided through the spaces in pursuit of the Blodsaukers. Some of them were resigned to their fate and extended their arms and met the brush of her pelt willingly. Those who sought to flee were forced back from the doorway by Athlan and mercenary weapons. And though mortal weapons could only momentarily hamper their movements, a moment was all the swan needed. At a single touch of her feathers they succumbed at last to the death so long eluded.

When the last decayed body crumbled to the floor silence prevailed like a returning king. No thunder resounded in the heavens, no lightning marred the slumbering night sky. The looming maw had folded into itself so that only a seam of grey mist remained over the torn roof, and this seam was disappearing swiftly into nothingness. The chanting of the Blodsaukers outside had ended; they likely had fled to the sanctuary of their haunted forest.

The warriors walked amongst the bodies, kicking with their boots the shriveled heads to ascertain no abomination of spirit lay in feigned death. It was then Cu'lugh saw the Darkling at the doorway, the one he knew, the archer who had spoken so crudely in the merchant's shop in Athla. At Cu'lugh's cry the others drew their weapons. But Helrose's command stilled their attack. They watched as he entered, carrying a small black-iron cage. No glance to mortal or Athlan he gave—certainly he avoided the eyes of the swan—and jumping onto the dais he stooped and lifted the fallen raven.

Cu'lugh saw her flutter, dazed but still quite alive; but he made no move to defend her as the Darkling shoved her into the cage and turned the key. Vanda seemed to liven as he rose; and as he strode back through the heaps of Blodsauker bodies she began to scream, a sound so terribly human that had it been another soul locked in the raven's form the dark elf could never have hoped to leave the Temple. But this one did; and for once Cu'lugh hoped his kind were as ruthless as legend told and would stuff the beak of this new pet on the fruitless grains of Jotunheim until her very craw burst.

Cu'lugh turned away, banishing her from his mind. He saw the swan perched on the soundboard, regarding him with her deep emerald-black gaze.

He was naked under those knowing eyes, eyes that had beheld his secrets and deepest fears, looked upon his virtues and faults. Here was the one soul he trusted enough to share both dreams and failures. No one had ever mastered him but this blithe and sunny creature. He set the sword down again and rose gently. He would let her rest a time before commanding her to disrobe of the pelted garment; and if she did not obey, this time he would wait until she chose to do so. The waiting lulled the terror that had ravaged his soul. Sweet suffering, he conceded, to wait to hold her again, to savor the moments until he caressed her again and scalded her intoxicating mouth with his kisses.

Helrose suddenly clutched his arm and tried to turn him away. "No, Cu'lugh, you must not touch her."

"What do you mean? She is mine."

"Above all else she battled for your life—do not think to take that from her now!"

Cu'lugh looked at the Mistress impatiently. "What do you mean? The Blodsaukers she took, for they were the undead. I have nothing to fear."

"She was already dead when she touched them. If you touch her now, you would succumb as surely as the vampire. Do not fail her by throwing away the life she set to defend."

Cu'lugh trembled, disbelieving, and shook Helrose's hand away. "No! This is not Athla! This is my world, and your superstitions have no strength here!"

Helrose tried again to stop him, but he flung her hands away brusquely and trotted toward the Harp. The swan's wings raised, and before he could blink she ascended into the air again.

"Odette!"

She did not look back, but spiraled higher and higher, through the splintered roof and into the sky until she was but a sliver of ivory on the black velvet heavens.

Cu'lugh's heart jumped fiercely, and his whole chest ached as if it would burst. He could not breathe and his left arm panged. He cared not when he stumbled, nor for anything else. If he were to never hold Odette again in life, perhaps in death he would find her again.

He spiraled down a long tunnel toward a golden light, and Helrose's chanting voice chased after him, beseeching him to fight against the descent.

* * *

For a day and a night Charles Martel had searched for the old route that would lead them around the forested boundary of Vanda's lands; but a wall of giant nettled vines had grown up about the entire fief since last he'd visited, vines that barred the accustomed passages. And when during the second night the sky broke open and threatened to devour the territory beyond his ranks broke faith, and neither promise of title or threat of retribution could entice them into journeying further. With only the company of his eldest companion and the half-wit standard-bearer Martel dared the forest.

The fear of excommunication was nothing to the horror of the dead forest. As if it had been struck by the angry hand of God Himself, some plague had befallen the once-lush woods. Vanished were the animals and winged creatures, even the borers of timber and the ants and flies. It was the trees and shrubs, robbed of all life and shriveled to but petrified stone that were most disturbing. And over every dead root and desiccated sapling, through log and about muted stone the razor-sharp nettles trailed.

One thing alone glittered amongst the lifelessness, and that he saw only now and then atop a stone or caught under the occasional bough. Feathers of startling white. When his horse passed under a particularly old oak he snatched one of the plumes from a deserted cobweb in the branches. It shone like silk; and its quill was damp to the touch, as if the bird that had lost it had just recently flown this way. When the forest vines were deemed too savage for the horses to surmount and the little party had to find the way out, Martel wished the bird would make some announcement, even a cry of pain, if only to break the deathly silence.

At length Martel's small party emerged from the forest. The sun lay well into the west as they tramped through the valley. Here, the land was barren, the grass so yellowed it was almost like looking across a great saffron-dyed blanket. But once out of the shadow of the forest Martel's anger for his cowardly men resurfaced. The only solace was the vision of their certain humiliation on his return. Like superstitious spinsters they all were, and he wondered how he'd not seen their cowardice before. Once they returned to Frankland they would pay for their cravenly disloyalty, he vowed, through taxes for the construction of the cathedral he'd decided to have raised in Aachen.

His eyes grazed dreamily over the sterile ground. Minutes passed before he realized he'd lost his companion. Turning on his saddle he saw the knight standing stock-still several paces behind. His old mouth gaped in wonder, and Martel followed his gaze down the valley to the entrance gates of the city. Behind them a crowd had gathered and these people watched as on the other side walked a second group, a dozen or so mercenaries and a few richly clad merchants. At the end of the line, however, garbed in her stiff black weeds was one of Vanda's old spinster serving women. In the air above them all something flitted. The gleam of it against the sun stung Martel's vision a moment. He blinked, and looking again realized the line had shortened. The rest continued to walk on, toward what he was not certain until he noticed something flying toward them. It caught the sunlight and his eyes smarted again.

He pressed a thumb to each corner of his eyes and looked again, and now he saw a swan flying in the firmament. It dove, rose and crested the breeze, watching as below it the assembly continued their odd stroll—to vanish one after another into the naked air.

By the time he'd regained his senses and taken his sword only one remained. The spinster. He yelled for her to stop, return to the safety of the city. Her head turned and she watched as he kicked his horse into a gallop. He saw her flash him a toothless grin and turn her face again. Those looking on from the other side of the gate neither attempted to coax nor to stop her; and when she, too, had vanished they watched the swan as it came to rest upon the top of the near watchtower. Martel shouted as his mount advanced, warning them all to get back from the beast of evil, to summon a priest to exorcise it back to whence it came.

They heeded nothing, and when it took wing again their faces looked as bereft of life as the desiccated forest.

Only one came out to greet Martel, a guardsman of her Ladyship, unshaven and weary, his sleeves slashed in several places and hardened by recent bleeding, though Martel observed no wounds beneath the shredded cloth. And as he knelt before Martel there shone an uncertain light in his face.

"Pray tell, man, what has happened to this city?" the Mayor demanded hotly. "Lady Vanda—is she safe?"

The guard grasped Martel's hand and pressed his bloodied lips to the Mayor's gauntlet.

"She has gone to reap the reward of God, dear Mayor," the man said in a voice tinged with madness. "He has promised to share His treasure with her, don't you know?"

* * *

Even the lights of Chaos had seeped back through the corridors between the worlds. They waited, Sigyn knew, for the next opportunity, for their anger would never be assuaged until Midgard and all the dreams of the precious living were obliterated and replaced by utter despair. That despair would they nurture and feed upon, too, until at last mortal life gave up; and either the hand of the Eternal wiped the returning hunger of Chaos under the final sweep of Hope or all the universe simply died.

Her candles were gone, blown away by the tempest of the Harp. Fenrir slept, dreaming the dreams of the mindless, and there remained not a single disillusioned Blodsauker or dubious Darkling to soothe the desolation of her Lord and husband.

And she, who would never forsake him, had heard the voice of Idun from the chasm entrance below, that secret entrance that had deliberately been left unsealed by the gods who had constructed this prison. They loved Sigyn and she loved them; and Idun, her friend, as She had been for ages uncountable, still brought the Apples of Youth. But Sigyn could not face Her and left the basket down the deep stairwell. Perhaps another day, or another eon, but not now would she eat.

Loki brooded in the darkness, screaming his curses at the swanmaiden but more so, as always, the Granddame, Freyja. His burst flesh had scabbed; and His true blood flowed, concealed once more, within the flesh of a god. And Sigyn wondered more than ever if now, without his minions to feed the desire for revenge, if perhaps, just perhaps, the godling flesh would at last and forever suffocate and override the essence of Chaos.

She had once heard it spoken by her old Mistress that with effort and will even the most tarnished vessel could be turned into a thing of beauty.

But she was weary now, and too long had she given all for nothing returned.

She rested, ignoring his tantrums. Like a pampered child sent early to bed he pleaded for her to return immediately.

"The serpent has awakened, Sigyn," he called, "and the vessel overflows!"

She lay alone in the small but comfortable room the Asa-gods had hewn just for her when she'd first told them of her choice to come into the cavern and attend her husband. Within the smoothed casket of granite she turned, beneath a quilt sewn of the fibers of irises from Freyja's gardens and stuffed with the wind-blown down of the holy swans used to make the Valkyries' mantles. Sigyn did not dream or stir to Loki's summons but reposed in the darkness sweetly distanced from hungering chaos.

* * *

As the portal to Midgard's routes closed Odette ascended the skies once more. The foul stench from the Blodsauker's corruption still clung to the air over the landscape, but as she broached the clouds the air grew crisp and clean. No mortal thing could touch her here, not Martel or Boniface, not Vanda's women who prayed for her to plunge headlong to earth. She was free now, truly a descendant of Freyja; and it was some instinctive yearning in her breast to fly to Vanaheim that piloted her up the ancient invisible route to the Bifrost Bridge, the route traveled by her aunts and by her own mother in the long-ago.

As she reached the foot of the mighty rainbow Odette could smell already the flowers of Freyja's gardens and hear the laughter of Her handmaidens. But before she had ascended halfway Heimdallr rode down to meet her. His brow was heavy as always, and He held a flail in His hand. Halting His steed He gestured her back, toward a route that flowed through the northwestern clouds. She flapped her wings, hovering hesitantly, and the god whipped the flail, lashing her tail feathers lightly, but enough to compel. She veered and followed as He bade, sensing nothing of where the route led, only that within the tunnel, white with mists, the merry echoes from Vanaheim grew distant.

Light elves populated the flanking spheres and they seemed oblivious to her, bound in the continual labor of their kind, singing their sylvan breezy hymns to sun and sky, the night and eternal stars, dancing and copulating over cloud and zephyr. Then, as she neared the winding end a beacon stretched toward her. A boy emerged from the light, clad in silver armor, a crest of bees upon his golden shield. She recognized the bashful smile and blonde tresses, the eyes that beckoned for her to follow.

He guided her out and accompanied her down the firmament. The clouds scattered before them, and soon she felt the sun warm upon her back. Great towering mountains loomed on all sides, cradling a fecund valley rich in trees and sprawling rivers. Onward they flew, coming at last to a beautiful city where the sun splashed golden even over the silver turrets. The boy directed her down to a certain tower, a window with shutters of smooth cedar. Odette buoyed her wings and accepted his caress, then watched as he turned and sped back toward the billowy ethers.

Odette slipped through the window to perch on the wide, dark-stained sill. The room within was not so lavishly furnished as most of those in the castle. A gleaming bronze sword, the only thing of intricate workmanship, hung beside the door. A glass vase of hyacinths stood upon a table, and runes crafted from mother-of-pearl lay strewn about every side of the bed. Beneath a clean linen sheet lay the room's occupant. His chest rose and fell evenly, and the lids covering his almond-shaped eyes did not stir.

Odette fluttered to the floor and intuitively wished the pelt away. The quills detached from her quivering pores, and the blood surged through her veins. The mantle loosened from her flesh, slipping over her naked legs to her ankles. With a toss of her golden hair she lifted her feet from the soft feathers and approached the bed.

She kissed his smooth brow, his nipples, his mouth, drinking in the taste of his breath, the dewy sweat upon his lips.

His dark eyes opened, and he stared at her, his brow knitting a moment.

"Odette!"

She purred as his arms folded about her and pulled her down onto the mattress. His mouth descended over her face, feeding upon her lips and tasting her cheeks, her chin, her ears. He cupped her breasts and suckled the nipples tenderly, and she massaged the smooth muscles of his arms eagerly and the strong back, the firm buttocks she loved so much. His stout eager manhood pressed her thighs and gently she stroked the eager fluids from the swollen head and sucked them from her fingers.

He kissed her again, invading her mouth with his tongue and grasped her buttocks and kneaded them firmly. Her legs opened, and his cock pressed upon her damp orifice a moment before invading her entirely. She moaned, writhing without protest as he held her arms down on the mattress above her head. His hips bucked roughly against her thighs, and her orifice seared gratefully under each thrust. He glutted her, gorged her, filling that ardent space within her that he alone could meet and make whole.

He came soon, jutting into her with an almost agonized moan. With his seed rushing into her core Odette climaxed. The light from the window faded with her rapture and her mind's eye soared to the clouds once more.

But his voice reined her home again, bound her with fetters sturdier than the mightiest steel.

"You are flesh and blood, my love," he wept, "and never again shall I let you go!"

She smiled up at his handsome, beloved face and melted into his folding arms. "My Master, my beloved, my Cu'lugh," she murmured. "I should not have returned had I for a moment thought otherwise."

Epilogue

As Cu'lugh made his rounds he stopped by Harold's shop. The man was still under close scrutiny by order of the queen, and Cu'lugh came by daily to insure the harp maker was not hiding away another man's rightful property. But Cu'lugh was touched by Harold's concern over his confiscated slaves and assured him again that they were well-treated in Lord Edred's household. The man seemed satisfied; and Cu'lugh returned to the street, snatching without trying the latest gossip over Queen Honi. Some said the High Priestess had already confirmed the babe in her womb was the returned soul of the king. Others proclaimed it was time she extended an official welcome to suitors.

Cu'lugh knew from Honi's own lips she had no intention of marrying again, not until Larsarian returned to her a man grown and prepared to enthrall her again. In the meantime, she mourned in her own way, keeping to her rooms and gardens, as she had little desire to witness in her court the pleasures that had been taken from her. Sometimes she went to visit Edred's manor. Helrose knew how to comfort her as no one else could; and the queen, he had observed, found a certain comfort to see her friend's passions incited and mastered at last by the devoted Edred.

The sun was just about to slip behind the mountains when Cu'lugh finally arrived at the little iron gate with the tinkling silver bells. He swung it open and stepped across the lush grass, thinking again he needed to purchase a goat or two if he were to keep the grass trim as he preferred. He paused a moment to admire the cottage anew. He loved the soft bluish stones and particularly the dark-blue-stained shutters. The tiled roof gleamed even in the twilight. Violets and baby's breath bloomed now on every windowsill. The door he had taken the greatest pains to adorn, latticing it over with birch swans and oaken bears. Ivy he'd transplanted at the base of the cottage and it was thriving alongside the climbing roses. The stones of the double chimney blazed golden under the setting sun now, and as he walked forward to open the door he glimpsed a pair of doves nestled in the little pear tree at the back of the lawn.

The cottage was cozy with shadows, for he'd not dared leave a candle or lantern burning when he set out that day. Of course, the neighbor's wife, little Matilde, had promised to come in and check on things. There was flint in the bedchamber, and he would light the lantern there before changing from his sentry clothes.

As Cu'lugh walked through the door he heard Odette's surprised whimper. She was just rising to her hands and knees and her face was bright and nervous at once. He contemplated her with deliberate sternness, and she bowed her head at once. Oh, how he loved her golden hair as it draped her milky-pale shoulders and spilled over the bronze floor plate of the cage. He drew a little closer and caught the reflection of her face in it. Wonderfully chagrined was that lovely face, the brow knit anxiously and the lips pressed together as she struggled against the urge to beg.

He wanted nothing more than to take her out and throw her over his lap and spank her thoroughly. The punishment would be over then, for he could not resist making love to her again. But she had been very naughty to utter that word during breakfast—a word crude enough on the lips of men, let alone a woman's. It had been thoughtless on her part, no more, but to be lax in punishment would only encourage the habit. And so he ignored her deliberately and took the flint from the niche over the bed.

She whimpered again as he went out to light the candles in the den, and the sound of it made his manhood swell urgently under his breeches. Taking a steadying breath, he walked into the small dining room and stood by the window that looked over the fields beyond the property. A man chased a damsel through the high green grass. The girl was naked but for the silver collar on her throat. Cu'lugh watched as the man at last grabbed a handful of her flying dark hair and pulled her to him. She turned her face to meet his kisses, her lithe body stirring fretfully against him.

Cu'lugh sighed as he turned away. A few moments he gave himself, forced himself, before striding again to the bedchamber. Inside the cage Odette knelt toward him with her face pressed over the back of her hands, her round luscious buttocks raised temptingly. She made an urgent, supplicating little sound now, and her plunging breasts swayed slightly and her hips strained to keep still. He smiled and lifted the golden key from his belt.

The End

About the Author

Model and writer Maria Osborne Perry was born in Kingsport, Tennessee and attended East Tennessee State University. She has received awards and acclaim in the genres of poetry, commentary work and fiction. Presently she lives in a small town in East Tennessee with her husband Robert and children, Evelyn, Byron, Autumn and Wolfgang.